MANGLED HANDS

MANGLED HANDS

Johnny Stanton

Introduction and Interview
by George Salis

Tough Poets Press
Arlington, Massachusetts

ISBN 978-0-578-85942-2

This edition published in 2021 by
Tough Poets Press
Arlington, Massachusetts 02476
U.S.A.

www.toughpoets.com

INTRODUCTION

BY GEORGE SALIS

"Ancient stories of black darkness and terrible falls
plugged the holes in my body ..."

Mangled Hands is a fantasy wound in book form, written without thumbs and employing an amalgamation of mangled manuscripts, including the stories of Conan the Barbarian, yet it reads as seamlessly as a dream, in which the dreamer never questions the oneiric logic, the lesional loggia, and one becomes a passive observer, an eager believer in this shared phantasmagoria of gored phantasms. As "words dripped from his wounds," all that we see or seem is indeed a dream.

The plot follows the plight of Tarcisius Tandihetsi, an adolescent Native American of the Huron tribe who is returning home with a French trading party via the Great River. In addition to having a traditional, biological father, he has a Father in a priest referred to as Blackrobe, for like most of the boy's kith and kin, he has converted to Christianity, a belief system that possesses as much power in this world as the mythologies of the tribes. In the middle of the river, the party sees the ill omen of a diabolical beaver removing its skin and it's not long until they are captured by their archenemies, the Poison Snake People. They're hairless except for fur on the soles of their feet and their palms and, supernaturally, they live in Tardis-like kettles and have the ability of ecdysis.

This tribe is led by a Judas or even Luciferian figure formerly of the Huron, Snake Tooth, an impossible apostate who had been "born during a festival of bad dreams, therefore everyone feared him. When he was three years old he was already building gigantic torture fires. . . ." During their journey as captives heading for the village of the Poison Snake People, they encounter other tribes and creatures, such as the naked stone giants: "Each of these monsters was as tall as a tree. The lower half of their bodies was large and heavy, their legs were as thick and solid as deep-veined stones. Their upper bodies were light and airy like tree branches growing out of their heads. Each branch was a long arm with many hands and fingers. Their heads were the middle part of their bodies, joining together the upper and lower halves. . . . [...] Their hairy manhoods were pointing straight out from just below their stomachs, but it was also just below their chins, which jutted out and down, so it looked like they had bushy beards and were about to smoke long tobacco pipes. Their skin color was a mixture of rock gray and tree brown." Oh, and they can breathe fire out of their 'pipes.'

Although the Poison Snake People join forces with the Killer Yellow Dogs and the Antler Face People, there is a looming enemy that is a threat to all, the mysterious invisible animals of oracular origin: ". . . as the Giant Snake in the earth dies, bits of its flesh fall off, and each little bit becomes an invisible animal." These sharp-toothed demons slowly become desensitized to their acrophobia and begin to climb like apparitional acrobats onto the terrestrial plane.

The Poison Snake People and their captives do eventually reach the village where Tarcisius Tandihetsi barely survives gory torture and transmogrification, though at times he is almost treated as one of them and even gets to observe and participate in some wholly strange games, such as Whip Lash and Snake Eyes. To play the latter exophthalmic game, "The Snake warriors knelt behind separate bundles of red and green feathers as tall as mounds of snow. There were no teams flying back and forth . . . every player depended on their own eyes, which seemed to be shaking inside their heads. Each warrior in his turned popped out his eyes as far as he could. [...] The Snake eyes would float ever so slowly to the wet ground, and while they were still in the air, the warrior from a kneeling position with a quick flick of the wrist tried to stick as many feathers as possible into his two or three eyes. They could also throw out as many dead eyes of eaten captives as they had saved . . ."

Indeed, there is animating cannibalism, bodies are dismembered and remembered, genitals are molested and mutilated, and amid the Poison Snake People's brutality, anatomy is its own necromancy, for—peace pipe war pipe—*Mangled Hands* is a hashish feather fever dream on the muscled back of a galloping night mare. Of course, the most symbolic maiming occurs in the form of Blackrobe's mangled hands, which echoes those of the historical missionary Isaac Jogues who interacted with the Huron as well as the Iroquois and other tribes, and the final echo is that of Christ's mangled hands after iron nails were ran in through his palms.

Is this first-person account of a beautiful and brutal paracosm true? All we know is the declarative sentence repeated almost mantra-like at the end of each chapter: "I, Tarcisius Tandihetsi, say so."

Soft-spoken and compressed with wonderful mythological and philosophical implications, this realization of hallucination reminded me of Ben Okri's *The Famished Road*, except Stanton's novel is about a Huron boy in the 16th century rather than a Nigerian boy in the 20th. Uncannily enough, the works of Nigerian writer Amos Tutuola are also evoked without intention.

Prose-wise, there is no wordplay here as such, for the words-phrases-sentences were mostly played with behind the "seens," fondled and nobbled to make a mosaic that sayeth surreality reigns supreme, featuring a quincunx of juxtapositions and a medley of replicating muses: feathers, slime, hair, teeth, smoke, blood, etc.

In somewhat Lynchian fashion, characters sometimes speak in semi-non sequiturs and mystical mumbo jumbo which is a product of eavesdropping upon a mythopoeic and confabulating confab. I was even at times reminded of the sparse and potent poetry of Barton Smock, such as when a character articulates this in relation to the looming threat: "If it's a word, it's not an animal. And if it's an animal, its voice won't reflect light, so you can escape from its language."

I found it difficult to escape from the mesmurmurizing language Stanton has crafted in this, his only novel, begun in the late '60s or thereabouts and finally published, thank the gods, by Sun & Moon Press in 1985, and of course such a masterpiece was ignored by the ever-unreliable literary community yet has now, 36 years later, been gratefully rescued from oblivion through the efforts of Rick Schober (Tough Poets Press). I can guarantee that if you breathe life into this invisible book, it will surely breathe life into you.

I, George Salis, say so.

George Salis is the author of the novel *Sea Above, Sun Below,* which was praised by Alexander Theroux and Rikki Ducornet, and is currently working on an encyclopedic novel titled *Morphological Echoes*. He is the editor of *The Collidescope*, where he also publishes a column called *Invisible Books*. He has taught in Bulgaria, China, and Poland. You can find him on Facebook, Goodreads, Instagram (@george.salis), and at www.GeorgeSalis.com.

CHAPTER I
SAVING WATERS

I am Tarcisius Tandihetsi. You must have known Eustace, my father, he was the bravest chief in the two valleys. I will tell you all . . . my father has gone to God. We were twelve in forty canoes, and we had seen wonderful things in French.

We were going home . . . the sun overhead could have jumped into our mouths, then we were sure the dangers would be greater. I am a Huron and we forget nothing in this world. When we started out I was a boy of fourteen and large, and like other Huron boys I kept a paddle near the silent shores of the Great River. Our greatest enemies were the Poison Snake People . . . they'd strike out when you least expected it.

"One, two, three," Eustace, my father, was counting on his fingertips. He was the leader of our trading party. . . .

He stood up and walked the length of the canoe, stretching his arms and watching the great fire along the river bank. He had to move carefully because he had only one good leg.

Many warriors had said that I look like Eustace, my father, and I have grown tall as a pine canoe. It is good to be a canoe . . . not like

Bernard Atieronhonk, my cousin, who was only a catechumen, not yet received Saving Waters.

Behind our canoes my other father was walking on the water. He didn't have blood like us . . . there were brown spots in it. His mind was filled with tobacco smoke. He had yellow skin and black hairs on his face, and sometimes when it was cold, hairs would grow on his tongue. He came to us from France, where people heal themselves with sharp sticks and medicine bones, while Hurons prefer to use birch bark, tree roots, and the summer rain. He was a Frenchman. I knew many other Frenchmen, but they were mostly like arquebuses . . . very quick to speak.

My other father drifted along under different ladders. His long black gown was wet . . . he was a Blackrobe. He took away my spoon and gave me a knife and fork . . . it was time to eat. The French eat and smoke in their own language, while my other father hardly ate at all along the Great River because his bottom lip was missing. . . .

I could still use my own tongue, and it was easy for me to speak Huron . . . I always knew it even from the days when I was a beady-eyed papoose. I remember when God's Will came, but not what was prepared for dinner. My other father had all the Huron medicine men strapped to his back. . . .

I opened my mouth to let in some air, but the sun burnt my tongue, so I exchanged hair and birch bark songs with Blackrobe. His songs were like smoke between silence and the bottom of the Great River. . . .

The canvas bags of the Mission were in front of me, and I started to chant to myself:

"Eustace can, and Bernard can, but I cannot yet. . . ."

In another minute my other father remembered his teeth, tongue, and throat. He climbed into the canoe, stretching his bare feet either side of me, while his hands splashed the water.

"It's not good to find leaks in your canoe, Tarcisius. . . ."

The wind and the sun disappeared behind some clouds. My other father stopped growing hair in the water, then he stroked my forehead with his breath and painted a dark blue picture. The earth trembled and the Great River shook in its place . . . Blackrobe looked at his hands and spoke to everyone:

"Huron braves, it is difficult to destroy the empty air. I have no relatives in this world except you, my brothers, this Great River, God, my superiors in France, and an open pouch of tobacco."

His words were like Saving Waters poured over our heads. I touched Blackrobe's hands . . . I always felt much better when I held his nice hands, for I knew that they had touched God Himself, and they made me a better boy.

My other father smiled. . . .

It was good to see Blackrobe smile, but he didn't have a big enough grin to smile often, and I was not to see him smile many more times. . . .

Then he told me about a fire long ago that burnt fifteen thousand villages in the air. He mentioned the names of monks and nuns who were changed into pigs, and he also described devil-dances, ruined palaces, dry snow, and man-eaters, who became mangy and lost their teeth.

My other father was very good to look at when his eyes were shining with blue fires.

He rested his arms on my shoulders and said:

"Your fiery look, Tarcisius, has reminded me of a poem I once wrote in honor of the Particles of Constantinople. . . ."

Many times my Blackrobe began this way . . . he wrote poems about everything. Huron braves only write poems about cabin fires in the winter time.

"In those days I could duck under lines only a finger's length from the ground."

Blackrobe's boyhood was so strange and interesting and not like mine. He fell into the water and finally I had to cough. . . .

"Tarcisius will pardon me my daydreams out here in the bosom of the Great River and I will tell you all at once. I was wearing my father's clothes when I wrote a poem from an old legend. It was a beautiful custom for the priest to call up the little boys and girls and give them the Particles."

He smiled again and I was silent, for I knew that Blackrobe had made the Devil in the water angry, but as our Huron custom is, I bowed my head between my knees. This meant that my temper had gone where the dead crabs go. . . .

In the middle of the river, not far from us, was a high and steep rock, and on its summit a full-grown beaver was taking off its skin. I did not like this because beavers are known to be allies of the Poison Snake People.

Blackrobe resumed as if he had not been interrupted:

"One day a little twelve-year-old boy whose father was a Jewish glass blower. . . ."

I remembered when I was twelve years old without blinking, and how I filled the world with tooth and claw fights . . . not making a sound. Now I listened to my other father like a gray squirrel in a high branch as it hears a noise below.

"This son of a glass blower opened the door of the furnace where the glass was melting like ice in the kettles in winter time, and he thrust his leg right into the flames."

I knew what would happen . . . many times when I was a pagan I had helped our warriors throw enemies into the fire. I was very bad then and carried the Devil in my pocket. . . .

My other father went on:

"For three days the little boy's mother went about the village looking for his leg. She thought surely her son's leg was lost and she prayed God to help her find it.

"On the third evening the poor mother was standing by the door of her husband's glass house, and in her grief she called the leg's name out loud many times . . . then the leg's voice called to her from inside the furnace."

I clapped my hands and jumped up saying:

"I too have heard voices in the flames of torture fires, and they aren't very nice."

"But the leg's voice was, and the frantic mother threw open the furnace door and saw the little leg dancing in the middle of the glowing coals."

"And not roasting?" I had to ask, for that is not the way.

"It wasn't roasting, Tarcisius," Blackrobe rubbed his hands together. "The leg came running and it was as healthy as any Huron leg."

My other father took me by the leg and threw me into the blue water. I splashed about helplessly . . . I heard hissing and rattling sounds and saw glittering scales leap out of the water.

Blackrobe quickly helped me back in and told me my body would rot if I stayed in the water too long, then he raised his right hand and drew a circle and two lines in the air. I wanted to ask these lines a question but I knew they wouldn't answer. I reached out to touch them and my hand stuck to these lines.

I became angry, more angry than any other time since Saving Waters were poured on my head, and with a swinging blow I hit the lines with my other hand, and this hand also stuck to the lines.

Instead of praying to God I said:

"What's the matter? Let go of my hands at once, or I will kick you."

So I kicked them with my right foot, but my foot got stuck there. Then overcome with a fit of great rage, I bumped the lines with my head and chest, but unfortunately these parts of me also stuck to the lines. . . .

Blackrobe glanced at me and laughed out loud. He poked at my body as though it were a storage basket . . . I was helplessly fastened to the lines. Now the water was very still and quiet.

My other father said:

"I will help you, Tarcisius, if you promise never to be so angry again."

I promised, but there would be other times when I would be more angry. Blackrobe suddenly covered his face and turned his eyes into holes. He had seen something that I couldn't. He mumbled to himself:

"My information is coming apart . . . its points are too mysterious now."

The lines disappeared and I fell, but the circle stayed in the air. Blackrobe didn't even give these vanished lines more than a single thought. My other father was indeed the best of all the Blackrobes in my nation. . . .

I, Tarcisius Tandihetsi, say so.

CHAPTER II
APOSTATE

In which the warnings from the Great River go unheeded by the trading party . . . two Frenchmen, René Goupil and William Coutre, rejoin the canoes . . . the Poison Snake People are described . . . a council is called under the reeds . . . Snake Tooth, the apostate and leader of the killer yellow dogs, is first mentioned . . . beavers break their dams, attack the canoes and are defeated.

The Great River was not where it had been last night. Dawn was silent about this . . . the currents had stopped moving. The fog was thickest among the birch trees where a canoe might be carved into stone.

Bernard Atieronhonk, my cousin, crossed his legs like a brave reading a poem and said:

"Is it possible that we are paddling our canoes and not moving? Some of us will die soon in the water. I have spoken to the Great River. The beavers grow restless under the surface of dreams."

I wish we had listened more carefully. Joseph Theondechoren, my uncle Ondonterraon, the old man Sweating Fish, who was still a pagan, Daniel Owanago, and Charles Tsondatsaa, who liked to carry my other father's prayer books and tobacco pouches, were in the water playing Huron water games.

Our boats made a chain of watchfulness across the Great River, but we only saw a few floating beavers.

"Beyond this bend," Eustace, my father, said, "three rivers came together last week and were wrecked."

"We lost the letters from France there," Blackrobe added.

Joseph Theondechoren was ready to burst into tears, but he

spoke quite clearly.

"The surface is broken only in ripples."

Up ahead smooth soft hills were obscured by the sky, but then the damp fog started to slip away.

Paul Ononhoraton, one of our bravest warrior scouts, waved his arms, eying the best arquebus in our village, then he pressed his toes and fingers together while he repeated over and over again:

"Nine ripples are treacherous."

"Eighteen ripples are twice as treacherous," said Ondonterraon, my uncle, whose nose was made crooked when the Blackrobes came to our village. The fur on his back had been shaved off. Now he was a catechumen. . . .

Our party spent some time dreaming together near polished black rocks. In the horror of my dreams I saw a brown hairy animal, red with streaks of anger, then a gray gloom shrouded the boundless world of the Hurons and Blackrobe. . . .

René Goupil and William Coutre paddled up and rejoined our party. These Frenchmen hadn't been seen in several days . . . they had dropped behind to talk in French. I liked William Coutre very much. He had taught me how to make a funny face and hold it lightly like a bow string. René built a rock statue . . . a naked swimmer about to leap into the Great River.

I wanted to go swimming but my other father objected:

"Small legs are better within the canoe. The naked clearness and beauty of this swimmer is for all of us a silent messenger of a truth beyond truth. We will wake up tomorrow morning with a different feeling of life and headlong movement."

Crows and ravens carried pieces of dried meat into nearby trees. A red glow appeared on Blackrobe's hands as I twitched my ears, pricked them up, then flattened them down. The forest vanished before my eyes, as I crouched low in the canoe and rested my small fingers on the nice hands of my other father. . . .

The Poison Snake People were a small tribe, but very hard to kill, and Eustace had said that this made them dangerous enemies, for they came like foxes and fought like bears and took flight like birds. Their warriors were hairless except on the palms of their hands, on the soles of their feet, and beneath their beady eyes, which gleamed with cruel intelligence.

I had seen three captured Poison Snake warriors in my village. One of them could take off his own head, and he was still able to breathe. This was before Blackrobe came to us. These captives lasted a long time in our torture fires, but now all our torture fires are put out forever. . . .

My other father gave me a mushroom . . . I swallowed it whole. The boys of my tribe never collect mushrooms, we eat them up right away. I can still keep my knees straight, bend forward from the hips, and touch not only the tips of my fingers, but the points of my elbows to the ground.

We all went fishing, and I caught five very large fish while William Coutre caught nine. There was something wrong with the taste of those fishes. . . .

I saw a reed and it had been freshly broken off, then I noticed a pile of broken bones with no tobacco. I pointed this out to Blackrobe. He didn't think anything was wrong with that, although he regretted no tobacco. He told me my taste was improving. He also said:

"One should look at art the way one looks at paper."

He wrote this down, put it in an envelope, and sent it to France. . . .

Eustace's head came through the bottom of our canoe . . . he was standing in the water. My father was very strong . . . it was said that he could pull a grown bear's head off. I never saw him do it because no bear would give him the chance. He was in the full vigor of life, and only sudden and violent death could have taken him away.

"There's a beach of paper around this peninsula," he said. "Come and truthfully read the message that's written there."

I had my knife with me, and it looked the same as ever so I

quickly repeated to myself the French alphabet. We read the different pages. Red earth paint was spread over the letters, and for a moment everything came back, even the sounds of foxes in the white and green forest.

There where the waves ended was the wet sand. Paul Ononhoraton jumped out of the canoe and examined it carefully. Blackrobe saw that I was curious to see more, but he put his nice hands on my bare shoulders . . . now I was squatting in the water.

"In the meantime," counseled my other father, "an arrow with its point of death might come to the curious. I once knew a pussy-cat. . . ."

I was curious to hear more about this pussy-cat, but Paul spoke:

"The sand has been here two days, Blackrobe, maybe an iceberg melted recently."

"We do not agree!" exclaimed Eustace, my father. "I have examined the water's edge, but there's nothing to drink there."

Joseph Theondechoren, whose mouth was grinning ferociously, interrupted:

"The dark night hid its passage from us."

His dark eyes lit up with that light I have often seen in a warrior's face, when I was a pagan and lived in fear of my life.

Now all who should be were here at the council under the reeds, except a vile Huron, who lived in the mountains with the killer yellow dogs.

"I know him well. He is an apostate."

"Snake Tooth! Snake Tooth!" said several braves, and I saw it made them carry the Devil in their mouths.

"Spit it out! Spit it out!"

"The chief without any hair?" asked my other father.

When they nodded, he added:

"Poor man!"

Snake Tooth was the only Huron born during a festival of bad dreams, therefore everyone feared him. When he was three years old he was already building gigantic torture fires. . . .

Bernard ran towards me shouting a demon chant of betrayal. Snake Tooth was once his warrior guide. Like many Huron braves, especially the youngest, when they are angry or trying to make themselves angry, Bernard stopped now and again to hammer on his feet with his fists.

He stood in front of me, then very quickly he grabbed the toe next to the little toe on my left foot and held it tight.

"I have heard it speak to me in the village of the Immaculate Conception. It told me that Snake Tooth's toe was hacked off and now he leads the killer yellow dogs."

I could see very clearly that William Coutre wanted to shoot his thunder-stick at my vile countryman, Snake Tooth. The killer yellow dogs had cut off one of William Coutre's ears and ripped out part of his nose, when he first came here from France and tried to pour Saving Waters over their heads. Killer yellow dogs were half-human and half-dog, they lived in mountain holes, and never washed their paws and feet. . . .

René Goupil got down on his hands and knees and inspected my toes for a very long time, then suddenly he threw up his arms to catch any signs of stray meat.

Beavers had broken their dams and surrounded us. The fight lasted for hours. The beavers had collected many tree branches studded with thorns and stones, and they knew where all the holes in the river were.

From one bank of the Great River to the other, beavers died, our fingers stuck in their hearts, so many useless shadows. I was able to break some of their bones in the air. I do not think an arquebus is as good as a war club when men fight beavers. . . .

After the battle Blackrobe spoke to us all:

"God has many arquebuses and bows and arrows. Now we rest with the sparrows. The empty toe was written many times in the sand, so we must guard ourselves in the white waters among the troublesome rocks. The Poison Snake People might not be your only enemy in this world.

"Remember . . . no one who rejects grace can be happy here, and God help him afterwards. When I opened my eyes this morning I saw streams of blood trickling from Tarcisius' toes. I wish I had examined them more closely. They would've told me what we should do now. We ran back to the canoes too quickly. The blood hadn't even dried, but no matter . . . we must all go on."

All affirmed what Blackrobe said. I, Tarcisius Tandihetsi, say so.

CHAPTER III
BIG FORK

The Great River narrowed to the size of a walnut, while flies were buzzing all around my eyes and hands and in the white water. They spoke fast words and I believed them. The invisible robe of grace I was wearing was as beautiful as a beaver pelt.

Paul Ononhoraton, Ondonterraon, and Eustace, my father, were straining forward in the water as though they were rocks with white collars. The canoes floated on fish hooks because there was no room to paddle. . . .

Eustace shouted to my other father:

"It's a hard life ahead . . . you must have the sight of an eagle to see the morning sky. I saw it come out of the water, but only for a moment."

I heard high and long cries with sharp bites at the end of them. Birds went diving into the water, and the thick tall green trees swayed towards the river for miles and miles. It was a furnace hot afternoon.

Through the birch bark side of the canoe a stream of water shot into my ear . . . our dreaded enemies, the Poison Snake People, started to attack us. Eustace jumped out of the water, and in one second was hidden in a cloud. He sounded our war cry which is

deep and strong, but cannot be heard when it's covered with forks.
. . .

Bernard Atieronhonk lay across the front of our canoe, very tired and weak, his arms and legs dragging in the water. A big fork was quivering in the middle of his forehead, fixing the back of his head firmly to a canvas bag. The canvas reddened as he struggled to pluck the fork out.

I saw my brother Hurons crumple up like paper and sink slowly. René Goupil and William Coutre were splashing the water as a fork flew towards me . . . I caught it with my teeth. Clouds drifted down and hid the faces and chests of my brothers. . . .

My eyes returned to Bernard, and as they did, he broke the fork off close and threw away his gaping wound. Now there was a large hole in his forehead. I became sick at heart . . . I was only fourteen and had not a man's strength yet.

I heard Blackrobe call out:

"Bernard, now is the time to open your mind and touch your shoulders to the sky."

Blackrobe raised his dripping hand and poured Saving Waters, which he kept under his robe, into the big hole in Bernard's head.

I went completely under water. A frightened screaming porcupine swam into my face, and I had to stick my fingers into its eyes. I could still hear the sounds of forks going into the flesh of my brothers. It is this way in the heat of battle . . . often have I heard our braves around the cabin fires tell it so.

Blackrobe swam down next to me and shouted in my ear:

"Tarcisius, you and I are not mad at each other. It is very difficult to kill the Poison Snake People when they outnumber you, and I still have this feeling there's something else even worse . . . so why don't we just lie low for a while."

We swam to the bottom of the river, which was so muddy that it was almost impossible to breathe. Frightened fishes screamed, but this was not the time or place to pay attention to them. . . .

When I straightened up I saw we had come before a large white tree, whose many leaves were as green as any land tree, and some fishes were asleep on its branches.

We hid behind this tree and watched the fighting . . . the Poison Snake People were very cruel. Off to our left two Hurons lost their breath, then I saw a birch bark canoe, broken and abandoned, drift down and strike a mass of raging braves and Poison Snake warriors . . . and always the forks and knives kept splashing in the water.

As Blackrobe and I watched, René Goupil and William Coutre backed into the deep water. Their arquebuses didn't speak as well in water as they did on land, they were only effective at close range.

A slimy naked enemy reached for Goupil's hairline, and as he did so, William Coutre's arquebus made bubbling noises, and the enemy's head separated from his body right there in the water.

Blackrobe started swimming around the river bottom tree like a bird . . . I knew he was praying hard. . . .

Different barking war cries suddenly sounded, and a new band of enemies was swimming down to fight. They were the killer yellow dogs with short tails, heavy shoulders, strong quarters, and bloody mouths. Their right side was human and their left side was yellow dog. Their human side was red, and their dog skin was covered by a dull yellow fur.

All Blackrobe said was:

"Maybe it's God's wish that we travel into the invisible West."

We quickly left the water. . . .

I climbed into a hole on the shore of the Great River, and watched a black bear putting mud on its face and paws. Bear's fat is very good to eat at this season of the year.

"Are you not coming in too, Blackrobe?" I asked.

"That I cannot do because I am like a bone with no muscle giving away prayers without any sticks."

Blackrobe wrote a poem on a small sheet of paper, ripped it up, and threw the pieces in the river. They floated away like tobacco leaves.

A wolf with no fur on its head, neck, and two front legs trotted up to my other father. It scratched its shoulders, yawned, spread out its paws, then brushed against Blackrobe's leg. Fur suddenly grew on the wolf's body where it hadn't been before, and all the colors of the rainbow seemed to be mixed into it, not like the other fur, which was only gray. There was a message behind this, but I didn't understand who the wolf was, or what it all meant.

Blackrobe playfully started rolling in the sand with the wolf . . . they growled and bit each other until blood flowed. Finally exhausted they stopped, then got up and walked into the forest together. I watched my other father's tattered wet black gown until it passed out of sight, and I feared that now my sight in this world would be lost forever.

Without a sound a shaved and greased killer yellow dog glided over my hole. The dog had strips of Huron skin across its stomach and a war amulet of beads and mole feet dangled from its neck. Its front fangs were painted a bright yellow. . . .

For the first time I realized that there was no more barking or yelling, and I had not heard any splashing for many long minutes. . . .

I came out of my hole . . . giant thunder clouds were racing across the sky. I saw countless beasts with strange minds and few words . . . they disappeared into blue smoke. I saw traces of my brother Hurons . . . the crooked nose of my uncle, Ondonterraon, was thrown out of the water . . . Daniel Owanago lost his voice . . . Bernard, my cousin, poor Bernard was floating in the water face down, while a sickening smell drifted through the air, very much like the smell of a big anthill on a hot day.

Ancient stories of black darkness and terrible falls plugged up the holes in my body, and overcome with invisible grief and infinite thoughtlessness I sat down on the dry sand next to an old splintered log. It was thinking about its life many years ago. . . .

Meanwhile I kept on breathing like a muskrat, and strange feelings ran through me as though I might be poisoned. I felt dizzy and sick at heart, so I put my chest behind my knees to think . . . and when I finally looked up I saw that the killer yellow dog had discovered Blackrobe's trail into the forest and was intently following it. . . .

Then it was that I fully understood for the first time that I was weak from hunger and the lack of food from my own country, and the Poison Snake People, our most feared enemies, and the killer yellow dogs had joined forces and defeated our small party of brave canoes. . . .

It was not good to realize this. I, Tarcisius Tandihetsi, say so.

CHAPTER IV
LANGUAGE

IN WHICH THE POISON SNAKE PEOPLE TORTURE AND EAT PARTS
OF THEIR PRISONERS . . . BLACKROBE RETURNS TO CAPTIVITY . . .
THE SANDS OF THE GREAT RIVER THREATEN THE RAIDING PARTY
AND SOME SNAKE WARRIORS SHED THEIR SKINS IN FEAR . . .
A FAT NAKED WHITE MAN WALKS OUT OF THE WATER AND
IS KILLED . . . SNAKE TOOTH PREVENTS THE BEACH
FROM JOINING FORCES WITH THE FOREST . . .
BLACKROBE IS CRUELLY TORTURED.

I struck up a conversation with the splintered leg, but it did not make much sense because it was dreaming. Hurons prefer to read their dreams through their open toes, so it was only a matter of time. If I had been a white brave I might not have seen the red and blue bushes or the Poison Snake People filling up every shadow. We Hurons are descended from trees and the open sky. . . .

A bird with a broken wing fell onto my shoulder and crawled quietly down my back. Three aprons of deerskin with yellow suns painted on them were banging in the trees. Arquebuses and war clubs that dripped were tied to the branches, and I recognized the helpless hands of Daniel Owanago and Charles Tsondatsaa. I also saw one of René Goupil's shoulders. . . .

These had hardly been eaten when the Poison Snake People dragged in front of me the brains of seven Christian Hurons. At first I did not notice Eustace, my father, but his brain was there, the last one. My heart told me to throw myself into the midst of the brains, but my brain said, no, wait.

I wished . . . not caring that it was bad to wish so, that a crazy full moon would destroy the reeds by the river bank. A branch, maybe ten feet long, was gliding among the bushes. The dirt began to rise, and slowly the air was filled with falling rocks. My brain kept saying to count the birch trees, but my heart remembered queer stories about my ancestors. For a moment the whole earth seemed to be as small as a footprint . . . I had hurt my arm but was still able to part my hair. I was marched a short distance along the shore to a larger torture camp. . . .

There the heads of six braves from a different Huron nation were lying on the sand in the shape of a triangle. I could tell they'd been tortured within the last few days because a dead squirrel was still tied around each head. I saw Joseph Theondechoren and Paul Ononhoraton stuck on giant forks that stood in the sand. I knew there were many more of our cruel enemies in the woods behind me, searching for their snakeskin satchels. Suddenly like a foolish thought my other father sprang over the trees into the sandy clearing. His robe was flung over his head, hiding his face. He struggled for a moment, then puffs of smoke like ghosts flew out of his head as he freed himself from his robe. He addressed his captors:

"Enemies of the Hurons, listen to me, I have not made it rain . . . I am the man who likes tobacco."

The Poison Snake People feared that Blackrobe had scratched holes in the sky with his warm hands, so they instantly hated his sacred fingers. Huge clumps of rotten hair tumbled down a hill, and I didn't like the smell of blue smoke that was hanging in the air.

Blackrobe went straight to the head at the top of the triangle. This brave was a very strange Huron. His head was long and pointed like an arrow, and he was hairless except for patches of fur under his eyes and around his neck. The head turned towards Blackrobe and poured forth rapid words.

I pressed my legs and stomach together. . . .

The open beach started advancing dangerously towards the camp . . . Snake warriors shook their forks with threatening gestures, but still the taller ones shed their skins and danced around on their empty tails.

Seeing this, with my hair tangled and a blue mist rising out of the Great River, I felt black night and the north wind in my heart. If only I, or Blackrobe, or any Huron could hide these skins in our mouths, or dung-holes, or under our armpits, then put them on over our own skins, we might escape from this torture camp. . . .

I heard war cries in the stream, and a naked white man came out of the water. I did not know him . . . small pieces of paper were stuck to his body. I thought he must be a Frenchman, but he wasn't from our party. A hand was painted on his chest, and tiny brown and yellow worms had crawled into his gaping wounds. The air smelled of dead beavers and butchered Hurons. The white man was fat and not nice to look at . . . I made out some words underneath the painted hand. THE WOUNDED HAND OF JESUS.

Many enemies leapt upon this white brave, and they screamed, not he, as they struggled like fighting wolves on the sand. When they fell back, Blackrobe went up and took this unknown white man in his arms like a papoose.

A fork transfixed the man's breast, in the palm of the painted hand. Blackrobe gently pulled out the fork. I saw the hand now holding four red flowers. There were brown spots on them . . . he must have once been a Blackrobe like my other father. The white man's blood covered some of the letters underneath the hand. The words were now: UN HAND US.

I had lost sight of the birch trees. They lingered too long in this place where the Poison Snake People and the killer yellow dogs had joined together. There were many torture fires, each one a different color. Half naked enemies were waving their tails as they danced in the flames. I almost stopped breathing. . . .

An enemy fire leapt onto my bare back and went deep into my neck . . . my face was buried in pebbles and earth. I plucked a thorny bush from the ground and flung it into the flames. I heard the moaning and rattling of long dead Hurons . . . their bodies rolled up like bundles in the fire. I decided that it wasn't very good to burn such a bush and watch its sparks die in the air. . . .

When I dug some of the earth from my eyes, I saw before me

an evil Huron . . . his body was stained with spit and urine, dirt and ashes covered his legs, and a blue slime encircled his neck. His face was almost flat, without a nose, just two holes, without hair but he had many scars and a cold dark slit across his face hid his eyes.

"Snake Tooth," I cried out. "Snake Tooth . . . the Apostate!"

He addressed me in the language of the Hurons:

"I lead the killer yellow dogs, you puppy, get up."

It is not right that an apostate should have such pleasure. A muskrat dropped dead right behind him while he laughed at my people's bleeding wounds. His teeth moved in and out of his mouth. He started to fall but regained his footing instantly.

"I would prefer a pagan who folds his arms to your forehead, you sinful dog." I said this to Snake Tooth.

He smiled, and I thought of torture fires in the wintertime. He said:

"Soon you will taste real food."

I let him see my growing manhood . . . I am a Huron and the son of a great chief. I was not afraid, even when he bound my manhood with many tight twisting snakeskins. . . .

Next Snake Tooth drove the sandy beach away from the trees. In the forest by the Great River when black night comes, a lynx or a wolf might jump into my dreams. I was like the flight of an arrow, which was always longer then my pagan name. My people were bleeding freely in many places. My other father was dumped next to me. Several Snake warriors beat him with their tails. Snake Tooth stood by and watched, prodding a lifeless muskrat with the end of his war club. A startled mallard flew out of the reeds.

Snake Tooth shouted so all the enemies could hear:

"Blackrobe, there's no sense in your vile language . . . I know it well. It's an unearthly curse brought back to life, and it makes you stare at spots of invisible darkness. It's like sheets of bark being stripped from birch trees, or beavers arguing over their dead."

It was then I realized that Snake Tooth spoke without a tongue. This was something no Christian Huron could do. The Poison

Snake People must have given him this power when they asked him to lead this torture raid. His false words were like fish cast out of the water . . . they writhe and fling themselves about until they dry up in the heat of the day.

An arquebus lay at the edge of the reeds . . . white and green moss had already formed on its wooden stock. Butterflies swarmed all around it, while robins and bluejays bumped into each other in the air. . . .

I wouldn't have cared just then if hundreds of demons fell out of the sky. I wouldn't have resisted their language or even tried to make my manhood grow bigger. Captivity was worse . . . I knew already that the Poison Snake People would not give their slave-captives much to eat. Then fear came into my heart when I remembered their customs of food gauntlets and mushroom smoke. . . .

The young warriors, one a Poison Snake and one a killer yellow dog, leapt upon my other father. It was raining inside their heads . . . another cruel language. Each of them grabbed one of his limp hands . . . it is very painful to have your nails torn out, and I knew my other father had never felt such a torture in France. He believed that Hurons work better with all their fingers and toes. At first when Blackrobe came to us, we did not understand him. . . .

The Snake warrior crawled into my other father's manhood . . . I saw the hair on the bottoms of the warrior's feet, then he popped up out of Blackrobe's mouth. Meanwhile the killer yellow dog twisted off a few parts of his sacred fingers and threw them into the dark and uneasy waters. Then like the sneaky village dogs that they were, they crunched in his forehead, until I, lying the space of three canoes away, heard the bones cracking. This is the way they speak to their fiercest enemies. . . .

Shadows melted into dust while stars started shooting into the sky from the Great River . . . the Poison Snake People always understood and spoke the language of the dead. They could control their own words faster than a brave with a rope knotted around his chest. Now since Snake Tooth and the killer yellow dogs had left most of their hair in the mountains, they learned this dead language quickly. . . .

Snake Tooth spoke to me in this language and I immediately understood him. He described future Snake tortures of Blackrobe and my people well beyond the stars and their sources of light.

Then I told Snake Tooth to speak in another language. . . .

I, Tarcisius Tandihetsi, say so.

CHAPTER V
BIRCH BARK

I was a shadow under the shore of the Great River. I tried to tattoo a coiled snake around my left breast . . . I had already tattooed snow, a birch tree, and a very small creek on my stomach. Clouds of dust had started to approach from long distances, and I felt dizzy most of the time because the air around me was swarming back up to the sky. . . .

The apostate, Snake Tooth, leader of the enemy war party, floated into the reeds upstream to catch his breath. Birch Bark, a killer yellow dog captain, the one I had seen follow my other father's trail into the woods, and Partridge, a Snake captain, went along with Snake Tooth, while the rest of the enemies bent down saplings and took off branches, which had been so skillfully concealed that when I gazed at the saplings before I only saw the leaves. . . .

Now the thick dusty clouds were forming into a wall over the surrounding hills. Just like the sands of the Great River these clouds hated the Poison Snake People. Suddenly all the animals went into hiding, but the orioles came flying back one last time to the water's edge. Then the clouds crashed to the ground spattering everything . . . rocks, birds, water, trees, a few killer yellow dogs, but not the Huron captives who were protected by Blackrobe, or the Poison Snake People who slipped away under the strokes of their tongues.

The solid bank of deadly clouds sprang back to the sky and a fine rain began to touch even the blue shadows. Our captors got up and quickly prepared our departure . . . invisible fears balancing on their tails. Tobacco leaves and slimy green feathers were stuffed into the mouth of each captor, except Daniel Owanago, who had lost his voice and hands for good.

All the booty was piled into one canoe on top of the two Frenchmen, and on top of this heap, staring in different directions, sat two killer yellow dogs and two Poison Snake warriors. One yellow dog held a bloody fork over his head, the other squeezed a snakeskin satchel between his legs. One Snake warrior carried the manhood of Eustace, my father, in his wide mouth . . . the other coiled knotted strands of Huron flesh around his body. Their thick hairless heads and tails were painted bright yellow.

I was flung into a canoe with Charles Tsondatsaa and the old man, Sweating Fish. Birch Bark was guarding us. The canoe was bleeding in many places, but you could easily see that it was still the best prisoner canoe there . . . it pointed straight ahead.

It was not always easy to observe these enemies as they traveled so silently . . . sometimes they got lost in the dark. They never stayed in one place very long when they were raiding Hurons. They dreaded losing their skins to some strong party of Hurons and French with many arquebuses and paddles . . . or to other things more dreadful. Everything in our world despised them, except the beavers. It wasn't safe for them to crawl along the Great River with their forks and snakeskin satchels. . . .

Late that night we secretly glided by our Huron villages. Snake

Tooth shrouded the Great River in fog. Next to me I heard the handless Charles Tsondatsaa trying to spit out the tobacco leaves and slimy green feathers and shout a warning to our villages. It was very painful, but finally he was able to clear his throat, and as he did a fork pierced his neck. Birch Bark laughed noiselessly in the dark. Charles Tsondatsaa died slowly through the night. I couldn't see, and my thoughts were very unpleasant because so many slimy green feathers were stuck under my tongue. Often I have heard my people say that the enemy will subject you to a hundred deaths before Death itself ensues. . . .

Three days later the Great River was no longer a part of autumn . . . the tobacco leaves and slimy green feathers were taken out of our mouths. We paddled through a mountain where the air was dark with dust and smoke and digging sticks were needed. The water here was much colder with many lengthening shadows and tricky currents of screaming words. . . .

The old man, Sweating Fish, the only Huron to keep calling me by my pagan name, Little Spoon, gave me a necklace of birch twigs to wear for protection.

Ahead of us beyond the mountain was a long beach with a thick fringe of birch trees. It was early afternoon and our canoe was the last one through . . . everyone else was already there, silent, husky and dry. Some of the Snake warriors were preparing to paint their feet, the water, and the wide open sky. . . .

Birch Bark threw me out of the canoe. Snake Tooth came up to me and ripped off a small clump of growing hair from around my manhood, but he didn't bother with the hairs between my toes. He was the only enemy who was completely hairless, and the Poison Snake People treated him with great respect and admiration. It seemed beyond dispute that Snake Tooth would become their great chief.

I was carried eight times to the spot where the enemies were tearing open some Huron bundles. I did not like this at all . . . they are worms, these Poison Snake People, and except for Snake Tooth no one had ever seen a beautiful birch bark chapel. No wonder the leaves began dripping blood and the birch trees themselves were fearfully streaked with invisible fire. . . .

Just in front of me Birch Bark, Snake Tooth's helpful shadow, who could feel and understand the mysteries of birch trees, ripped open a virgin Huron girl. She had envelopes tied in her hair. She was captured by him on his way to the Great River, and he had hidden her well, but now a Poison Snake captain saw this prize and wanted the helpless girl. Both started to pull her as village dogs do sometimes with a stolen bone, yet she didn't break into two pieces as I expected she would.

They tugged at her and snapped at each other . . . Birch Bark was using his sharp finger claws. Once they fought so close to me that I heard them panting and hissing and I fell back into the water. . . .

When I got up Birch Bark missed a swipe and his claws slashed a long tear in the girl's chest. Hissing flames came out of the Snake captain's mouth . . . among the Poison Snake People only warrior captains possess this power to breathe fire. I saw cunning creep into the Snake's eyes, and he made believe to tug very hard at his end of the virgin, but he let go and Birch Bark tumbled backwards with her, then as an eagle swoops, the Snake captain landed on Birch Bark, breathing fire from his throat and coiling himself around Birch Bark's chest.

I felt glad under my own breath that anyone of our captors, especially Snake Tooth's second in command, might fall into the flames that never go but, but at this point I saw Birch Bark rub his war amulet. He opened his mouth wide and caught the Snake captain's head. The Snake uncoiled his limbs and his body quickly turned stiff, and for a moment it was standing straight in the air, then all of him sank into Birch Bark's mouth . . . I could still see the end of his hairless tail at the back of Birch Bark's throat.

Birch Bark kept pawing his neck as he ran into the water. He leaned over and out popped the dead slimy Snake captain . . . its skin already shed. The body floated away surrounded by awful-smelling blue shadows. . . .

Birch Bark now had the power to breathe fire from his mouth . . . the first killer yellow dog to be able to do this. He picked up the virgin girl and put her over his head, then burned a hole through her stomach and gathered the black smoking ends of her body around his shoulders like an elkskin robe. His barking war cry trailed into the growing night. The birch trees were not asleep. It had been a long time since they stayed awake into the gloom of dusky owllight. . . .

Birch Bark triumphantly joined a mob of howling enemies who were dancing and shouting with snakeskin masks over their heads. One young Snake demon had cut off a Huron's head and put it on over his own. The Huron's three eagle feathers bobbed and weaved as the Snake leaped and hissed. The Huron head once belonged to the gentle Daniel Owanago.

Another hissing Snake warrior took off his own forehead . . . many blue stems stuck out of his head, and they pointed like arquebuses at my other father, who was surrounded by his own bundles, until the pain was too much for the Snake devil and he was forced to shake his head wildly. Spots of fat were splattered on Blackrobe's bundles. One crazy Snake savage pulled out a small bell that the altar boy rings at Mass and put it inside his head.

Many enemies started to batter some of us captives with sacred wax candles and shining crosses . . . these tortures were as heavy as war club blows. I saw Joseph Theondechoren fall, and I knew he would never get up. . . .

Beyond the circle of dancing demons, everywhere in the darkness of the forest came deep angry invisible sounds. I had never heard them before . . . they went right through my body and made my feelings jump high in the air, even several killer yellow dogs lost their heads.

"From despair to despair," chanted the old man, Sweating Fish. "Hot, uneasy, and snatching."

It was a good thing Snake Tooth was too busy trying to digest the invisible rumblings, or the prisoners would have felt his great wrath, when a dancing Snake warrior was invisibly kicked in the face . . . a very great insult.

"Little Spoon," Sweating Fish pleaded. "I can no longer breathe through my nose . . . find Blackrobe and tell him that the earth shakes in the birch trees and wings are losing their feathers."

Behind the old man the uncertain darkness seemed spotted with flashes of teeth or ghostly fingertips that were alive like half-formed feathers, masks and shadows. . . .

Snake Tooth hunted everywhere for a vision as wide as daylight. He ordered the mask-dancers to stop, then dug a hole and buried all the differences between animals and the Poison Snake People. I thought it wouldn't work, and I was right. Now he began poking around the outer edges of the birch trees. Snake warriors peeled off barks from the nearest trees, while Birch Bark trembled as ladders and doors appeared in the sand. He took up the least possible space on the beach, not breathing more than was absolutely necessary.

Birch Bark suddenly lost a piece of his backbone . . . it rolled into a beaver pelt. A Snake warrior picked up the fur and threw it at the birch trees. Then out of the black nowhere a storm wind swept through the forest, but nothing moved on the beach. I heard the noises of countless birds flying up into the dirty sky. It started to rain . . . each raindrop was surrounded by a bright blue light, and as they fell to the ground and into the Great River they made very loud smacking sounds as though from an enormous spit-filled mouth. . . .

The enemies went crazy with fear . . . their skins were steaming like sun-baked earth in the rain, and their mouths were full of weeds. A bundle of feathers was still alive despite the bloodstains. Birch Bark stood up straight . . . he replaced his chunk of backbone with a tiny silver chalice. He could reach down and fathom the ancient thoughts of roots and branches. He came right up to me and ripped off my necklace of birch twigs and it stopped raining. The wind roared off into nowhere. . . .

Everyone except Birch Bark, Snake Tooth, Partridge, Blackrobe,

Sweating Fish and me tried to bury themselves under forks or whips or in the dead slime of several minutes ago. Blackrobe drew closer to me . . . he tried to paint a picture, but Snake eyes had been tied to my other father's remaining fingertips, and lips were squeezed between his shoulders and pressed into his palms. Words dripped from his wounds.

"The birch trees are indigestible . . . some are even poisonous, and Sweating Fish told me that they will burn more brightly."

I thought my body was being divided into many ladders and doors as we stood quite still in the deep silence. Then the birch trees burst into flames, very hot, but the trees didn't burn up. Instead they picked themselves up and marched into the Great River, leaving behind a hole in the earth a mile wide. . . .

I felt very small staring out at the place where the birch trees had been and I had to ask Blackrobe:

"What does a birch tree taste like?"

Before my other father could speak, the old man, Sweating Fish, cried out with all his might:

"Not like snakes and yellow dogs, Little Spoon! Geese go mad for birch trees. I am an old goose now and am eager to go with the trees."

Invisible fingers were pestering the birch trees in the waters of the Great River as Birch Bark's eyes returned to us from the ripped up ground. He understood what was happening, and he was like a burning flame under a pile of leaves at deertime . . . even Snake Tooth noticed the change. Sweating Fish threw up his arms and hobbled towards the Great River, yelling insults over his shoulder.

"Tree dog, geese do not like to visit invisible countries when it isn't necessary."

Birch Bark howled as the dark ground came out of the sky . . . a crazy full moon. He took a short run, as the boys in my village do when we play leaping games, and still in the air he buried a sack of slimy green feathers under the sand. He was wearing my necklace of birch twigs. The old man, Sweating Fish, collapsed, but the feathers did not fly away.

Birch Bark's head was dripping with feathers . . . the waters of the Great River had stopped moving. Blackrobe prayed in his secret language, his face and arms turning blue. The enemies were in a hurry to leave this invisible place. They also secretly feared what Blackrobe's dripping words might do. . . .

Leaves and feathers had already gathered in Sweating Fish's mouth . . . pieces of string, some red, some blue, hung from the stems. There was a great band of stars on the old man's cold forehead. Blackrobe covered him with handkerchiefs . . . perhaps Sweating Fish will never rot because his skin will dry out so quickly.

We soon started for the country of our enemies. I had much to think about, and my thoughts were not pleasant. . . .

I, Tarcisius Tandihetsi, say so.

CHAPTER VI
MEAT

Eight days of captivity and I was still stumbling against feathers as wild wooden points came into early afternoon, and every afternoon my belly was like a gray wolf . . . no, it was more like three gray wolves.

We hadn't seen any more birch trees. My people were stretched helpless across the afternoon campfires, while some of the killer yellow dogs amused themselves by irritating our festering wounds with their long sharp yellow painted fangs.

Blackrobe blessed me with his mangled hands, and for many minutes I remembered gray dawn, marvelous night, and the restful spaces of evening. . . .

That morning Snake Tooth with Birch Bark and Partridge had destroyed the heavy dams and walls, which were built long long ago in the Great River to keep out the Poison Snake People and other evil tribes of monsters and odd stone creatures. When the

French first came to the Hurons, we thought they were really blood-less fiends from beyond the Great River dams, but Blackrobe had changed all that. . . .

Our real enemies did not change, even though Partridge could look like a paddle or a bow and arrow. These shapes amused him whenever he tortured my wounds. . . .

My dreams were asleep in a broken canoe. It was a calm after-noon as I watched invisible hands twisting numerous whips and forks. Partridge rolled over and spoke to me like a village dog.

"Does the sun stream too hotly into your dreams, Huron puppy, let me cool off your insides."

He tore some flesh from my blistered side with a whip, and shot my flesh at the sun. This was very painful but I tried not to show Partridge what I felt. Daylight was bouncing off my forehead, and swollen dreams inflamed my arms. I quickly bit off a piece of my flesh and threw it in the water, then I stared at Partridge as bad as I could . . . never once blinking my eyes.

Partridge was not happy with my tricks . . . strings of blue smoke poured out of his body. He smelled horrible as he hissed at me:

"Tomorrow there will be another fork, and another, and another, Huron puppy, so you like to bite. We shall see what Snake Tooth thinks of this."

Lying on my side where it was not necessary to look at the greasy mushroom-colored flesh of my tormentor, I attempted to read any messages in the gray clouds of smoke that appeared and disappeared along the silent shore. . . .

The canoes turned west. Hurons had never gone this far before on the Great River. We came under a lonely point . . . it was small, very high in the air, and made from a shiny metal. Beyond this point there was a high rock wall surrounded by burning fire. A sturdy birch tree had grown up in a crack in the sheer brownish rock.

We watched its roots and branches grow in the rock until they reached the flames. Snake Tooth stood up in his canoe, wiped off the blue slime encircling his neck, then shot up above the high wall. He had grown very powerful . . . an unearthly light was glowing around him as he pointed both hands at the sturdy birch tree, whose branches and roots suddenly burst into large red and yellow balls of flame. Nearby Blackrobe was praying in his secret language, the only sound I heard in deep silence of several long breaths. Then the wall collapsed, the shiny point fell, and the Great River started to boil. . . .

As I stared into the boiling river, the swift current suddenly changed. My other father leaned towards me in the canoe and told me that I was dearer to him than any burning tree. I felt much better at once. . . .

Meanwhile the Snake canoes were stopped dead in their tracks, no matter how hard the warriors were paddling. They started tearing into their own stomach-trunks, hoping it would help their canoes move faster. It was no use. The river current change made no difference. The northern shore of the Great River was painted a different color, and a new band of enemies loomed up. These strange warriors moved deeper into the water, trying very badly to mimic snake movements, but they danced more like enormous bears disturbed in middle of long winter sleep. Each one of these monsters was as tall as a tree. The lower half of their bodies was large and heavy, their legs were as thick and solid as deep-veined stones. Their upper bodies were light and airy like tree branches growing out of their heads. Each branch was a long arm with many hands and fingers. Their heads were the middle part of their bodies, joining together the upper and lower halves. . . .

It was a good thing for the raiding party that there weren't very many of these stone giants . . . this was the last known tribe. The ancient dams and walls were built to keep their ancestors out. They were still feared by everyone, pagan and Christian alike, and now they had acquired new invisible power to stop all canoes in the Great River. . . .

These stone giants weren't wearing any clothes that I could see. Their hairy manhoods were pointing straight out from just below their stomachs, but it was also just below their chins, which jutted out and down, so it looked like they had bushy beards and were about to smoke long tobacco pipes. Their skin color was a mixture of rock gray and tree brown. Their manhoods were strange instruments of power . . . they could no longer make babies for their tribe, but they could stand at attention for great periods of time. Now if a stone warrior forced a giant breath through the back of his manhood, a stream of fire would shoot out the front. The only weakness of their manhood-weapon was that its fire would go out if splashed with water, and their manhood would collapse and force them to bend over. Sometimes they lost their balance, if they didn't dry their weapons quickly. . . .

These stone giants slept in long low lodges, one right after another along the northern shore of the Great River, which was now calmly flowing west, but it was the calm of just before a storm. The Snake canoes had disturbed them and brought them down into the water. Usually they stood in front of their huge kettles, which faced the river outside their sleep-lodges, and shot their streams of manhood fire at each other. . . .

Partridge told us that their kettles are filled with rotting fish, maize, mushrooms, bears' fat and dead captives. The stone giants never eat this food, instead they throw it into the Great River as a sacrifice every full moon. . . .

Then the stone giants attacked our canoes . . . they all moved like ladders, which seemed to be invisibly controlled. Some of them started shooting fire out of their manhoods, while others ripped off chunks of their bodies and threw them at us. . . .

Snake Tooth piled layer after layer of blue earth on the surface of the Great River, then he knocked it over, and water splashed on the stone giants. Some of them lost their balance and fell. Suddenly the canoes moved faster than any cloud . . . we quickly shot ahead. We were well out of range of those crazy stone giants before we stopped. Snake Tooth pushed my other father into the bottom of a basket and jumped into the air like a grasshopper without touching the cold water. His fingers were as sharp as knives and could swim away like otters. He spoke to the raiding party, his booming voice a deep wave of sound rolling through the sky.

"Hey-Ho-Hey! . . . my new brothers, when is a Huron canoe like a pile of snow?"

As if in answer the body of an unknown Frenchman popped up out of the water. There were four big holes in his stiff blue body and he was dressed like a Huron. He was wearing a beaver robe ornamented at the edges with mooseskin and a collar of porcelain beads, and was holding a prayerbook against his chest. Snake Tooth did not know of a more direct sign. He dumped my other father out of the storage basket as the Snake warriors stopped sliding around in their canoes. They quickly left this terrible country, not stopping that night and most of the next day. . . .

"Berries do not fill your belly!"

I was chanting this to myself, like answering a litany, when we paddled into a new country where the birch trees were silent and did not burn or move. We came to a narrow island in the middle of the Great River. We made camp here for several days. . . .

I was looking into the half shadows at my feet . . . something struggled there, then seemed to sink down and disappear. Maybe the fever of cold water was on me. I tried to shake it off like a duck, but memories soft as sunshine were being torn from my feet.

I wished very much that I could own a new arquebus and a rock I could look through. The French can make the far away come near . . . it is not really magic. My other father can take off his feet and grow back his fingers, while some Snake warriors can take off their heads. . . .

Then I was sure there was something living in my feet. I called to Birch Bark:

"Vomit dog, look down right away at my feet . . . where the hair is thick, something strange struggles there."

He saw nothing for it was now quiet in the hairs between my toes, then Partridge came up to me and was about to cut off some of my hairs, when he caught sight of a movement in my quivering feet.

I craned my neck to see, and in the half shadows there was a sharp noise, a mere blur in my surprising dreams, but now something was trying to rise up out of my hairy toes.

Birch Bark and Partridge instantly leapt towards me, growling and hissing. I saw their noses disappear into the shadows of my feet, which wouldn't stop kicking. The evening air was filled with broken dreams. . . .

"Aaaaaaiiiii!"

I knew by their cries that they had come upon meat and it made me very hungry . . . I wanted the soft heart. I began to think about Blackrobe and how his heart was now much more beautiful than his face and hands, and this made me feel better in my heart, but it didn't stop my feet from shaking.

Birch Bark menaced my face with a sharp fork, until I thought my time to go to God was here.

Birch Bark burned off the strips of Huron skin from across his stomach, then he said:

"The Huron puppy has keen sight and he will fill our bellies with meat."

I was not able to talk because Birch Bark was stamping on my chest as though it were an ancient forest path. I gazed with ferret eyes at the freshly killed meat . . . it was a huge muskrat. My feet stopped kicking, but my manhood kept rising and falling until at that night's cooking fire I ate a small share of the muskrat's shoulder. . . .

The next morning Partridge picked me up with his slimy hands and held the soles of my feet to the embers of the campfire. The hair under his beady eyes gleamed with cruel intelligence, then just as the hair between my toes was about to catch fire, he drew me back, but I knew what he really meant. . . .

I was to learn that my captors were not only savages and pagans, but demons as well.

I, Tarcisius Tandihetsi, say so.

CHAPTER VII
SUPERSTITION

Our dreamless sleep and the damp wind continued . . . the boats were useless, sometimes they were no bigger than acorn shells. It was Partridge's turn to guard Blackrobe and me. Our slippery feet were caught on the edges of some broken rocks, which were as sharp as teeth and even a little bit hungry. We felt like two specks in the distance. . . .

We met fifty more enemies, Snake warriors, getting ready to go on another hunting raid . . . they had already shed and replaced their skins. Some warriors were making forks out of tree branches, while others covered themselves with strings of blue smoke.

Their cruel whispers were those of delight, and their hairy eyes brightened when Partridge told them about their new allies, the killer yellow dogs. He described Birch Bark's fight with the Snake captain. He pointed to Snake Tooth with awe, then he spit towards Blackrobe and the rest of us slave captives. All the new Snake warriors showed great respect for Snake Tooth and instantly hated my other father.

They wanted to know more about Blackrobe's secret language, but it was time for them to go. The killer yellow dogs departed with these enemies except for Birch Bark and two others, Hot Dog and Yellow Breath. . . .

The Huron captives were being crossed into sections like speeches and thrown back painfully into the canoes for the night. It did not make me feel good to hear Partridge taunt me:

"Your world is flying apart, Huron puppy, it's too bad you'll lose your eyesight and your fish belly will have more than one hole in it."

I did not like Partridge and I did a foolish thing . . . I swallowed an oar, and my right foot kicked out sharply. My heel caught the canoe . . . it was upset as my stomach flew overboard.

Partridge buried many sharp-pointed nails and knife-edged flints into my bare shoulders. I was helpless as he grabbed me by the ankles, and with his slimy thumbs pressing my toes, he kept bending them upward, and also kicking my face in the shallow water. I choked and smothered. . . .

I did not sleep much during the night. My dreams were spotted with muskrats. My toes ached and my ears were stuck to my belly. Like the stars over the Great River, I only thought I was wet when my hands fell out of the sky. . . .

In the morning my ears were back in their rightful places, and I saw Eustace, my father, and Blackrobe, my other father, sleeping in acorn shells next to each other. I hadn't seen my father since the first days of captivity, which seemed so long ago now. He looked horrible like a pile of bones. His manhood was missing, and I knew his brains had been taken out, but not if they had been put back in. . . .

All the Poison Snake People had slept together in an enormous hole. With some of the other prisoners I heaped up piles of flint until the afternoon. No one had given me any real food since Partridge and Birch Bark killed the meat coming out of my feet.

Columns of blue smoke and a disgusting smell were rising out of the ground. The Snake warriors were removing all traces of yellow paint from their hairless tails. Some Snake captains burnt off their littlest fingers, flung them into the pit, and began to sing with their eyes closed.

"I am the Giant Snake who never sleeps. I am the Giant Snake who never eats."

It was then I realized that this place was sacred to the Poison Snake People.

Partridge teased me:

"Are your hands sore, Huron puppy, do you think our dreams are meaningless? We followed a dreadful trail between your toes, and it said many things. . . .

"Snake Tooth is a different Huron. You call him 'Apostate.' He possesses magic powers . . . like a Snake captain he can shoot flames from his body, but he can also fly, which no Snake captain can do. Soon he will be accepted as a very great Snake leader, and since he's an apostate, the Giant Snake will give him greater powers and strength than any Snake captain. . . ."

Now all the enemies stood on the edge of the pit. Horror of what was ahead came into my heart as I noticed pieces of torn and bleeding Huron flesh being tossed onto the foul smoking flint. Snake Tooth, the Apostate, stood in the center of the pit between two piles of charred and broken limbs, one mostly Huron, the other mostly French. Many snakeskins were scattered about his feet. A bunch of white-tipped eagle feathers covered his stiff manhood, and streams of blood wandered over his hairless body. At first I could not figure out what he was doing there, but then my stomach threw up flies and bundles of straw. My head was turning around as if on a piece of string. . . .

Snake Tooth was bending over the Huron pile of bones. He was rebuilding a captive . . . this was a magic power I had never seen before. I didn't yet recognize who the captive was. Snake Tooth was connecting the body parts with discarded snakeskins. He did his work quickly. The dead Huron was alive . . . it was Eustace, my father, and his manhood was back where it belonged, but it was as raw as red meat. . . .

I jumped into the pit . . . blind with rage I ran towards Snake Tooth. I saw my father's thumbs hurled into the smoky air. Snake Tooth had eaten the shoulder of the huge muskrat . . . he was replacing my father's shoulder with it. I noticed a piece of it missing . . . the piece I had eaten.

I bent down to pick up a flint to throw at Snake Tooth, and as I did this a great rushing roaring noise swept down from the sky, but I felt no wind.

Partridge screamed out a command from somewhere . . . all the enemies dove into the pit, and in front of me flashes of blazing fire and the head of a Giant Snake shot through the ground covered with flints. Red and blue and yellow sparks flew up to the sky like stars. Waves of flame surrounded the Giant Snake's head, yet didn't scorch or shrivel its slimy black skin. The rest of its body was somewhere else, only its head and neck just stood there, a very ancient evil thing, horrible in size and smell, looking down at the French pile. The Giant Snake spoke, telling Snake Tooth something in a crazy language, whose words sounded like sparks scattering off a full moon.

From under the ground I heard the moaning and rattling of the invisible dead. They sounded like they had no teeth and could barely move. Partridge yelled at the other Snake captains and they formed a circle around the Giant Snake. They were as naked as my hands. . . .

Meanwhile some Snake warriors put on tattooed snakeskin masks and tortoise shells, half full of pebbles. They began a leaping hissing dance . . . strings of blue smoke drifted out of their bodies. It was then I realized that this beach was a place of wicked superstition.

I shouted to my other father:

"Help me, Blackrobe, someone else's ears have moved into my

head."

"Don't worry, Tarcisius," he replied. "This is a pagan trick. Come here and help me, then the Giant Snake can't harm you."

I glided over to my other father and gave him a helping hand. He had his hands full swatting away swarms of blue flies, wasps, and yellow-jackets that gathered around the white brave, René Goupil, who had been rebuilt by Snake Tooth to only half his former size. . . .

I watched Snake Tooth bowing very low to the Giant Snake, then he picked up a large rock and threw it against the Snake's filthy neck. The rock broke in half, and blood and clumps of quivering flesh poured out. Several Snake captains started to rub this stone flesh against their manhoods. They went down in a line to the water's edge, then each one cut off half of his manhood and threw it far out into the Great River. There were no splashes in the water or wind through the trees . . . this was the very old and shameful manhood magic.

Blackrobe whispered to me:

"It seems our pagan captors have found out that there are invisible animals in this world whose power may be greater than theirs."

René Goupil shouted in Blackrobe's face:

"Another world . . . invisible . . . underground!"

Poor René, now he could only speak in half sentences.

My other father spoke:

"I'm beginning to understand why the Poison Snake People are such a wicked Nation . . . they don't believe in God. They believe that long ago this Giant Snake built their part of the earth around itself, using the soft ground from the stars . . . that's why, they say, the stars sparkle so little now. When the Snake had finished its house, this world, and was resting inside, fire then rain poured into its universe. As the fire cooled the ground was formed into hills, mountains, and valleys, while the rain made the rivers and lakes. Then the Giant Snake hid its own manhood in the deepest part of the earth. Over many hundreds of centuries the Giant Snake has slowly suffocated, only its head and a small part of its neck are still alive, and sometimes it pushes through the ground and breathes fresh air. . . ."

Suddenly René half fell to the ground, and Blackrobe and I helped him back up to his one steady foot. He had no shoulders to speak of . . . one had already been eaten during the first days of captivity. He started to cry as my other father went on talking.

"These pagans also believe that there are invisible animals underground, and as the Giant Snake in the earth dies, bits of its flesh fall off, and each little bit becomes an invisible animal. They have become the Giant Snake's mortal enemies, and search for its manhood underground. They are evil and cannot be seen, and unless they are driven by powerful feelings, they won't climb up into our world because they believe they will slowly become visible and die. Underground they are immortal. In this world they are deathly afraid of heights. . . ."

Silence except for René's half sobbing . . . I started to wonder if this Giant Snake had anything to do with our God, but then I remembered who I was and spoke up:

"Isn't this worse than Huron superstition . . . there are no such things as invisible animals. The Poison Snake People are indeed only pagans and cruel savages, and they are going to burn forever."

I must have said this too hotly because Blackrobe went on:

"Tarcisius, what can we do? You are right of course. I must report to my superiors in France that the Poison Snake People in their blindness believe in strong smells, strings of blue smoke, and now invisible animals."

All about us Snake warriors were hissing the high notes of some sinful chant and dancing as though they were stepping on glowing coals. I had it in my mind to wish that this superstitious place was on fire, but I quickly put the thought away because my other father, who understood so much, would also be burnt. Snake torture fires had already scorched his hands and feet. . . .

The pagans stopped dancing and opened their tobacco pouches embroidered with porcupine quills . . . they threw bits of tobacco at the Giant Snake. They did this three times with each bit of tobacco sticking to the Snake's slimy skin.

I felt pity in my heart seeing Snake Tooth, who had Saving Waters on his forehead, doing these invisible practices. Our pagan captors didn't know any better, but this apostate did.

René Goupil touched Blackrobe's knee with half a hand:

"Full of . . . ladders . . . tobacco . . . a deep hole."

Blackrobe shrugged his shoulders.

"Should we complain if this Giant Snake gets a very vile tobacco . . . the Poison Snake People are not catechumens. Another year perhaps . . . René, René, something is missing."

The white brave wept, then he started to pray:

"Holy . . . holy . . . holy . . . Snake babies dying . . . invisible . . . end of everything . . . Amen!"

His breath was almost on fire, and his one good eye rolled and stretched into the air. My other father said:

"These are pages from my own heart, René. I too have no desire to reach sixty feet in height. We sow and others shall reap. Thus it has always been and there will be no exceptions.

"René, you know I have traveled in many distant countries where ferocious beasts live, and life is always threatened. Until now I have made it a rule never to examine every footprint in the sand . . . but then what about the delicate foot or the light imprint?"

René's raw wounds puzzled me, but I couldn't put my puzzle into words because my dreams had suddenly split up, and a large part of René's footprint had also disappeared . . . it is hard to be both a victim and not free. . . .

That evening the Huron slave captives ate berries and roots while the Poison Snake People talked and argued about the invisible animals around a council fire. Hey-Ho-Hey! Snake Tooth admitted that these enemies had been unknown to him as a Huron. The Snake Giant told him many things. . . .

Meanwhile the sounds of nature whispered through my thoughts, and my mind was torturing my stomach like an invisible enemy. I finally fell asleep and a large white man the size of a vision wandered through the hairs between my toes, and every once in a while he shot out mindless explanations into the night. I woke up suddenly. Our captors were afraid and held onto their snakeskin satchels. Large holes were dug and carefully guarded because a great light was growing under the river, but when it reached its full height it disappeared into the crazy full moon. . . .

Next I saw smoke rising from Blackrobe's swollen hands . . . stars dashed across his forehead and many lines of light were buried underneath the sand. My other father groaned in his dreams . . . he saw God walking into the side of a burning mountain. He felt that his own body was rolling through some birch trees. . . .

I took off my clothes before it became too hot . . . then I fell back to sleep and dreamt of fires. . . .

I, Tarcisius Tandihetsi, say so.

CHAPTER VIII
MANHOOD

"Is it possible, Little Spoon, that you wish to remain all your life a Huron, a Christian, more despised than a fox, more repugnant than a village dog, who only eats what is rotten?"

Snake Tooth asked me this. We had left the narrow island, and the Great River disappeared. I was fastened to the upper branches of a young tree. I couldn't see more than an arrow's flight away, or keep in touch with my dreams. Snake Tooth plucked out a few hairs from between my toes and spread out my legs as if wishing to pull out a devil . . . he tortured me often during the march. . . .

The next day we were marched into another new country. Two forks were stuck under each captive . . . we were beasts of burden. We grew tails, our footprints were destroyed along the narrow Snake trail, and our livid shoulders carried bulky snakeskin satchels and pushed baskets of flesh not fit to eat, pagan food stripped off their enemies. . . .

The rest of the morning came through a strange thick woods . . . beautiful streams went between every tree and never left the forest. Some of the trails had fallen behind deer meat, so we threw up everything we ate, which wasn't very much. . . .

I saw Snake Tooth drop his weapons in an open field, his naked body was swollen and filled with air. His manhood was not as big as my father's, or as big as mine can be. Snake Tooth floated in circles until he fell through a snake hoop and struck a mound of earth above his ribs. He had received many new magic powers from the Giant Snake. Warriors crowded around him like drops of water . . . they rubbed their hairless heads and shouted to the sky. They all insisted that he would be one of their greatest leaders. They wore beaver pelts and blue fox furs stolen from the Hurons and French.

My thoughts fell by the wayside, not on top of each other because I did not yet understand Snake Tooth's full powers. He stood on my shoulders and answered all the warriors' questions . . . then he looked down on me and said:

"Little Spoon, even now listen . . . the landslides have stopped, tobacco has been thrown into snakeskin satchels, and Snake babies have settled into their cocoons, and will soon be demanding fresh meat."

Early afternoon growled painfully in my stomach as Snake Tooth pushed us slave captives even harder. I thought I was losing my quick moves because my arms and legs kept slipping into the ground. Then new feelings of fear reached down into my bones . . . we were now in the countries of our enemies. There were many camp fires on a hill across a wide lake . . . the Poison Snake People called it Mushroom Lake because wild mushrooms grew very thickly there.

Suddenly I heard a sound as though a branch passed softly over paper. Paul Ononhoraton had grown tired of captivity . . . demon warrior madness possessed him. He attacked Partridge with his tortured hands and teeth. Partridge stabbed him many times with a fork, then cut off his manhood and tied it around his own slimy neck. Blackrobe pointed to Paul's manhood and said:

"The health a great scout carries there will attach itself to the ground because that is desire, but several days later it will be gone."

Our captors began stripping us bare as stripling poles in a palisade. We were pushed into the lake, while their fierce thoughts scratched holes in the water. Crawfish started to gnaw at my fingernails, and other more hideous water creatures surrounded Blackrobe's stomach. He bowed his head . . . he could swim, and I could swim of course, but the sharp forks and black digging sticks, and most of all the bad meals had brought us Hurons closer to death. . . .

I went across with Partridge, who could hold his breath a very long time underwater. Once I looked up and saw a young Snake warrior struggling to hold his breath.

I couldn't help . . . I was a slave captive, and Partridge had a strong hold on me. . . .

Finally we reached the other shore . . . it was covered with water moccasins, bundles of flesh, and dried demon meat. I heard a stone knife sharpening a bear . . . then the sound rumbled like thunder inside my ears, as the Poison Snake People came swarming down the hill, screaming and roaring behind their colorful forks and whips. I saw skinless warriors, hissing children, and hairy fat Snake women with porcelain collars and moon pendants. They had come to Mushroom Lake from the nearby village. . . .

A fork was pushed through my heel and the hair between my toes was almost burnt away. I do not remember what was said . . . it was not easy to fix my mind on anything in particular without being overcome by a damp fear. I had to rub my hands along my manhood so I wouldn't forget.

The Snake children stood as tall as their largest forks. They were pointing up the hill to piles of dark mushrooms and the curves of their soft shadows, but I didn't show any fear in my face. Of this I am sure . . . yet under my breath I said:

"God, make me strong and silent like a favorite meal."

An ancient Snake captain with a necklace of keys plundered

from French doors sniffed loudly. I could see all the way to a ditch without losing my head as a piece of flesh sailed into my mouth. The captain spoke:

"It was the Sun who gave you a mouth, Huron puppy . . . then you knew fear, fatigue, and pain. Your ancestors built mighty dams along the Great River, but the Giant Snake built the river itself, also the lakes, forests, and stars in our country. Your backs are different than your stomachs . . . your shoulders are red. You must be weary of your new tails . . . cut them off. Have the Blackrobes taught the Hurons to fly yet?"

Birch Bark suddenly jumped out of nowhere and threw a handful of slimy green feathers on my manhood. He growled:

"Huron puppy, a great Snake captain urges you to grow . . . courage belongs only to the greatest warriors. Once I led a pack of killer yellow dogs against a Huron village, and I could not march from place to place unless it was on the corpse of a dead Huron."

Like the waves of a lake that rise during a storm, like the dry leaves of autumn that are blown away by the wind, like the reeds of the Great River that bend and straighten in a sudden flood, like a herd of animals sniffing on the edge of a forest, the Poison Snake People stirred and murmured. . . .

Snake Tooth spoke to me:

"Little Spoon, heaven is a loathsome disease, but courage might be under your feet, if you join us. I am a greater captain than Blackrobe, who promised you everything. Now look, he lies on the ground . . . grovelling, helpless, and inert."

A mask of calmness settled on my face so I did not show the murder that was in my heart . . . it is the best way to deal with Snake venom.

Black Magic spoke to all the slave captives:

"Listen Huron enemies, we believe in filling up every hole in the naked woods. From your face to your manhood legs are useless. We now think that the Giant Snake in the Earth might be overcome by the invisible animals, and then it will never appear again. Our people might be replaced, or every layer of our skins eaten away by our new enemies, or maybe we might be drowned by so many pieces of invisible flesh. Who knows? . . ."

It was dark night in the forest across the lake as we stood in late afternoon sun and watched the Poison Snake People forming themselves into two lines. They were as intent as so many lynx about to spring on a fallen deer. . . .

Blackrobe put his battered manhood on my shoulder, something he very rarely did . . . then he spoke softly in my ear:

"Tarcisius, do not believe the pagans. The darkness across the lake is not due to the struggles of any powers, or even the invisible animals, but to the effects of the sun's heat."

The two yelling lines closed in like waves rushing together in a storm, only a narrow lane was left between them. A group of grandfather warriors, whose deep lines of age writhed like worms across their faces, painfully pulled out our prisoner forks. There was a moment of silence ahead of me . . . many years were wiped out by the terrible smell, while flint-sharpened forks prodded the few remaining slave captives of our party. Snake women bowed to the empty air. Everything roared while Blackrobe kept repeating a line from one of his poems:

"Byzantine flowers of thought. . . ."

Meanwhile my manhood became swollen and red . . . my body felt like it was stuffed with leaves. Swarms of flies hummed and whirled around the Snake children as their bellies swelled then sank with rumbling noises. Red lines had joined the corners of their mouths to their wet eyelids.

"Puppy. Puppy. Huron puppy," they chanted.

I staggered into a whirlpool of blows and kicks that stung and stung until I could have shrieked. Tangled bushes of thorns were stuck inside my head. Once Black Magic hit himself with a blow which was intended for me and he did not like it. My body had become one stinging sore, and I was forced to wipe blood off mushrooms on the hill. . . .

They pinched and lashed my feet, small forks were stuck in my chest, so much blood that I couldn't see any of my tattoos. Another kind of darkness was cracking my shoulders like the bottom of a French glass. My flesh was open and my bones stuck out, and they were covered with sand, then mud, then splinters of wood. . . .

Snake Tooth was carrying a sling with an iron ball that must have weighed at least ten pounds at the end. Slimy feathers longer than any shadow were shooting out the slit of his eyes. It was then that I saw my other father . . . his body was covered with nails and thorns. Snake Tooth swung his iron ball and let it go at Blackrobe . . . it caught his manhood, which was ripped off his body like limbs torn from a tree in a gale. His mangled hands shot out from his shoulders and almost touched me. . . .

I shall never forgive this apostate no matter what it means to be a Christian. . . .

My people were twisted red and yellow in the setting sun. We had grown smaller, and there were large spots on our skin. Our warriors would never find their arms again or even cut their feet behind them . . . most of our trading party were already dead.

A purple and gray mist surrounded the hill. Frogs started to flock together and jump in our footsteps. There weren't any designs in our hearts or food in our stomachs. The day had turned sideways and was examining our bones. . . .

I, Tarcisius Tandihetsi, say so.

CHAPTER IX
SLEEP

IN WHICH ALL THE OTHER SLAVE CAPTIVES OF THE POISON SNAKE
PEOPLE ARE BROUGHT TO MUSHROOM LAKE . . . CURLY HEAD,
A CRAZY SNAKE WARRIOR, WANTS TO BE A CAPTAIN . . . HE PULLS
OUT BLACKROBE'S REMAINING FINGERNAILS WITH HIS TINY BODY
FORKS . . . A BEAUTIFUL SNAKE WOMAN SUCKS UP CURLY HEAD'S
ARM AND SHE MAKES TARCISIUS' MANHOOD GROW LARGE . . .
SNAKE TOOTH FORCES JANE TO CUT OFF BLACKROBE'S TONGUE,
BUT BLACKROBE GETS IT BACK ALONG WITH HIS MANHOOD . . .
BLACK HAIRS START FALLING OUT OF THE SKY . . . SNAKE TOOTH
SMELLS TARCISIUS' BODY FOR ANY INVISIBLE MESSAGES . . . HE
ORDERS HOT DOG AND YELLOW BREATH TO FIND NEW ALLIES
FOR THE POISON SNAKE PEOPLE . . . A LARGE NUMBER OF SNAKE
WOMEN AND ALL THE SLAVE CAPTIVES ARE SENT TO THE CENTRAL
SNAKE VILLAGE . . . FEAR OF THE INVISIBLE ANIMALS IS
GROWING AMONG THE POISON SNAKE PEOPLE . . .
MORE MIDDLE OF THE NIGHT SNAKE CHILDREN
TORTURE.

We had been sleeping a very long time . . . . our legs buried in earthenware jars surrounded by brightly painted snakeskins, while all the other slave captives of the Poison Snake People were brought here to Mushroom Lake. Clouds moved slowly across the sky, and Snake children were taunting us like whistles.

Jane, a Christian Huron slave, captured two years ago, gave us fish heads and rotten mushrooms to eat, while Blackrobe was forced to eat from a pile of very old Snake slime. A Snake boy drove a nail into my other father's head with a fork. I heard Partridge call this boy, Jumping Snake . . . he was the one who had been struggling to hold his breath when I crossed Mushroom Lake. He was also one of the few of the Poison Snake People to have three eyes. I did not like him and I was to like him even less. He yelled many insulting and false words about Christian Huron girls sleeping at the feet of killer yellow dogs. . . .

Snake Tooth put wings and dusty pieces of paper inside his head, then he dragged his skin along the ground where the invisible animals were more like lines dropping in the darkness. It started to rain . . . the invisible shouting and wild dancing under the ground stopped. Finally Snake Tooth raised his voice:

"Snake warriors, you need not fear the French dogs or their Huron puppies. See how they lean back once their stories are shaken. They simply stop talking, then it's easy for us to fling them over our shoulders like muskrats. Do not trust a Blackrobe . . . all he really wants are beaver pelts and tobacco, and his shadow will plead with you better than any goose."

Blackrobe just shook his head and wiped the swelling tears from his eyes with a thumb he had found at the bottom of the hill. . . .

A Snake warrior named Curly Head danced by himself on an ancient mound of earth. His moving feet were like fierce sharp bursts of fire, his tail was like a nail studded war fork . . . sometimes he would leap off his mound and go bumping into the prisoners. He could take off either one of his arms and beat you with it. . . .

He danced over us Hurons, never touching his tail . . . a sure sign that he wanted to be a Snake captain. When he came to my other father he seemed to go mad with hate. It showed mostly in his feet. Blackrobe still had some of his fingernails left. Curly Head rubbed his open palms down his sides and wherever he touched tiny forks tumbled out of his body. They moved like spiders along the ground and soon covered Blackrobe's arms. . . .

When I looked again my other father had lost his remaining fingernails. I tried to protect my manhood with my knees. Curly Head threw down one of his arms . . . it turned to snow. A beautiful Snake woman covered with feathers came along and sucked it all up. She picked little forks out of her feathers, and touched my manhood, which suddenly grew very large. Then she disappeared into the shadows of the many mushroom piles. . . .

Curly Head held a fragment of a shell in his hand . . . a thumb and living eye were in the shell. I looked into the eye and felt within my breast that this thumb might be stuck inside my head. Suddenly he threw the shell into the air and the living eye was thrust into my unwilling hand. I was sure it was a Huron eye . . . maybe even my father's, the color was the same.

Snake Tooth shouted out:

"Curly Head, I am your new chief . . . make the Huron puppy feed the eye to Blackrobe and you can have this Huron slave girl."

Snake Tooth pointed to Jane. Curly Head opened my other father's mouth as wide as he could with one hand and held it open with a sharp fork, which was clenched between his teeth. But instead of dropping the eye into Blackrobe's mouth as Curly Head was now ordering, I flung it into a howling crowd of Snake People. It hit the naked side of Partridge, who was standing on a ladder . . . his side opened and swallowed the eye. Then he threw up an elbow, probably a Huron's, and ate it again.

All the Snake People laughed at his stupid tricks except Curly Head who was furious. He had looked bad in front of Snake Tooth, his new chief. Curly Head took his anger out on me. He chewed on my forefinger until I crossed my knees, and everything was lying at the bottom of my heart. Red clouds, a blue and green sun, crumbling yellow trees, and floods in bare white fields . . . I could understand orange lips and bursting showers. Cruel and unknown pains had stretched themselves out and covered all my bones. . . .

Finally Curly Head put my nose between his slimy legs, and the nails on his tail cut my face. It is a Snake custom to destroy an enemy's nose with strong smells and filth, but I held my breath and Curly Head, feeling disgraced, gave up and went off into a mushroom field. The other Snake demons hurled themselves at the captives, and the hill was covered with ladders. . . .

My other father was stretched across a blanket of snakeskins, and Snake Tooth was forcing Jane to cut out Blackrobe's tongue with one of Curly Head's small forks. She did not know how to hack it off and that made it more painful. My other father was very brave and did not utter a sound.

His tongue fell beside me and I reached for it. I wanted to kiss it, but a mangled hand was between the tongue and my lips. Blackrobe had it back himself. I was sure that his magic was greater than Snake Tooth's. . . .

The hill was reduced to a single dark snake. Blackrobe went up in the air . . . in one hand he held his tongue, in the other he held his manhood, which somehow had come back to him. Snake Tooth was surprised. Then Blackrobe swallowed his tongue and placed his manhood back where it belonged. For an instant he reminded me of the Giant Snake, his neck had become so incredibly long. Black hairs were falling out of the sky, while lights were plunging into feathers. My other father raised his arms like the points of a fork and cried out:

"Living God, I've never been thrown out a window. Now I'm beyond language, a monument of superstition, although my tormentors still remain impatient. They haven't given me any real food for days, only words . . . that's why I'm floating in the air."

Snake Tooth rose up like a storm that whipped and thundered across the sky. Strings of blue smoke poured out of his body like snakes and mixed with the falling black hairs. Then he hurled many sharp-pointed stones at my other father, who didn't struggle to get out of the way. Snake Tooth's voice seemed to come from the middle of his hairless body:

"Listen Blackrobe, the Poison Snake People are the greatest warriors in this world. They believe that dreams move like river banks along invisible lines. They and their allies, the killer yellow dogs, will destroy your muddy religion."

Blackrobe dropped his head . . . I heard beasts snarling between the cracks of his skin. It was a windy evening and the black hairs had stopped falling. Foul, greasy, and unsavory Snake women with battered heads were roasting some captives' ears. Snake captains were lying on their backs vomiting up large fishes, muskrats, and Huron bones. . . .

I was tied to a mound of porcupine quills. I was dreaming of heaven . . . thrushes flew out of my wounds, while Snake Tooth was smelling my dirty flesh. To him my smells as well as my body hair were invisible messages. When he was finished sniffing, he told Hot Dog and Yellow Breath to go out and find new allies and take the white brave, William Coutre, with them. Snake Tooth also ordered that the slave captives and a large number of Snake women be sent immediately to the central Snake village. . . .

The Snake women smeared pitch all over us, then Snake Tooth and a picked number of Snake captains cut us up into small pieces so we could fit into snakeskin satchels with many shells, hair, and dark veins of animal meat. Jumping Snake carried my cut-up pieces of flesh in his satchel. He liked to drop me hard whenever possible. My thoughts were like large words painted as big as my arms. Torches were burning slowly on every Snake warrior's chest and stomach trunk. Trails of blue smoke kept wandering in and out of their skins. . . .

It was the early part of the night when we reached the central Snake village. Snake Tooth thought it was safer because there was no large body of water nearby and he believed that the invisible animals liked cold water. Jumping Snake dumped all of me next to a cooking fire, then he returned to Mushroom Lake. When I opened my eyes I saw wild plants stretched through snakeskins and shallow baskets. Babies as big as Snake eyes were hanging in the smoky air, while discarded snakeskins and pieces of charred flesh were being swept out of a fire.

A crowd of Snake warriors huddled around me. They were opening their sides, taking out their hearts and emptying them of mushrooms, slimy green feathers, snakeskins, and the wind that blows through the reeds.

I became very hungry as they crawled over each other and told fearful stories. One Snake warrior said:

"I just came back from a large raiding party. The invisible animals were swimming at the bottom of the Great River."

Another said:

"A slimy green feather, the size of my tail, sank four Snake canoes the other day."

I thought in my heart that it had been the old man, Sweating Fish . . . perhaps he had turned invisible. Meanwhile the Snake women who had come with us built their sleeping platforms next to the large kettles that were everywhere in the village. These small platforms looked like they had been thrown together by ducks. The women wrapped themselves in snakeskins and also smoked on long hemlock pipes, gifts from Snake Tooth. When they were satisfied with their new pipes each one climbed up into her own platform and slept with the red and yellow stars. . . .

One by one the many cut-up flesh pieces of the slave captives were staked down to the ground. We were given something to eat, but in the dark I couldn't tell what it was and I really didn't want to know. We ate this cooked filth with our feet and hands in different directions . . . in these positions it was hard to move and shake off the burning coals. . . .

I was lying next to the many pieces of Eustace, my father. Except for Blackrobe, who had many different strengths, none of the captives had been more cruelly torn apart. I looked at him, but he could not see . . . his eyes were missing. I spoke and my father tried to smile, but his features were lost on the ground in horrible grimaces and noises that did not sound like words.

Suddenly Birch Bark leaped out of nowhere and landed on my father's lips. Out of a small yellow pouch he dumped the half pieces of René Goupil, then he emptied the flesh pieces of Ondonterraon out of a snakeskin satchel.

My breath opened holes in the ground and all the pieces of my flesh turned a very dark blue. My head was free and I started to put myself together, but Birch Bark bit into part of my shoulder and kicked away the other pieces.

"Huron puppy," he said insultingly, "you'll never be a warrior chief . . . you're more like a plant, a frog, or a discarded elbow."

He gathered me up and threw me on a pile of Huron wounds . . . there in pieces I had to watch Birch Bark pick up the pieces of my uncle, Ondonterraon, put them back in his snakeskin satchel, then throw it into a large torture fire. I saw the wild red flames eat up my uncle . . . the smell was awful. But worst of all was seeing the frightening blue whips that grew out of the faces and body trunks of Snake warriors as they laughed and applauded Birch Bark's trick. . . .

Now only five of us remained from the peaceful trading party going home along the Great River many moons ago. And we couldn't be sure whether William Coutre was still alive and well, but I would pray very hard that he might escape from Hot Dog and Yellow Breath. . . .

The middle of the night torture was chiefly for children. When I was Little Spoon and still a pagan I painted trees in the hair of our enemies and opened many foreheads. It was different and much worse here in the chief village of the Poison Snake People. . . .

The Snake children started driving in thorns that hurt but did not kill, and pushing hot forks through pieces of naked Huron flesh. Only the near dead could stand to have their bodies tied up in so many knots. . . .

Then I was rebuilt by Snake Tooth . . . he stared for a long time at my young manhood. The first thing I saw complete was a shower of pine needles and a flock of mallards dropping out of the dawn sky. . . .

A vision started to grow out of my head . . . a slimy green feather moved from rock to rock. Suddenly from a distance I made it turn into a gray old man, whose body trembled and whose arms could not even lift a handful of broken shells. He could do nothing but sleep and dream. . . .

It is good to sleep. It is good to dream. I, Tarcisius Tandihetsi, say so.

CHAPTER X
TOBACCO

IN WHICH TARCISIUS QUICKLY DESCRIBES THE TORTUROUS FIRST
WEEK IN THE MAIN SNAKE VILLAGE UNTIL THE FOUR TOBACCO CAP-
TIVES SHOW UP . . . THEIR TOBACCO STORY . . . BLACKROBE
LOSES THEN REGAINS HIS ARMS . . . HE POURS SAVING WATERS
ON THE FOUR TOBACCO WARRIORS DESPITE STRAIGHT LEGS
STANDING GUARD . . . PARTRIDGE PADDLES UP AND KILLS
STRAIGHT LEGS . . . THE FOUR TOBACCO WARRIORS ARE SMOKED
TO DEATH . . . TARCISIUS DIMLY SEES AN INVISIBLE WAR IN THE
FUTURE . . . THE MANY PIECES OF EUSTACE ARE TORTURED TO
DEATH BY SNAKE TOOTH AND A HOST OF SNAKE WARRIORS . . .
BLACKROBE HEALS HIS OWN MANGLED BODY . . . HE'S
GIVEN EUSTACE'S SPIRIT . . . TARCISIUS IS VERY
PROUD OF HIS BRAVE FATHER.

Our first week in the enemy's main village had so many awful things crowded into every day and every night that I do not remember them all, but there does remain in my mind that bright cold morning at the end of the week, when we captives were dragged through twenty cooking fires. . . .

Blackrobe didn't have the strength to argue. It was too difficult for him to talk, yet he was able to whisper that so far the invisible animals didn't like to fight when it was too hot, but that could change. I wondered how he knew, or for that matter, how Snake Tooth knew that they liked cold water, but I didn't have time to ask because once I was out of the last cooking fire, I was thrown on a stage in the center of the village, inside a double circle of torture fires. I saw four enormous tobacco pipes and piles of tobacco, and at first I didn't notice the four pagan warriors because their skin was so brown and cracked.

"Who are you?" I cried.

The answer echoed on and off the stage:

"We are from the Tobacco Nation, the first of our tribe to be captured by the Poison Snake People. They were surprised at our size. They have never tasted our flesh. They'll find out that our thoughts can turn ugly underneath our tobacco leaves. . . .

"We were attacked on the Great River and defeated by a large Snake raiding party, even though we were able to use our feet as extra weapons. We were dragged here as slave captives, and now we are buried up to our necks in tobacco. . . ."

Another Tobacco warrior continued:

"A few years ago a Blackrobe visited our country. Every day he demanded beaver pelts and smoked more tobacco than the previous day, and he would only eat his own slime . . . finally he drifted away."

When my other father heard this, he asked for some tobacco, and the flesh on his face became as wrinkled as dried leaves. Blue smoke strings poured out of many Snake bodies and surrounded Blackrobe . . . they encircled his arms and pulled them off. My other father didn't scream or show any other sign of pain. He didn't move as his arms were carried out of the village, past the mushroom fields, and into a clearing with large rocks, where the blue smoke strings dropped them at the foot of a single dark gray tree.

The slave captives, except Blackrobe and the four Tobacco warriors, were quick-marched into the clearing. A naked Snake warrior sat on top of this tree and wouldn't come down. Small birds were in his skin, and their feathers fell down and covered Blackrobe's arms, whereupon a beautiful Snake woman, not the one who had disappeared with Curly Head's arm, but another, stood up like a shadow over a tobacco pipe.

She wore a dress of dark feathers, and her shiny black hair was shaped like a spider. She climbed up the tree, and when she reached the Snake warrior, he quickly jumped out of the tree and ran away. Several pools of blood appeared on the ground, while the Snake woman was trying to encircle her own body with her arms and tail. She rocked back and forth in a frenzy, but finally got tired and crawled into a box of teeth on an upper limb . . . her eyes full of feathers, shiny stones and yellow spruce cones. Later she fell out of the tree and was chained to the bottom of a large rock . . . I never saw her again. . . .

We were marched back to the stage, and just as we got there, Blackrobe's arms popped back in where they belonged. He staggered over to the four Tobacco warriors. I heard him under his breath telling them about God and His beautiful daughters in the flames after a night of prayer. It is easy to think of God's daughters when you are soon to meet them, and they are so much stronger than you . . . they will not cry out or moan when you are in pain. I felt good that I was not a pagan anymore and had never lost my head in an earthenware jar. . . .

Straight Legs, a peculiar Snake boy, who had sand running all the time from under his three eyes, had been told by Partridge to watch Blackrobe very carefully and not to let him touch water. . . .

I knew my other father would do everything in his power to touch water and help the four Tobacco warriors wear robes of grace and live in a well-protected village when they were dead. . . .

Straight Legs' feet were not like any other Snake's . . . they were shaped like brooms, yet his body was able to stretch in many places. His stomach trunk was shaped like a spider's web, and slimy green feathers were falling from under his arms. . . .

I could tell that Straight Legs wanted to know what my other father was doing at each tobacco pile, so I tried to turn his attention away. I asked him what was under his feet. This made him very angry . . . he answered:

"Maybe some damp clay and your face spinning back and forth."

Then he put his slippery hand down my throat, but I remembered how my other father would act . . . no hot words rushed out of my mouth. All I did was hold down his arm for awhile . . . I was not so foolish. . . .

Blackrobe had already touched Saving Waters from the nail

hole in his head to the forehead of each Tobacco warrior. Partridge paddled furiously through the tobacco leaves. He was still wearing Paul Ononhoraton's manhood around his neck. He was the only Snake captain who liked to use a canoe on dry land. Birch Bark was with him in the canoe. Straight Legs stood frozen like a small bird at the sight of a tribe of hawks darkening the sky by spreading their wings. His spider web stomach was blown to the ground, where snakeskin satchels hid the dirt under his feet.

Partridge asked with his whip:

"Do the roots of trees have hair, Straight Legs, or were you asleep?"

Partridge continued beating Straight Legs . . . Partridge knew right away what Blackrobe had done. Finally he threw his heavy paddle at Straight Legs, who fell to the ground like a closed door. Yellow scratches on a stone, medicine bundles, and slimy green feathers in a snakeskin satchel . . . that was all that was left of Straight Legs. No pagan Song of Mourning was chanted . . . a very big disgrace among the Poison Snake People.

Snake Tooth suddenly landed on the stage, looked around slowly, then spoke like pagan earth to the gathering Poison Snake People:

"My children . . . didn't you see the warriors from the Tobacco Nation throw up their insides after Blackrobe touched their foreheads with water. I was at the bottom of Mushroom Lake and yet I saw what happened."

I thought what Snake Tooth said was a wicked lie, and I made a face at his back. Then he turned around and smiled at me like a wicked apostate. He asked me again to join him as a warrior-chief. I fell instantly sick, and didn't feel better until the afternoon, when the slave captives were fed wild mushrooms and snake slime. . . .

That night all four Tobacco warriors were put inside the huge pipes, and each Snake warrior and woman took a turn at smoking them. The Tobacco warriors were brave men . . . they didn't utter a moan of pain throughout the long hours of smoke, not even when their fingertips were all red with heat. . . .

Time was lengthened with water, beaver pelts, and tobacco . . . for the rest of the night Snake children chewed on bits of the victims' flesh like hunks of tobacco. When they were finished sucking and chewing, they would spit out the shriveled flesh. . . .

After the four Tobacco warriors had gone to God, Snake Tooth gathered together my father, my other father, poor René Goupil, and me . . . we were the only ones left here from our trading party. William Coutre was with the two killer yellow dogs. It was just before dawn. Snake Tooth said:

"Village dogs . . . your flesh has lost most of its taste, but we will treat you better than tobacco. We'll let two of you live, but the others will have to die very slowly. Look . . . the air is the color of faded chestnuts, and this will be the last time at least one of you will see the ground that's not so far away."

Snake Tooth did not have to tell us more. We could see all the Snake designs. For a moment I saw the future . . . an invisible war fought in water jars and a huge tower until Snake flesh boils and their old skins are flooded. . . .

Snake Tooth cut up my father into many pieces. Eustace was never braver . . . his manhood lay bound and helpless in some warm clay surrounded by the rest of his body. He was staring blindly at the dying flames of a torture fire, and it was difficult for him to open his mouth and speak because Snake Tooth had thrown away his lips, but it was necessary.

"Tarcisius, my son, I am already a dead Huron, old and tired and blind, and giving up all my powers. I am ready to go to God . . . soon my life will vanish into a sacred mountain. . . .

"In the old days, Tarcisius, before Blackrobe made us give up hunting with spoons, when you were Little Spoon, and I was Rainbow Wolf the Hunter, I taught you the best ways to torture your enemies. You were very young and eager . . . your powerful dreams would cut open their necks and your cold shadow would crawl into their mouths. We could smell their fears in your body, which gave us more information. Then we used their dried bones to build our villages . . . for these bad things forgive me, my son, my lips were really born in a walnut. . . ."

My father was exhausted . . . I picked up the remains of his face and put it in the clay with his manhood. He was desperately trying to tell me more, but without much luck, when Snake Tooth jumped on his chest and turned it inside out. . . .

Snake Tooth's powers were rising everywhere like the sun . . . his teeth were gliding like white stars above his broad shoulders, which were so different than the Poison Snake People's. A dozen warriors wearing snakeskin masks started to crowd around the naked pieces of my father. They were searching him inside out for his brave spirit. One of them picked up my father's manhood and the others stuck hot forks into it over and over again. Bits of his flesh were rubbed into shells, his ears were pushed upwards, but he made no sounds of fear or pain. . . .

Snake Tooth was flipping out in a rage . . . blue smoke strings were flying out of his head. He was brainsick . . . furious because he could not learn why Eustace, my father, was so brave and still a Christian.

More shrieking Snake warriors swarmed around my father. I knew in my heart they were going to gnaw at him forever, then no one's magic would be able to put him together again. Snake Tooth grabbed my father's shredded manhood from the masked warrior, and lifted it above his head, then dropped it into his wide grinning mouth. He ate it noisily right in front of my face, then he asked me if I would join him eating my father's heart. . . .

I prayed to God. An avalanche was in my fingertips, but I kept myself under control, while snakeskin satchels were opening inside my head. I was on my hands and knees, crying, but I said nothing to that apostate, Snake Tooth. A hand touched my shoulder, and I suddenly felt much better in my heart because I knew that hand had touched God Himself. It was my other father, his eyes shining with blue fires, his bottom lip no longer missing, the nail hole in his head gone, and his mangled hands were beautiful again. Blackrobe's magic was strong medicine, even his yellow skin brightened, and his beard was thick and full once more. His voice came from heaven:

"Tarcisius, try to be holy . . . Eustace, your father, has gone to God. He gave me his spirit before he passed away, and asked me to keep you holy. For a while I can protect you from Snake Tooth. . . ."

Snake Tooth walked away, slimy green feathers dropping off his manhood. Never did I feel more proud of my father than I did then . . . he had gone to God. . . .

I, Tarcisius Tandihetsi, say so.

CHAPTER XI
RAIN

In which Tarcisius is already a slave in Wrinkled Black Skin's kettle ... Blackrobe is slave to Kettle Skin ... Snake Tooth has given Jane to Curly Head, Wrinkled Black Skin's husband ... their son, Frog Snake, kills Jane in a fit of madness ... he rubs his tail with his hands, a very bad thing among the Poison Snake People ... during the night Snake Tooth rips off Tarcisius' left shoulder ... a muskrat takes its place ... the next evening Frog Snake becomes deathly sick ... a monster tongue grows out of his stomach ... his warrior uncles and their Snake magic are no help ... René secretly touches Frog Snake's forehead with Saving Waters ... the tongue disappears ... Black Magic demands René's death ... Snake Tooth swoops down from the sky and kills René ... a gang of Snake children cart away the body ... the sadness of Blackrobe ... Frog Snake gets better.

Wrinkled Black Skin boiled my wounds into her family kettle and wrapped my manhood in leaves of corn. She had a needle and thread and tried to make me whole again....

My other father was also a slave ... his mistress was Kettle Skin, wrinkled and gray-skinned every half year, and the only Snake woman without a head of hair. She seemed to have been young when the stones on the ground grew wings and silently rose into the mountains.

Sometimes when I thought of Eustace, my father, I wished that God would torture to death all the Poison Snake People....

Wrinkled Black Skin's husband was the cruel warrior, Curly Head, whose arm had been returned from the snow by Feather Skin, one of the few beautiful Snake women. Also Snake Tooth gave him Jane, whom I liked very much. Like me she had hair between her toes, and ears like a puppy, although the rest of her was like any other Huron girl, except her shiny fish-colored hair.

She was always recalling her past . . . like when she painted sharp-edged designs on deerskin cradles with blue and yellow earth paints. . . .

Wrinkled Black Skin's son was named Frog Snake, a crazy savage boy with webbed feet, holes in his face, and red and gray fur growing around his wrists. He hated me and often tried to stretch my head above the sky. . . .

One afternoon I was tied to the edge of the kettle, while my wounds were gathering strength from the food inside. I watched Frog Snake crawl after Jane, catching her by the hair and holding it firmly even though it was very slippery. He rubbed a thorn bush over her tongue and ears. He was jealous because he didn't have any ears . . . just holes in the sides of his head.

Then a dreadful thing happened . . . Frog Snake threw Jane out of the kettle. She flew by me, screaming, streaked with blood and water. I was helpless as I heard her voice retreating to the edges of her hair. I looked back inside the kettle . . . Frog Snake had opened his stomach, which was as wrinkled as an old handkerchief. He started rubbing his tail with his hands . . . it seemed to excite him very much, but now he would never be a Snake captain. He shouted:

"The sun is a dream! The sun is a dream! I escaped by cutting through the ribs and taking a piece of the heart."

Then he leaped out of the kettle, rolling his eyes in search of Jane. I saw he had little sense . . . he was tearing the fur from his wrists. When Jane saw him she rushed madly through the Snake baby cocoons that were now hanging in the air.

Soft breasts surrounded by white feathers made sleeping noises inside the cocoons. Jane looked everywhere for the right path, but couldn't find it. Frog Snake jumped after her, his eyes quickly climbing up a ladder as he started to hop sideways. He thought the invisible animals were outside the village waiting for small game.

He shouted:

"The dreams in my stomach are surfacing like dark circles of blood. I haven't seen the invisible animals, but I know for sure that this Huron slave is their helper. . . ."

He grabbed Jane by the toes and dragged her through a big torture fire . . . after the fifth time through she was dead. I went mad, breaking the snakeskin ropes that held me to the top of the kettle and splashed to the bottom. Luckily this calmed me down and my thoughts scattered wherever they could. . . .

Frog Snake dropped Jane's body back into his family kettle. I was face to face with her legs. Jane! Jane! Her limp body was a rose-bush, a spruce cone, and her eyelashes beautiful colored porcupine quills . . . then she vanished. . . .

Later during the black night I lost my left shoulder. Snake Tooth ripped it off because I had pushed some crazy Snake women out of the kettle. I did not want to know what was inside their slimy bodies. I was only a boy of fourteen, not yet a man. . . .

I felt very miserable and alone trying to rest in a warm pool of water. My other father was in his kettle. I wished he could be here with me and put his nice hands near my missing shoulder. Then a thought came to me that I preferred to miss my shoulder rather than my forehead. I felt better with this thought and reached over in the dark to find out how much of my shoulder was missing. . . .

I touched a muskrat, and instantly I felt for certain it was the one that had been part of Eustace, my father. The muskrat had grown out of my body in the water, replacing my shoulder, and it could not move because its rear paws were hidden near my heart. Its tail started whipping the back of my neck. . . .

The next evening Frog Snake fell sick . . . he had fallen into a deep furry dark blood swamp pit. He had touched his tail, but I was the only one who had seen him do this. Slimy green feathers were coiling their way out of the holes in his face. Many warrior uncles led by his father's brother, Kicking Snake, jumped into the kettle and danced through the night on clouds and roots crawling out

of Frog Snake's stomach trunk. They mostly stayed away from me
. . . the silent muskrat in my shoulder surprised them. No one
would touch it . . . they were waiting for some sort of sign. Some of
them wore the heads and skins of defeated enemies, while others
scattered mushrooms and bits of tobacco in the water.

Small squares, pictures of the French alphabet, beavers, piles of
tobacco, and wingless birds squirming helplessly in tree moss . . .
all appeared and disappeared on Frog Snake's mushroom-colored
flesh, as he shivered in the kettle. Then I saw the white brave René
Goupil float by under a small circle of sticks . . . his blood was mixed
with water, he was still only half a man. When he saw Frog Snake he
mumbled:

"Some disease . . . tongue . . . half-medicine . . . the birch trees."

Piles of tobacco were thrown away as a large tongue pushed its
way up through Frog Snake's stomach. Then the Poison Snake People realized that this kettle was more than just a fireplace. . . .

René Goupil and William Coutre, my other father had told me,
loved to swim. They were coming to our Huron villages to live there
for a year and practice swimming every day. Poor René, now he
could only swim halfway across a river.

René turned to me and said:

"Cold muskrat dreams . . . Snake Tooth . . . broken arms . . . your
missing shoulder . . . mushrooms and tobacco!"

I looked at Frog Snake . . . he looked dead. The tongue had
grown bigger and it was cleaning pictures off his body trunk . . .
only the French alphabet was left. I moved closer, no one stopped
me. Frog Snake's face was an immense wind, he was nearly finished
dreaming.

René crawled halfway behind me . . . . I knew he would try to
help Frog Snake. I moved away, and René drew a muskrat with
muddy paws on the sick boy's chest . . . it was running through
the French alphabet and around the monster tongue. René did his
work quickly and quietly . . . he secretly touched the boy's forehead
with Saving Waters, then he half crawled and half jumped out of the

kettle. Meanwhile the muskrat devoured the tongue, plunged into a pool of water, and swam away.

Frog Snake screamed in great agony. Kicking Snake ordered me to leave. He said that Snake Tooth and Black Magic would be coming here shortly to take council. Outside it was raining lightly. I watched a rabbit munching on some leaves and a clumsy young bear rolling in the wet grass. It was the start of a fine day for a hunter. . . .

As I walked around the Snake children called after me:

"Look . . . there goes our next meal."

I did not like that until I remembered what Blackrobe had said:

"The rain will grow weary of these mushrooms. What suffering! The Poison Snake People don't know much about eating."

I bumped into Partridge . . . his body was shaped like a paddle. His chest was gleaming in the rain. He made me paddle his canoe. The rain soaked the muskrat's fur. . . .

Black Magic came into the village wearing his winter dreams. Leaf designs and spider webs were carved into his skin. He stopped the canoe and asked:

"Partridge, is it really true that my nephew, Frog Snake, is near death in his family kettle?"

After Partridge answered, "Yes he is," Black Magic continued:

"Partridge, I want you to find that French half-worm, whose rain magic is slowly destroying Frog Snake. A new downpour is needed. I will go and demand that Snake Tooth kill him. I am too old to do it myself."

"I am greatly honored, Black Magic . . . I will gladly find him," Partridge replied. "It's easy to tell who René Goupil is . . . his tongue is cut in half, but his single breast is four times larger than any Snake woman's. He lives in a different world that's only one color . . . there he means to burn or roast us, if he can."

How can René do this now, I thought, if he's only half a man. Black Magic nodded to Partridge.

"I went there in my youth with my cousins. We all had grown red fur on each wrist."

Partridge said:

"Last week I rebuilt another French captive to only half his size . . . Snake Tooth gave me this power. The Frenchman was a dirty old man with sore eyes and a beaver face. We left the village and paddled up the face of a mountain. I made a campfire and shoved hot rocks and pieces of an old robe down his throat. Then he curled up and died."

"That was not good!" I exclaimed.

Partridge opened my wounds again, shaping his body like an arrow. He dug his long nails into my neck. My head was full of dark acorn worms.

"Huron puppy, you should keep your tongue in a kettle."

Partridge shot me out of his canoe. I landed in a heap of snake slime, and as I got to my feet Black Magic screamed:

"There . . . between that prisoner's toes I hear the invisible animals making evil noises. Partridge, before you start, go and get my other nephew, Snake Nose, Kicking Snake's son. Then I want the both of you to find that French half-worm. Maybe the invisible animals are looking for him . . . if they are, Snake Nose will sniff them out."

The western flight of an arrow had been captured and it was smeared with grease. Partridge held it above his head as he figured out loud that René would go to Blackrobe, who had been given the task of spinning a pile of tobacco over the body of a lifeless dog.

I turned and ran away. Everything came rushing up through my eyes until I saw René, half-naked, gazing up through the rain and challenging the argument of chains. He was lying on his back in the open, while Blackrobe tried to squeeze into his armpit.

Quickly I told them Black Magic's command.

René's single breast was dripping as he quietly started to read from a prayerbook. I had to lie on the ground to hear my other father whisper:

"Tarcisius, I was born in dense tobacco smoke. Come as close to me as you can without touching me."

Blackrobe smoked my fingers and silently petted the muskrat in my shoulder, but not asking me a thing about it. Instead he recited a poem about fish smashing out their brains . . . they were trying to drown each other. What an argument for Absolution!

I spied Partridge and Snake Nose paddling our way . . . then Snake Tooth with Black Magic on his back passed overhead like a shadow without any oars. . . .

Snake Tooth spoke without his tongue:

"Blackrobe get back to your kettle right away!"

My other father obeyed, and we all followed him. When we reached the kettle Snake Nose handed me a mushroom. I devoured it . . . it was wonderful . . . the earth trembled and I saw a burning birch tree from a great distance inside my head. Joyful singing started, but it didn't last very long. Everything became worse and before I could say a word, René started to half lose his flesh. He was rooting under a white stone for names not connected with any shadow. I knew he had come to a sacred name from the way smoke curled up out of his eye and skin peeled off his shoulder. There was a bright flash, incredibly swift out and down . . . like a tremendous sweeping claw, cold, stubborn and sharp. René's arm fell off, writhing like a wounded snake. . . .

My other father cried out:

"René! René! My faithful René! My unhappy René!"

It stopped raining . . . a gang of Snake children carted away René's half body, then Partridge, Black Magic, and Snake Nose paddled away. Snake Tooth stood there laughing like an Apostate, while my other father wept without shame. Blackrobe spoke to me inside my head:

"Tarcisius, liberty is a wonderful thing in the afternoon. Innocence in this darkened land depends on invisible animals and forgotten ideas. You possess the power to rebuild yourself, no other Huron has it, so you have a better chance to escape inside a discarded snakeskin."

I did not say anything because I did not know what to say. I couldn't ask him now about the silent muskrat in my shoulder, yet it frightened me to lose one of my biggest bones. It was a vast disturbance from my breast to my throat, like birch trees falling around my ears, or the sound of my other father's crying. . . .

Kicking Snake, Blackrobe's master, climbed out of his family kettle. He was Black Magic and Curly Head's brother, an ugly Snake captain, who had burned off his littlest finger. He kicked my other father right in the heart, then said:

"Your heart doesn't beat like mine. Get inside the kettle or I'll kick you again."

Blackrobe did all he was told . . . he was still half crying over René, when Kicking Snake started to pull out big clumps of his beard and chewed on them like tobacco.

I turned away and wouldn't look. . . .

When I finally got back into my slave kettle, it was late afternoon. Wrinkled Black Skin and Curly Head were very happy because Frog Snake was up and hopping around again. The clouds and roots crawling out of his belly had left him forever. Wrinkled Black Skin told me that Snake Tooth and Black Magic had destroyed the invisible animals, but I knew better. . . .

I, Tarcisius Tandihetsi, say so.

CHAPTER XII
HAIR

In which Snake Nose sheds his skin for the first time . . .
Blackrobe and Tarcisius talk about hair . . . at the bottom
of Wrinkled Black Skin's kettle is a fairly wide stream
with a thick sloping ravine . . . Tarcisius sees René Goupil's
body in the water . . . Snake boys are fighting off invisible
animals . . . Snake Tooth magically appears and single-
handedly beats down the invisible animals . . . Tarcisius
steals some stray hairs from Frog Snake's manhood . . .
two days later he and Blackrobe go searching for René's
poor body . . . hair magic . . . they follow the trail of
Frog Snake's hairs . . . they open the side of a birch tree . . .
they find Frog Snake surrounded by a tight circle of
invisible hairs . . . Blackrobe realizes that René's body has
been captured by the invisible animals . . . Snake Tooth
performs the ritual of hair magic . . . the next day the
stream disappears even in Wrinkled Black Skin's kettle . . .
several days pass . . . Tarcisius overhears Frog Snake
telling Snake Tooth how he and Snake Nose found René's
useless body behind a door made of hairs . . . Blackrobe
and Tarcisius search again for any remains . . . they
find some half-gnawed hairs and a small part
of a skull . . . they bury these solemnly,
then Blackrobe preaches about
the distant future.

All through the next night Snake Nose attached himself to me and threw stones into my hair . . . a hasty dream was seeking an exit through his torn and bleeding nose. Black Magic had ordered him to search for invisible animals. He was going blind because he couldn't find any. He was about to shed his skin for the first time . . . his uncle, Curly Head, abruptly threw me out of the kettle. I wasn't allowed back for hours, while Snake Nose sat by himself on a comb made from porcupine hair, and changed his mind into animals and birds. He told me later he was not surprised when they flew away. . . .

Still later, when I told this to my other father, he said:

"Tarcisius, your eyes are mad from studying the stars, the mystery of unimaginable hairs. The cunning and crazy Poison Snake People are just like hairs on our bodies without permission but not without cruelty."

I looked at Blackrobe and there were still some hairs left on his yellow face from when Kicking Snake yanked off his beard. I gently plucked them all out. I wondered why the hair on his tongue had stopped growing when he left the canoes, but then I remembered the kettles were much warmer in the evening. . . .

"Tarcisius, build a chain of invisible dreams in the direction of a precipice and pull up the ladders so escape is impossible, then let your hair fall down . . . it will be long and beautiful."

My other father must have seen my puzzlement and the war in my hair. He said:

"You must be careful, Tarcisius, when you look in a mirror because there are bones in your black hair . . . and chestnut trees and a quiet spot by a blue lake to sacrifice dead warriors.

"When you lie in your slave kettle at night, talk plainly to the silent muskrat who's replaced your shoulder. Curl your body so your face is down near your manhood, and in the morning you might have a new head of hair."

This was the first time my other father mentioned the muskrat in my shoulder. I felt Birch Bark crawling around in my hair so I went back to the kettle. That vomit dog might burn my hair with his breath if he knew I thought of him too much. . . .

At the bottom of Wrinkled Black Skin's kettle there was now a thick sloping ravine and a fairly wide stream where I was sent to cut wood for my mistress's hair. Halfway down I heard the fearful shouts of many Snake boys, but a clump of hair hid them from my sight. The circles of magical effort, breath, and the invisible animals penetrated into hairs and deep wishes.

I swallowed some hair to find out how it tasted, but it was not pleasant in my stomach, and I sighed to myself like a boy, not yet a man. When I looked up I saw the body of René Goupil shaped like a broken water jar with a rope coiled halfway around his neck. Tired Snake boys had been floating in his hairs all morning long, fighting off a steady wave of invisible animals. This was the first time I saw any real parts of them . . . all that could be seen of each one were four rows of cutting sharp teeth. . . .

Snake Tooth wouldn't let René be buried like a Frenchman, I thought, because he was using the body as an invisible trap. Frog Snake popped into the hairs of René's nose, then gave a signal with his tail, and he suddenly popped out . . . a hair sneeze. Snake Tooth appeared out of nowhere armed to the teeth. Frog Snake started hopping around . . . brave again, having his cruel fun. He hopped very close to me. Several hairs dropped from his manhood. I secretly picked them up, then whispered:

"Frog Snake, help me and I won't tell anyone you touched your tail. Ask Snake Tooth to let me bury René in a canoe or a small kettle. Tell him death is impossible in a water jar, also hair raising and letter writing."

Deep down in the skull of that boy no one was listening. Snake Tooth stepped towards me, then pushed me back into a pile of tobacco. I watched as he beat down the invisible animals . . . he did not show them all his powers. Frog Snake and Snake Nose carried away the lifeless body of René, and as they dragged him along, they were chewing on his hair. . . .

It was two days later in the early afternoon before I had a chance to speak to my other father . . . I had filled up a deep hole with hair and tracked down every turning point. Blackrobe climbed into my slave kettle and we sat down together near the stream. His face was twisted in sorrow. The wind above our heads was lost in our hair. He said:

"Tarcisius, we must find René's hair!"

Blackrobe rubbed his hands across some stray hairs on my manhood. I cut these off, swallowed them, then heard myself say:

"I think René's surrounded by hairs or captured by the invisible animals, but he's not in this kettle!"

Blackrobe stroked the muskrat in my shoulder as he told me:

"Tarcisius, there are not enough hairlines in your words. I don't think you could write a poem describing a large sleeping platform or a pile of tobacco."

Suddenly I remembered the stray hairs from Frog Snake's manhood, and said:

"I saved four hairs that fell from between Frog Snake's legs. They'll bring us to Frog Snake. He and Snake Nose carried off René's poor body while Snake Tooth defeated the invisible animals. But Blackrobe, it is going to hurt me very much here."

I touched my hair, but instead of pain there came to me feelings of peace and gladness that I never felt before when I touched my hair. These feelings were finally interrupted by my fat Snake mistress sliding into the kettle. Earlier in the day she had climbed into my hair and tried to talk to the muskrat in my shoulder. It wouldn't talk to her. Now before she could try again, I asked her to let me wander outside the kettle. She thought it over for a moment, then picked me up by the hair and threw me out . . . Blackrobe and I followed the trail of Frog Snake's hairs . . . we passed through old mushroom fields crossed by flying walls, roaring fires, and heavy mounds of hair and tobacco. We talked about muskrats until we met Blackrobe's mistress, Kettle Skin, who was standing near a large stream, the one that passed through the bottom of Wrinkled Black Skin's kettle. Kettle Skin said:

"Blackrobe, can you steal tobacco from hair? You've been driven crazy by your secret language, so now you go hunting near this stream for hairs and a burial ground."

My other father touched his face. He answered:

"I will have less and less hair."

Since no prophecy could forbid us we floated on Frog Snake's hairs, while the sun was looking up out of the water. Kettle Skin continued on her way. I didn't see any Snake children, who usually ran all over the place . . . maybe they were out chasing gray hairs that had been sighted in older mushroom fields. . . .

Then the trail of Frog Snake's hairs took us out of the water. We opened the side of a birch tree, searching for where the hideous Snake boys might have dragged the poor corpse of René Goupil. Although we rooted around the trunk and all along the branches, we still couldn't find René's body . . . all we found were some stray body hairs and the invisible marks of many Snake children. . . .

Then I saw Frog Snake surrounded by invisible hairs, his teeth broken, he was squatting on a small mound of tobacco. Now I thought it was safe to throw a stone at his ribs, but in a snap with many cracking noises he hunched up his legs and small shoulders, leaped over the tight circle of invisible hairs, then quickly got away. . . .

Blackrobe and I tried to follow, but we tripped over the heap of tobacco abandoned by Frog Snake. My other father began to weep when he knelt and disturbed some directions underneath the tobacco pile. Many hairs flew out and disappeared. He cried out:

"Poor René! Poor René! He has lost more than his hair! What little remained of him was captured by the invisible animals. Your prophecy was right, Tarcisius."

I shrugged my shoulder, then we picked ourselves up and carried a stream across my chest like a heavy stone . . . sometimes I had to swim and sometimes Blackrobe did. I lost only a little hair. Finally we climbed back to the other shore, but my other father kept looking back at the tobacco. Then he whispered something in his secret language, which I did not understand. . . .

My hair started to smell like tobacco while everything around us turned fearfully silent. I pretended not to listen. Blackrobe was on his knees counting hairs. Time seemed to pass by like a French mirror as Snake Tooth paddled into sight. He was performing hair magic with Birch Bark and Partridge, and some Snake women, who were walking on both sides of the stream. These women were parting their hair on the ground while Birch Bark and Partridge planted hairs and took invisible measurements.

My other father and I were forced to leave this place, but the next day I went back by myself. I found no traces of tobacco . . . the stream had disappeared, even in Wrinkled Black Skin's kettle. All that was left were small pools of water and shadows across some hairs. . . .

Several days later I overheard Frog Snake telling Snake Tooth how the invisible animals had captured the remains of René. But after Snake Tooth performed the hair magic ritual, Frog Snake and Snake Nose returned to the invisible spot and spotted some hairs floating on a pool of water in the shape of a door. They opened it and found the useless body of René inside. They devoured as much as they could, although there wasn't much left anyway. Snake Tooth embraced Frog Snake like a warrior, a very great honor for a Snake boy, who had touched his tail. . . .

I told this to my other father, and we quickly started hunting for whatever might be left of poor René . . . all we found were half-gnawed hairs and a small part of a skull with many holes in it. These Blackrobe gathered up most solemnly, while I dug a hole. We buried what we had discovered at the base of a birch tree. All around us birds were flying as thick as hairs. I remember exactly what my other father said as we moved slowly back to the kettles:

"Tarcisius, some day long after you and I are forgotten, a consecrated people will come into this world of tobacco and discover the secret heart of everything, the perfect form of hair vanishing from tree to tree. Invisible animals will pass through their heads, and legends will be collected."

Everything I knew about hair passed in front of me like a vision. I thought my other father could have his hair cut off at any moment, or his head, or his manhood, or his sacred hands. But that didn't bother him at all, he just continued what he was saying from the other side of his hair.

"Tarcisius, even now the invisible animals are blowing through your hair. They are creatures from the Giant Snake, and it's dying, so they can't fill up their own strength with ecstasy like us. All traces of their hairs will vanish in time. . . ."

I did not really understand what my other father meant . . . I moved from side to side, but did not feel anything under the surface of my hair. I could not build shadows, and surely the Poison Snake People will not pile up any more hairs. Were the invisible animals that awful? Would the Poison Snake People and their allies, the killer yellow dogs, survive? Or would there be another awful people in these awful lands?

I could not answer any of these awful questions. . . .

I, Tarcisius Tandihetsi, say so.

CHAPTER XIII
ROOTS

After many days and nights evening disappeared from among the shadows, and it no longer smelled like bad tobacco. The fire between the earth and moon had sputtered out and groups of small platforms had replaced some of the colder kettles . . . it was way past summer, the end of fall. Only Blackrobe and I were left from the trading party . . . we had not heard any news of William Coutre. . . .

In their restless sleep the Poison Snake People crawled through their dreams, wishing that the invisible animals were only a dream. I was weak from hunger trembling in my bones. I let my arms hang in pools of water, which darkened my shadows. . . .

One afternoon Blackrobe was sitting outside his mistress's kettle, talking to Full Moon and Black Magic, and trying to guess which one was hiding a snakeskin satchel inside his dreams. He pointed to Full Moon, a faceless Snake prophet with maggots instead of brains and a round and bumpy head. Full Moon had painted red dots around his eyes and he was always playing with his tail . . . he was not even allowed to be a warrior.

My other father said:

"Let me explain the roots of my hair and what that means in my secret language."

When he started to explain the word "stem," Black Magic interrupted him:

"Blackrobe, before you envelop yourself in the misty fragrance of your secret language, you must know that I have the strength of many dreams and know the ecstasy of all language. Once I flew over your lands and saw a tree that didn't have roots."

I smiled . . . Black Magic went through the motions of a ladder, the pleasures of a snake with slime coming out of his mouth and nose. He pointed to the muskrat in my shoulder with his necklace of keys. The muskrat's whole body shook . . . Full Moon was right behind me rubbing my other shoulder like a stone. He was singing:

"I have no forks,

I have no arrows,

And I carry my head

In a snakeskin satchel."

At first I thought it was one of Blackrobe's poems. Black Magic told Full Moon to go and get Snake Tooth. Full Moon walked away, carrying his head in a snakeskin satchel. It was repeating the song. . . .

Black Magic waited until he could no longer see or hear Full Moon, then he said:

"Blackrobe . . . once we thought the invisible animals didn't exist . . . now we know better. They were afraid to come up to our world because they would die, but something happened to them. What it was we don't know yet. And now they are coming up out of the ground, and not dying. They have become our enemies, out to destroy us as a people. And we don't understand the difference between what is visible and invisible. We haven't figured out what shape they might form around their rows of teeth, or if they are a tribe like us with women and children. Full Moon is the only one who can figure out the differences. And as you can see he's real crazy, so now we must go on hunting raids hoping to find a stray invisible animal, who is taking on some definite shape. We need to see both the visible and invisible parts. Then we can torture it, and maybe cut out its secrets. They might be able to form themselves into anything . . . a cold campfire, a contemptible Huron, a snail, a raccoon, but Hey-Ho-Hey! it will be hard to kill the Poison Snake People. . . ."

Many Snake people had gathered around, listening to Black Magic's speech, and as their custom is, they hissed their approval. Then some warriors shed their skins all at once and threw them into the large hole I had filled with hair. While everyone hissed Black Magic stood face to face with my other father. I heard what he said:

"You stand in our way, Blackrobe . . . I hate you very much."

Then I watched Black Magic bite off Blackrobe's bottom lip. My other father didn't cry out . . . he is very brave. He tried to stop the blood with a discarded snakeskin. Suddenly my attention was turned completely around. I saw Snake Tooth, Full Moon, Birch Bark, and Partridge paddling through the kettles. They paddled right through Kettle Skin's family kettle . . . Partridge was using a white paddle. Birch Bark was still wearing the necklace of twigs he had stolen from me. His dull yellow fur had grown longer as the Snake village grew colder both inside and out of the kettles. His human side was now covered with thick hair. He was carrying a yellow painted otter skin pouch, and he carried it very carefully.

He spoke to my other father:

"Blackrobe, I know you use words in the strange ways of a country full of ledges. . . ."

"This is the effect of wings and the way we cut up words," Black-robe replied as blood dripped off his chin. "I have been inside a terrible mask with a doubting mind, sunken eyes, and flaring nostrils. What visions! My bottom lip is missing again, but I can still smoke all the tobacco left in the abandoned kettles. Birch Bark, what is it you don't understand?"

"This is it!" Birch Bark lifted up the otter skin pouch. On one of its sides was a design of a birch tree secured with many locked doors. He continued:

"When Snake Tooth was leading us killer yellow dogs along the Great River, we heard many invisible rumors and kept our eyes in the air like a long string of birds searching for an opening in the woods. Then we saw a shining birch bark canoe . . . it contained a French lamp, a white paddle, a book, and this otter skin pouch. We had heard that four rivers, deeply moved by night, had destroyed a Poison Snake raiding party there. . . .

"Suddenly hundreds of pine needles grew up our legs and slimy green feathers were stuck between our paws. Snake Tooth fell across my back so he was the first to discover the invisible animal that's inside this otter skin pouch."

Snake Tooth took off a necklace of invisible teeth that he made after the battle over René Goupil's body. He threw it up to Kettle Skin, who was leaning over the edge of her kettle watching and listening to everything going on. She put on the invisible necklace. Snake Tooth spoke to my other father:

"Blackrobe, I know all the animals in the rain, but this isn't like any of them. It knew our names and our destination. It spoke to us, but now I think it's dead. Its voice was like a shrub branch, a whip, like all our insults and taunts disturbing a great stone mask."

Black Magic stepped forward.

"I too have heard their language with its long roots like blue smoke strings." He took a deep breath, then added: "It's not of this world!"

All the Poison Snake People gathered here were frightened. They yelled:

"Let's bury it in the mushroom fields . . . that is safer."

"Let me see it," demanded Blackrobe, stopping the flow of blood from his missing bottom lip. "If it's a word, it's not an animal. And if it's an animal, its voice won't reflect light, so you can escape from its language."

I was more than curious to see this so-called invisible animal. Some Snake women thought that the muskrat in my shoulder was an invisible animal, but Full Moon hadn't said it was when he rubbed my other shoulder. And Snake Nose hadn't sniffed it out. Both Snake Nose and Full Moon thought it was just another muskrat trapped in a missing shoulder. . . .

I was standing near my mistress, Wrinkled Black Skin. She was the first to see the invisible animal. I saw Snake Tooth invisibly bury her scream in a French lamp. At first I couldn't see the invisible animal, not even its rows of cutting sharp teeth. All I heard was a mournful singing from underneath the ground and the beat of many kettle drums. The Poison Snake People were afraid, but Snake Tooth took their fears and shook them into silence. Finally Birch Bark dumped the invisible animal out of its pouch. My other father went down on his knees to examine it. He said:

"Birch Bark, Black Magic, Full Moon, Partridge, Curly Head, Kicking Snake, Wrinkled Black Skin, Kettle Skin . . . you all need Saving Waters poured over your heads, or else the invisible animals will attack you again and again, making Snake Tooth, your chief, their most hated enemy. The invisible animals haven't appeared in your dreams, so it's only natural that you don't know what they look like yet, or what different shapes they might take. . . .

"Now if you'll let me, I think I can make this invisible animal come alive again and speak a few words . . . maybe it can tell me why you are hated so much."

Blackrobe was squeezing his blood from the discarded snakeskin, his hands twisted over his wrists with the hairless soft flesh turning blue like a wicked pagan's. No matter what he said his words always seemed new to me. . . .

My mistress, Wrinkled Black Skin, called out:

"Blackrobe, be careful, don't pick it up or your voice will crack in wintertime. You may lose your blessed fingers again, then what would you do?"

Some Snake warriors laughed, but I didn't . . . I thought that she was right. But Blackrobe picked it up anyway. Now I was ready to jump into winter, grayer than a fallen twig, a tremendous leap supported by the circular sky. I wanted the muskrat inside my shoulder to jump with me, but it didn't move. . . .

Full Moon brushed by me, grinning the way those who have no sense grin. He grabbed the invisible animal from my other father . . . I had never seen anything like it in my hands. It could grow in mud, grass, or in the sounds of swarming bees, but it wasn't surrounded by rain like an evil fox trail. It could disappear into the soft wood of a freshly cut door. Its round dirty white face was eaten into, and two of its four legs were shorter than the others. At first it didn't move . . . of this I am most sure.

It didn't look really dangerous, but you can never tell about an invisible animal. It is probably better to kill it with a sharp fork or a war club and then examine it in safety. . . .

Full Moon folded up his head and returned the invisible animal to my other father, who then said:

"Watch now, Poison Snake People, and listen."

He held the invisible animal in his hands, then shook it violently . . . its tail broke off and fell to the ground.

He turned to me and said:

"Tarcisius, don't be afraid to listen to its invisible words . . . they have more wisdom than roots and stems. You will be a prophet!"

"I am a chief's son, not a prophet," I replied. And though my heart didn't disturb the tail on the ground, I knew that many little roots were quivering along my back and they felt like drops of invisible slime. . . .

Blackrobe said:

"Tarcisius, take the tail I broke off and put it in your stomach, then let it crawl through your body until it comes to your head. It may fly away, or it may live in your head, and you'll never die of starvation."

I took the tail . . . it was shaped like a flattened kettle. I put it into my stomach. It was moving in circles through my body, when the muskrat in my shoulder finally screamed out:

"I'm losing my skin! I'm losing my skin!"

These were the first words it ever spoke . . . next another strange thing happened . . . the invisible animal began to breathe loud and fast, then so did all the Snake warriors. I saw Wrinkled Black Skin brush some roots off her hair, while the invisible animal's tail flew out of my head and disappeared. I suddenly felt very hungry. . . .

The invisible animal's breath smelled awful, worse than a pile of worms living in the darkness of decaying plants, wounds, and snakeskin satchels. I noticed that two long thin paws with rich fur mittens grew out of its face. One went into the ground and the other almost touched the sky.

"Now listen, everybody!" said my other father, and he was smiling. "You will hear it speak."

While everyone listened I saw the invisible animal's paw, the one that reached into the sky, move, very slowly, but it moved. The invisible animal spoke one, two, three, four, five, six words, then it stopped.

"That's what it said on the Great River," shouted Birch Bark. Then the invisible animal spoke some more, but I didn't understand a word it said . . . each word sounded the same to me. . . .

"What happened to you when the invisible animal spoke?" Blackrobe asked Snake Tooth.

"My back was covered by bits of flesh and the head of a muskrat hanging from a birch tree was suddenly tattooed on my arm." Snake Tooth's hairless body snapped forward, and his voice bristled with rage . . . clearly he did not like to remember mistakes from his past. "What difference do these past things make, Blackrobe? The tattoo on my arm has disappeared, and I want to know what the invisible animal is saying now."

"It says that wherever there are roots the invisible animals are expanding into pieces of flesh. Their legs are very old, but they can still balance things on their teeth."

"They are more powerful than you thought, Snake Tooth," Black Magic declared, ignoring Snake Tooth's anger. Then he turned to my other father and asked:

"Could you always speak its language, Blackrobe? Why don't you question its roots?"

"No, I've only recently learned its language, but I can understand every new word," answered my other father. "Their words have stems and roots in every other language. . . ."

All this time the invisible animal's two paws were moving towards each other. It was talking and breathing, but it couldn't bring itself to walk on its four uneven legs.

The Snake people were silent . . . they were looking at the violent designs created by the roots between every word of the invisible animal. When it stopped talking, Black Magic stepped forward and said:

"Blackrobe, the invisible animals seem to be more than a splash of words . . . they are a new storm in our world. We must capture another one, then maybe their words will start growing, and their language will no longer be a disease.

"We've seen this invisible animal come to life and heard it speak . . . now I say let's bury it! Bury it before we hear the last noises of our own language. . . ."

Everyone looked at Snake Tooth . . . he slowly nodded his head in approval. Black Magic picked up the creature, pierced its tough skin of dreams, and put it back in Birch Bark's yellow pouch. Then he and Birch Bark along with Full Moon buried the invisible animal deep in the damp ground of the mushroom fields. . . .

Later when I was alone with my other father, I asked him about some things that were puzzling me.

"Blackrobe, was that invisible animal just so many secret words? Were its face paws just two more devil tails? Does every invisible animal look like this one? Or was it just one brief mask on a changing shape?"

I took a deep breath before I went on:

"And what did Black Magic mean when he said, 'the last noises of our own language?' And why did they bury it so deep?"

"Little Full Moon!" exclaimed my other father. "Don't you know that there are objects felt to be essential . . . powers that need to be protected. Long thick hair, the sun, fire, beaver pelts, water, and pipe tobacco.

"You know that you can never separate the invisible animals from their roots and stems. . . ."

"But I heard words begin to breathe!" I interrupted. "The invisible animal started them going in my head when you gave me its tail."

"Tarcisius, don't you understand yet that you're a prophet? The Poison Snake People think it's me, a poor Blackrobe, but I think Snake Tooth knows better. You are the one with a muskrat in your shoulder, but soon it will jump off. . . ."

My other father's eyes were jumping around in his head . . . they were filled with important things. He told me he believed God was speaking through me. . . .

It was then I knew for sure that the invisible animals were ready to show themselves and fight . . . all the things Snake Tooth, Black Magic, Full Moon, Birch Bark, and my other father had said about them were true, and it was only the beginning. I didn't know what to do, so I curled my head into the roots of my manhood and asked the muskrat in my shoulder for a new head of hair. . . .

Blackrobe picked me up and carried me back into Wrinkled Black Skin's kettle. He put me down near the bottom, where the large stream had disappeared. I was trying hard not to think of the invisible animals. I was trying to sleep and dream, for that is the right way. But I knew that this was next to impossible . . . and that it was also very strange and invisible.

I, Tarcisius Tandihetsi, say so.

CHAPTER XIV
FULL MOON

The next day Wrinkled Black Skin's kettle was crowded with Snake warriors, uncles and cousins, forced out of their own kettles by the invisible cold. It was the middle of the dreamless night . . . suddenly everyone woke up, hissing, afraid, startled by a loud invading uproar. It could not be kept in one place, but spread out instantly from every starting point . . . for a moment I hoped the Hurons and French were coming to avenge us. . . .

Soon the kettle was boiling with Snakes and wild guesses, then everyone climbed outside. A full moon was moving in and out of the clouds. Snake babies hung in the air and they were silent as always. Snake women had come down from their many small platforms, and Snake children started throwing clumps of hard earth at me, once their eyes became accustomed to the dark. . . .

There near the signal fire at the center of the village was Full Moon, crying, trembling, spitting, shouting from the powerful anger of too many dead crabs. His legs were shaking as if they were on fire, and at the same time he was waving away some horrible dream . . . he never had any sense, but this was even worse.

The older Snake women, ancient greasy hags with hardly any shoulders, scurried around and picked up warriors' deadly forks and their own torturous whips . . . things might get dangerous. The Poison Snake People were now sure that the invisible animals would try to kill Full Moon, especially since he was so helpless and had no sense, and therefore could recognize them. I had heard Black Magic say that Full Moon would be able to recognize what shape most of the invisible animals would take. Full Moon had said that the buried invisible animal was an unusual stray, and its shape belonged only to itself. . . .

Blackrobe's mistress, Kettle Skin, started heating up a night drink for Full Moon . . . it was made from owl's blood and bits of mushrooms. I looked for my other father but could not see him. Full Moon's body was burning like coals . . . he lay there kicking and biting and emptying the night air, and always screaming senseless things. Black Magic held him tight . . . when you are overpowered by anything invisible at night you do not like to stay in a place where other torture games had been played in the daylight.

Black Magic wasn't wearing a thing except his string of French keys around his neck . . . his manhood was nearly invisible. Leaf designs and spider webs were carved into his ancient skin. In the dim light I saw a grin of hate and rage working up his shriveled face. The muskrat in my shoulder saw it more clearly . . . for a moment I felt I was as near to my dreams as I ever would be. Black Magic had complete control over Full Moon and this made him very powerful, only Snake Tooth had a stronger magic among the Poison Snake People.

Black Magic was stroking the shadows on Full Moon's blank face. He told Kettle Skin not to give Full Moon the night drink until he told her to. He spoke to all the Poison Snake People:

"A few hours ago Full Moon and I dug up the otter skin pouch to look again at the stray invisible animal with the sky reaching paws. When we opened the pouch the invisible animal leaped into the sky . . . its whole body was alive with light, yet not burning up like our torches. It was plain to see . . . in one paw it held one half of that dead Frenchman, René Goupil . . . in its other paw, the other half. Then the paws joined the parts together . . . all that was missing were several hairs and a piece of skull. Once René's halves had settled into place the paws let go, and he fell right on Full Moon's head and plunged through his neck, then slid easily into his stomach like a duck into warm water. . . ."

Full Moon was breathing hard. He rubbed his stomach trunk, then tried to rip it open, screaming out:

"He's in there now, and cannot get out!"

Surely Full Moon is missing his brains, I thought, and cannot do very much head work. Had he forgotten that Frog Snake and Snake Nose had wolfed down everything left of René except a few hairs and a small piece of skull, which my other father and I had buried. Black Magic kicked apart an old firestick, his feet were very upset. He looked through a pile of discarded snakeskins, then he straightened up and announced:

"The powers of the invisible animals are great. Everything in Full Moon's stomach is now their allies . . . a duck, a dead Frenchman, and even the remnants of last night's meal."

Full Moon calmed down and spoke quite clearly:

"But that Frenchman in there, Black Magic, is alive . . . both halves of him. He's in there all right . . . I can feel him pressing the inside of my stomach. And you are dead right when you say he's an ally of the invisible animals . . . but I don't think the duck and whatever remains from my last meal are their allies."

I shook my head slowly, very sad. The Poison Snake People must have no sense if they believe such things. I watched Snake Tooth walk through the Snake crowd giving strength to his people with his magic. I didn't see my other father anywhere. Snake Tooth called together a Snake council of fire-breathing captains. He did not like this Snake custom, and he was to like it even less. The Snake captains stuck their heads in a circle, hoping not to splinter their thoughts. It was no use . . . curved lines tumbled from their bodies. They couldn't be sure one way or the other. . . .

Black Magic finally spoke into the dying air:

"The world is less and less visible since the Great Snake came up through the sacred ground to bless Snake Tooth as chief among chiefs of the Poison Snake People."

He looked around several times before he continued:

"Wind currents have suddenly jumped into our skins causing us to lose our strength, but at least now we know that invisible animals can be swallowed whole or eaten alive. . . .

"Full Moon is one sick mushroom . . . we must cure him quickly by taking that Frenchman out of his stomach trunk, or he might lose his head in his snakeskin satchel, or he might drown the next time he gets into a canoe."

When Black Magic finished, Full Moon took off his head and put it in his snakeskin satchel, while some Snake women started to build a small sleeping platform. Black Magic nodded to Kettle Skin, who offered her bloody night drink to Full Moon, but his head cried out:

"No, no, wait . . . I've just had a vision. The Giant Snake told me what to do. Pour it over that muskrat which sits and watches everything from the Huron boy's shoulder . . . then pour it down the boy's throat."

I did not like to hear such talk so I tried to disappear, but Frog Snake jumped on me and held me down like a decision. He put his slimy mouth over my ear and started to chew. This didn't hurt me much because the invisible animals had broken his teeth. Finally Snake Tooth kicked him away and said:

"Frog Snake, stop acting like a turtle."

Snake Tooth quietly asked me again if I would join up with him and the Poison Snake People. I refused to reply . . . I spun my head completely around, but could not see my other father. The moon was hidden behind a cloud. Snake Tooth dragged me closer to Black Magic, Full Moon, and Kettle Skin. He shouted into the smoky darkness:

"The Poison Snake People are ready to fight whether our enemies are visible or not. The Giant Snake told me the secrets of storage baskets and the meaning of things far away from this village. I am ready to grow more than any other sign. I am not afraid of the invisible animals. To me they are only dark spots behind my eyes."

All the Poison Snake People were amazed at Snake Tooth's courage, even Black Magic was impressed. I struggled helplessly against Snake Tooth's iron grip. He spun me around by the feet until I was dizzy, then he said:

"Little Spoon, that muskrat in your shoulder might be dangerous . . . . Full Moon needs protection. To me, you and every Huron and Frenchman are less than a drop of mud hanging from the end of a stick, so don't even attempt to struggle."

He dropped me on the ground, and I was quickly surrounded. I saw Kettle Skin coming closer, and I heard her telling me that the hot night blood drink would be good for me, but I knew better. I struggled and as I struggled the muskrat jumped out of my shoulder and hotfooted it away. . . .

For several moments everyone froze and just stared at the invisible darkness, but then Black Magic broke the silence.

"Hurry, hurry . . . Full Moon may go off the deep end, Kettle Skin, pour it down the Huron boy's throat and over his missing shoulder."

My legs went out from under me like rotten meat. Horrible smells hung in the night air. I thought I was about to go to God. The vile-tasting owl's blood burned my mouth, tongue, throat, neck, and missing shoulder. . . .

Snake Tooth watched my pains intently, even getting down on his hands and knees to examine between my toes. He smiled.

"Very good, it is easy to read any invisible messages there . . . that French half-worm is indeed in Full Moon's stomach."

Full Moon's head was still in his snakeskin satchel, and it was laughing crazy. Snake Tooth walked over to him, pulled the satchel open all the way, and took out the talking head. He poked at its two red dots, then he placed it between Full Moon's shoulders like a crown. Blue smoke strings poured out of Full Moon's neck, then he climbed up onto the small sleeping platform that some Snake women had just built. He carried along his snakeskin satchel. All the Poison Snake People there began to shout and dance around the platform, while Black Magic licked up any of the hot night blood drink that had dripped to the ground. Full Moon was looking down on this sudden madness. He started rubbing his tail and laughing crazy again. He took off his head once more and put it in his snakeskin satchel. His head shouted:

"QUACK! QUACK! QUACK!"

Full Moon flapped his arms like wings in flight . . . all the Poison Snake People around the small platform picked this up, starting a sacred Duck dance. Most of the fat Snake women like Wrinkled Black Skin and her sister Belly Skin looked more like waddling ducks than graceful snakes. The quacking dance was kept up for quite some time. Four times they stopped, breathing hard, then Snake Tooth would shout up to Full Moon:

"Where are the invisible animals?"

The first time Full Moon's crazy head answered:

"To the South!"

Then to the North, then to the East, and finally to the West. The sacred Duck dance ended as it began!

"QUACK! QUACK! QUACK!"

Most of the Snake warriors started peeling off their skins. Black Magic wrapped his tail around himself as he asked Full Moon:

"Has that French half-worm left your body?"

"Yes!" Full Moon replied. "It has gone up in the air like puffs of foul smelling smoke. . . ."

A cold wind rolled through the night, scattering the heavy clouds and bad smells . . . the crazy full moon reappeared. It was very bright, and now it was shaped like a snakeskin satchel. Fear spread through the ground. Snake Tooth walked among the exhausted duck dancers. Finally he stopped by the small platform and spoke like a great chief:

"I want everyone to go back to their platforms or kettles and sleep it off . . . tomorrow morning is waiting in your dreams. And you, Full Moon, come down here to me right away, and bring your snakeskin satchel."

Full Moon did as he was told, and while Snake Tooth put his head back on for the last time, Snake women tore down the small platform. Strings of blue smoke dripped from Full Moon's neck and shoulders as though he had fallen into the Great River, but at least he wasn't trembling or mumbling all sorts of wild talk. . . .

Everyone left . . . Frog Snake pushed me back into his kettle with a long fork. He was very excited and asked me:

"Did you see what Full Moon did up on the platform?"

"Yes . . . his head was jumping in and out of his snakeskin satchel."

"No . . . I mean something less visible than that."

"What?"

"Didn't you see him deep breathing in each foul-smelling puff of smoke that was the French half-worm, René Goupil?"

"So what!" I was angry at the way Frog Snake described René, who had gone to God.

"Huron puppy," Frog Snake addressed me with scorn. "Don't you see the danger? Your French half-worm has become an invisible animal. Full Moon discovered it, then got rid of it, but now has inhaled it back in. . . .

"Maybe the next time Full Moon takes off his head and puts it in his snakeskin satchel, no one will be able to put it back on . . . what would happen?"

He answered his own question when I wouldn't speak.

"Full Moon's brains will rot like so many blue smoke strings!"

"Frog Snake, you are just as senseless as Full Moon." I split my tongue with venom. "I'm going to sleep just like Snake Tooth told us to do."

I lay down in a small pool of water. Frog Snake left me alone. The water was warm and made me feel safe inside the kettle. I thought I would ask my other father if he knew where the missing muskrat was. I missed it greatly. . . .

I was half asleep in my head when I saw Full Moon again. He was jumping up and down on my chest, and his tail was slapping the warm water. I prayed to Eustace, my father . . . I asked him to make me as strong as a brave canoe. I also asked him to keep my head from flying off, and not to let my brains rot. . . .

I felt a sudden rush of strength as my manhood began to get hard, and I whacked Full Moon with it. He fell off my chest. He was very frightened. I had seen that invisible look of death before around our old Huron torture fires, when I was a bad pagan, not yet received Saving Waters.

Full Moon quickly climbed up the side of the kettle. Before he sprang away, he shouted back at me:

"You are a Little Full Moon like me, and you'll know before the others . . . the invisible animals will be everywhere. . . ."

I thought about this for awhile, then I swore an oath to Eustace, my father, never to breathe in my own farts again . . . even though since I was a papoose I sniffed them up like a village dog smelling

food at dinnertime. I too was afraid of the invisible animals.
I, Tarcisius Tandihetsi, say so.

CHAPTER XV
POEMS

I had been crawling in the mushroom fields all day, collecting bruises and keeping a sharp lookout for invisible animals. I didn't see any, but they could be anywhere, I thought. They might be lurking in the rock walls, or by the dying signal fires, or in the hairy mounds of tobacco. . . .

Wrinkled Black Skin had sent me out to search for invisible animals. She believed in their fantastic appearances, but she didn't think about them every minute. She was really hiding me away as much as possible from Curly Head, who had become very crazy since René had slid in and out of Full Moon's stomach. Curly Head thought that anything he dreamed of might be an invisible animal. . . .

It was late in the afternoon and I was so sore and stiff that it hardly mattered I was talking to myself and wishing my other father could be here to answer me. My legs were filled with messages, and my stomach had grown tired of hair and tobacco. Inside my head invisible voices kept repeating:

"Huron puppy . . . you will be our favorite meal!"

For a while I sat on the damp ground and fashioned a muskrat from some old snakeskins I found in the fields . . . all their powers had long since disappeared. When my day's work was done I carried this muskrat figure back inside the village. I would give it to my other father to keep and we could eat it if things got really desperate. . . .

Right in front of me playing in an open space were Frog Snake and some other Snake boys. Among them was Jumping Snake, the boy from the Mushroom Lake village . . . I was sure that he had come here to torture me because he was already good friends with Frog Snake.

The Snake boys were playing with the dead hearts of their enemies, blown up to three times their real size. They were also given the manhoods, which the Snake warriors wouldn't eat because the captives weren't brave enough. The boys had divided into two sides of a snakeskin hoop . . . just wide enough not to touch their tails, then they started rolling on the ground with their forks. Each side would try to touch several manhoods together in the center of a hoop and pile up discarded snakeskins behind them.

Full Moon had taught the Snake boys this game . . . it was fun and it also helped them find out if there were traces of new words or any invisible thoughts in the uneaten manhoods. I saw that Frog Snake and Jumping Snake were the best boys at this game, never once did they stop to aim. They were more like warriors, and I could not help but think that many Hurons would be tortured under their skill when these two had long enough tails to join the Snake war parties. . . .

Now I thought that I could be a better player in this manhood game because in my own village I have practiced with beads and carved stone figures. My aim is true . . . my power can fly in four directions during any game I play. I put this thought away with other such thoughts. It's not good to play Snake games, especially ones made up by Full Moon, my other father had told me, so I turned away. I held my carved muskrat with both hands and thought I could sneak off without anyone speaking to me, but Jumping Snake called out:

"Huron puppy, come here!"

I walked over as slowly as I could . . . I didn't like to be called "Huron puppy," especially by Snake boys. When I reached Jumping Snake, he took out a torn book from his growling stomach trunk and put it under my nose.

All at once I remembered quite clearly an afternoon two winters before when the air smelled like French tobacco, and Blackrobe read to me from a book of his poems. I remembered how my other father loved to make words come out of pictures.

Jumping Snake said:

"Huron puppy, Birch Bark threw this away, and I picked it up . . . can you make it speak?"

"I won't tell you a thing," I said. "Unless you stop calling me 'Huron puppy.'"

"All right, Little Spoon," he whispered with his three eyes jumping.

Little Spoon is better than Huron puppy, even though it is my pagan name, so I told Jumping Snake:

"Only Blackrobe can make it speak with its magic words."

"Then it must be an invisible animal!"

The invisible madness of the Poison Snake People was growing by leaps and bounds. The fear in Jumping Snake's voice split through the air . . . soon even the silent Snake babies that hung in the air would be afraid. More sadness and pain would be inflicted on me, the last Huron captive . . . of this I was sure. . . .

I grabbed the book from Jumping Snake, and he didn't bother me because he was now terribly afraid of it. I would give it to Blackrobe as a present with my carved muskrat. My other father was not in his mistress's kettle. I finally found him up on Belly Skin's wide platform. Belly Skin was Partridge's Snake woman and Wrinkled Black Skin, my mistress, was her sister, and like her sister, Belly Skin was covered with layer after layer of Snake flesh.

A young Snake woman, who wasn't fat, was also on the platform. Her name was Feather Skin. She was the one who had taken up Curly Head's arm when it turned to snow. She had feathers instead of hair hanging like clouds around her shoulders. Many different colored feathers were stuck in her tail . . . very beautiful. She was Snake Nose's favorite.

Many Snake babies hung silently in the air around this platform. Soon they would all come out of the cocoons . . . Wrinkled Black Skin had told me this. Feather Skin was their guardian. Belly Skin was talking to her:

"Let Blackrobe just touch your nieces and nephews and the invisible animals will never harm them."

My other father was sitting between the two Snake women. A beaver pelt was wrapped around his shoulders, and in front of him a pipe was stuck in a pile of tobacco.

Feather Snake shook her head.

"Snake Tooth told me that Blackrobe must not touch them. He might take a pain out of his mouth and put it with the Snake babies, or else eat them up in the direction of the rising wind."

I secretly gave my other father the torn book and my snakeskin figure. They took his breath away, then he turned to Belly Skin and said:

"Feather Skin is afraid of Snake Tooth's magic. I will not touch her nieces and nephews, Belly Skin, and they will never be protected from the invisible animals."

My other father suddenly reached under my clothes and broke off my manhood . . . there were no agonies of pain, only surprise. He touched it to my forehead, my missing shoulder, and my stomach. The Snake babies didn't fall out of the air or make a single sound . . . they were still perfectly healthy.

Feather Skin stared at my manhood, which Blackrobe continued to hold like a torch, stiff and straight. She reached over and snapped it up, touching every part of her body with it, especially her feathery hair and tail.

Now the pains below my stomach started twisting around, while my teeth were clicking and my tongue was hanging all the way out of my mouth. Feather Skin gave back my manhood to Blackrobe, who bent over me and put it back where it belonged. He pulled out a lump of beaver fat from underneath his beaver pelt and rubbed it over my manhood. All my bones seemed to be weeping together and hideous pains streaked across my naked arms.

Feather Skin said:

"Little Huron, you speak and act like a small paddle, but your manhood is very interesting."

I knew that I didn't look like a tree trunk or a canoe. The Poison Snake People were still very far from helpless, weary, broken, or bloodless. They wouldn't let their feet be caught in a heavy rain, or speak in a secret language.

Blackrobe was shaking his head, going through some ripped pages of his book, then he looked up at the red and yellow stars and cried out:

"Here I am, dear God . . . do you wish my life to be under water again?"

My other father was gazing at my snakeskin figure . . . his eyes brightened up with a shine I hadn't seen in a long time. He held my two gifts up to the sky and spoke to me:

"My Little Huron Son, these gifts are more wonderful than tobacco that takes my breath away."

All of a sudden I felt no more pains . . . this was the first time my other father called me his 'Little Huron Son.' He set my gifts down, then pointed at my toes, saying:

"Hair grows very thickly there without any secret edges. I see it clearly . . . your gifts will go through my body three times, then one of them will burn away."

I watched with frightened eyes as the book and snakeskin figure went through my other father's body for the first time. He seemed to be sitting outside his body like a bundle of feathers. Night time had stepped into his eyes and he was listening to something inside his belly. I heard these words:

"Roast it! Eat it! My stomach is empty, crying out with each breath."

Again the book and snakeskin figure passed through my other father.

Feather Skin started shrieking and howling, jabbing her head like a fork at the pictures that were floating into the air from Black-robe's torn book. They disappeared like shapeless rolls of flesh as soon as they were formed. Belly Skin filled her arms with dreams and was hiding her face in fear. The whole village was now shouting up to the platform.

Snake Tooth and Birch Bark climbed up the ladder in time to see the book and snakeskin figure pass through Blackrobe's body for the third time. Snake Tooth yelled:

"Birch Bark, grab that muskrat . . . it might be an invisible animal. And throw away that beaver pelt."

Birch Bark threw the beaver pelt off the platform, then he tied up my carved muskrat with long strips of twisted snakeskin. Black-robe had made his book disappear. Snake Tooth was very angry, his hairless body was gleaming like a fireplace, and his sharp teeth were moving in and out of his mouth like a hissing snake.

"Blackrobe . . . this muskrat is an invisible animal, and we will torture it with horrible smells. If it doesn't tell us its secrets, it will die in the flames."

We were dragged from the platform and brought outside the

Snake village to a mushroom field. In the middle of the field there was a pit about five feet deep and ten feet wide. In the center of the pit was an eight foot high platform.

Around it many Snake warriors were already standing with torches burning in their stomach trunks. I looked at them very carefully, for this was one of the few times I saw fear in the eyes of the enemy. . . .

We were dumped into the pit. Snake Tooth held the snakeskin muskrat in his lap. Crowded around a kettle, which was underneath the platform, were Birch Bark, Partridge, Black Magic, Full Moon, and two other Snake captains.

Snake Tooth gave the carved muskrat to Full Moon, who started chanting:

"Invisible animal, why are you here
And not underground?
Will the Poison Snake People
Die in your belly?
You better answer us,
Or you'll burn in the flames."

The carved muskrat started running around and around in Full Moon's lap, trying to bite its tail. Full Moon easily picked it up by the back of the neck and threw it towards the kettle, overflowing with filthy Snake slime and many enemy bones. In mid-air Snake Tooth hacked off its tail without stopping its flight.

The carved muskrat boiled in the churning kettle, while each Snake captain chewed on its tail, and at the same time they ceremoniously passed around a sacred snakeskin robe, decorated with hair and manhoods cut from many Hurons. It was handsomely painted and trimmed with bright blue beads of porcelain. My mistress, Wrinkled Black Skin, was its guardian.

My missing shoulder began to itch and it rolled back to a place under my heart. I heard all my other father's poems beating there, then my bones started shaking at something I thought might be missing inside my shoulder. . . .

Finally everyone climbed out of the pit, while Full Moon took the muskrat out of the stinking kettle and tossed it on the platform. Next Snake Tooth flung the sacred robe over the muskrat, then Black Magic set fire to the platform.

My other father mumbled in his secret language. He pushed me aside, and with a running leap he jumped over the burning platform. He was able to pour Saving Waters over part of the snakeskin robe where the muskrat was burning.

A circle of blue sparks spun out from under the robe and flew off into the night . . . it was my carved muskrat. It spun around in the air, then dove into the ground. . . .

Snake Tooth raged like a starving village dog gone mad. He jumped on my other father and beat him with many firesticks. Snake Tooth did not stop until every stick was burnt away, and Blackrobe's beautiful hands were mangled again. . . .

I knew that Snake Tooth always carried the Devil in his heart, and I did not need anyone to tell me this. . . .

I, Tarcisius Tandihetsi, say so.

CHAPTER XVI
SNAKE EYES

In which Tarcisius goes on food hunting party led by
Birch Bark . . . they set up their base camp near a sacrificial
rock . . . the Snake warriors play a game called Snake
Eyes . . . Jumping Snake wins . . . the hideous Antler Face
People show up . . . the youngest Antler Face has a muskrat
on his shoulder . . . he asks Birch Bark if he could play
Snake Eyes . . . he is faster than Jumping Snake . . . he is
friendly towards Tarcisius . . . Jumping Snake and Tarcisius
play Snake Eyes . . . Tarcisius wins when he pops out his
heart . . . Antler Face's muskrat stops Jumping Snake from
blindly attacking Tarcisius . . . it talks to Tarcisius . . .
the oldest Antler Face dies . . . his flesh is roasted and
made into a feast for everyone except Tarcisius . . . Birch
Bark and three Snake warriors play a team game against
the Antler Face party . . . the game stops with the Poison
Snake team slightly ahead, but Birch Bark has played badly
. . . he blames Tarcisius . . . blindfolded Birch Bark throws
forks and hatchet spoons at Tarcisius, who's tied to an
uprooted birch tree . . . they land between Tarcisius'
legs and on either side of his neck . . . everyone
cheers . . . Tarcisius is unafraid . . . Birch
Bark praises him.

The next day it was snowing in the kettles . . . black smoke was
rising and falling in the air behind the sun, and my stomach
had run down to a handful of mushrooms. I tried to wash my hands
at the bottom of Wrinkled Black Skin's kettle, but the water was so
cold so it hurt my fingers. . . .

Wrinkled Black Skin told me to find Birch Bark and go with
him. It was all arranged . . . a hunting party to bring back food for
the Snake babies was leaving the village. Meanwhile Curly Head

was throwing his body forks into the air, hoping to kill a stray invisible animal, so I climbed out of the kettle as fast as I could.

I found Birch Bark sitting outside his dog-hole . . . he wouldn't sleep in a kettle. He was calmly rubbing the small chalice in his backbone with pieces of Huron flesh the size of my fist. His fangs were painted a bright yellow. He looked big and strong, and I knew he could fight like a swarm of angry bees . . . that's why he was Snake Tooth's captain among the killer yellow dogs. His necklace of birch twigs was now his sign of power . . . it had been rubbed with snake slime by Snake Tooth. . . .

Birch Bark pointed to a small pair of snakeskin feet, then he pounded on my chest as if it were a basket of dirt. I crossed my hands as he said:

"Huron puppy, you would make very poor food for the winter time . . . I would rather eat long slabs of dog meat. Put on these snakeskin feet and come with me. If you try to run away, you won't come back with any of your skin left . . . I will drop your flesh all over the place."

I did as I was told . . . the snake feet would guide me over the snow, but they were very tight and itchy, and with them on I could not touch the bottom of my back with my elbows. . . .

We passed my other father surrounded by a group of Snake boys, who were writing their names across his back with sharp sticks. I would have liked very much to stop and speak with Black-robe, but Birch Bark wouldn't let me. . . .

Outside the village we met a party of Snake warriors . . . each one was rolled into four bundles, and their tongues were licking the morning snow without moving their lips. Snake Nose was there, and that hateful Jumping Snake. This was his first mission . . . his tail had grown, and he was restlessly waiting for us.

We started at once and tramped for many many hours. The way was long and pathless through the savage wilderness of birch, fir and pine trees, and on the snow-covered ground there were many odd-shaped rocks and fallen branches. My snakeskin feet got tangled in the sharp underbrush. I was shivering from the snow and the lengthening shadows, and some trees started to look like they were covered with long gray hairs.

Finally we halted in a clearing near three fallen birch trees and a large rock shaped like a footprint . . . it was white with green and yellow veins. Some of the warriors whispered that it might be an invisible animal, until Snake Nose sniffed it carefully and shook his head. This crazy invisible madness of the Poison Snake People grew and faded like the moon. . . .

Suddenly Birch Bark threw me over this white stone . . . I saw many scraps of animal and human skin around it, while he brushed my legs and tied the back of my neck. I closed my eyes and thought of a young deer cooking over a slow-burning Huron fire. The wet rock smelled like a food platform in my old village. My mouth was watering, incredibly hungry . . . I was ashamed of myself daydreaming like a pagan. . . .

The Snake warriors started cleaning the snow around the rocks with their tails. Very swiftly they peeled off their skins and new ones started to grow. Birch Bark picked up the old skins, stretched them, and formed them into a large upside down kettle shelter over poles stuck in the ground on both sides of the white rock. Then he carved a door on the side facing the Snake village.

When Birch Bark was finished building the snakeskin cabin, he dug a hidden dog hole for himself outside, behind one of the fallen trees. Next he crushed a large basket of snow with his head, and sweating he came back inside the snakeskin kettle. He turned me over with a fork and gave me some pine needles and roots to eat, then he untied my legs and neck, and let me go from the rock. . . .

It was still snowing, so the Snake warriors decided to play a game they called Snake Eyes, which is very different from any game Huron warriors play, but I liked it. The Snake warriors knelt behind separate bundles of red and green feathers as tall as mounds of snow. There were no teams flying back and forth . . . every player depended on their own eyes, which seemed to be shaking inside their heads. Each warrior in his turn popped out his eyes as far as he could. Birch Bark and blind Snake Nose were the only ones who didn't play. The Snake eyes would float ever so slowly to the wet ground, and while they were still in the air, the warrior from a kneeling position with a quick flick of the wrist tried to stick as many feathers as possible into his two or three eyes. They could also throw out as many dead eyes of eaten captives as they had saved . . . this extra part of the game I did not like. Whoever drove home the most feathers into his floating eyes was the winner. . . .

The last player to throw out his three eyes was Jumping Snake. Birch Bark treated him like a son, teaching him how to growl and bite. If Jumping Snake learned this, he would be a powerful enemy in raids and fights. He might even be chosen a Snake captain sooner than expected.

Jumping Snake covered his own eyes with numerous feathers . . . his wrists were so fast I could barely see them move. Birch Bark howled blindly and puffed up his chest when Jumping Snake's eyes at last hit the ground. Jumping Snake smiled and bowed, then he took something out of his snakeskin satchel . . . it was the half-eaten eye of a Huron warrior. Birch Bark had given it to him as a present. I felt uncontrollable hate in my heart for Jumping Snake. I wanted to cross his three eyes together and eat them for breakfast, but I remembered that Blackrobe taught me this was wrong, so I tried to think of the way my other father's hands used to be . . . so very nice, and how they made me feel when they touched my head and shoulders. But, dear God, their touch was mangled now. Jumping Snake covered the half-eaten eye completely with sharp feathers before it reached the ground. I wished my thoughts could be as sharp as a hundred forks piercing deep into every part of Jumping Snake's body. My mind began to crawl into my eyes, half boy, half man, and talked with the devil there for a very long time. . . .

Then a group of strange enemies marched into the clearing. Five of them were picking their way carefully through the feathery Snake eyes, but when they came to the Huron warrior's half-eaten eye they all knelt down and jabbed at it with the antlers that grew out of their faces. . . .

They were the hideous Antler Face People, incredibly tall, thin, and straight with one hoof and one foot, one arm and one hoof. Their mouth was in the middle of their chest . . . two eyes on each shoulder . . . their manhood grew out of their necks right under their chins. Their bodies except their head, neck and manhood were covered with a shining green moss. Their manhood was colored blood red, and their head and neck were skinned like birch bark. Their ears were long and pointy, and their nose and chin stood out as the only features on their face besides the knife-sharp antlers, which grew each year until old age when they toppled off just before death. . . .

Behind these hideous Antler Face People was the killer yellow dog, Hot Dog, Birch Bark's cousin, howling with delight. He had been sent out by Snake Tooth to search for allies with another killer yellow dog, Yellow Breath . . . back when the few remaining slave-captives and many Snake women were brought to the central Snake village. . . .

Hot Dog said that he was bringing these new allies, a treaty party from the hideous Antler Face People, to make an agreement with Snake Tooth, the great leader of both the killer yellow dogs and the Poison Snake People. . . .

Birch Bark spoke for everyone except me . . . asking the Antler Face party to hunt with them first, then everybody could go back to the Snake village together. The Snake warriors hissed their approval, while they put their eyes back in their sockets after cleaning off the feathers. All this time the hideous Antler Face People had put their antlers together and were trying to make loud noises with new words and small footprints. The sky was filled with ladders and doors, while winter birds cursed the snow with horrible names.

When all the Snake eyes were back in, everyone was solemnly introduced. Each one of the hideous Antler Face People had the same name . . . Antler Face. I was not mentioned, or Blackrobe, or the invisible animals. . . .

One of the Antler party was a boy my age, but taller . . . sitting on his shoulder was a live muskrat with its paws crossed protecting two of the boy's four eyes. All the Snake party said that this muskrat was a good luck sign. . . .

The young Antler Face asked Birch Bark if he could play Snake Eyes. Birch Bark gave him a bundle of feathers. Four eyes popped out of Antler Face's shoulders and lazily floated down with the snow. In the time it had taken Jumping Snake to cover completely three eyes, Antler Face had feathered four. Jumping Snake leaped in the air screaming, and fell on his head, which was buried in a mound of snow, with his legs and tail flailing about in the empty air. Everyone laughed. . . .

I liked this young Antler Face boy because I had this strange feeling that the muskrat on his shoulder had once been inside my shoulder. I also felt that he was very different from the others in this Antler Face treaty party. I was impressed by the way he acted when he finished playing Snake Eyes. He bowed and prayed in four directions, but then I couldn't figure out to what God he directed his prayers. Also while the other hideous Antler Face People were shaking with laughter, he helped Jumping Snake to his feet. He said:

"Jumping Snake, there isn't any paper in your head or under the ground where you sleep."

Then he turned his muskrat eyes to me . . . there was a question there and I answered it.

"No, I am not another ally of the Poison Snake People . . . I am a Huron, the son of a great chief, Eustace, who led our trading party on the Great River. We were attacked going home . . . first the Poison Snake People had beavers battling against us, then they and the killer yellow dogs captured and tortured us, especially my other father, a Blackrobe. They are afraid of his magic so they often set him on fire."

I could tell that the hideous Antler Face People were deeply impressed with the powers of the Poison Snake People, who could control beavers, feathers, and mushrooms, and with the power of the killer yellow dogs, who controlled all the wild hill creatures. But who controls the muskrats and the birch trees?

Antler Face spoke to me very carefully:

"Yes, I have heard of your other father. Isn't he the one who can rip the head right off a grown bear?"

I smiled at Antler Face's mistake. Next he asked me if I could play Snake Eyes? I nodded yes, then Antler Face turned to Birch Bark and asked:

"Why don't you let Jumping Snake test this son of a Huron chief?"

Jumping Snake leaped to the challenge . . . we knelt opposite each other, separated by around fifteen feet. Again and again we popped out our eyes . . . Jumping Snake popped out only two of his three eyes, and each time our feathers were equal.

I felt good inside my manhood, but Jumping Snake was very angry . . . his face was breaking into tiny shells and pebbles. He could not believe that a Huron slave might be his equal, especially me, who was two years younger than him. . . .

Finally Birch Bark said:

"Throw all your eyes out one more time, and no more."

We were both steaming like wet earth at the edge of a meadow in springtime.

Birch Bark commanded:

"Snake Eyes!"

Jumping Snake seemed even faster than before. He threw out his three eyes, but my heart also popped out with my eyes . . . a special gift from God. It stayed in the air a long time as I covered both my eyes and one side of my heart with feathers.

Birch Bark and the young Antler Face counted the feathers. The muskrat was smiling at me . . . it seemed as though it might speak, but it didn't. Birch Bark pointed to me and some of the Snake warriors hissed menacingly.

I had beaten Jumping Snake at the warrior game of the Poison

Snake People. I shouted:

"Snake Eyes!"

My heart returned to my side and my eyes went back into their sockets . . . just in time to see Jumping Snake flying blindly towards me. But suddenly the muskrat jumped off the Antler boy's shoulder, it landed on Jumping Snake's face and started biting all three of his eyes.

Jumping Snake flopped around in horrible pain on the cold ground like a freshly caught fish, no longer permitted to draw strength from the bottom of everything . . . then he was quite still, mouth closed but still breathing.

No one there paid any more attention to him, but me, who wanted to pounce on him instantly and tear out his life. I kept thinking and thinking about this, and it was some time before I could chase this wicked desire out of my dreams. . . .

Meanwhile Birch Bark ordered some Snake warriors to pick up one of the fallen birch trees, and put it upright in a mound of snow. Long gray worms dropped off its underside and quickly disappeared into the muskrat's stomach.

I was tied to this tree with knotted snakeskins, while the muskrat licked the damp muddy bark. My legs were cold, my missing shoulder quivered, and my thoughts were somewhere up in the air. In a moment the muskrat scampered up to my shoulder . . . I thought the world would turn over in my head. The muskrat whispered to me in Huron:

"You are a very foolish Huron boy. Don't you know that you've been an enemy captive for as long as four journeys? You cannot get anything done with such an extra uproar in your heart . . . instead you should try to live your life without getting stuck in the snow."

I almost laughed . . . I glanced all around. No one seemed to know that the muskrat was talking to me . . . only the young Antler Face stared, but said nothing.

The muskrat continued in a thoughtful whisper:

"Huron boy, do you know William Coutre?"

I nodded . . . my heart felt as wide and as large as a signal fire. . . .

"I am a friend of his also," the muskrat was licking the inside of my ear. "I have a message from him for your Blackrobe. Remember my words and give them to him when you see him next. Say, 'Black-robe, William Coutre says to go back to France.'"

I repeated the message word for word, but my heart wasn't in it. Then the muskrat scampered off my shoulder and back onto the young Antler Face's shoulder, its paws crossed protecting the Antler's eyes. When it was finally settled and seemed ready for anything, all the hideous Antler Face party except the oldest leaped into the air and exchanged their legs, arms, and hoofs. Then the oldest just toppled over in front of me, his antlers bouncing in the snow, his face as blank as a rock. . . .

The other Antler Faces started singing songs of death and dancing at the same time, horns locked in a circle around their dead brother . . . they thought their after-life would be very pleasant if their bodies were made into a feast. . . .

Birch Bark and Hot Dog built a spit and started a roaring fire . . . everyone but me enjoyed the roasted meat of the dead Antler Face. My mouth was to remain dry even in the snow. After both parties were satisfied, they decided to play another warrior game . . . a team of Snake warriors against the hideous Antler Face treaty party. There were four on each side. Birch Bark and three power-ful-looking warriors were the Poison Snake People's champions.

The teams formed separate circles on the ground no thicker than my wrist. Two other groups, all of them Snake warriors . . . they were called the Weapon Keepers, made two squares, one of hunting forks, the other of gleaming hatchet spoons, which were as sharp as tomahawks and were the weapons of the hideous Antler Face People. They were similar to the Huron torture spoons of old pagan days before Blackrobe. . . .

The warriors in the circles started yelling and barking fearful war whoops, sometimes only once, sometimes maybe five times, then one warrior from both teams ran over to the weapon squares, stooped down, picked one up and hurled it at the nearest opposing warrior, who must try to catch the weapon. If he catches it, one of his Weapon Keepers take a weapon from the other team's pile. If he is hit by a fork or spoon, then one of the other team's keepers takes a weapon. . . .

There were many spoons and forks in the circles . . . the game lasted until twilight when it also stopped snowing. The Poison Snake People were slightly ahead, but Birch Bark had played very badly. He started crawling on his belly, scraping his necklace of birch twigs in the snow, while ladders were folding close to his sides. He felt miserable.

Birch Bark saw me watching him and said:

"Huron puppy . . . it's all your fault."

He got up, rubbed his necklace of power, then took two forks and two hatchet spoons. I was facing him, but couldn't see the details of his face. He was far away, yet I could see him put the weapons down by his paws, then fasten a strip of birch bark over his eyes.

"Keep your eyes on me, Huron puppy," Birch Bark commanded. "Don't you think I'm even more handsome than a real birch tree, or a smooth fringed skirt?"

What could I say?. . .

I watched him pick up a spoon and fork, sniff the icy air, then I stared at the weapons as they came whistling towards me. I am the son of Eustace, a brave Huron chief, who has gone to God . . . I did not close my eyes. The hatchet spoon and hunting fork both hit the tree I was tied to at the same time . . . in the little space between my knees.

I was laughing . . . Birch Bark threw again. A fork and spoon were barely touching each side of my neck, but still I didn't close my laughing eyes, and now my mouth was wide open. My head was spinning in the tree trunk, but I was not bleeding.

Birch Bark took off the bark strip . . . everyone cheered, hissing their approval. The Antler Faces locked their horns again, and seemed more like birds turning around and around in the air. Birch

Bark ordered that I be untied from the tree, and I was brought to him. Standing behind him in one line was the rest of the party . . . he looked me over back and front, as though he were seeing me for the first time. He even felt my heart, but it wasn't beating any faster than usual.

Birch Bark spoke:

"Huron puppy, you will be a noble chief of great strength and courage, if you live . . . maybe even among the Poison Snake People. For they will now always choose their chief leader from outside their own tribe."

Birch Bark hadn't told me anything I didn't know already. I was growing up fast . . . to become a man with special powers and gifts. But every piece of me knew with absolute certainty that I would never help in any way the Poison Snake People or their allies.

Of this I was sure.

I, Tarcisius Tandihetsi, say so.

CHAPTER XVII
BABY FOOD

The next morning Birch Bark with most of the Snake warriors and the four hideous Antler Faces went out hunting for winter food. The Snake babies would soon be coming out of their cocoons, and they would need plenty of fresh meat.

I was dragged along with this party of hunters to help collect the carcasses. Jumping Snake didn't come along and Birch Bark told me why.

"Huron puppy, you made Jumping Snake sick. He thinks his manhood will run off from between his legs if he comes near you too quickly."

I had no fear of Jumping Snake now, but I still could not chase the hate I felt for him out of my dreams. . . .

Morning vanished into more snow as my stomach grumbled like a pack of hungry wolves. We traveled on snakeskin snowshoes, and there was a smell in the air that seemed to be stamping out the earth. We climbed over edges and crawled through holes, never stopping to rest . . . we were in such a hurry that I couldn't even roll my hair into a knot to keep it from getting in my face. . . .

We finally stopped where there were many pine needles under the snow . . . we camped here for three days. I ate very well because I collected most of the dead animals . . . everyone ate from the same kettle. In the afternoons the hunters outlined their paths with snow and searched for invisible animals. Each night I slept on Birch Bark's shoulders or near the chalice in his back.

In the first afternoon Birch Bark and the young boy, Antler Face, brought down a birch bark chapel that was fleeing through the woods. Why was it escaping so far from Huron country . . . I didn't want to think about it. There were many leaves blowing across the chapel windows . . . this was very surprising to see after the first snow of winter.

I watched helplessly as some warriors pulled off the chapel's door. The only things inside were a beaver blanket, a snakeskin box, and a stick lying in a corner. I was forced to pull out every log and pound the wood until my arms ached, then the chapel was set on fire, and the smoke penetrated into every part of my body. When the chapel was completely burned away, I had to fold and make packages of the ashes . . . this is the work of the lowest slave captive and I did not like to do it. . . .

In the evenings the Snake warriors would play their favorite hunting game, Whip Lash. The hideous Antler Faces also joined in the action. They were very good in any kind of game, and were always willing to play new ones even if the games were bloody or deadly. . . .

On the second evening of our stay in this hunting ground 1 saw Birch Bark do a wonderful thing. In Whip Lash a squirrel's skull a little larger than a walnut is attached to the end of a whip. The whip is then wrapped around the neck of the player, who is blindfolded, and as it uncurls itself and falls to the ground, the blindfolded hunter must throw a fork, knife, or sharp hatchet spoon through the squirrel's head. Whip Lash is a very dangerous game. . . .

At the end of this game only two players weren't scratched . . . Birch Bark and the tallest Antler Face, who was also a captain of his people. To settle the contest they were placed facing each other, still blindfolded, around ten paces apart. Two whips with squirrel heads were cracked together between these great captains. Birch Bark threw his fork an instant before Antler Face tossed his spoon, and they both dropped quickly to the ground, but only Birch Bark's fork hit a squirrel's head. As a matter of fact his fork went through one head and stuck in the other catching both heads at the same time.

All the warriors shouted loudly without stop, rapidly praising Birch Bark in every direction. I shouted too. What he had done was a very difficult thing to do . . . I told him this. He smiled at me and rolled his teeth.

But I went on to say that it was too bad he wasn't a Christian or a Huron. When I finished Birch Bark wasn't grinning anymore, and feathers had started to fall out of my eyes and I felt that I would be a captive forever. . . .

During the third evening while the warriors were again playing Whip Lash, the camp was suddenly surrounded by invisible animals. Howls of hunger, demon yells, and other unpleasant sounds twisted around the trees . . . mere blurs in the surprising shadows. Two Snake hunters were torn from their feet, and their screams would still wake me a long time afterwards in the cold darkness. Then the evening dipped into the great circle of night. No one could figure out the secret of this movement. The invisible animals vanished in an instant . . . all we saw were their rows and rows of cutting sharp teeth. They were trying to get the fresh meat and blood needed for the Snake babies. . . .

The next morning we returned to our starting point near the footprint rock and the fallen birch trees. Snake Nose told Birch Bark that the invisible animals had passed through the camp. The hunters collected their belongings in an instant, and we were heading back to the Snake village. . . .

All the warriors were faster than any cloud. It was a very crisp winter day, the air was so pure that the world seemed a hundred miles away. It was a long trip . . . we were gliding along in a pack. Everyone was afraid of the invisible animals, but Birch Bark trotted ahead.

I saw it all . . . Birch Bark was attacked by a stray invisible animal. None of the Snake warriors saw it, of this I am sure. The only other person to see it was the young boy, Antler Face. I noticed that the muskrat on the boy's shoulder was missing. I scratched my head, wondering if all muskrats were the same. The wind blew through the trees as if it were cooling off some freshly roasted meat.

All I saw of the stray invisible animal, besides its four rows of cutting sharp teeth, were its hands and feet, which were webbed, and part of its head, which had a big tuft of hair sticking out like a horn. I did not see the rest of its body . . . it was invisible, but the longer the invisible animals stay in this world the more visible they become. . . .

Birch Bark rushed in among the branches of a birch tree, shaking off its snow, then he slipped on the icy ground. The invisible animal jumped on his legs, and strings of blue smoke melted in the cold air as its slimy webbed hands slid down his flesh. The world seemed to shoot out of Birch Bark's screaming voice . . . a mountain rolling into the Great River. He tried to breathe fire, but his mouth looked like it was swallowing water.

The Snake warriors were frozen like ducks, who had lost their sense of flight. The Antler Faces rushed up and put their antlers together swiftly and silently, trying not to spill any water.

Then blind Snake Nose started sniffing the air suspiciously, while the other Snake hunters were asking each other what was wrong with Birch Bark.

"Maybe he is changing into a digging stick as the sun goes under his mouth."

"Maybe he tripped over a storage basket."

"Perhaps he ate too much meat."

Finally the Antler Face boy shouted:

"Don't you see what's attacking Birch Bark?"

When all the Snake warriors except Snake Nose shook their heads, the young Antler Face threw his hunting spoon at the head of the invisible animal. As it pierced the hard bone under the invisible animal's tuft of hair, both it and the hunting spoon disappeared, leaving behind only a few slimy green feathers.

Birch Bark was tearing at his leg which gave him great pain, but he did not yell again. He covered his mouth with his paw to keep out the hair . . . his neck was rolling in the snow. Birch Bark would never run straight again. . . .

He was struggling furiously inside his head. In one breath he came out with:

"We must hurry back to the village . . . the invisible animals are going to attack it . . . maybe all the Snake villages will be attacked."

All the Snake warriors suddenly shed their skins. My mind dragged itself through tangles of imaginary hair, then it was flying as fast as my blood. I went into a ceremonial pagan trance and pretended to fall out . . . I fell on a warrior's freshly-shed snakeskin and swallowed it whole.

My heart was beating like a speck of light against the speed of flashing darkness . . . none of the Snake hunters had noticed what I had done, only the young boy, Antler Face, had seen me. . . .

We pushed our way back through the snow. Birch Bark's wounds were wrapped in snakeskins and many layers of beaver fat . . . his eyes had turned into traps as he looked everywhere. Hot Dog carried him on his back as much as possible. . . .

From a great distance away we could see black smoke rising out of the Snake village . . . the Snake warriors and the hideous Antler Faces started to run. I felt gladness touch a piece of my heart for the first time in many moons, but I quickly lost touch.

Birch Bark was very angry and he had the temper of a naked bear in wintertime because he couldn't go full blast with the others, so he knocked my face against the bark of a tree. I thought to myself that I had better keep out of Birch Bark's way or he might really hurt me. . . .

We entered what was left of the Snake village in the evening . . . overturned kettles, broken platforms, sharp pointed nails, and half-eaten bodies . . . the mushroom fields had been pulled up and torn to bits. My eyes, which didn't make a sound, poked through the ruins. It was then I realized there were no Snake babies hanging in the air, and I remembered that René Goupil had half-predicted it. . . .

I heard strange voices muttering under the ground, and my heart was dusty and wrapped in snakeskin. Snake Tooth was also returning to the village with a band of Snake warriors . . . lights were breaking all around them, and their feelings were such an awful thing to see. Blows had been exchanged and wounds inflicted, and they left a bloody trail of footprints in the snow.

All the Poison Snake People, who had fled the village, came back and gathered around Snake Tooth and his warriors. Many Snake women started shrieking in madness, while some of the older Snake men like Black Magic were lying on their sides striking their manhoods against the ground in a frenzy.

Black Magic shouted:

"Brothers, our flesh died out long ago, but now our spirits are being shoved under water."

Suddenly his mushroom colored skin turned black like a torture kettle, and it would always remain that way. He got up and bowed to Snake Tooth, then he continued:

"Our women are tearing out their hair . . . all the Snake babies are dead, they never came out of their cocoons. This raid was well planned. The gray hairs sighted in the mushroom fields changed into invisible animals . . . poles were picked up without moving, and warriors quarreled with smoke. Our bodies are rolling towards us . . . we are the last of our race. Our future has been wiped out. . . .

"Snake Tooth, after you left with most of our warriors to try to capture the invisible animals, who had so boldly killed Full Moon, while he was paddling in Partridge's canoe . . . more of them charged into our kettles. They had three purposes for their raid . . . destroy the mushroom fields, kill all the Snake babies, and maybe help Blackrobe escape from our torture fires . . . but then again, they might want to torture him too. Without Full Moon I just don't know."

Snake Tooth was still too amazed at everything . . . all he could think of asking was:

"Did Blackrobe really escape?"

"Yes . . . he went underground with the invisible animals."

Snake Tooth rubbed his hairless head.

"Maybe Blackrobe will never come back with his secret language to plague us up and down for our tobacco."

Black Magic shook his head.

"It's a small victory, Snake Tooth, when all the Snake babies are dead. You were not born a Poison Snake, and the invisible animals are many. They may have attacked every Snake village at the same time, and all our survivors will be crowded here."

The Snake warriors started chanting their song of mourning, while the hideous Antler Faces locked horns without spilling a drop of water. The Snake women continued to tear out their hair, except Kettle Skin, who stamped on her awful feet.

The muskrat on the shoulder of the young boy, Antler Face, hopped off and sniffed around in small circles. Next he buried his face in a pool of blood, and I knew it was my other father's blood because there were brown spots in it. Then the muskrat came right over to me in between all the confusion of the Poison Snake People, who had started to wander about, either searching for lost possessions, or looking for new ones. The muskrat jumped on my missing shoulder, smearing Blackrobe's blood on my neck and face, and whispered in my ear:

"Blackrobe is going to France! The invisible animals did not help him escape . . . I know them too well. Most of the muskrats living around here are their allies."

The young Antler Face lifted the muskrat off my body and put it back on his own. He stared at me for a very long time, then put his hand under his chin and touched his manhood. The mouth in the middle of his mossy chest seemed about to speak, but didn't. I wanted to clutch the boy's short antlers and shake them, but he was too tall for me so I pulled myself back by the hair. Now I was wishing that I could go to France, or to places even closer like my own Huron village, or at least start shifting back and forth across the Great River.

Sadness was filling my heart, and a breeze started to blow through the overturned kettles . . . I suddenly realized that I might never see my other father again. It is hard to be a man and not a boy. . . .

Young Antler Face interrupted my feelings, he spoke to his muskrat:

"My Little Cousin, you should tell your Huron friend that I know what he swallowed and all its remaining powers. It once belonged to the blind warrior, Snake Nose. I also know your friend wants to see his Blackrobe again. . . .

"For everyone else the situation here is hopeless. I cannot say anything, I am the youngest of our party, and now the Antler Face People are the allies of the Poison Snake People. Our word is sacred and cannot be broken or traded away. . . ."

Antler Face stared straight at me as he went on:

"Little Cousin, tell your Huron friend that I won't try to stop him from escaping, but he better look out for the other Antler Faces. They'll grab him like a rock and pound him into feathers."

I was barely breathing . . . my eyes were wide open and there were pounding noises inside my head. My body had turned into chipped stone as I helped the Poison Snake People chisel and scrape, rebuilding their village. I felt sorry for these pagan people for the first time in my life because they had lost their future. . . .

That night floating in Wrinkled Black Skin's half broken kettle I asked God to show me the way out of here. Outside my mistress and her family wept and sang their Snake Song of Mourning. I looked up at the sky . . . the stars were shining like French buttons. That night my sleep was awful and my dreams were not pleasant. It was even much worse than that. . . .

I, Tarcisius Tandihetsi, say so.

CHAPTER XVIII
ESCAPE

In which Tarcisius wakes up from a long nightmare sleep
... all the other Snake villages have been destroyed ...
Kicking Snake's skin has turned black ... three stray
invisible animals are captured ... young Antler Face's
muskrat brings Tarcisius a message to escape quickly ...
the situation is getting worse ... Tarcisius changes into
blind Snake Nose ... Partridge mistakes Tarcisius for
Snake Nose and Tarcisius gets into Partridge's canoe ...
Tarcisius smashes Partridge over the head and escapes in
the canoe ... he meets young Antler Face outside the
snake village ... they eat Snake Nose's skin the first time
they stop ... they are brothers in Christianity ... they
paddle on through the night ... the muskrat on Antler
Face's shoulder tells Tarcisius a story about its encounter
with a Blackrobe outside a birch bark chapel ... a large
rock emerges from the ground, but the muskrat forces
it back ... Tarcisius and Antler face are attacked by
invisible animals ... the muskrat runs off so Tarcisius
and Antler face can escape by hiding under the canoe ...
a stray invisible animal jumps on Antler Face by surprise
... Tarcisius kills it and loses his hair from around his
manhood ... they paddle away ... they find the muskrat
dead, and when they start burying it, the invisible
animals make themselves known and strike up a
deal ... Tarcisius and Antler Face follow
Blackrobe's invisible trail.

There were nine days of bad dreams before it was the middle of the night again. All the other Snake villages had been destroyed. I had dropped my voice to the point of a stick ... my head rolled out of a tobacco pouch while my heart was stuck inside a snakeskin. I felt as if I had died and my body had gone where the dead crabs go.

I rubbed the dreams out of my eyes and looked over the rim of the kettle.

It was snowing, and the cooking fires burned low in the village. Blue smoke strings poured out of the Snake warriors' bodies, and it didn't smell very good. The few remaining Snake children, really no longer children since the Snake babies had been killed, collected feathers and matched them with their heads and tails. Warriors were everywhere, shedding their skins in bits and pieces. . . .

Black Magic was lying in curves waiting for the snow to melt away the color of his skin. Kicking Snake's skin had also turned black. He would bend over backwards and inch toward his dreams, hoping to find a power that might cure his darkness. Nothing could change it, I thought, except the invisible animals themselves, and that didn't seem very likely. . . .

War parties had been sent to all the other destroyed Snake villages. Three stray invisible animals were caught . . . they all looked like the one who had attacked Birch Bark. The older Snake women had built a huge torture fire that would not go out until the coming of dawn. I knew in my heart that these invisible animals were pretty tough enemies and would not utter a sound in pain except at the moment of death.

I slipped back down into the kettle. I heard something growling. I knew I was the only one left inside . . . everyone else was out helping torture the stray invisible animals. My thoughts were crowded into snakeskin satchels while my lips trembled. I was throwing up flies and bundles of straw. A small figure moved across a strip of birch bark . . . softly it brushed against the shadows and rolled over in the smoke. I heard my name mentioned:

"Tarcisius. . . ."

It was young Antler Face's muskrat.

"Is your master well, little cousin?" I asked in a loud voice, while one hand felt the keen edge of my thumb, and the other touched my manhood.

"Keep your face down, Huron puppy."

My face burned with shame. As the muskrat crept closer and closer to me, I saw that it was chewing on a stick.

When it sat down next to me, the muskrat dropped the stick in my lap and said:

"I sat near the torture fire with my young master. We listened as Snake Tooth preached to the Poison Snake People and led them in all the worst tortures, but so far nothing. We overheard some warriors whisper that Snake Tooth didn't speak as powerfully as he once did before Full Moon and all the Snake babies were killed. They think he should have seen through the invisible trap. . . .

"Now he sees invisible animals everywhere like Curly Head and many others. He's afraid the French might become their allies and sell them good arquebuses. He argues with Black Magic. The situation is getting worse. That's why Antler Face sent me with this message . . . escape. Use the snakeskin you swallowed in the snow before it's too late. . . ."

I interrupted:

"Wrinkled Black Skin told me that Snake Nose has gone out again on a food hunting party."

"Yes," answered the muskrat. "But the party was called back for the torture of the stray invisible animals."

I nodded my head and lost myself in thinking what to do. . . .

The muskrat bit me on the neck and said:

"Hurry up, little cousin, the snow is melting on my fur, and I'm beginning to see through your shadowy body. The village is being repaired and surrounded again by icy mounds of hair and tobacco. Take my stick and paint a red dot at each end, then get out of here. Don't you wish to see your Blackrobe again?"

I said:

"I have wished that in many dreams."

I painted the red dots on the stick as I was told. Next I put my arm down my throat along an old line of mushrooms, then pulled out the powerful snakeskin. There was a white mark across the skin where the body trunk had once been. And as I shook out the skin like a blanket, the muskrat disappeared, saying:

"We will meet you outside the village."

I looked over the edge of the kettle . . . no one in sight, so I quickly stepped into the snakeskin. This had to work, there was no turning back now . . . I could only do this skin trick once. I closed my eyes, then opened them . . . I could barely see the white mark above where my stomach used to be. My slave captive Huron body was changed into the body of the warrior, Snake Nose, but not his mind or spirit.

I climbed out of Wrinkled Black Skin's kettle. I was blindly trying to find my way through the snow, when Partridge paddled by in his canoe. He yelled at me:

"Snake Nose, hurry up and get into my canoe . . . I'll bring you back to the torture fires."

I noticed that only a piece of string was left of Partridge's necklace . . . Paul Ononhoraton's manhood had disappeared. Partridge seemed to look through me as he asked:

"Have you found the Huron boy yet?"

My voice was ready to jump outside my nose and throat. My Snake arms and legs and tail were shaking as I answered in a strange voice:

"No, he wasn't in Wrinkled Black Skin's kettle . . . I couldn't find him anywhere. What should I do?"

My feet were cold from searching outside myself . . . my head hurt and my manhood was trying to disappear.

"Get in here, you sightless fool," Partridge shouted. "There are enough bites on your forehead to turn war paint into spit. Hurry up, let's go. Snake Tooth will have his teeth sliding in and out of your arms. I'm tired of paddling by myself. Come on . . . grab a paddle with your tail and start helping."

I grabbed a paddle . . . it felt strange to hold it with a tail. I gazed through my newly acquired skin. My own sight returned a little bit. There were many snakeskin satchels in the canoe, and I saw myself helping Partridge with all my strength. The canoe glided straight ahead, moving in and out of the kettles and sleeping platforms. We went pretty fast . . . we could easily have won a canoe race together.

I was laughing to myself as I twisted and raised the paddle, then smashed it down on Partridge's head. There was no rope to tie him up, so I dumped him out of the canoe like the village dog that he was. I could feel the air around me growing warmer until my tail smelled of wood smoke and my stomach was cramped with hunger. I thought eagerly of the muskrat. . . .

I paddled through a small opening. The tracks of the canoe were as stiff as deer hide, and the canoe itself smelled like so many old ladders. The young Antler Face was waiting for me behind some rocks. There was a piece of wood tied around his neck just under his manhood . . . it was dotted with red paint at each end like mine. The muskrat was on his shoulder, its paws crossed protecting his eyes.

The moment the Antler boy joined me in the canoe, I felt his thoughts jump to the edges of his feet, which were so thin they looked like spoon handles. I also felt many small circles gathering around his antlers. We paddled through a clump of trees and across a frozen stream . . . we kept on going into a lifeless forest.

My tail was numb by the time we finally stopped. I took off the stolen snakeskin and ripped it apart . . . my memories were never very far behind my stomach. I gave half to Antler Face and chewed my half very slowly. I could see quite clearly in the moonlight when I looked up from my meal . . . Antler Face was sitting in front of me, his antlers making remarkable shadows. Then out of nowhere I made a funny face and held it lightly like a bow string. Antler Face smiled and his arms moved with his words . . . he said:

"Tarcisius, your face that way reminds me of William Coutre. Did he show you how to make it?"

"Yes he did . . . on the Great River just before we were attacked by the Poison Snake People and their allies."

I tried to stare deeply into all the eyes of Antler Face as I asked:

"Are you really a friend of William Coutre?"

"Yes, Tarcisius, I am . . . I am a catechumen, not yet received

Saving Waters," he spoke from the middle of his chest. "When we find your Blackrobe I will ask him to pour Saving Waters over my antlers."

My mind was rolling around in astonishment like a canoe in a storm . . . I had to hold on to my stomach. I did not like to feel so uncertain, so I tried to remember all my other father had taught me about God and His Magic.

A look of deep understanding touched Antler Face's mossy shoulders and chest . . . his head did not move yet his antlers made small circles in the dark air. I was sure he knew what I was thinking about. . . .

We embraced like Christians, like brothers, sparkling eyes and magic fingers. Then we were moving again, but this time we paddled more slowly. We needed to protect our energy, or our thoughts might disappear beneath cold flat stones.

Antler Face was in the front of the canoe directing its path. Trees were breaking down into baskets and pushing away the earth, while its surface seemed to weigh less than my arms. We paddled into a deserted Poison Snake camp that had been set up to hunt for stray invisible animals. An apron of skin with lines of shaggy hair across it had been left on the ground, and it made my mouth water and stick to my eyes. Antler Face and I chewed on this skin until it was tiny and narrow and had no more juice left. It was good to spit into ashes of the Snake fire.

We paddled on, never looking back . . . over our heads the moon was shaped like half a snakeskin satchel. I was stretching out my legs, wishing I could order up a warm cabin to go across the hills, when my feet began to shake . . . something moved in the hairs between my toes. My heart started spinning to the top of my head. I heard small animal noises as I picked up a hunting fork that had been lying in the bottom of the canoe. With it I killed two rabbits coming out of my feet. I felt there would be plenty more where they came from. . . .

Many things were shifting around in my head . . . I shouted at the back of Antler Face:

"No matter where we must go, no matter how many circles we make in the snow, we won't starve or have to sing hunger songs or lose our shadows."

I knew then I was stronger than any pagan magic, but Antler Face didn't turn around . . . he was busy up ahead with his growing antlers. With one hand I held up the two rabbits and exclaimed in the rich full voice of visions:

"See these, Dear God, and bless me with many others." Then with my other hand I lowered a hunting stick midway between a point and a hole and said:

"This is a magic place where I can trade with many different roots . . . in the future I may even find pieces of invisible flesh here."

A shadow fell across Antler Face's back . . . it was the beginning of dawn in this cold and lifeless forest. We had been paddling most of the night, and the ground itself seemed to soar into lifelong dreams. The muskrat turned around and said:

"Little cousin, my body shakes . . . you shouldn't speak about invisible animals here. You really know next to nothing about them. They are very dangerous enemies, who might boil you alive in the snow. Me . . . I've always tried to drop bits of flesh in the water, but remember . . . you have to catch them by surprise. . . ."

The muskrat continued this way for a while, but I didn't listen until it started telling about an adventure it had when it was only a young muskrat. I heard Antler Face laughing to himself, but the muskrat paid no attention to him . . . sweat was pouring down its round face as it spoke:

"When I was a young muskrat, only half my full size, leaping in and out of the water, circling all the traps and snares, I had the curiosity of a cat and like a village dog I would steal anything I could eat right away.

"I didn't wander much in the dark or swim in lakes and streams where the beavers lived. They didn't like me one bit, but I did travel in many different lands and my body would sometimes glow with an intense blue light. . . .

"Once I visited the land of the Hurons . . . I had been traveling a long time. My stomach was hanging out, waiting for my eyes to turn into dried meat. I came upon a birch bark chapel in a small clearing outside a Huron village. I saw no humans around so I went in through the front door to see what I could steal. . . .

"All I found inside was a beaver blanket, a snakeskin box, and a stick the size of Antler Face's manhood. Inside the snakeskin box there was a dish with small circles of food, and a shiny cup with red liquid in it. At once I dipped my eager mouth into the cup, then heaped up what was in the dish. I didn't stop until everything had disappeared into the pit of my stomach."

Antler Face laughed right out loud because he was only a catechumen, not yet received Saving Waters. Everything was pulled into place under the morning sun, and the muskrat's body was glowing with a bright light as it continued:

"And after a minute I felt all different inside . . . one of my legs was lying on the ground while another went hopping all around. In my head I heard a rising wind and a tremendous rush of flapping wings . . . I wanted to do something great."

Antler Face was shaking with so much laughter that the muskrat nearly fell off his shoulder, but it straightened itself up and resumed its story:

"I crawled out of the birch bark chapel, and it began to rain. Did I cause the rain? I thought I could teach the world to live under different roots. I was suddenly able to speak in any language or network of signs. I was certain that I was the greatest muskrat to ever live on the face of this earth. Maybe I would never die! . . .

"Then without thinking I ran headlong into the trunk of a birch tree. My head and shoulders went through the tree and were sticking out the other side. I was stuck in that tree trunk for hours while it kept raining furiously.

"Finally the rain stopped and a Blackrobe came by. First he laughed at me, but when I started crying and telling him what had happened, he parted the tree trunk and pushed me out. Right away he poured Saving Waters over my head and sent up prayers of tobacco smoke to the sky. . . .

"I am very grateful to this Blackrobe, and Tarcisius, I think that your other father is the same Blackrobe who saved me."

Antler Face was no longer laughing. He was rubbing his antlers, which were suddenly hanging down from his head like snakes. I hadn't understood why he was laughing in the first place. I heard myself speak to the muskrat very reverently:

"I have also tasted God's body and blood, and they didn't make me feel like beating up my dreams. I felt calm and happy and protected with a warm glow inside my whole body."

A soft light crept into the muskrat's eyes as I went on to praise him:

"Indeed, you will probably be the greatest muskrat in heaven."

Antler Face turned around to me and said:

"It is better to be quiet in this cold land . . . it is filled with invisible animals. My antlers feel their presence."

We settled down in the canoe and paddled forward into the heavy brooding silence of snow. We kept moving, stopping only twice. Once on the surface of cold water, and once to cook and eat the two rabbits that I caught in the hairs of my feet. . . .

In the evening a blue mist started trailing in and out of the snow like signs of bad tobacco. By nightfall it was very difficult to see, so we got out of the canoe and slowly tracked the wind. The muskrat dragged the canoe after us. . . .

When we stopped to rest a streaking sliver of light suddenly passed through our eyes. Something rock-hard rose out of the ground . . . something sleek and dark beneath my frozen feet. My knees started pounding together like a war drum. I was sure that this stone thing had tough sinewy roots, which curved deep into the earth. As I jumped to one side, I saw the muskrat drop the canoe and with its paws trace strange patterns above the emerging rock. . . .

The rock was forced back into the ground . . . I wanted to run and not stop running, but I couldn't make up my mind. I reattached myself to my head with one leg behind me. I felt as weak as a rotten stick, and I couldn't understand why Antler Face was tapping his manhood so impressively.

He started telling me something but a strong wind suddenly blew the words back into his chest. I only heard the sound, "Hiiiii!" Then he pointed to some hidden edges behind me. I saw ghostly shadows in the wavering blue mist . . . it was the invisible animals. Two of them stepped out of the trunk of a birch tree. I saw four blank eye-holes under their tufts of hair. A third invisible animal was controlling the mist . . . their feet left prints in the snow, but you could see right through their shadowy bodies. . . .

Antler Face and I just stood there unable to rush back to our bones, but the muskrat got our attention by making noises that sounded like a roasting fire . . . the heat of his words finally drew in our spirits. We turned the canoe upside down and formed a circle on top of it. We knew that the invisible animals were hunting for blood and strength-giving meat. The muskrat spoke without words inside each of our heads. I thought I heard a death rattle in its throat.

"Younger cousins, there is only one way to escape. Listen closely . . . there's no time to repeat. First all of us will jump off the canoe. I will dart away making as much noise as possible, while you two hide under the canoe. Try to stay off the ground as much as you can. I'm sure the invisible animals won't turn over the canoe to look underneath."

Both Antler Face and I felt like lumps of meat no smaller than a wall . . . I could even feel the smallest hairs on my manhood standing up. Our breath came in long gasps as we dropped to the ground. Our chests were heaving and our legs trembling as we maneuvered ourselves under the canoe. Meanwhile the muskrat took off like a log plunging down a foamy river. The noise he was making sounded like a waterfall roaring out of his wide open mouth. . . .

Antler Face and I straddled the dividing sticks under the

turned-over canoe . . . we had to remain still for a long time. It was very hard to hide quietly from the invisible animals when your feet weren't firmly planted on the ground. . . .

They prowled silently around the canoe but did not touch it . . . of this I am most sure. They spoke to each other in an invisible language I didn't understand . . . maybe my other father could. Now he seemed as far away as dinner, and I could hardly swallow. . . .

The invisible animals took up the muskrat's trail, and they didn't stumble along one step at a time. I feared that our little cousin would be the greatest muskrat in heaven before dawn. We stayed under the canoe until we saw a black shadowy tree stump evolve into a single feather of light. It took us quite a while to straighten up our backs, especially Antler Face, who was so tall. . . .

We ate some black shriveled mushrooms, which fell out of the canoe when we turned it over. We also chewed on pieces of cold bark. Nothing tempting was coming out of the hairs between my toes. . . .

We had to decide what to do . . . we couldn't just stay where we were until our arms fell off or slimy green feathers covered up our manhoods. Antler Face started to stretch his legs over his words like the ends of tree branches. Suddenly he doubled up and yelled out, surprised by great pain. A stray invisible animal was pulling down on the boy's antlers. I could only see its webbed feet, so I dove down like an otter and sunk my teeth as far as they could go into one of its stray feet.

The invisible animal let go of the boy's antlers and tumbled over . . . it made a deep impression in the snow. I hacked off its webbed feet and rolled over its invisible body. I saw its face . . . the tuft of hair growing out of its forehead like a horn, two wide evil grinning mouths with four rows of cutting sharp teeth, and four blank eyeholes, one at each corner of a mouth. I could hardly believe my eyes, but then suddenly it disappeared and much to my horror so did what little hair I had around my manhood. For a moment I thought I too might become invisible. . . .

Antler Face quickly pulled himself together. We set up the canoe, climbed in, and paddled away. After several hours we found the muskrat . . . our little cousin was all chewed up like a leftover meal. Its tail was missing and its head was hidden in snarling shadows. . . .

As we buried the muskrat, we heard many sounds in the ground underneath us. They seemed to echo through our heads like language. We tried not to listen, but then these words started to make sense. The invisible animals were giving us a message. What they said was something like this . . . they wouldn't bother us again if we didn't bury the muskrat in the ground. Take it out of its grave and let the insects feed on it . . . then they told us that they might know where Blackrobe was hiding and would point out the way.

Antler Face was furiously digging his antlers into the ground and at the same time kicking the air. A circle of birch roots was pushing its way up through the ground. Antler Face and I quickly agreed to do what the invisible animals asked, even though they were worse than pagans. We took the muskrat out of its grave and dumped it into the circle of birch roots. My desire to see my other father and Antler Face's urge to have Saving Waters poured over his antlers overwhelmed our faint hearts. But I think we committed a grave sin. . . .

The invisible animals did leave us alone, and as they promised they pointed out the way to my other father. Antler Face and I paddled away and didn't stop until late evening. We camped in a small clearing near a stream. While Antler Face filled a snakeskin satchel with water and made a fire, I killed a turkey that tried to fly out of the hairs between my toes . . . .

We ate and drank our fill and settled down by the comfortable fire. It was nice to be warm again, and I soon fell asleep, thinking pleasant thoughts that I hoped would lead me to my other father. . . .

It was good to think that I might see him again. I wondered if he was stronger than the invisible animals, who are more powerful than a paddle in every direction.

I did of not like the invisible animals because I couldn't see very much of them. I prefer to be able to see my enemies than for them to be invisible.

I, Tarcisius Tandihetsi, say so.

CHAPTER XIX
BIRCH BARK CHAPEL

IN WHICH TARCISIUS AND ANTLER FACE CONTINUE TO FOLLOW BLACKROBE'S INVISIBLE TRAIL TO A SACRED MOUNTAIN . . . THEY GO INSIDE TO A VERY WIDE AND DEEP CAVE, WHICH IS FILLED WITH BIRCH BARK CHAPELS . . . ANTLER FACE'S HEAD, MANHOOD AND ANTLERS ARE KNOCKED OFF AND THEY RUN AWAY . . . TARCISIUS FORMS A CLAY MUSKRAT INSIDE HIS HEAD AND IT JUMPS OUT TO HELP SEARCH FOR THE MISSING PARTS . . . THE MUSKRAT FINALLY LEADS THEM UP A WHITE LADDER THEN JUMPS BACK INSIDE TARCISIUS' HEAD . . . THEY CLIMB OUT ONTO A WIDE LEDGE WHERE THERE IS A LARGE BIRCH BARK CHAPEL SURROUNDED BY A WARM STREAM . . . AS THEY CROSS A BRIDGE THEY SEE PICTURES FROM EVERYWHERE IN THE TRAILS OF STEAM AND THE HAZY DEPTHS OF THE STREAM ITSELF . . . BLACKROBE WARNS TARCISIUS TO GET HIS HEAD OUT OF THE WATER . . . TARCISIUS INTRODUCES ANTLER FACE TO BLACKROBE . . . THEY ALL GO INSIDE THE WARM BIRCH BARK CHAPEL . . . BLACKROBE REJOINS ANTLER FACE'S HEAD, MANHOOD AND ANTLERS TO HIS BODY . . . HE POURS SAVING WATERS OVER THE BOY'S ANTLERS . . . BLACKROBE TELLS TARCISIUS THAT HE MUST GO BACK TO FRANCE, BUT HE PROMISES TO COME BACK . . . TARCISIUS AND ANTLER FACE LEAVE THE BIRCH BARK CHAPEL . . . IT FLIES OFF THE MOUNTAIN WITH BLACKROBE INSIDE AND DISAPPEARS INSIDE THE GIANT RED MOUTH IN THE SKY, WHICH QUICKLY VANISHES . . . TARCISIUS LEADS THE WAY BACK DOWN THE LADDER . . . ALL THE BIRCH BARK CHAPELS HAVE BEEN DESTROYED BY THE INVISIBLE ANIMALS . . . TARCISIUS AND ANTLER FACE LEAVE THE SACRED MOUNTAIN AND ARE INSTANTLY RECAPTURED BY SNAKE TOOTH AND A LARGE PARTY OF SNAKE WARRIORS . . . THE POISON SNAKE PEOPLE LED BY SNAKE TOOTH HAVE DEFEATED A GIANT WAR PARTY OF INVISIBLE ANIMALS . . . TARCISIUS IS BEATEN UP BY PARTRIDGE AND JUMPING SNAKE . . . SNAKE TOOTH SMELLS TARCISIUS' BODY FOR SECRET INFORMATION . . . A SACRED INVISIBLE ANIMAL IS TORTURED ON A LADDER . . . ITS NECK BECOMES VISIBLE AS IT'S FORCED UP THE LADDER . . . DAYLIGHT

IS EXTINGUISHED . . . THE SACRED INVISIBLE ANIMAL EXPLODES
INTO MANY SLIMY GREEN FEATHERS . . . TARCISIUS TRIES TO
ESCAPE IN THE DARK BUT HE'S CAUGHT BY SNAKE NOSE . . .
SNAKE TOOTH'S BODY BURNS LIKE A BRIGHT LIGHT IN THE
IMMENSE DARKNESS . . . THE SNAKE WARRIORS START DESTROYING
THE SLIMY GREEN FEATHERS . . . SNAKE TOOTH FALLS TWICE
AND THE BRIGHT LIGHT INSIDE HIM GOES OUT . . . HE PRAYS
TO THE GIANT SNAKE FOR HELP . . . LIGHT RETURNS
TO HIS BODY . . . HE LEADS THE WAR PARTY
BACK TO THE SNAKE VILLAGE.

Antler Face and I paddled for several days in the distance . . . through snowy fields, over icy cliffs, and around frozen trees. We sang many songs behind our backs, and I drew pictures in the snow that could be taught not to disappear underground. Sometimes we had to travel on our knees in order to follow the invisible trail. Antler Face was in the front of the canoe, he seemed to know which way to go, and I was kneeling in the back watching behind us. We suffered many hardships on the ice. . . .

Finally we came to a sacred mountain . . . it was sacred to all pagans. I remembered hearing the eldest Hurons talk about it. They had never seen it, but stories had been passed down. Now I was looking at it . . . its rocks were mostly smooth, white and shiny, but near the top it had a few wide ledges, which cast long shadows down the sides. We circled the mountain three times before we noticed a small opening in the solid rock. Antler Face knew of this secret entrance and the necessary ceremony. I felt sure that the invisible animals hadn't figured it out yet, but they did know Blackrobe was hiding inside the mountain. . . .

We hid the canoe in what we considered a secure place because we still feared the Poison Snake People might be tracking us. I knew Partridge could smell it out in any open place. Then we crawled into the narrow passage, to whatever evil or safe distance it might lead. I thought we were very brave like Eustace, my father, or René Goupil.

The tunnel was long and slimy, and if your body brushed against the sides, the damp walls would start sucking at your flesh, but at least the ground under us was rough and solid.

We crept along for many long minutes not knowing which way we were going . . . I followed close behind Antler Face. When we finally emerged, we straightened up and looked around. Antler Face started making noises like roots breaking through a rock, and he pointed up to a ridgepole that was continually burning. We were in a very wide and deep cave. The ridgepole, which had startled Antler Face so much, went the whole way across the cave and provided all the light. It wasn't very bright, but you still could see that the cave was filled up with sturdy bark chapels all looking the same. . . .

I opened one of the doors and peered inside . . . nothing was there except a beaver blanket and an open snakeskin box. I felt a rush of thoughts that rubbed me the wrong way. I saw a stick, dotted with red paint at each end, lying on the floor behind the snakeskin box . . . suddenly it shot a stream of water at my head. I thought of signs scattered across the floor like bits of paper. I ducked, and the water knocked off Antler Face's head, manhood and antlers, then the piece of wood flipped into the snakeskin box, which instantly shut itself tight. Meanwhile the head rolled away . . . I tried to jump on it, but instead I fell on my face. Red and white war paint alternated to the bottom of my breath as I made a circle and looked between my legs, but I couldn't find any trail.

The head was nowhere to be seen . . . Antler Face staggered aimlessly down a row of birch bark chapels, bumping into doors and windows until he finally went into one. They were all the same inside . . . he sat down on the beaver blanket, holding in his lap the empty snakeskin box. He cried out after his missing parts, touching the air where his head, manhood and antlers should have been. . . .

I started scratching out the hairs inside my nose. I coughed and sneezed and little mounds of clay were growing bigger inside my head. They formed a figure that was shaking hairs off its back. Another muskrat . . . not on my missing shoulder but in my head.

It quickly leapt out and broke the stick that was lying on the floor, then it shook its eyes at me. My eyes dashed up and down twice over, looking at the muskrat, but this time it wasn't flesh and blood, it was made of clay. . . .

The muskrat threw the broken stick at my feet, and started sniffing the ground. It padded its way towards the door and seemed to be tracking some mysterious path. I helped Antler Face up, held onto him, and sometimes had to drag him along to stay in sight of the muskrat.

There were at least twenty birch bark chapels in the cave. I think we followed the clay muskrat in and out of most of them. We didn't meet anyone, or even catch a glimpse of Antler Face's missing parts. If Antler Face or I made any extra noise with our feet, the clay muskrat would turn around and stare at us coldly. Of course I made very little noise and did not need the muskrat's warnings to tread lightly. I am a Huron and always walk like a cat. I could silently brush against your legs, arch my back, and spit in your face before you could even call out my full name.

But Antler Face's legs had become badly swollen after his head, manhood and antlers were knocked off, so he had lost his warrior's sense of balance. It was very painful for him to change direction suddenly, and the muskrat seemed to change his steps every few seconds. Poor Antler Face . . . it was such a terrible thing for him to lose his head so quickly. . . .

After much wandering about we reached a small open space near the center of all the birch bark chapels. A white ladder went up in the air, past the burning ridgepole and into the solid rock of the mountain. Unseen tortures or delights . . . I tried to keep my mind open and my stomach full. It was easier to keep my mind open since I had no way of knowing when dinner might come out of my feet. . . .

The clay muskrat scampered up a few rungs on the ladder, then unexpectedly jumped back inside my head. It faded back into smaller mounds of clay, then completely faded away. Too bad . . . I had hoped it would jump into my missing shoulder and stay there. I was even wondering if the muskrat might taste good although it was made of clay. I guess I'll never know. But at least its message to Antler Face and me was clear . . . so far we had only scratched the surface of things that didn't belong to the Hurons, or for that matter the Poison Snake People, or even the invisible animals. . . .

Antler Face and I slowly climbed the white ladder, past the cave's ridgepole of light and into the cold darkness of the sacred mountain itself. I was in the lead. Once I turned my head back to whisper some bit of advice to Antler Face, but the sounds of my words faded into the noiseless stone as the face of Eustace, my father, appeared and disappeared on the wall. I turned back and kept on moving steadily upwards until my head popped through an opening that was covered over by dirt and snow.

It was daylight in this unknown place . . . I saw many cracks and deep holes in the ground, and only a few patches of snow. We had surfaced on a fairly wide ledge of the mountain. In front of us was a birch bark chapel exactly like the ones in the cave but much larger, and it had no windows. Things here seemed isolated and out of place with many noises in the short distances.

I shook my head in amazement when I caught sight of the wide stream that surrounded the chapel, and the log bridge that stretched across it. Warm lines of steam were continually pouring out of the water. They were immensely long and could almost touch the sky.

Near the bridge I found an empty snakeskin box, which I shoved into the water with my foot, then Antler Face and I started to cross over, and at the same time we could not help but peer into the hazy depths of the stream.

We saw outlines of Partridge's canoe, invisible animals, and another sturdy ladder. I also spied two giant eggs that looked like someone's lips. We knelt down for a better view . . . pictures from everywhere in our world and other worlds were caught in the trails of steam and the water itself . . . constantly fading and changing and reappearing again.

We saw Partridge boldly sniffing the air, but also rubbing a large lump on the back of his head. I laughed out loud, then lay down on the bridge with my head over the side for a closer look. Antler Face was behind me, looking down at the water from his shoulders.

Invisible animals were gathering around Partridge's canoe . . . we could only see their webbed hands and feet . . . they were talking things over invisibly. Something awful had happened to them so everything they said sounded even more evil. . . .

They now hated my other father with a great passion. I was thinking that Snake Tooth would like to know this. The invisible animals had pointed our way to this sacred mountain, and I was sure they had followed us . . . maybe they were even now inside the cave.

I knew this stream could tell me more, so I stared even harder. I found out the invisible animals hated Snake Tooth most of all. He had destroyed a sacred invisible animal, who had been learning to climb up into higher places for all of them. It had been killed when Snake Tooth was coming down from the hills with the killer yellow dogs. Its spirit was the stray invisible animal Snake Tooth and Birch Bark had shown Blackrobe in the Snake village. The invisible animals wanted to destroy everything connected with Snake Tooth and when he was finally completely alone, they would begin to really torture him. . . .

Their invisible words started to run together and get muddled like tiny bits of flesh, then wild shafts of unearthly light were shot through the water. What the invisible animals were saying got harder and harder to see and hear, changing and fading in the warm stream. And now they were talking about their own dreams . . . both Antler Face and I were very interested in listening to this part more closely, so we dipped our bodies toward the heated surface of the water.

Out of nowhere a voice exploded:

"Tarcisius, get your head out of the water or you'll drown in it."

I knew that voice and gladly obeyed it. I pulled back Antler Face who was about to fall in. He was trying to understand the invisible animals, but without his head it was next to impossible, and without his antlers he couldn't control his own body.

I rushed up to my other father and was kneeling by his side, holding his mangled hands and resting my head against his soft thighs. The stumps of his sacred fingers caressed my hairless manhood, making me feel like a good boy again.

We talked in whispers, sitting there in front of the large birch bark chapel. I told Blackrobe everything that had happened to me since I had last seen him many moons before. He especially wanted to know how and when I lost the hair around my manhood. I told him all the good things, which weren't many, and all the many bad things, and I confessed to him my secret feelings. . . .

My other father wanted to know more about William Coutre and the hideous Antler Face People, so I let Antler Face do the talking. He related the history of his people from their dark beginnings to the arrival of Hot Dog and Yellow Breath and their slave-captive William Coutre with an offer of alliance from Snake Tooth and the Poison Snake People. The Antler Face People had their own invisible creatures, who hung in the sky like shadows afraid to come down. . . .

Here my other father stopped him and asked:

"Young Antler Face, did anything happen to your head? Why is it missing, or are all of your people without heads?"

Antler Face pawed the air where his head and antlers should have been, while I touched my other father's sleeve and shook my head. Then Blackrobe continued:

"Just before, when I was working here in my master chapel with the door open, a head with antlers suddenly rolled in. It's inside now . . . I knew it was lost, but it has no mouth to talk with. . . ."

Antler Face cried with delight . . . he never expected to use his head again. I was sure my other father knew whose head and antlers they were. Antler Face thanked him many times over, then said:

"Blackrobe, you are more wonderful than William Coutre told me. I was bringing you his warning to escape to France. I came here with my little cousin, a muskrat, who sat on my shoulder and was killed by the invisible animals. It was helping us escape from them, and we did not bury it!"

"Do not worry, Antler Face . . . your little cousin is now the greatest muskrat in heaven."

Blackrobe motioned us to go inside the big birch bark chapel. He didn't want us to talk too much near the warm water with its long trails of steam. He thought like an owl hiding in the lower branches of a tree, and he always thought of magic whenever he looked underwater.

I did not mind . . . it was cold and windy on this ledge except by the pool of water, and afternoon had already skillfully passed into its place. I looked up toward the top of the sacred mountain, but it was wrapped in mist that seemed to be crawling down into my eyes. I had a vision of Eustace, my father, in heaven surrounded by God's daughters, and my mother, Bright Windows, surrounded by God's sons. When this vision vanished I turned my eyes away and let them linger on my other father. I could not help but notice the broken teeth that were stuck in his mutilated arms, so before we entered the chapel I pointed to them and asked:

"Blackrobe, did Snake Tooth or the invisible animals do this to you?"

"The invisible animals, Tarcisius," he replied after a long pause to rearrange his arms. "Snake Tooth's teeth are sharp, but not as long as counting sticks. I have learned that many birch bark chapels shouldn't be crowded into one cave, and the invisible animals are more fierce and cruel than the Poison Snake People. They did not help me slip away from the Snake village, although the Poison Snake People might think so. The invisible animals hate me now almost as much as they do Snake Tooth because they are afraid of my secret language. I know that their eyes can only see straight in front of them, and their mouths say the same thing, even though their memories are never faulty. . . .

"All I did to escape was march between a double line of invisible animals. I was the blind spot in the middle of their second thoughts. Only their dreams of revenge against Snake Tooth disturbed their silence. It was easy for me to cut loose from them by climbing a tree. They didn't even see me disappear. . . .

"But let's go inside and talk some more. I'm afraid the invisible animals followed you here, and might now be inside the cave, but don't worry, they'll never attack us up here. Come, Tarcisius, and you too, Antler Face. You will be safe and warm in the chapel."

He took a few steps over to me and put his mangled hands on top of my head and closed his eyes. He whispered:

"My Little Huron Son, I have many curious and fantastic things to tell you."

We walked in . . . the inside of this birch bark chapel was very different from the ones in the cave below. It was like nothing I had ever seen or heard about before . . . the noise of a powerful river rushed through the air, and there were no windows to let it out. Around the walls many circles were spinning and countless colored lights without fire flashed on and off.

On the floor, which was warm and shiny, next to a pile of tobacco lay Antler Face's lost head. My other father bent down and picked it up . . . . it glided into his hands. He put it back where it belonged. Antler Face shook his manhood and antlers many times, then he fell on one knee and said:

"Dear Blackrobe, William Coutre taught me the secrets of your religion. How your God cracked open the rivers and mountains of this world and every world, as though they were great big eggs, then He rested His hands in France, where Blackrobes live behind every tree. I believe that there is a magic power in God's fingertips, and I feel drawn to Him by this magic. I wish to be more than a catechumen. . . ."

My other father took Saving Waters from under his robe and poured it over the boy's antlers. His manhood stood at attention.

We all embraced like Christians. Tongues of fire rested over our heads. . . .

We sat down on the floor . . . Antler Face and I facing Blackrobe. I felt very happy and holy inside my feet, but nothing came out for dinner. Everything was down to earth, even the wind, and the floor underneath us kept on shaking and purring on either side.

The light in this chapel was the same as on a cloudy day, and it didn't seem to change at all. I had already forgotten the time of day outside and how really cold it must be. There inside this warmth and light I heard my own voice, and it sounded as though it might be coming from the bottom of the sky like a heavy wind.

"Blackrobe, are you really going back to France?"

"Yes," my other father nodded, his mangled hands sweeping out into the dull light and making a wide circle of brightness. The river noises in the chapel stopped. He went to the door and looked outside, turning his head around a few times, then he came back in and said:

"Yes, I must go back to France to report all these new circumstances to my superiors. None of us really knew anything about the invisible animals when we first came to this new world . . . they were completely invisible . . . and we had thought we were well prepared."

Blackrobe gazed at the spinning circles, first one way, then another, but hardly ever at the same time. His eyes became large and vacant, and I had to cough three times before he remembered me. He seemed surprised that I did not understand why he couldn't send this message to France in an envelope. He took some tobacco and slowly blew smoke over it. His bottom lip was still missing, so it was a long time before he answered me:

"Tarcisius, I do not belong only in France. This world has been my country during my tobacco years . . . my poems here were my best, and the Poison Snake People might have become my brothers as well as the killer yellow dogs. I studied their habits for a long time. I knew that they had forgotten their ancient ways and were trying to neatly lay out their days like blankets."

Blackrobe took a deep breath and held on tightly to the edge of his robe as he went on with what he was saying:

"Even five years ago when I first looked up close into the minds of the Poison Snake People, I found hardly any traces of the invisible animals in their memories, except maybe in Full Moon, but I thought he was just crazy. I didn't understand the invisible patterns until after we were captured on the Great River, and then I understood everything at once. But it was too late, so now I need new instructions. A different plan may be developed, or a whole new tribe of people sought out. . . .

"But don't worry, Tarcisius, I promise I will come back to you. I have to return to this spot inside this birch bark chapel. Go back to your village with young Antler Face, and I will meet you there."

My other father looked at me . . . his eyes were shining with love. He touched my missing shoulder, which healed instantly. He said:

"Tarcisius, your shoulder will never again be missing, and in years to come your manhood will be protected by long prayer sticks. You will be a great person . . . a mighty warrior chief and a holy man. Of this I am sure."

I felt extra happy with these words. I waved my arms and feet without getting up, rubbed both of my shoulders, and took a deep breath. The air smelled extra clean. . . .

The river noises started up again as I glanced over to Antler Face, who was stretched out on the floor, asleep like a long wooden paddle. I swayed towards the wall of swirling circles, watching Antler Face's dreams rise up out of the black nowhere like a flood of shameful pagan practices. . . .

My other father gave me some water to drink. It had no taste to speak of, but it left my mouth wide open. He started reading my mind like a big gray duck. His voice splashed cold water inside my head. He wasn't speaking out loud, yet I heard him very clearly.

"My Little Huron Son, what I want to tell you now is for your ears alone. You can do great things with your body, especially in the dark or on a sleeping platform. My plans were to build birch bark chapels everywhere in this world. . . .

"I am from a different world altogether, where crowds of people rush after tobacco, and where everything is allowed to lie at the bottom of your heart for years . . . very cold, hidden and cruel. Tarcisius, you have to use your imagination. I know you used to think of the stars as small bright buttons on a dark robe, but that's not so. They are worlds just like yours or the Poison Snake People's. And many are even larger than this whole earth, but you see their lights from very far away."

My other father threw a stone into a water jar, which was standing in one corner. I stood up to gaze at its ripples, and when the water was still again I sat down. Blackrobe continued inside my head:

"I have been sent here from very far away, where each small distance is measured by description and uncertainty. You never heard me speak of this particular place before. I know you can't understand it unless it burns in the sky like tobacco, but at least you know I came in peace and was sent here to protect the Hurons, even the ones who haven't received Saving Waters, from the designs of the Poison Snake People, who need to have balance stretched into their heads. I was going to pour Saving Waters on their tails and shave the hair from beneath their beady eyes. . . .

"But things here have gone crazy . . . I did not expect anyone, least of all the invisible animals, to dare attack the Poison Snake People. And now the Snake babies are dead . . . there's no future in thunder or small round stones.

"I have mixed feelings about the surface of a world that might be ending. I must get new instructions through France. That's the center point for all my plans and agreements . . . it's like a large pipe for tobacco leaves."

I stared at the hair between my toes . . . I did not like to worry about so many words. Blackrobe's mysteries might become stuck inside my head like the steps of a ladder. . . .

A noise like the hum of many flies buzzed around my head. I stamped one foot down on top of the other. I said:

"Blackrobe, I do not understand what you're trying to tell me, and why the Hurons and French should live in peace with the Poison Snake People, especially since they are even crazier now."

"Tarcisius," Blackrobe sighed. "You are still Little Spoon in so many ways. Don't you realize how old I am . . . I must live by different rules."

"But do you think differently?" I asked.

"Yes, Tarcisius, I must think things through differently. Remember, I have traveled from far away where other people are more like leaves on a stem, protruding a finger's length from the ground. My mission here was to help develop your tobacco, spread out our birch bark chapels, and eventually control the Poison Snake People. William Coutre was to take care of the hideous Antler Face People. Our work fell into fragments when the invisible animals showed up. Their power is very great, and no one can control them when they are on a rampage. . . .

"Some of them have come up out of the earth and are slowly becoming frighteningly visible. They are cut off from the Giant Snake, who wants to see them destroyed forever. It rumbles like thunder in the night and gives all its advice to Snake Tooth, who is despised by the invisible animals. . . .

"I could not foretell when I baptized Snake Tooth that he would become a sacred warrior chief of the Poison Snake People, although I did know that they were bound to pick a leader from outside their tribe.

"Something was fouled up with my information . . . I hadn't got it straight before I gave myself a hair shirt and a black robe to wear. Now I must go back to France . . . that's the only place on this earth where my words can be repeated and drawn closer to my dreams. . . .

"If I went back to the Poison Snake People now they might sacrifice me to the invisible animals. They will never become Christians, and they certainly won't rest on long flat rocks until they die out. What would happen to all that tobacco? My plans for your world need to be refilled."

Again my mind snapped . . . the part of me that was still Little Spoon was screaming in fear. I felt like a big rock and an empty pouch at the same time. The walls of the birch bark chapel began to shake more violently. What did all these spinning circles and flashing lights really mean?

On the floor I suddenly noticed several slimy green feathers. Had they been there all the time? And if so, why didn't I see them before? Did they belong to Blackrobe or to the invisible animals? Antler Face rolled over but did not wake up. When I looked towards the feathers again, they had disappeared. I was very frightened . . . had I just imagined them? My voice started cracking like a discarded snakeskin and it barely came out. . . .

"Can I go with you to France?"

My other father got up, went to one of the spinning circles behind the pile of tobacco, came back and sat down again. He gave me some pieces of freshly cooked deer meat. He said:

"No, Tarcisius, only one person can be in the birch bark chapel when it goes through the Big Mouth in the Sky. And this is the only one that can travel long distances . . . the others in the cave were just built for short jumps."

Blackrobe sighed, looked again at the spinning circles around him, then said:

"I would like to return you and young Antler Face to your village, but I can't do this. I'm not allowed to help you with any future magic. It would make the bottoms of my feet crack. . . .

"Now get up and take Antler Face outside . . . be careful. I can tell that the invisible animals are growing, grumbling, and destroying things nearby, and the Poison Snake People are also on the move. I must be leaving now so I won't be able to protect you."

He helped me put Antler Face over my shoulders. I noticed his tattered book of poems under his robe. He spoke firmly:

"My Little Huron Son . . . you must leave right away, but don't forget to gaze up at the changing sky."

Blackrobe's words seemed to float out of his body. I knew he was sad inside his heart because he never liked to be hurried away by outside forces. . . .

I opened the door and took Antler Face outside. For a moment I felt like a poem, and lines formed on my body. It was evening, but not yet dark . . . then I saw something which made me drop Antler Face, and he quickly woke up. I pointed up to the sky . . . a gigantic Red Mouth was there. My manhood began to grow . . . it was like the beginning of a long poem. I really don't know how to describe it, this was the first time it had grown so big. I forgot all the dangers around me because I was discovering so many new pleasures. . . .

My other father was going somewhere beyond the clouds. How far away was France? Or where was Blackrobe's real home? Was it inside the Big Red Mouth in the Sky? I didn't know, but I was remembering that only in the days when Saving Waters were poured on my head and feet, did my manhood feel the same as it did now. . . .

Suddenly I heard a thunderous sucking noise . . . I watched the birch bark chapel fly up and disappear into the Giant Red Mouth, which then closed by itself and vanished . . . bound for France and maybe even further away. . . .

My memories and imagination floated away, emptying me out like a water jar. I didn't really understand why my manhood collapsed . . . perhaps it was because I had no hairs there. My stomach was growling. Antler Face opened a bundle of food, which my other father had wrapped around his antlers, and ate up half of it in an instant. His voice rang out as though from the edge of a dream:

"It is dangerous to hide here for the rest of our lives, Tarcisius, my brother. There are others who can instruct and comfort us.

"I heard some of what your Blackrobe said in my dreams. They were strange and powerful words, which took several turns into the sky and beyond. I didn't understand half of them, except that Blackrobe was going to France and he promised to return to you."

Antler Face started to rub his manhood and antlers, then coiled himself together like a tight rope. His teeth chattered as he went on:

"I too saw the birch bark chapel and the Giant Red Mouth disappear. What does it all mean, Tarcisius? I don't know . . . yet I do know that it's very cold here and the wind follows you around like a school of fish. . . .

"Before Saving Waters was poured over my antlers, I never would have figured out that sometimes you might be dying to get off a sacred mountain. There is a story told among my people about how long long ago, when we had more magic to shake up our manhoods, we came out of this mountain from another underground world and built the cave below, before we left for our present home. Maybe it was this memory that knocked my head and antlers off."

I just shook my head. Antler Face uncoiled himself and started talking differently:

"Also, I think you should wait a year or so before you let your manhood perform holy tricks. Now let's get out of here and find our way back to your village."

I led the way back down the white ladder. I had marked the place where it came through the hollow mountain with a small mound of clay. When we got to the burning ridgepole, we saw right away that all the birch bark chapels had been totally destroyed. We both knew instantly that the invisible animals had figured out the sacred mountain ceremony. They were searching for Blackrobe, and if they caught my other father he would surely go to God, a little at a time. . . .

I was beginning to understand the invisible animals' only fear . . . they are afraid of heights. Only a few of them so far had conquered this fear . . . just to get revenge on Snake Tooth and all his connections. Now they also wanted Blackrobe, and they didn't care if they became completely visible and died . . . revenge was their most sacred emotion. . . .

Snake Tooth deserved revenge, he had killed a sacred invisible animal, who was learning how to climb for all of them. Under the earth of Snake country there were countless invisible animals, but only a few had been brave, shrewd, or crazy enough to come to the surface. The rest weren't able to overcome their unbearable fear of heights yet, even underground where everything is the same. . . .

Antler Face and I carefully searched the ruins in the cave, wondering about every small noise until we found the narrow tunnel back into the world of the Poison Snake People, the hideous Antler Face People, and the killer yellow dogs . . . and maybe, if we were lucky enough, my Huron world. . . .

After we tumbled out and straightened up our backs, we headed straight for Partridge's canoe. We were recaptured without a struggle by Snake Tooth himself. His skin had turned bright yellow with streaks of red. It was nearly dawn . . . Antler Face and I had been up all night in a different world.

We were used up and knocked out and would accept anything but death. No one who is a Huron and not yet a warrior can accurately carve a death mask or describe a lesson in manhood. My body curled up as if in a bad dream. We were kept close to Partridge's canoe. All around us and even beyond, which was not quite hidden from our eyes, were signs of a recently-fought battle. I heard some Snake warriors singing their own proud song of victory over the invisible animals. I could hardly believe it, but it appeared to be true. Snake Tooth was once more the absolute devoted leader of the Poison Snake People and their allies . . . there was no doubt about it now. . . .

Many warriors whose skins were getting darker started to pound their tails on the snow and sing together about Snake Tooth's magic and his holy tricks . . . how they helped defeat a large war party. He was more than just sliding teeth and a shiny body . . . he was a proud and sacred warrior chief. . . .

Partridge crawled up to me and hit me on the head with his white paddle several hundred times. I kept my mouth shut tight and my hands over my ears, while my eyes touched my chest and my shoulders started to shake. Skin was peeling off my manhood when Partridge finally stopped hitting me, but then Jumping Snake bounded up and jumped on my back until he fell off too tired to hit me again. . . .

Antler Face did not suffer as many blows as I did because he was claimed by Kicking Snake to take the place of my other father as a slave captive.

Snake Tooth poked my face with questions about the cave inside the sacred mountain, the invisible animals, and mostly about Blackrobe. I could see nothing in the slit across his face where his eyes were hidden. I did not answer any of his questions, and only smiled at his insulting remarks about my hairless manhood. I would never say anything . . . I am a Huron, and the son of a great chief. . . .

Snake Tooth became furious. No one could hold back his unstoppable anger as his skin turned a dirt brown, more loathsome than a disease. He rolled over and over on top of my battered body. Sometimes he would stop dead and put his head near my toes . . . listening for something to stir there and maybe leap out. He hoped it would tell him all my secrets.

At first nothing came out, but after much pounding on my beaten body I started to smell like mushrooms left in a cooking pot too long. I was overflowing with hate for this apostate. He made the devil bigger in my life. I knew in my secret heart that he wanted a muskrat to jump out of my feet, but he had to settle for my bad smells. What a stink! He nearly choked on my smell. . . .

He walked back and forth in front of me. Three times he smiled towards the sacred mountain, but many more times he just shook his head. I didn't dare touch my feet as Snake Tooth spoke to his numerous warriors:

"My brave Poison Snake People . . . we have won a smashing victory over the invisible animals. They do not live forever when they're visible, and I played tricks on them during the battle. Now I know they have at least one incredible fear. . . .

"Birch Bark, Hot Dog . . . bring me the sacred invisible animal that was just captured. We will torture it. What I want to know will float to the surface and flow in only one direction if it's true prophecy. Otherwise it will be meaningless."

This kind of torture might take a long time so everyone ate a big meal but me. I looked in vain at the hairs between my toes. Afterwards Snake Tooth rubbed my manhood with snow. At the same time he called out to Jumping Snake:

"I want you to get the tallest ladder you can find in our supplies and bring it here . . . and be quick about it."

Jumping Snake returned in a hurry with a ladder. It was so long that he was able to bury part of it in the ground, so the rest of it could stand by itself.

Meanwhile Birch Bark and Hot Dog tied the surly invisible animal across Partridge's canoe with knotted snakeskins. It appeared to be much larger than any I had seen before. Its webbed hands and feet and big tufts of hair were visible . . . and like the stray invisible animal I had killed by the overturned canoe, when I lost the little hair I had around my manhood, its two evil grinning mouths and four blank eye holes were also visible. . . .

Snake Tooth selected four of the most powerful Snake warriors. First he made them bite their own tails to draw blood, then he gave them each a present of a shell necklace. He told them:

"Untie the invisible animal carefully and take it firmly in hand, then hold it in front of the ladder and move it up when I tell you to."

They did what they were told . . . the four of them were holding the invisible animal at the foot of the ladder. It struggled fiercely yet invisibly.

Birch Bark, Partridge and Hot Dog constructed a large circle of burning rocks around the tall ladder. Their hands, feet and paws were wrapped over and over again with wet snakeskins. Meanwhile Snake Tooth had climbed more than halfway up the ladder. His voice boomed out like an arquebus:

"Invisible enemy, I want to know if the Poison Snake People can jump behind your people when they are altogether visible. And will

Snake babies ever hang in the air again?"

All I saw were waves of sparks rolling in the air . . . the Snake warriors held back their dreams, either in their tails or under their feet. Their hearts could not help but leap like lightning above a forest. But when the invisible animal did not answer Snake Tooth's question, they shouted in anger and shook their forks over their heads. Birch Bark and Hot Dog were growling close to the ground and puffing out their cheeks. Only Snake Tooth remained calm and this was not at all like the apostate.

He signalled his people to be quiet. They did this instantly, their minds closed in every other direction. Snake Tooth's body was now the color of a smooth barkless birch log. He asked:

"Invisible enemy, if we sacrifice the Blackrobe, whose mind is filled with tobacco smoke, then can we move our trails with you below the wind or at the foot of a ladder? And will Snake babies ever hang in the air again?"

Again no answer, but many sparks exploded in the snow. Snake Tooth told the four huge warriors to stand the invisible animal on the fourth rung of the ladder. It took them a long time and much effort to force it off its webbed feet, but finally they did.

A vast dreadful moan plunged through the ground, and the afternoon sky danced above the swaying trees. The invisible animal's neck became visible . . . long slimy feathers tied together at the bottom with a knot of black flesh. Its head sat on top of these feathers, its quivering lips almost brushing against them. . . .

I knew then without a doubt that all the invisible animals, both below the earth and those fighting in this world, were being pounded and chained together like tables and chairs. I also realized that wherever there are pagans, there are invisible animals. Each one of the invisible animals felt the rising, choking fear of this sacred captive forced to stand on a ladder way above the ground. Finally it cried out . . . a hideous noise.

Snake Tooth had to shout to be heard by his people. All these horrible sounds made my nose bleed.

"Invisible enemy . . . if you don't answer my questions you'll be forced even further up the ladder. Your body will become more and more visible, and when you reach me it will explode into slimy green feathers. Escape will be impossible. For every feather we crush many of your people under the earth will die a fearful death, and you know this has never happened before."

There was a dead silence for several moments, then the invisible noise was out of this world . . . the moaning soared up to the sky. The Snake warriors were so frightened that they all nearly shed their skins at once . . . Snake Tooth barely kept them under control. Two warriors actually fell apart . . . their stomach trunks were stretched into blankets. Their bits of flesh were gathered up and put into storage baskets to be eaten when this war party returned home. . . .

Blood from my nose was still dripping on the snow . . . I threw my head back to stop the bleeding. My heart was burning like one of the stones around the ladder. While my head was back and my body warming up, I was wondering whether the other hideous Antler Face People had remained in the Poison Snake village. Snake Tooth signaled the four massive warriors to bring the sacred invisible animal all the way up the ladder. The Snake warriors around me started yelling, pounding their tails on the ground, and sometimes spitting on the burning rocks.

Black clouds were darkening the afternoon sky as though they had hair, and had been sweating all day over a cooking fire. Daylight was interrupted by dark thoughts and dreadful noises. . . .

As the struggling invisible animal was pushed and pulled up the ladder, black darkness settled more thickly there at the foot of the mountain than anywhere else in this sacred land. The snow on the ground was completely flattened out of sight. My heart was touched by secrets that seemed to belong only to the sky. My nose stopped bleeding. . . .

All around us it became blacker than a pagan burial mound. I was sure that Snake Tooth had not foreseen this heavy darkness when he threatened the sacred invisible animal. I heard the gruntings and groans of the four Snake warriors, who were fiercely struggling up the ladder.

Snake Tooth started singing in the dark:

"In the sky

I am Waiting

For my new Maker.

Can the Invisible Animals

Have Snake Babies?"

The only source of light for any distance was the circle of burning rocks, but the heavy darkness was now eating up this fire spark by spark. I could not see what Snake Tooth was doing when the sacred invisible animal was finally forced up to him, yet I knew whatever it was, it was something awful. . . .

The sacred invisible animal suddenly exploded . . . the air was alive with hundreds of falling slimy green feathers. Their bursting lights faded out as they touched the ground, and the burning rocks were smothered by the deep down darkness that seemed to be everywhere. No sun, no moon, no stars . . . now not even a spark from the fires. Every sound but our breathing was washed out by the heavy blackness.

I instantly thought of escape. I hoped Antler Face was thinking of the same thing, but I couldn't see him, so I turned completely around and started to move forward as quietly as I could. I saw nothing at all. I accidentally stepped on some feathers which were also trying to escape in the darkness. They screamed out in pain, and their cries were echoed underground. I started to run, and immediately bumped into something long and slimy. It took me only a few seconds to realize that I had let myself be captured again, but this time by the blind Snake Nose. I could feel his immense rage boiling over, but before it could burn me, Snake Tooth jumped off the ladder, shouting:

"We have to get out of here and find daylight again . . . there's only one way."

His body was suddenly a burning light as bright as a hundred fires. He landed on one of the slimy green feathers, crushing out its life and many invisible lives underground. I saw many of these feathers scurrying around. Snake Tooth's voice boomed out as he picked up the crushed feather and held it over his head.

"Step on them, break them in half . . . crush out their invisible life. It will kill the others underground, all of them if we can get all the feathers. I can give you plenty of light."

Snake Tooth began chasing the slippery feathers and stomping down hard on them. The air burst with screams and weird cries echoed up and down the sacred mountain, which was still hidden in thick darkness.

All the Snake warriors started destroying the feathers, but then Snake Tooth slipped, and it didn't seem like he wanted to get up. The fire burning through his body made him feel very heavy, almost like he was asleep, so some of the feathers escaped. The warriors would not venture beyond the visible light of Snake Tooth. . . .

Snake Tooth had fired himself up with the power of his dreams. He was dreaming, and in his dreams he thought he could see through the darkness and understand the invisible animals. He struggled to his feet, he had to get up . . . no one could help him, he was too hot. The snow in a large area around him had melted away.

He slipped again on some crushed feathers, and before his burning light went out when he fell back into a puddle of slimy water, I saw out of the corner of my eye Jumping Snake making soup with melted snow and some broken feathers. He would be a very curious warrior, maybe like Full Moon. . . .

Snake Tooth pulled strings, which were glowing in the dark, out of his stomach as he strained to get up again. I must admit that Snake Tooth was a very great warrior chief, even though he was an apostate. He got back up by himself, but now his body had lost its light and it was totally dark out. He started to pray:

"O Giant Snake under the Earth,

Can you See Me?

Have Pity on the Poison Snake People.
We will Water Your Bones and Offer much Tobacco Smoke,
If You Light Our Way back to Our Village,
And Clear Our Path of Invisible Animals."

I watched as Snake Tooth's magic floated to the surface. It was starting to give off light . . . it began in his wet feet and shot up through his hairless body. It was growing quickly and had everyone's attention. He spoke calmly:

"It's all over here. We can't gain another victory . . . some of the slippery feathers have escaped. We have killed many, but we must leave right away. The invisible animals underground have stolen our daylight, and they will try to hold on to it as long as they can. I have spoken to the Giant Snake. . . .

"I know the way back to our village. Hold on to each other's tail and follow Partridge's canoe. . . ."

Several Snake warriors yelled out in surprise. I heard Curly Head say:

"Snake Tooth, what if you want to become a captain . . . you're not allowed to touch your tail."

Snake Tooth answered:

"Curly Head, it doesn't matter anymore . . . . I alone will decide who becomes a Snake captain. Now make sure the Huron puppy and the young Antler Face are tied up securely. Drag them after us on a short rope. I don't want them to escape because I know Blackrobe will come back for them, and then we will get him."

Partridge tied me to his white paddle so I could not escape, then he made a terrible noise in his throat. I also heard Kicking Snake call out that he had a firm hold on Antler Face.

Snake Tooth spoke with authority:

"Antler Face, you have disgraced the solemn treaty your people made when they allied themselves with the Poison Snake People. Your uncles left our village boiling like meat and blinded by their own antlers. Do you really want to be a Christian, no better than an anthill on a hot day or a village dog at mealtime?"

Antler Face was able to shout out four words before Kicking Snake shut him up but good.

"I am a Christian. . . ."

Snake Tooth did not get angry . . . for a moment he seemed like a very different person from the old apostate. All he did was hit Antler Face once and laugh a little to himself, but then he spoke again and his voice was slimy and bitter.

"Poor Antler Face, your people no longer want you among them. You will be our slave captive for the rest of your life. You won't enjoy it . . . Kicking Snake and Snake Nose will see to that."

I wished so hard to see Snake Tooth die that my head began to hurt along the edges of my thoughts . . . it was worse than a nose bleed. Snake Tooth told his people to keep stamping their feet with all their might, maybe they would kill some stray green feathers. This was also a good tactic because the noise of marching, stomping feet might draw some of the missing light from underground up to the surface where it belonged.

The war party broke camp in a hurry and left the sacred mountain, following Snake Tooth, who sat alone in Partridge's canoe. They were a long winding procession of warriors holding each other's tails. I thought of a poem my other father used to read me about God's bloody torture procession to the top of a hill. . . .

I did not feel good because there was no chance for me to escape. I was tied to Partridge's paddle and dragged along by my manhood, first by Partridge, next Hot Dog, after him Birch Bark, blind Snake Nose and Jumping Snake. . . .

Fragments of light were cracking through the ground behind Snake Tooth and the canoe, then flying up to the sky. I knew that it was just a matter of time before dawn. After a while I forgot the pain, then I dreamed of my other father and how he built a house inside my heart, and how it grew longer and wider until it was the size and shape of his special birch bark chapel.

I woke up and felt glad that my other father had escaped both the Poison Snake People and the invisible animals. He had gone to

France for secret instructions, but he'd be back because he promised me, and his words were much stronger than any of Snake Tooth's magic. Everything seemed far away, yet there was a growing light in the distance. . . .

I suddenly remembered the whole afternoon and part of the evening on the ledge near the top of the sacred mountain. It all seemed like a very long time ago. I whispered to myself Blackrobe's promise to return to me, his little Huron son. . . .

This was a memory I would need to recall in the many disastrous days of captivity ahead of me. . . .

I, Tarcisius Tandihetsi, say so.

CHAPTER XX
TARGET SPOTS

IN WHICH SNAKE TOOTH MAKES TARCISIUS' LIFE MISERABLE
DURING THE REST OF THE WINTER . . . THE INVISIBLE ANIMALS
MAKE ONE LAST BIG ATTACK AGAINST THE SNAKE VILLAGE AND
ARE DEFEATED . . . IT'S THE BEGINNING OF SPRING . . . THE
WARMING EARTH DOESN'T BOTHER INVISIBLE ANIMALS . . . THEY
ATTACK A FISHING PARTY . . . OPINIONS ABOUT THEM ARE DIVIDED
. . . BLACK MAGIC AND SNAKE TOOTH HAVE HAD MANY WINTER
DISAGREEMENTS . . . NOW THEY AGREE THAT CONTACT SHOULD
BE MADE WITH THE HURONS AND FRENCH BUT FOR DIFFERENT
REASONS . . . BLACK MAGIC LEADS A LARGE FISHING PARTY TO
THE GREAT RIVER . . . TWO DAYS LATER PARTRIDGE HEADS OUT
WITH A SMALL TREATY PARTY . . . DARK TARGET SPOTS APPEAR
IN THE SKY . . . THE TWO PARTIES JOIN UP ALONG THE GREAT
RIVER AND MAKE CAMP . . . THE NEXT DAY WILLIAM COUTRE
AND THREE HURON CHIEFS SHOW UP TO TALK PEACE . . . THE
DARK CIRCLES IN THE SKY SPREAD OUT EVEN FURTHER . . . THE
TERMS OF A TREATY ARE DISCUSSED . . . YOUNG ANTLER FACE
ASKS WILLIAM COUTRE ABOUT HIS PEOPLE . . . KICKING SNAKE
PROPOSES AN EXCHANGE, YOUNG ANTLER FACE FOR BLACKROBE . . .
BLACKROBE WALKS OUT OF THE GREAT RIVER WITH A HUGE WOLF,
THEN BIRCH BARK, HOT DOG AND SNAKE TOOTH WITH HIS OWN
HUGE WOLF WALK OUT OF THE TREES . . . THE DARK TARGET
SPOTS IN THE SKY ARE THE INVISIBLE CREATURES OF THE HIDEOUS
ANTLER FACE PEOPLE . . . SNAKE TOOTH SENDS CURLY HEAD
BACK TO THE VILLAGE TO TELL SNAKE WOMEN TO START BUILDING A
GIANT SLEEPING PLATFORM . . . BLACKROBE SUGGESTS DESTROYING
THE DARK TARGET SPOTS IN THE SKY AS PART OF THE PEACE TREATY
. . . BLACKROBE AND SNAKE TOOTH COMBINE THEIR MAGIC
TRICKS IN THE SKY . . . WILLIAM COUTRE'S SPECIAL BLEND OF
TOBACCO . . . TARCISIUS FINDS OUT HIS MOTHER, BRIGHT
WINDOWS, HAS GONE TO GOD . . . WILLIAM COUTRE, PARTRIDGE
AND BLACK MAGIC GO OVER THE DETAILS OF THE PEACE TREATY . . .
TARCISIUS CUTS A POISON FLESH PADDLE, A SIGN FOR THE GREAT
RIVER TREATY, FROM PARTRIDGE'S THIGH . . . BIRCH BARK STARTS

BOUNCING AROUND IN THE DARK, FRANTICALLY SIGNALING
TOWARDS THE GREAT RIVER . . . PARTRIDGE TAKES TARCISIUS
BACK TO FROG SNAKE . . . TARCISIUS GOES CRAZY AND BEATS UP
FROG SNAKE . . . THE NEXT MORNING THE BIRCH TREES ARE
MASSING IN THE RIVER . . . SNAKE TOOTH SHOOTS OPEN THE
BLOATED BELLIES OF THE TWO WOLVES AND SWARMS OF BURNING
FLIES RUSH OUT INTO THE BIRCH TREES . . . THE POISON SNAKE
PEOPLE FLEE IN FOUR DIFFERENT DIRECTIONS . . . BLACKROBE AND
TARCISIUS ARE CUT UP INTO SMALL PIECES OF FLESH AND TOSSED
INTO THE SAME SNAKESKIN SATCHEL, WHICH IS TIED TO THE
BACK OF PARTRIDGE'S CANOE . . . BLACKROBE AND
TARCISIUS ARE DRAGGED BACK TO THE
SNAKE VILLAGE.

I was a slave captain once again in Wrinkled Black Skin's kettle. Snake Tooth dragged me around the village by my manhood. He made my life miserable . . . he often made Antler Face bury me like a seed in the hard earth, and during the rest of winter this was very difficult. . . .

Twice I tried to escape and twice I was brought back by Curly Head, whose mind had become more and more invisible. Both times Snake Tooth tortured me the whole night, while streams of blood wandered over his hairless body. He cut me up, cooked me in snake slime, ate me, then threw me up and rebuilt me again. His favorite trick was to take my head off and brush it against his smelly manhood. It was awful. . . .

The invisible animals attacked the Snake village one more time during the winter. The Poison Snake People were well prepared and defeated them easily, but after that nothing happened the rest of winter. The Snake warriors just sat around and let their skins turn black. They scattered themselves among bundles of discarded snake skins, slimy green feathers, and broken forks. They hugged their narrow shoulders, and let the harsh winter penetrate their lives like moss in the cracks of rotting trees. . . .

Now it was the beginning of spring . . . the edges of the ground had been picked up and carried away during the night. Grasshoppers were jumping into my eyes like drops of rain, while my feelings were splattered around tree trunks and small plants. A fear was growing inside me like a mushroom, but at the same time my head seemed full of life, and seeds were tumbling out of my feet. . . .

I was watching the forest lean from side to side, and the narrow trails, which might lead me to freedom and my other father, lose their sharp outlines. I could also hear the vines rustling with insects. . . .

Last week the invisible animals attacked a fishing party. The warming earth didn't seem to bother them at all. The warriors who came back all agreed that the invisible animals were getting stronger. Snake Tooth thought they might have regrouped in hidden places and were sending out their most visible and sacred captains to gain allies anywhere, but especially among the Hurons and French. There would be a grand assault against the less numerous Poison Snake People.

But opinion about the invisible animals was divided in the Snake village. Black Magic, the Snake women, and most of the younger Snake warriors hoped that the Poison Snake People might be able to create Snake babies again with the invisible animals. To me, this was all more invisible Snake madness.

There were many winter disagreements between Snake Tooth and Black Magic. Now they agreed that the Poison Snake People must go out and find the Hurons and French, but for different reasons. Snake Tooth wanted to prevent a treaty between them and the invisible animals. Black Magic was spoiling for a fight with an enemy he could see. He didn't care who fought the Poison Snake People as long as it wasn't the invisible animals for a while. . . .

I thought Snake Tooth was crazy to think that the invisible animals would become allies with any people who live on the surface of the earth, especially the Hurons and French. The invisible animals were too ugly and unreal for anyone in their right mind to smoke a peace pipe with them.

Their chief interest was revenge on Snake Tooth and all that's connected with him. They were very tricky in their own way . . . their first target of attack was not Snake Tooth himself, instead they killed Full Moon and destroyed the mushroom fields and all the Snake babies. In one clean swoop they denied a past and a future to the Poison Snake People, and I thought that the hideous Antler Face People might be next.

The invisible animals wanted Snake Tooth to be old and by himself . . . all alone, absolutely no one to turn to, then they'd finally settle in and start to torture him. . . .

My mistress, Wrinkled Black Skin, forced me down from the upper reaches of the thoughts gathering inside my head. The sun had stretched through the air after taking its morning bath in the damp mist, but now silent dark spots were growing in the sky like targets. My mistress's long black hair was shaped like a dying beaver . . . she was wearing a porcelain collar and a moon pendant. She held in her arms a ceremonial snakeskin robe, which she was repairing. She told me:

"Little Spoon, paint your manhood red and go with Partridge's treaty party. I have made Frog Snake your new and complete master, his tail is finally long enough. You will do everything he desires, do you understand me?"

I nodded my head and as I did so I saw more target spots appear in the shaking sky. Cruel lights were bouncing through Frog Snake's eyes as he stood there listening to his Snake mother. I was sure he would never let himself realize, no matter how many times I told him so, that René Goupil had poured Saving Waters on his head when he was strangely sick and near death. I felt that there would be many things for me to do, and many stiff backs and painful necks. It is not nice to be a captive, and worse to be a slave to a Snake that hates you. . . .

I painted my manhood red, then bundles were piled on top of me and I was pushed outside the Snake village . . . this treaty party was in a hurry. Belly Skin sewed a lump of meat into my forehead, and I was forced to dig a hole. It was filled with snake slime and discarded snakeskins. It might become my grave if I tried to escape. The plan was for Partridge's treaty party to join up with Black Magic and his fishing party, which had left two days ago. Antler Face had gone with the fishing party as a slave to Kicking Snake. Snake Nose hadn't gone with his father because they weren't seeing eye to eye. His skin hadn't turned black like his father's. . . .

I was wishing that the Poison Snake People might find spoons instead of forks on the Great River, or nail-studded war clubs instead of beavers. I hoped the Stone Giants might attack them, or better still, a strong Huron and French war party with plenty of bows and arrows and many arquebuses. And I was secretly hoping to see my other father again . . . back from France with new plans, tricks, and instructions. I was sure he would be whole and not mangled. He would know how to take care of the invisible animals. . . .

Partridge had gathered together only ten warriors for the treaty party. Curly Head was second in command. They had scratched their faces and put splinters in their tails. Each one brought a fishing pole because Black Magic had dreamed a winter vision three nights in a row that eating fish would lighten his black skin and also arouse his desire beyond the limit of his manhood.

Partridge was sitting in his canoe with Curly Head. Before we embarked Partridge passed his open palms down a deerskin wrapped around an ear of corn. This gave him great power . . . he wouldn't need to eat for the whole trip. He would drink water and smoke his own special blend of tobacco. . . .

It took three weeks to reach the Great River. Those dark target spots grew slowly in the sky and followed us all the way. The Snake warriors were very careful to look where they were going . . . no invisible animals jumped into their footsteps. But Snake Nose couldn't always see where he was going so frogs jumped into his footsteps, and he would be helpless for at least an hour. . . .

Sometimes Partridge's canoe was set up as a decoy for any small party of canoes . . . but none came near. It was our third day along the Great River . . . we were searching through a clump of pine trees, which Partridge thought might help uncover some invisible trails. While they were rooting around, Black Magic and his large hunting party showed up at the bottom of their feet. I saw Antler Face carrying Kicking Snake on his back. Kicking Snake held the boy's protruding manhood. This party had eaten lots of fish, which were smeared over their faces and tails. They were hoping to put the color back in their skins, but instead they looked more frightening. . . .

We made camp around a bend in the Great River. It was early afternoon and drizzling . . . Black Magic was anxious to get under cover, in case the fish slime might wash off. The red paint on my manhood had started to fade. Everyone but me ate fish for dinner . . . the Snake warriors cooked them up quickly with their tails. I ate some wild roots and rolled in the river mud, but nothing came out of my toes. . . .

That night I was tied to Partridge's paddle and stood in water up to my waist . . . my legs were crossed in the reeds. Many fish jumped against me in the dark trying to reach the lump of smelly meat stuck to my forehead. If only I could've grabbed at them, but I wasn't able to move much. I looked downstream, and it was some minutes before my body showed up at my side.

It was very hard to sleep . . . the smell of Frog Snake's body was unbearable. He kept biting my manhood trying to rip it off, but it was no use since the invisible animals broke his teeth. When I finally fell asleep he jabbed me with his fork as hard as he could. Then he swam around me saying:

"Huron slave, I'm tired of you sleeping . . . it isn't right. Wake up and smell the fresh air. You are helpless, remember that, or your manhood may fall in the river.

"The Poison Snake People are still a powerful nation. We will roar through the sky like the wind, our faces and tails painted for war. If the Hurons and French don't make peace with us, we will torture their women for pleasure. Your braves will twist in torment and their groans will be heard underground."

I could hardly stand up as I listened to this invisible madness. I laughed like a muskrat, but finally Frog Snake gave up torturing me and we both fell asleep in the water.

The next day something incredible happened. . . .

It was early morning and already warm. Partridge was showing Frog Snake how to use me as a fishing pole. Frog Snake held me by my manhood and made me catch fish with my mouth. He would pull the fish out of my mouth before I had a chance to take another bite. Suddenly two canoes floated into sight . . . beavers surrounded them instantly. Three Huron chiefs and the Frenchman William Coutre were in one canoe, and in the other a giant pile of tobacco . . . a sure sign of language at long distances. The canoes moved closer to shore. I heard Antler Face scream out in joy of recognition. My muscles ached and I was breathing heavily. I noticed that part of William Coutre's nose was still missing, but his beard fell down to his hands. I heard him loud and clear:

"Hey-Ho-Hey! Poison Snake People, we've been sent as ambassadors to seek you out and discuss a peace treaty. Let the captains of your party come out and tell us if you are ready to talk."

Partridge, Black Magic, and Kicking Snake got into Partridge's canoe and met the Huron and French peace ambassadors. I could hardly believe my eyes . . . after many words and gestures that seemed like small stones skipping over the surface of the water, all three canoes came back to the shore. This meant a few things . . . that water was still a part of each day, and a peace treaty would be discussed in council. . . .

Suddenly the dark circles in the sky spread out even further, blocking out the warming sun, except for bright shafts of light between each target spot. The world quivered halfway up a mountain, and the fish in shallow water began to bark like dogs.

The peace party landed. William Coutre opened a large snakeskin satchel and gave Partridge, Black Magic, and Kicking Snake each a muskrat skin and a small doll in a white robe, like the ones

I've seen in the decorated homes of Frenchwomen. . . .

Inside my head a birch bark chapel was being built with the bones of my people. William Coutre and the three Huron chiefs sat facing the three Snake captains. In between them were two piles of tobacco and a council fire. Frog Snake had tied a snakeskin rope around my neck and was holding it tight . . . I wondered if I might be used as a tobacco pipe.

William Coutre spoke:

"Hey-Ho-Hey! We hope there can be peace on the Great River between the Hurons and French and the Poison Snake People."

Partridge pointed his thumb in the direction of the sky. The targets were still there, and the rays of divided sunlight were like tree trunks or logs in a palisade. He said:

"Hey-Ho-Hey! Snake Tooth has said that if you want peace you must stay away from the invisible animals . . . not even to trade with them, and you must give us hostages."

I watched Black Magic very carefully. I knew he wanted to fight, but he could not forget his fishing rights, and underneath that the tribal dreams which were soaking in every Snake kettle. He spoke like a village dog:

"Maybe peace would be better . . . if we can always fish on the Great River during the spring, summer and fall. The Hurons and French can fish in the winter."

Several moments raced noiselessly over the piles of tobacco. William Coutre was chewing on his beard, while Kicking Snake licked his new muskrat skin. The beach along the river was slowly disappearing into a snakeskin satchel.

Antler Face threw himself into one of the piles of tobacco . . . his brains were aching from staring at the target spots. The green moss on his body was no longer shiny.

"William Coutre," he cried out. "Are my people still part of your breakfast?"

William Coutre shook his head like an empty ladder, and his eyes shifted back and forth across his feet. After a few deep breaths he grabbed the young boy by the antlers and spoke solemnly:

"Antler Face . . . you are the last of your people. Behind those target spots in the sky are the invisible animals of your people. They have totally destroyed your parents, uncles, aunts, cousins, brothers, and sisters. Their antlers melted in the air, and their hooves were chipped away like stones. I was the only one to escape . . . even Yellow Breath was killed."

The cries of grief from the last of the hideous Antler Face People shot straight through trails of blue smoke. He continued howling madly along the pagan edges of life.

After he had calmed down, Antler Face said:

"William Coutre, I shall bend my antlers to the sacred mountain."

Meanwhile Kicking Snake's eyes had become clear and round like porcelain beads. He had put away the French doll and stopped licking the muskrat skin. Slime streaks covered his black head and tail. He cried out:

"Hey-Ho-Hey! William Coutre, you may have this boy, the last Antler Face, if you know where Blackrobe is and give him back to us."

My heart settled down some fifty feet away. I said to myself:

"Don't cry . . . don't cry!" But I felt dizzy all over and my body was flying apart . . . parts of me floated in the river, while other parts of me were caught in updrafts of a hot sickening wind. . . .

Out on the water, walking towards us, completely dry and whole again, came my other father and a huge wolf . . . the one that had rolled in the sand with him when our Huron trading party was captured on the Great River.

I could not help myself . . . there were no more spots of red paint on my manhood, but the piece of foul-smelling meat was still stuck on my forehead. I tried to run into the Great River, but Frog Snake stopped me with one fast yank on his snakeskin rope. I struggled in the sand as I shouted out:

"Blackrobe, please go away . . . don't be foolish. The Poison

Snake People don't like you. They'll mangle you for sure, or they might sacrifice you to the invisible animals."

But my other father kept coming. I knew I couldn't stop him with anything I might say. I was only a boy, not yet a man decorated with beaver pelts and tobacco. I looked at William Coutre. He was crying in his beard, but he answered the question foremost in my mind.

"Tarcisius, nothing can make Blackrobe change his mind . . . he loves us too much, and will do whatever he must to protect us."

At the same instant that my other father and his wolf stepped onto the warm sand, Birch Bark, Hot Dog, and Snake Tooth himself with a wolf at his side jumped out of the pine trees and headed towards the council fire. Snake Tooth's wolf was the complete opposite of Blackrobe's. It had a grey head, neck, and front paws, while the rest of its fur was rainbow colored.

I was on my hands and knees like a village dog, yet I was dreaming about the beautiful world at the bottom of a ladder. Everything was upside down and gone crazy . . . my other father was returning to the people who had mangled his hands and tortured him so cruelly.

I could not dream anymore . . . my tongue was split down the middle of the Great River. What I might say scarcely mattered, so I watched and listened. . . .

The slimy Snake warriors started to dance and leap over their tails . . . each one was slapping a fish against his own manhood. Snake Tooth, his wolf behind him, sat down between Partridge and Black Magic, while Kicking Snake got up and went off dancing with his son, Snake Nose. They were no longer angry at each other. They were joined by Curly Head and Hot Dog. Birch Bark took Kicking Snake's place at the council fire, then Partridge told Snake Tooth everything that had been said.

Blackrobe, his wolf behind him, sat down next to William Coutre, but before these great captains and chiefs started delivering speeches or smoking tobacco, a song was heard everywhere, from out of the spotted sky and under the ground:

"The Center of this World
Is Where We are From . . .
Where the Waters are Calm
And the Earth Invisible."

William Coutre savagely spat out:

"That's the song I heard those invisible creatures sing when they destroyed the hideous Antler Face People."

Everyone here at the Great River, except Blackrobe, Snake Tooth, and their wolves started shaking with fear. Birch Bark and Hot Dog were growling over Yellow Breath. . . .

Snake Tooth finally spoke:

"Hey-Ho-Hey! Are these invisible creatures changing sunlight into shade or only missing a few spots?"

He dropped down to his feet and seemed to listen at a great distance inside his head. . . .

"Curly Head," he yelled. "Come here, I want you to travel top speed back to our village and tell the Snake women to start building a sleeping platform at least ten birch trees in height and very wide. The Giant Snake has spoken to me."

Curly Head took off faster than a discarded snakeskin, while Snake Tooth returned his thoughts to the council.

"Poison Snake People, is it not clear by now that council fires are worthless, and that the invisible animals are tireless in their patterns of attention? But maybe we can form a new pattern of invisible strategy."

He started petting his wolf, but kept his hidden eyes fastened on Blackrobe. My other father paid him no mind, instead he shouted to Antler Face:

"Young Antler Face, are these dark target spots in the sky really the invisible creatures of your race?"

His antlers nodded sadly up and down. My other father filled his pipe with tobacco, then asked another question:

"Are these circles like the effects of an idea chained up inside the past minds of your people?"

"Yes," Antler Face answered. "They are circling through the sky without any signal fires wrapped around their effects. They burn up easily. That's why they want to control the Great River, building it up to its final stages with bones, antlers, leaves, shells, fish, and mud . . . then they'll be able to signal each other and be very dangerous under water."

Blackrobe smoked his pipe and scratched the rainbow-colored neck of his wolf. He spoke to everyone seated around the council fire:

"Let's say we agree on a peace treaty and exchange hostages. Shouldn't we also do some tricks together as an additional pledge of faith. . . .

"Why don't we build some fires and set up a breathing line from the trees to the water, then blow away these dark target spots in the sky before the beach disappears into a snakeskin satchel."

Everyone at the council was seeing eye to eye . . . and at that moment the small fire burst into a larger one. I saw William Coutre smiling without his teeth. He said:

"Hey-Ho-Hey! Even the fire agrees with Blackrobe."

My other father lit up another pipeful of tobacco. He spoke with authority:

"First we should smoke some more tobacco . . . there's plenty."

There was no hurry with the details of the treaty . . . all the Snake warriors were talking about the target spots. They whipped out their pipes . . . everyone there on the shore of the Great River, even Antler Face and I, smoked some of the Huron peace tobacco. Only Partridge and William Coutre smoked their own special blends.

My other father handed me his pipe to smoke. I was so amazed to be near him after such a long time of captivity that I nearly choked on the tobacco. . . .

After many pipefuls everyone in the camp lined up in a single row. Blackrobe, a cloud of tobacco smoke still curling around his head, and his wolf were at the front of the line nearest the Great River, and Snake Tooth and his wolf at the other end nearest the forest.

A circle and two rows of blazing torture fires were heating up the air. I was standing in the line in front of Frog Snake, who still held a snakeskin rope tied around my neck. Standing in front of me was Curly Head, whose nail-studded tail banged into me like a fire stick . . . every once in a while he took off his arm and hit me across the toes. . . .

Snake Tooth gave a signal . . . everyone got ready to blow their hardest and force the torture heat up towards the black circles. I took a deep breath and so did all the Snake warriors, but first they took off their heads and held them out closer to the fires.

We all forced out our breath together and nothing happened. The Snake warriors put their heads back on, then Blackrobe and Snake Tooth and their two wolves roared up to the sky. Down on the ground we kept blowing the heat up towards the dark circles . . . strings of blue smoke were pouring out of every Snake body.

Meanwhile the wolves were pulling apart the black spots, then crowding them together, and for the first time ever, Blackrobe and Snake Tooth combined their magic tricks and started tearing the target spots in half and half again, then throwing them back to the wolves. Snake Tooth's hands shot fire in all directions. . . .

This took the rest of the day and the whole night, which blazed with many fires. On the ground we were waiting patiently . . . everyone split up into small groups. I didn't mind at all. Birch Bark had untied the snakeskin rope from around my neck and let me go to William Coutre's fire. Kicking Snake let Antler Face go too . . . it was all very pleasant as long as I didn't glance up at the four growing figures in the crazy full moon sky. If I did the insides of my mind would be swept towards a door. . . .

Antler Face and I talked to William Coutre, but he wouldn't answer any of our questions about Blackrobe. He said that Blackrobe had new orders from his superiors in France . . . new plans and secret instructions.

Antler Face asked William Coutre about the last invisible fight of his people. It was a horrible battle, William Coutre told us . . . the invisible Antler Face creatures weren't afraid of heights. I could barely keep myself from looking up at the sky, as my thoughts were being swept towards a door. I also began to wonder out loud if all the invisible animals of the Poison Snake People were learning how to overcome their own incredible fear of heights. Then countless numbers of them, like hairs that need cutting, might pull themselves out of their underground roots. . . .

William Coutre's eyes gazed off into the Great River . . . three Huron chiefs suddenly came out of the night water with many fish. They cooked them while William Coutre, Antler Face and I prayed to God to help and guide Blackrobe in his dark hours of need. Then we ate all the fish until our stomachs were dying to get out of our salty bodies and find themselves fires where corn, squash and deer meat were being cooked. Of course the taste of fish would never be the same as long as I knew that the Poison Snake People had acquired a tremendous desire for fish, but still I ate a great many because my hunger was always increasing. . . .

After dinner William Coutre pulled out a wooden doll, like the ones he had given to Partridge, Black Magic, and Kicking Snake, from his large snakeskin satchel. He laid it on the ground and took off its white French robe, then with his hunting knife he cut open its small chest and stomach. The inside of its body was stuffed with a special blend of Huron and French tobacco, which was thick and gummy with many small black spots.

A secret light quivered and grew in William Coutre's eyes like the sparks in a dancing fire. My ears moved an inch or two inside my head. The Huron chiefs looked at the tobacco and slapped their thighs in recognition . . . they made themselves comfortable.

"We will smoke this," William Coutre gasped, swallowing hugely once or twice, then he puffed up his throat.

"We smoke this in honor of Blackrobe," Antler Face intoned

and crossed his four eyes in bewilderment.

Ignatius Owanago, the father of Daniel Owanago, who had been beaten to death by Snake warriors in a sacred frenzy, was the only one of the three Huron chiefs that I knew. He took the pipe from Antler Face, puffed up his throat until it seemed about to burst, then leaning his face back and closing his eyes, he said:

"Let this smoke stay in our heads so we may remember our meeting here."

I thought about my village, my family and clan . . . all my relatives and friends. The tobacco smoke mixed them up in my mind as I puffed up my burning throat and smelled the awful lump of meat stuck on my forehead.

My heart was aching as I remembered a poem my other father wrote about my mother taking me one day to a stream outside our village. He called the poem, "Bright Windows," my mother's pagan name. When I left our village with Eustace, my father, and Blackrobe, my mother was still a catechumen, not yet received Saving Waters.

"Tarcisius, you are walking . . .
Where? To a stream with
Your mother, Bright Windows,
Holding her hand
Trying to remember
What you promised . . .
But you can't remember,
And your mouth is wide
Open on both sides."

I asked Ignatius Owanago if he knew anything about my mother. While he spoke to me the other two chiefs quietly clapped their hands and chanted:

"The clouds are speaking in the sky . . .
Bright Windows has been welcomed into heaven."

Ignatius Owanago told me that after the news spread to our village that Eustace and I were slave captives of the Poison Snake People, Bright Windows, my mother, died in her sleep surrounded by five days of great sorrow, goodwill, and many knotted prayer beads. Saving Waters were poured over her head . . . she went directly to God. . . .

I fell into William Coutre's arms and cried on his long beard. I could not help myself . . . my heart felt as though it had been sharpened and scratched by many poison digging sticks, then a large hand dropped down from the sky. I was afraid to look . . . it touched my shoulder, the one that had been missing. I knew instantly whose hand it was. I heard my other father's voice inside my head:

"You are the son of a brave Huron chief. You must always try to get up in the morning and enjoy your breakfast, no matter who tortures you underground."

There on the shore of the Great River, with my other father and Snake Tooth playing tricks together in the air, I promised myself never to grieve or even think about Eustace, my father, and not ask what my mother's new name was, until I was free again in my Huron village . . . and not a slave captive of the Poison Snake People. Also I couldn't help but know in my heart that my mother and father were together again . . . dreaming with God. . . .

The two other chiefs stopped chanting, and everyone was quiet as we continued to smoke and peer into the last embers of the cooling fire . . . all we heard was the tearing and growling from the sky. . . .

I was almost asleep when Partridge paddled up with Birch Bark, who carefully climbed out of the canoe. One of his legs was always in pain since that time a stray invisible animal brought him to his knees as he was leading the winter hunting party. He spread out the last glowing embers and put more wood on the fire, sparking it up with his breath.

Partridge peacefully curled his whip around his neck, then he put his tail in his mouth and touched it with his hands, which were slowly becoming webbed. The Snake custom of captains not touching their tails had been given up. It was now supposed to be a gesture of goodwill and understanding. I was breathing deeply . . . I hated this show of peace and friendship, the opposite of the Poison Snake People's real agitation and direction. They would much rather capture, torture, and kill all the Hurons and French, especially my other father, but they were afraid we might make a treaty with the invisible animals.

Partridge was smoking his own special blend of tobacco . . . it smelled different. He spoke to William Coutre about the details of the treaty. While they were discussing it, Black Magic came by . . . it was fast becoming an all night pow-wow. He detailed exactly the fishing rights he wanted for the Poison Snake People along the Great River. . . .

Blackrobe would become a hostage and Antler Face would stay with William Coutre. I would remain a slave captive to the kettle of my mistress, Wrinkled Black Skin.

Partridge grinned at me and ordered:

"Huron puppy, come here and cut a paddle out of my thigh. It will be a sign for this Great River treaty . . . a poison flesh paddle."

I gladly cut the paddle out of Partridge's flesh, which was soft and grainy, but I made extra sure not to glance towards the sky while my eyes were digging along with the knife into Partridge's thigh. I was thinking that the night sky might go up in flames and I knew that I could not keep the devil in my pocket very long when Blackrobe was on the ground.

There was no movement in Partridge's leg when I gave him the poison flesh paddle. He looked it over solemnly then said:

"Most excellently done, Huron puppy."

He put it in his canoe and smiled . . . he was wearing a bracelet of Huron and French teeth on each slimy wrist. He bent his thoughts into a bow and arrow, while mine were shaped like target spots. It was hard to grin at Partridge, but I managed and this made him furious.

"Huron puppy, you will be dragged back to our Snake village behind my canoe. Birch Bark and I will torture you, so you better not try anything funny or you might have your head knocked off forever."

I could not show this hateful Snake captain how I really felt so I said:

"Partridge, your mouth is too big . . . words drip out of it like invisible slime."

Partridge took the poison flesh paddle out of his canoe and hit me over the head with it, and would have hit me many more times, if he hadn't noticed Birch Bark's head, legs and paws shaking so violently. Fear was jumping through Birch Bark's whole being, yet he was as silent as a puff of blue smoke. Many flies had started buzzing around his yellow fur, and before Partridge could begin to help him up, Birch Bark started to roll towards the river.

He bounced around helplessly every which way in the dark, his thoughts were only a foot above the ground. He shook his head like a rabbit because his voice had been stolen. He signaled frantically towards the Great River, hopping about on one paw as if bitten by a crab, but no one could understand what he was trying to say. He finally stopped shaking from side to side and fell down from heavy exhaustion.

Partridge stuffed Birch Bark's mouth full of beaver fat and dragged him into the canoe. For a few moments Partridge looked up at the sky and listened with immense satisfaction to the tearing and growling. . . .

He motioned me into the canoe. My mind jumped in forty directions . . . endlessly making up other paths that did not fit together on the surface and seemed to travel away from the Great River. I knew something awful was going to happen . . . the flies were starting to bother me, buzzing in my ears. My feet were under a rock and my eyes implored William Coutre. I cried:

"William Coutre, did you know that staying in one place is like wandering all over the world for me? I could become very confused and disturbed in my dreams."

William Coutre didn't answer, but he gently touched my manhood until it stood up straight . . . hairs had started to grow back between my legs. I searched for Antler Face, but he had already gone away.

I felt like throwing myself into the fire, but instead I got into the canoe as Partridge had directed me. He solemnly waved the poison flesh paddle over his head before we glided away from William Coutre and the three Huron chiefs. . . .

I was all alone again . . . a slave to my worst enemies, a hostage returning to cruel work and constant torture.

The canoe stopped. Partridge curled a snakeskin rope around my neck and tied it to a stake in the ground outside Frog Snake's shelter. My ears were folded down to my face. The edges of the earth were very cold even though there was a glowing fire next to me.

Partridge paddled off with Birch Bark, who was still falling into swift gestures large enough to be seen and digging into his own flesh. I could feel it in my bones that something awful was going to happen. . . .

I hooked my legs around my head and sat close to the fire. I was very hungry, thinking about this hateful life . . . going, coming, following, working, scratching, going. Fresh deermeat dropped out of the sky . . . I was sure it was a gift from my other father. I started to roast it over the bright fire. . . .

Frog Snake crawled out of his shelter, sniffing the air. He quickly pinched a piece of my flesh and forced it through a needle. I howled in pain . . . I did not care anymore if I lived or died as long as I could eat. I wasn't afraid of beavers or a good night's sleep. My thoughts were disappearing into pagan shadows, making my neck almost invisible.

Frog Snake would have nothing to do with the ground . . . he was holding his dreams against the wind. His tail was caught in my feet, and my hands were in better shape than his because I had carried many rocks out of the mushroom fields.

Bad thoughts were following up my anger and pain. I picked up a sturdy branch from the woodpile and banged Frog Snake upside his head. I beat him within an inch of his life. I cut the skin between his legs with my slashing fingernails. I think I would've killed him if my neck hadn't been tied to the stake, and if that same hand as before hadn't slid down from the sky, touched the lump of meat on my forehead, and made me suddenly peaceful. . . .

Frog Snake was out cold, and the deermeat was gone . . . it must have fallen into the river. I called out to my other father, but he did not answer. I put more wood on the fire, and holding my breath I pulled off the lump of meat on my forehead, cooked it a lot, and ate it with my eyes closed. Then I fell asleep listening to my stomach, which was buzzing like all the flies around me. . . .

I dreamed about my mother and father. I was a little boy again with butterflies hovering around my body, and tree limbs dropping silently to the ground as though it were a soft green robe. My manhood grew into a tree when Saving Waters were poured over it by a giant hand, surrounded by light in the middle of the falling sky. . . .

The ground was shaking up and down when I woke up in the morning. Frog Snake was black and blue all over and crying like a baby. My other father and Snake Tooth weren't floating in the trembling sky, but the wolves were still there howling to each other. They were barely held in place by stout snakeskin ropes tied to two ancient tree stumps . . . both animals wanted to rise into the heavens. Their whole bodies were bloated from chewing up so many dark target spots.

Partridge quickly paddled up while the earth kept dancing to the click of bright feathers. Long strings of blue smoke erupted from his half-webbed hands and long wooden neck. He handed me the poison flesh paddle, the sign of the Great River treaty, and told me to get in the canoe. To Frog Snake he said:

"Hurry up and get your thoughts together . . . you can follow the path of my canoe. Snake Tooth's orders . . . we must leave here immediately or be trampled underground forever."

He turned back to me and said:

"Birch Bark finally warned us what was wrong, after he had

smoked plenty of William Coutre's special tobacco. With his breath of fire he was able to tell us that the birch trees are coming here to take root. They have been branching out up and down the Great River, looking to crush any raiding party.

"Snake Tooth fears that the birch trees could become the new allies of the invisible animals, and he says that it is better to run than fight birch trees. There are too many of them and they are hard to kill. Birch Bark agrees with him."

He whacked me with his white paddle, then concluded:

"Even Blackrobe agrees with Snake Tooth and Birch Bark."

Thick smoke whirled out of the river, and a sickening smell started to rise up out of the ground. There were many more flies buzzing in the air. I looked down at the hair between my toes . . . soft wings seemed to brush the air.

I peered into the Great River. Rows and rows of birch trees were turning the bend in the water and beginning to head for shore. Partridge shouted at Frog Snake:

"Hurry up slow poke . . . take down your shelter and run after us."

Frog Snake didn't move. He was sitting on his bruised tail, his mind collecting nothing with his thoughts. He was like a person turned to stone . . . solid, hard, and irresistibly drawn to the ground. The lower folds of his body were already immovable. I started to wonder if Frog Snake might sit there too long and be crushed by the birch trees. . . .

All the Snake warriors were assembling around the two tree stumps, which were still holding the snakeskin ropes around the upward floating wolves. Snake Tooth was standing on one tree stump while my other father sat on the other. Both of them were smoking special tobacco, and their bodies were streaked by firesmoke and burns. My other father's robe was scorched, and Snake Tooth's scars were bright red.

They peered anxiously at the growing number of birch trees. The closest ones were swaying in the water, but not moving. They were actually squatting in the river, their branches moaning and cracking in the disappearing haze, waiting until all the birch trees were massed. Then they would take root where we stood on the shores of the Great River. . . .

I did not see William Coutre, Antler Face, or the three Huron chiefs anywhere. They must have already left for Huron country . . . a treaty settlement with the Poison Snake People . . . Blackrobe a hostage and I still a slave captive. An invisible madness was spreading through my body. A wind started blowing across my face and my fingers had turned stiff just below my hip.

There was only one good feeling stranded in my heart . . . that Frog Snake might never bother me again. I had disgraced him by beating his brains out. I was sure Partridge knew what I had done, but he never said a word about it. Maybe he thought the Great River treaty or the advancing birch trees were more important now. I thought that was very strange. . . .

In the Great River more and more birch trees were gathering together. Different smells and colors twisted through the air. Birch Bark looked like a broken shell . . . less than a handful each day. His head and front paws were burned pretty badly.

He was lying on his stomach, stretched out like a fallen tree. I could see part of the tiny silver chalice, which had replaced a chunk of his backbone back when he had killed the old man, Sweating Fish. . . .

Snake Tooth's voice suddenly boomed out like an arquebus:

"I will quickly tell you all . . . during the night while I was tearing up the dark target spots in the sky, I found out that all the invisible animals of different peoples are allies of each other, but the invisible animals of the Poison Snake People are the most powerful. Now I'm wondering if the birch trees have joined up with our most fierce enemies."

He pointed at the massing birch trees, then his arms shot up higher than I'd ever seen them go before. His hairless body, grown coarse and tough from so many fights, was raised to the sun. He shouted even louder than his breath:

"Even if the birch trees aren't allies of the invisible animals, we should still get out of here fast. Let's separate into four groups and head back to the Snake village four different ways. Partridge will lead one group, Black Magic another," he paused and glared at Kicking Snake. "Snake Nose will lead the last group, and I will lead the first. Kicking Snake, you will come with me in Partridge's canoe, and since Blackrobe helped me so much, I will take him with me."

Blackrobe smiled and asked Snake Tooth if I could also go in the canoe. Snake Tooth said, "Yes."

My heart started pounding like a war drum. My arms and legs were stiff and my teeth were chattering as I heard horrible noises in the shallow water. The countless birch trees were slowly coming ashore. . . .

Snake Tooth was handed a bow and two arrows. He shot open the bloated bellies of the wolves . . . out came swarms of burning flies. For a few seconds they gave form to the surrounding impressions, then they blocked out the sky in the shapes of countless snakeskin satchels. They flew into the birch trees. . . .

I watched all the Snake warriors dancing around, scraping off fish scales, mud, and dead flies. They formed themselves into Snake Tooth's four escape groups. The noise rolling ahead of the birch trees became unbearable. Their roots could grab a hold of anything and crush it in an instant. . . .

I was with my other father in the canoe with Kicking Snake, the injured Birch Bark, and Snake Tooth. It was crowded in there, so Snake Tooth ordered Kicking Snake to tie my other father and me to the back of the canoe. We were dragged along the ground for several hours. . . .

My body had already turned over a new leaf when the canoe finally stopped. Snake Tooth got out and laughed in our faces, but he also knew that if Blackrobe and I were dragged much more my other father would surely die. So Snake Tooth cut us up into small pieces and tossed us into a snakeskin satchel. I was mostly at the bottom near my other father's sacred hands. I wept for joy.

I felt the many pieces of his hands soothe my many different pieces of flesh, and they made me feel good again like a Huron boy about to receive Saving Waters. I knew I would not die although I also knew that I had been cut up and rebuilt too many times.

The snakeskin satchel was tied to the back of the canoe. I practiced my sign language. I sensed something coming out of the hairs between my toes, but I couldn't see what it was. Blackrobe later told me it was a pen and some paper. He wrote a poem. . . .

The canoe started off again . . . a long bumpy journey back to the Snake village, but I did not mind because I was lying under my other father's sacred hands. And this made me forget all my troubles, even my great hunger. . . .

I, Tarcisius Tandihetsi, say so.

CHAPTER XXI
INVISIBLE TRICKS

In which the treaty party returns to the Snake village . . .
Snake Tooth rebuilds Tarcisius very slowly . . . he replaces
Tarcisius' stomach with two stones . . . Snake Tooth
calls a Snake council and proposes building a giant Snake
tower and walls around it . . . Wrinkled Black Skin has
adopted Jumping Snake as her new son, she treats Tarcisius
miserably . . . spring and summer pass into fall . . . Tarcisius
helps the Snake women build the tower and walls . . .
Tarcisius is able to eat anything with his new stomach . . .
he sees very little of Blackrobe during this time . . . by
late summer all warriors' skins are black . . . the invisible
animals tighten their grip around the Snake village . . .
the Great River is cut off to all but the largest fishing
parties . . . an unusual evening near the end of fall . . .
bits of tobacco are falling out of the sky . . . peculiar
Snake behavior . . . Blackrobe gives a few drops of his
blood to Tarcisius . . . not to be outdone Snake Tooth
and Black Magic cut their wrists . . . the Giant Snake
suddenly appears and talks to Snake Tooth then disappears
forever . . . Blackrobe offers to bring the Poison Snake
People the gift of understanding the invisible animals'
language . . . an invisible tricks contest starts with
Blackrobe, Snake Tooth, and Black Magic and their
chosen helpers . . . Tarcisius stretches himself around a
torture kettle . . . Partridge swallows the sacred poison
flesh paddle, but it doesn't fit back in his thigh . . .
Blackrobe gets what he wants by tricking Kicking Snake
. . . he carves the real treaty paddle out of Partridge's
thigh and gives it to Snake Tooth . . . a Snake council
approves Blackrobe's plan . . . Tarcisius falls asleep and
dreams a hungry muskrat is inside his stomach . . . the magic
inside his feet is gone . . . Blackrobe tries and fails to
buy Tarcisius from Wrinkled Black Skin . . . he advises
Tarcisius how to evade the invisible animals if they attack

Just before we arrived at the Snake village I asked my other father to tell me his secret instructions from France, but he didn't answer. His bottom lip was missing again . . . Snake Tooth had thrown it away. Blackrobe scraped the bottom of my feet and pointed to the holes around his mouth. If my flesh hadn't been sliced up into small pieces, I would have lost a lot of blood. I tried to move my arms, but there wasn't any space left in the snakeskin satchel. . . .

I heard Snake Tooth say that he had tricked Blackrobe into helping him destroy the invisible Antler Face creatures. What a lie! He also said that Blackrobe would have to do all the dirtiest jobs in the village, even cleaning out the slimy torture kettles. . . .

The canoe finally halted and we were dumped on the ground. Snake Tooth wrapped his face with tobacco leaves, then he rebuilt my other father. He mangled Blackrobe's hands and numbered all his bones. Now my other father's dreams were heavier than his own shadowy body. He was a bloody mess. . . .

Next Snake Tooth turned his attention to me. Streams of blood wandered over his hairless body. He rebuilt me as slowly as possible . . . he dragged me around the village by my manhood and tried to stretch it out. I watched him put a drum inside his chest, which he could open like a box. He threatened that every morning he would dance on my chest as though taunting the invisible animals. His tricks were always very dangerous even when they were meaningless, but sometimes I think they were accidentally helpful

. . . like in the middle of putting me back together he tied my stomach to one of the poles on the Snake women's new giant sleeping platform. They had started building it when Curly Head frantically rushed back from the Great River with Snake Tooth's instructions. My stomach was crying out loud in the distance. It hurt me terrifically when I was forced to move closer, then my stomach melted into the platform pole. My tattoos were stuck on the surface . . . snow, a birch tree, and a small creek. My mistress, Wrinkled Black Skin, brushed her hair against the pole. I thought to myself that I would never survive by just fishing alone. I was very frightened . . . my mistress had changed. Her hair was shaped like so many tortoise shells, then I realized that she must know what I did to her son, Frog Snake. Since the invisible animals had destroyed all the Snake babies, the remaining children were being treated even better than Huron grandchildren.

There were many blue smoke strings pouring out of Wrinkled Black Skin's hair and body. They made disgusting images as they circled around the pole, but then they disappeared like secret prayers as soon as they touched my stomach. Wrinkled Black Skin painted some of these prayers with invisible signs. She took my stomach back to her kettle. I didn't see it again for a very long time. Snake Tooth substituted two flat gray stones in its place, which I didn't mind at all because later that day Jumping Snake tried to kick me there and hurt his foot. . . .

The last things Snake Tooth sewed back on me were my feet, but first he ceremoniously burnt off the hairs from between my toes. Nothing came out of them except smoke, which Snake Tooth eagerly sniffed up, then blew out his mouth in the shape of a snakeskin satchel.

He immediately called a Snake council.

"Hey-Ho-Hey! . . . I am tired of Snake councils, but I have smelled wonderful things in French. We should build a giant tower and wall around the new sleeping platform and live inside it next winter to protect ourselves from the invisible animals."

Not surprisingly everyone agreed with him. . . .

I looked down at my feet . . . they felt very hot and very empty just like my new stomach. I was dragged back to Wrinkled Black Skin's kettle. She did not treat me very well. She hid my dreams at the bottom of her kettle and rattled my teeth with her hair. She had adopted Jumping Snake as her new son, and I had to sleep behind her kettle in a hole partly filled with snake slime and discarded snakeskins. . . .

It was several torturous days later before I could show my other father what Snake Tooth had done. Blackrobe said nothing about it. He asked me if I remembered what he had told me on the ledge of the sacred mountain. When I nodded my head, yes, he told me to forget it . . . it would not help me in the Snake village. I agreed . . . I did not think anything would.

I started dreaming about sliding into a discarded snakeskin. I curled up like a piece of fat at my other father's feet. He said:

"Tarcisius, while I was in France I spoke to my superiors about the invisible animals and what they have done to the Poison Snake People, and how that affects everyone's dreams. We discussed it thoroughly, and it was decided that whatever I do now must remain a secret. I was granted special privileges. No matter what I do, it will be the right thing in the end."

My bones had been scratched by rocks. My shoulders rushed up to the sky. I thought my mind might become as long as my manhood. . . .

All day every day during the spring and summer then into the fall I worked on the stone walls, which were going to enclose the sleeping platform into one giant Snake tower. Hour after hour I was forced to work extra hard with the Snake women, who were filled with great desire and strong purpose and could use their hair as digging sticks, while my body echoed against the limits of my dripping manhood. At night I wasn't given any tobacco or snakeskin satchels. Sometimes a piece of fish or a few mushrooms would come my way, but it didn't matter because I could eat almost anything with my new stomach. It all went in one hole and out the other when Snake Tooth dragged me around the village in the morning. . . .

Only for a short time in the evenings could I see my other father, who would often take pity on me and let me lick his mangled hands. I would leave my voice a few feet behind him. . . .

By late summer the skin of every Snake warrior and captain except Snake Tooth had turned black and stayed that way. I was sure no amount of fish would change that. The only Snake woman whose skin turned black was Belly Skin. She'd smile and talk to me whenever she could, which wasn't often. Now Birch Bark and Hot Dog's yellow fur was always wet and slimy, so they couldn't cut any of it off, no matter how many times they rolled in the dust. . . .

All the Snake warriors went about their business preparing for winter, dragging around a terrible strength that could fly up in the air like a legend, but this gave them little comfort one way or another. They kept talking and disagreeing about the invisible animals, the enemy birch trees, Blackrobe, and what they should do in the future. Anytime a party of warriors jumped to their feet and left the village, it was attacked by an increasing number of invisible animals, who were all the time becoming more ferocious and visible. After a while the Great River was cut off to all but the largest fishing parties. To me this invisible strategy was very much like seeing a dirt trail disappear one step at a time.

The few times the Snake warriors did not seem very shaken or crazy were when they were touching the poison flesh paddle with their tails or seeing it dance across their dreams. It was Partridge's privilege to keep this treaty paddle in his canoe, and it made him think he was better than his brothers except Snake Tooth. He even thought his skin wasn't as dark as the rest . . . invisible madness! . . .

The Poison Snake People were very much divided about how to treat Blackrobe. Snake Tooth wanted my other father to slide along the ground as though he were holding a ladder in his hands. Snake Tooth would abuse Blackrobe and even beat him, but he made sure not to kill him because his life represented the Great River treaty. My other father would die when the Poison Snake People decided to go to war with the Hurons and French, or when Snake Tooth thought that Blackrobe himself had broken the treaty. . . .

Black Magic, who now always wore a headdress of slimy green feathers, thought my other father should be sacrificed to the invisible animals to find out if Snake babies could be reproduced with invisible help, even though Snake Tooth had said that this was impossible. Black Magic would drag his slimy green feathers from kettle to kettle, and every chance he got he would wonder out loud if an invisible animal could crawl inside a Snake woman's belly. Whenever I heard Black Magic say this I would think that an invisible animal certainly couldn't crawl into my stomach, and then I would pick up anything handy and eat it. . . .

After the first big attack on the Snake villages by the invisible animals, when Full Moon and all the Snake babies were killed, the remaining Poison Snake People had joined together into one large village. Now they hoped by winter to fit themselves and all their kettles inside their giant Snake tower. Many forks were collected but there were no more signal fires . . . their tribe was getting smaller and smaller. . . .

During the autumn days of fire Snake women dug up ledges while I helped straighten the tower. I connected many ladders from one kettle platform to another. In the evening after the day's work was done, the Snake women gathered on top of the sleeping platform . . . they were gifted climbers. They slept in circles one inside the other. I still had to sleep in the slime hole behind Wrinkled Black Skin's kettle, and Blackrobe had to sleep in the only kettle he didn't clean, Kettle Skin's . . . no one ever cleaned it. Ugh! It smelled like my other father. . . .

In the cool evenings under the shadows of the growing tower walls and the sleeping platform, groups of Snake warriors would eat enormous amounts of fish, or play magic games, or just talk and argue together, which I thought they really liked to do. It was here that I sometimes saw my other father. The growing tower had already become the center of the Poison Snake People's activity. Beyond the destroyed mushroom fields, where only a scattering of mushrooms grew where many had grown before, we began to see more stray invisible animals slithering or stopping in front of the ground. Sometimes when they turned sideways, their long necks would disappear into a straight line like a branch or a dirt trail. . . .

My other father was always more than willing to talk to the Snake warriors, even to the many who hated him more than anything, but he still wouldn't tell me his secret instructions from France. . . .

It was an unusual evening, very quiet and warm, near the end of autumn . . . that morning Snake Tooth and Black Magic returned from a very successful fishing trip in Mushroom Lake. Only one more large food-gathering trip there would be necessary, Snake Tooth said, before the dreaded beginning of winter. There was a basket of fish near every group of warriors. I felt enormously hungry . . . wood ornaments and a small fork were ground to mush in the pit of my stomach. . . .

I wasn't ready to fall asleep even though I had worked mighty heavy since early morning. I was standing under the Snake tower. Bits of tobacco started falling out of the sky . . . both Snake Tooth and Black Magic warned everyone not to smoke or chew this tobacco. They said it might be a trick of the invisible animals or the Hurons and French. Snake Tooth said it was the invisible animals, and Black Magic said it was the Hurons and French.

The tobacco touched everyone . . . many warriors tripped over invisible roots and shouted up to the Snake women on their platform. They were continually scratching themselves. This was unusual behavior for Snake warriors. To me they sounded more dead than alive as though their voices were floating upstream instead of shooting up the air. My mind went under water, and as I came closer to these warriors I saw that there was no hope for the future in their eyes. Was it the tobacco? It didn't affect my other father, who smoked as much as he could.

He was sitting on a snakeskin satchel painted white. He was scratching himself, talking and arguing with anyone who would listen and react. I listened to my other father. I could hardly move.

"I am seriously considering giving away some of my blood. It's not fair that I have so much of it."

Was this my other father?

I screamed out:

"Blackrobe, don't give away too much of your precious blood!"

And without realizing what I was saying I added:

"And remember my thirst."

I pressed forward and at the same time let my manhood fall to the ground. Snake Tooth had already stretched it a lot dragging me around the village and dancing on its head. Now he wouldn't allow any hair to grow back on my body. He wanted to show me how much we looked alike. He even burned off hairs inside my nose. . . .

Blackrobe collected some tobacco from the air and shoveled a handful into his mouth. He finally noticed my manhood as he spit.

"Tarcisius, come here. My blood is not precious. Here . . . you'll be the first to taste it, then the Poison Snake People can see the immediate results."

My other father cut open his wrist and let a few drops of his brown spotted blood fall into my wide-open mouth. Suddenly a beautiful elkskin robe covered my shoulders, and the tobacco stopped falling out of the sky. All the Snake warriors standing around cried out in amazement as my manhood grew underneath the robe. They followed it for the length of my arm. . . .

Meanwhile Blackrobe took a small wooden cup and let his blood drip into it. In a flash Snake Tooth and Black Magic cut their own wrists and let their blood drip into wooden bowls. They didn't want to be outdone by Blackrobe. My mind passed beyond any invisible recognition. Some warriors were shedding their skins as though they were invisible, but underneath each new layer of skin the same color remained . . . black as moonless sky when the sun has disappeared. Everyone was sweating, and an awful dead smell was choking the air. . . .

All of a sudden the Giant Snake, who was still worshipped by all, pushed half its head up through the ground. It had not forgotten the Poison Snake People. Red and blue and yellow sparks flew up to the sky. I heard hissing songs in the dark . . . from above on the Snake women's giant sleeping platform. Three times Snake Tooth threw bits of tobacco that stuck to the Giant Snake's slimy black flesh, quivering underneath its hissing skin. It spoke to Snake Tooth with magic signs of animal teeth. A beautifully designed snakeskin box was stuck in the center of its mouth. Snake Tooth pulled the box out and emptied the contents . . . three snakeskin satchels made from rare old skins of the Giant Snake itself popped out. He made a gift of the box to Kicking Snake who handled it reverently. Snake Tooth kept the satchels for himself . . . magic gifts for a contest. He tied them around his waist. I knew what the Giant Snake had said to Snake Tooth and I was sure my other father did too. The Giant Snake wanted Snake Tooth to call a challenge for an invisible tricks contest. It wanted to test its powers of godhead . . . to trick other gods into doing or saying something stupid through their sorcerers without any realization. It had no idea how far gone its powers were. . . .

The Giant Snake tried but couldn't make a circle with only half its head and no body. It was truly a powerful god but now no match for my other father and his God from France. The dark hissing songs from the Snake women's platform suddenly stopped. The Giant Snake gave a few last instructions, which I didn't understand, to Snake Tooth, then crashed underground, a noisy disconnection from the life of the Poison Snake People.

I glanced past the mushroom fields in the dark and noticed some trees that looked like they were on fire. I thought of the swarms of burning flies. I saw a trail at the beginning of the forest . . . its borders of fire went straight up in the air as two clear cut lines. . . .

Like an invisible fire Snake Tooth drew everyone's attention in the dark. He danced around a burning pile of tobacco and untied one of his new satchels. He shivered slightly as he threw it over his shoulder . . . a beautiful elkskin robe just like mine popped out of it. He called out a challenge for an invisible tricks contest. Blackrobe and Black Magic listened carefully . . . a magic fight excited the air . . . a final break for Snake Tooth with everything in his Huron past.

He called a Snake council and spoke to his people:

"My people, we must find out if the invisible animals outside our village are planning anything. Some birch trees are on fire beyond the mushroom fields. They might be allies of the invisible animals and therefore dangerous enemies . . . they have come from the Great River. The Giant Snake warned me about their burning moments of silence that last a long time. It told me to fight one enemy at a time, and our greatest enemies are the invisible animals, not the burning birch trees, and certainly not the Hurons and French. We should keep to the Great River treaty at least until springtime because its poison flesh paddle is now a sacred object to the Giant Snake, part of its afternoons and evenings. . . ."

Snake Tooth took a deep breath as he looked around to see the effects of his speech. I had not heard the Giant Snake tell him all these things. He took off his elkskin robe, rolled it up, then shoved it back into its snakeskin satchel. He raised the satchel over his head and shook it as he said:

"And remember, my people, it is the growing numbers of invisible animals who are cutting us off from the Great River, not the Hurons and French. . . .

"Partridge, bring us the treaty paddle. Black Magic, Blackrobe . . . get ready."

Partridge paddled through the burning pile of tobacco. Birch Bark, who could only talk in signs, was with him in the canoe. Birch Bark made a sign to the ground where the Giant Snake had poked through. Partridge was carrying the poison flesh paddle of the Great River treaty . . . it made him push his shoulders up towards his eyes, and the space above his head seemed to be cut into feet.

My other father, Snake Tooth, and the reluctant Black Magic touched the poison flesh paddle. The night air was filled with magic whistling. Six forks were thrown up into the bottom of the sleeping platform . . . two were black, two were red, and two were white.

"When I wake up in the morning," Snake Tooth yawned, "I open a black door."

Black Magic rattled his mouth:

"If anyone rushes across my shoulders, I see red."

With his mangled hands my other father worked the snakeskin satchel he'd been sitting on into a large white ball, then he threw it up to the sleeping platform, saying:

"Poison Snake People, I will show respect to our treaty and bring you the gift of understanding the invisible animal's language, then you will be able to pin-point their stray invisible thoughts."

Black Magic grunted and rattled his necklace of keys. Blackrobe stared at him.

"Black Magic, you always think I'm trying to trick your people, but I'm not. . . ."

Snake Tooth interrupted:

"Hey-Ho-Hey! Each of us will choose a helper and pin our shadows on one another's bones. Our magic contest will decide what to do."

Snake Tooth called Partridge to his side. In the past he would have nodded to Birch Bark, his oldest captain, but Birch Bark had grown silent from scratching at the invisible roots of language. Black Magic picked Kicking Snake up by the head and filled him with bits of paper. If Full Moon had been alive and wanted to think for a moment, I'm sure Black Magic would have asked him to be his helper. Kicking Snake was very practical in everyday schemes, but not with magic tricks. My other father smiled at me, for him there was no doubt.

It was decided that they would try to trick each other's helper. More fires were started. Snake Tooth took another snakeskin satchel from around his waist and looked inside it.

"Little Spoon, can you kneel down and bend back invisibly around a torture kettle?"

I knew if I didn't stretch back and around a torture kettle like soft flesh or tobacco smoke, there would be very little movement left in my arms and legs. My manhood would be stuck on a giant fork and my nose pulled straight out for five feet. I answered carefully:

"Yes, if Blackrobe helps me."

Partridge brought over a torture kettle. He was still wearing a bracelet of Huron and French teeth on each slimy wrist. I knelt down and my other father let me lick his mangled hands. I thought my body had suddenly moved far away, but still I didn't feel out of place although the ground did start crawling backwards. Many Snake warriors gathered around the torture kettle and they were sniffing at it until hundreds of sparks suddenly flew out like porcupine quills. I was hoping that the torture kettle would disappear, but no such luck. I took one last lick of my other father's mutilated fingers . . . his blood had dried all over his hands. I bent over backwards from a kneeling position. My body went invisibly around the torture kettle, and my tongue was able to lightly touch the back of my manhood. Blackrobe's blood had given me the power to do tricks with my body. . . .

Black Magic's slimy green-feathered headdress shook with rage. His winter dreams were still stuck under his tongue, and his fingers were shaped into cruel pointing forks. He stuck them into the torture kettle, took them out quickly, then would have stuck them in my manhood if Kicking Snake hadn't pulled on his feathers and whispered in his ear while pointing at Partridge. It was several long moments before Black Magic's head was eye-to-eye. He spoke to Partridge:

"I will give you the power to do it. Swallow the poison flesh paddle and it will fit back on your thigh."

Partridge's skin crumpled like old tobacco. The poison flesh paddle quivered outside his mouth. His lips were cracked with scratches and his voice needed sleep.

"I'm not afraid. I've been chosen by Snake Tooth to be the guardian of the Great River treaty. I don't even care anymore about the loss of our Snake babies."

What hissing pride . . . I almost laughed out loud. But at least his mind had not sunk into the slimy bellies of the Snake women. He was looking at his half-webbed hands, and at the same time uncovering small bits of flesh. Then he swallowed the paddle . . . it reappeared in his thigh, cracked into three pieces, much smaller, and no longer the real treaty paddle. . . .

Black Magic was disgraced, he walked into the abandoned mushroom fields. Meanwhile Blackrobe was pouring Saving Waters on Kicking Snake's tail, much to his horror, then I too was splashing down around his ankles and dreaming under his armpits. I heard Blackrobe whispering in his secret language . . . it was like tiny footprints scattered along a dirt trail. Sweat was pouring off Kicking Snake's body and mixing with his blue smoke strings. One side of his skin was rolling into his bones while his eyes tried to look down below his chest.

Snake Tooth suddenly interrupted Blackrobe's trick. He grabbed my manhood and bent down to sniff between my toes. I did not move, not even to scratch myself. My other father told me to keep still without saying the words out loud . . . a vision swept through the door. I saw that the invisible animals were starting to gather themselves together like a solid wall or some dreaded winter disease. It was important to find out their plans, even if it meant helping the Poison Snake People. Blackrobe also wanted to know more about the burning birch trees. Were they really allies of the invisible animals?

Snake Tooth finally got up from between my legs. He brushed against my elkskin robe. I knew he had been listening to me inside my head . . . that was what my other father wanted. Then Snake Tooth gave Partridge a good drink of his blood, much more than Blackrobe had given me. He waved his hands in the air until they hung suspended like half moons, then he said:

"Partridge, you no longer need to hurry your thoughts along the edge of your tail. Now all you need to do is throw back up the poison flesh paddle."

At first Partridge tried to breathe hard and push it up through his body, next he violently tried to throw it up, no luck, then he tried to carve it out. He got a lot of bloody flesh but no paddle. Blood was pouring from his thigh like a fire. All his needs and desires were stretched into his tail. He started flipping out piece by piece. He shaped his whole body into a large wooden paddle, but still it wasn't the white treaty paddle. . . .

Snake Tooth groaned and spit out a few of his teeth. He hadn't concentrated enough on his magic trick . . . he was more interested in what he had heard inside my head. Blackrobe picked the teeth out of the air and gave them back. He had everyone's attention as he asked Kicking Snake:

"Who should face all the invisible dangers? Haven't the Poison Snake People suffered enough? Your lives are more important inside the Snake tower. Should any of you be needlessly sacrificed? Haven't I escaped from the invisible animals before, and won't I trick them again?"

Kicking Snake answered solemnly:

"Yes, you are right, Blackrobe. Our shadows are fading into a snakeskin satchel, which no longer contains any dark pieces of meat. You are the only one here who can go underground and then escape."

Snake Tooth shook his head. He realized how my other father had tricked him. Blackrobe spoke to all the Poison Snake People.

"I don't carry a string of beaver pelts under my robe anymore because they smell so bad even in the dark. For a long time you treated me like a tiny hole, so you must know by now that I like to work in more than one place at a time. That way I get to try out many different kinds of tobacco."

He coughed up puffs of stale tobacco, then he dragged each puff back into his lungs. Fear splashed through the kettles . . . the Poison

Snake People were definitely afraid of the invisible animals, whose destructive powers were visibly growing. Blackrobe took a few deep breaths, then slapped his legs to get some extra air. His words were so clear that they seemed to have climbed over a small hill, crossed a stream, then wandered into an open field. He had attracted a lot of attention which grew in whispers through the village.

"Snake People, listen to me . . . I've tricked the invisible animals before. If I go underground they might not see me at all. Snake Tooth, you don't know any more secret information. I can penetrate to their invisible center and there secretly listen to everything. I might even find out if they can reproduce with the Poison Snake."

My other father went over to Partridge and carved the real poison flesh paddle out of his thigh. Everyone agreed that this paddle was the real thing, part of the Great River treaty. Ceremoniously Blackrobe handed the treaty paddle to Snake Tooth, who held it with both hands. He wouldn't let Partridge protect it anymore. Snake warriors started stretching their movements into pointed nails, then circling back like animals. Everyone there agreed to let Blackrobe, as hostage of the Great River treaty, search out and spy on the invisible animals any way he thought best. The Poison Snake People were tricked into this decision by my other father because he had won the magic tricks contest. He convinced them to let him turn invisible.

Forks dropped from the mouths of Snake women and melted into hissing noises that lasted a long time. I was very hungry. I was thinking about eating my elkskin robe, when my other father gave me a long stick, which I snapped into small pieces and gobbled up. Then I drank more of his blood . . . this was my greatest privilege. Blackrobe started laughing at me. He had already separated his body into a new language, and yet he still could laugh at my big boy appetites. It felt good to hear him laugh again . . . he hadn't laughed as far as I knew since the Snake women waddled through their funny duck dance. . . .

For a moment I forgot I was a slave captive and thought I was rolling through a hoop without any feathers. The sun rose like magic. I forced myself to remember the large birch bark chapel near the top of the sacred mountain and the noises it made. For the rest of the day Partridge and Kicking Snake took turns dropping into smokeholes and making me lick the dirt off. Finally I couldn't move my tongue. Snake Tooth and Blackrobe walked by discussing invisible strategy. My other father stopped, bowed to Snake Tooth, then picked me up and carried me back to the slime hole behind Wrinkled Black Skin's kettle.

I watched the different colors of sunset paint a picture of a snakeskin satchel across the evening sky. My elkskin robe slipped off my shoulders. I felt tired but happy because my other father had carried me to bed . . . another thing he hadn't done for a very long time.

I fell asleep . . . dreams drifted up from the layers of slime at the bottom of my hole. I was inside a birch bark chapel, inside the huge cave, inside the sacred mountain. A muskrat was inside my stomach. I was trying to stuff my elkskin robe inside a snakeskin satchel, but I didn't have enough strength to do it. The muskrat inside my stomach was telling me how hungry it was. I started chewing inside. . . .

I woke up chewing away at my elkskin robe. I decided to bury it at the bottom of my hole, then I cleaned the snake slime from between my toes . . . the magic inside my feet was gone. It was just after dawn when I heard noises inside Wrinkled Black Skin's kettle. I listened carefully . . . I could barely make out the sound of my other father's voice, which was talking to the voice of my mistress. Their voices together sounded like the rustling of many tobacco leaves, so I couldn't understand them very well.

In a flash I was dragged out of my slime hole. Snake Tooth raced my manhood through our village run. He was in a hurry. I could tell because I was thrown back into my hole in practically no time at all. Snake Tooth didn't even bother to open his chest and dance on my manhood. . . .

I watched my other father climb out of the kettle. He walked towards me. He helped me out of my slime hole and let me lick his mangled hands. Clouds of tobacco smoke surrounded his head . . . he told me some bad news.

"Tarcisius, I've been talking to Wrinkled Black Skin. She is very difficult to please since Frog Snake disappeared. She knows where she's planted and she suspects you know more than you're telling."

Blackrobe tossed one of his mangled hands in the air and pulled down a poem about tobacco falling on the Snake women's sleeping platform during the night . . . a special blend. He was chewing some tobacco but spit it out before he continued:

"Yes, Tarcisius, I control tobacco leaves, but I do not control the Snake women. I tried to buy you from Wrinkled Black Skin. Even Belly Skin helped me, but your mistress didn't want you to go with me to spy on the invisible animals. But after I come back, I will tie red sticks on your manhood and turn you around. Then I'm sure she'll change her mind. I'll offer her many pieces of invisible flesh. . . ."

I started to cry . . . it was hard to be a man and not a boy. I think now that if my other father hadn't been there telling me these things, I might have thrown myself into the nearest fire. My other father put his mangled hands on my shoulders, and his voice touched my manhood.

"I will pray for you, my little son, I have tried my best with your mistress. Snake women can't be persuaded so easily anymore . . . maybe when I come back I won't even need to ask her. . . ."

He put his arm around my shoulder and we walked together.

"Tarcisius, if the invisible animals happen to attack while I'm away, don't forget to always move between their invisible parts, and never turn your head in any direction without first looking straight up. Then you should try to breathe silent and deep. Don't move quickly, and not right in front of them. It will be very difficult to control your desire to run away, but you must. . . .

"The invisible animals can hear fast movements at a distance, but their eyes can only see things directly in front of them. And I think that their bad eyesight is one of the reasons why they're so afraid of heights."

Bits of tobacco fell out of Blackrobe's poem. He threw back his head to open up his mind and dumped some tobacco into his mouth. He chewed on it while we continued walking, then he spit it out:

"Tarcisius, it might be a good idea for you to have something hidden away to protect yourself. Perhaps a beaver blanket or better yet a book of poems. I wonder if the invisible animals have overcome their extraordinary fear of heights yet. Have their eyes adjusted to our light? I'm not sure anymore, I've been pounding my hair into too many holes. There are so many invisible tricks I want to learn. And information."

Blackrobe leaned his head back again, letting some more bits of tobacco from his poem fall into his mouth. He seemed to be talking to himself:

"In what way are the invisible animals connected to any future Snake babies? Do the invisible animals believe in God? Should I pour Saving Waters wherever I see an opening? . . ."

My other father's eyes fell to the ground, so he bent over and picked them up, painted hairs on each of them, then put them back in their sockets. I heard invisible voices calling out magical names in the distance, as these words marched out of Blackrobe's mouth:

"Tarcisius, sometimes I think the invisible animals are more evil than the Poison Snake People . . . and at other times I think the opposite. But the future of tobacco is more important than either tribe. The invisible animals are a very ancient race and have rejected their own creator, while the Poison Snake People, also an ancient race, have been rejected by their own creator. And it is the same creator, the Giant Snake, so it's hard to know who will lose their footing first in the slimy darkness of this life. But when I come back, I'm sure I'll know more. . . ."

We were under the shadow of the giant platform, three sides

were walled in, but there were clear spaces around the dirt. I felt like Little Spoon again with long hairless legs hanging down over my feet, my skin rushing up to the sky. I spoke out of the clear blue:

"If you go, Blackrobe, I will run away from here."

My other father let his arm drop from around my shoulder, which felt like it was missing. He moved away from me . . . there was no protection in his eyes. He spoke firmly to me:

"Oh pagan Little Spoon, it is a long way back to your Huron villages, and the way is blocked by the invisible animals. You have seen or heard about the terrible things Snake warriors have suffered lately on their hunting and fishing parties. . . .

"I want you to wait here for me. I promise you I'll be back, you can be sure of that. Then you can stay with me and be my helper."

My other father did not need to tell me more. My eyes were looking between the spaces in my head, which had moved a considerable distance during the past few minutes. Blackrobe started laughing again . . . he knew I had changed my mind. He said:

"Ah Little Spoon, Little Spoon, I see a green light in the center of your eyes."

I did not think this was possible without body paint because my eyes were as black as the new skin of a Snake warrior. But a voice in my head kept saying it must be true, Blackrobe said it. Kicking Snake walked up to Blackrobe, bowed deeply and handed him the beautifully designed snakeskin box, which belonged to the Giant Snake. My other father thanked Kicking Snake very ceremoniously. I was sure he had tricked Kicking Snake into giving it to him. After Kicking Snake left, I watched my other father put his book of poems in the snakeskin box. I hung my head down to my long manhood. I felt an invisible spot in the back of my neck. I am the son of a great Huron chief, but sometimes I acted like a lost little boy.

"Tarcisius, after I become invisible take this box back to your slime hole and bury it at the bottom. I will return to you before the first snow and before anyone gets a chance to drown you in a water jar."

My other father looked over the edge of my forehead and let me lick his mangled hands for the last time. He had broken open my dreams and rubbed tobacco over my heart. . . .

Partridge paddled up and Blackrobe and I got into the canoe, pressed between him and Birch Bark, whose fur was still wet and slimy. A ladder and many snakeskin satchels were lying at the bottom of the canoe. Birch Bark wiggled his head back and forth and clapped his paws . . . I didn't understand the meaning of his new sign language.

We didn't go very far. I had my other father's snakeskin box under my manhood, which felt almost magical. I walked funny, but no one said anything about it. We joined a circle of Snake captains, the ones who had cut off their smallest fingers. Now their manhoods were half missing.

Snake Tooth was there of course, and Black Magic, Kicking Snake, whose eyes were lost in distances, Hot Dog, and Curly Head, who was now a crazy captain of his people. Wrinkled Black Skin and the ugly hag, Kettle Skin, who was wearing the necklace of invisible animal teeth given her by Snake Tooth, were there to look out for the interests of the Snake women. Both of them had cut off their slimy breasts, and the wounds were covered over with beaver fat. . . .

Snake Tooth told Partridge to get the ladder from his canoe and stand it up in a circle of snakeskin satchels. When this had been done, he spread his shoulders from a whisper to a single loud word.

"Blackrobe! . . ."

Hissing voices began an invisible song on top of the sleeping platform, first one voice, then another, and another. They sang about their invisible hardships, the loss of the Snake babies, and their uncertain future. Then the Snake warriors sang about Snake Tooth's great victories over the invisible animals. Snake Tooth made a long speech about how he was beginning to dislike Snake councils, how important it was to find out what the invisible animals were planning, and also to finish building the Snake tower and walls before icy winter strikes the village. . . .

My other father stepped into the middle of the snakeskin circle. Snake Tooth gave him a large pipe full of special tobacco, a blend of snakeskins, bark, hair roots, and young tobacco leaves. Blackrobe smiled and smoked away until the pipe was gray and empty. Then he asked Black Magic:

"Do you have any tobacco that needs to be smoked?"

The other Snake captains laughed when they saw the expression on Black Magic's face, but when I started laughing too, Partridge hit me over the head with his paddle. Snake Tooth climbed up the ladder, then he pointed to the ground in front of Blackrobe . . . that was my other father's invisible spot. Hot Dog and Curly Head dug it up swiftly. They made a wide circle hole, half my size deep. . . .

Snake Tooth slipped off the last snakeskin satchel from his belt while Blackrobe stood perfectly still in his hole, his body going flat against his chest, his face halfway out of his head. Snake Tooth opened the snakeskin satchel, then jumped with it onto my other father, who melted into the ground or into the snakeskin satchel. I wasn't sure which . . . Snake Tooth closed the satchel before I could peek in, and he ordered it to be buried immediately in the circle hole. Hot Dog and Curly Head filled in the hole, making piles of dirt and quickly tapping them down. . . .

If I had only known then what I know now, I would have at least tried to jump into the snakeskin satchel and become invisible. Too bad I didn't understand the true meaning of my other father's poems. . . .

I, Tarcisius Tandihetsi, say so.

CHAPTER XXII
SNAKESKIN BOX

In which Curly Head leads a large fishing party to Mushroom Lake ... Tarcisius develops a terrible fear between his legs ... Kicking Snake raids Tarcisius' slime hole many times, but never finds the snakeskin box ... Snake baby visions ... furious building work ... Belly Skin and Wrinkled Black Skin try to smell out the future ... invisible fears ... Jumping Snake's dreams ... his middle eye kills a stray invisible animal ... Curly Head and Snake Nose are the only ones left from the Mushroom Lake fishing party ... their story and their skin color change ... Snake warriors are amazed at the growing size of Tarcisius' manhood ... Tarcisius discovers from Curly Head who really attacked the fishing party ... Snake Tooth is impressed ... he declares the last Snake council ... he will lead a big fishing party to the Great River ... he remembers a fight with Eustace ... the last crazy Snake council lasts all night ... Black Magic speaks up ... Snake Tooth beats off an attack of invisible animals in the mushroom fields ... Kettle Skin talks to the Snake council ... she jumps off the sleeping platform and lands on the council fire ... Wrinkled Black Skin eats Kettle Skin's heart ... Black Magic's dream vision ... Snake Tooth goes fishing on Tarcisius' manhood ... he lands a fish sent by the Giant Snake ... he swallows it whole, then tells the Poison Snake People what the sacred fish told him ... Snake Tooth captures Black Magic in a skin cocoon ... he sucks off Black Magic's face ... he fashions a new paddle-club ... Snake Tooth ends all disagreements ... Snake warriors shed their skins ... Tarcisius' rising manhood again ... this time Snake Tooth makes it shoot out fiery liquid ... Snake Tooth fortifies the Snake tower with magic ... he tells Birch Bark and Hot Dog to find out for sure if the burning birch trees are allies of the invisible animals ... Birch Bark is

BURNED UP LIKE A SLAB OF FAT . . . SNAKE TOOTH
COMMANDS HOT DOG TO BRING BACK THE
KILLER YELLOW DOGS . . . TARCISIUS
GOES TO SLEEP.

Everyday after Blackrobe became invisible my heart would spill out of a water jar or my mouth would roll under my stomach like the bottom of a cloud. It was cloudy nearly all the time and more invisible animals and more burning birch trees surrounded the Snake village. I was not allowed to leave under any circumstances. . . .

Snake Tooth still dragged me around by my manhood every morning, but now he was letting my hair grow back. All day I worked with the crazy Snake women on the giant tower and walls. Snake Tooth had ordered a group of Snake warriors with Hot Dog as their captain to help. He gave them secret magic . . . the warriors could roll heavy stones without losing the other side and beat them with their tails for many hours until the large rocks were made soft and sticky. Fish bones, broken forks and discarded snakeskins were stuffed between the stones with dirt, twigs and Snake slime. It was a heavy job, but the Poison Snake People were driven to it by their invisible madness . . . they were trying to prepare a perfect defense against the invisible animals. Snake Tooth also ordered Curly Head to lead a large fishing party to Mushroom Lake . . . this would be the last big one before winter. . . .

After my other father became invisible one side of the sky started to move around in circles. I was worried. A terrible fear developed between my legs. I was always hungry, so at night I dug up my elkskin robe and chewed on it until there was only a small piece left. I finally threw it into Blackrobe's magic box, which was now very cold to the touch. Many times Kicking Snake raided my slime hole looking for the magic box, but it would disappear then come back when he had left. . . .

Sometimes when sunlight broke through the clouds, visions of Snake babies appeared in the sky and shook like tortoise shells. They reached deep down into the inner spirit of every Snake woman and always came up with a favorite meal. It was weird to look over your shoulder and watch them blindly staring straight ahead. You would lose your balance if you stared at them too long. . . .

All the Poison Snake People treated these visions as a parting gift from the Giant Snake . . . Snake Tooth had told them this. But I thought these visions were a trick of the invisible animals. They had a slimy way about them as they floated to the limits of the Snake tower, just before they disappeared into the clouds. Several times Partridge tried to chase and capture one of these visions, but he always paddled through them like doors, his face pounded on, and his chest nearly broken. . . .

Work on the giant tower and walls became furious with the excitement of trying to finish them before winter. Many times Belly Skin and Wrinkled Black Skin buried me between two stones, started a fire over me, trying to smell out the future under different layers of Snake slime. Sometimes they saw visions of the Giant Snake diving through the earth, searching for its buried manhood, never sleeping and never again coming back to its sacred places. . . .

I remember one cold morning when Wrinkled Black Skin and Belly Skin met up with a different vision. They glimpsed the Giant Snake's beautifully designed snakeskin box and they knew it was hidden somewhere in the Snake village, but exactly where the vision didn't tell them, neither did it tell them that I had something to do with it.

Belly Skin went off to tell Snake Tooth, while I continued to work with Wrinkled Black Skin. Her hard fingers seemed to be falling out of a snakeskin satchel. My head was spinning around and around. An invisible animal drifted under a ladder. Whole chunks of it were missing except for its four rows of cutting sharp teeth. It disappeared into slimy green feathers before it was three steps up the ladder. I wondered if this stray invisible animal had pushed its way up through the ground, or if it had been outside the village.

I asked Wrinkled Black Skin if she had seen the stray invisible animal. She told me she hadn't seen anything go up the ladder. A snake hoop rolled silently through my head. I thought I was being very tricky as I asked:

"Wrinkled Black Skin, how do you know it wasn't going up the ladder, if you didn't see it?"

I paused to let a cloud of tobacco smoke drift by, then I rolled my thoughts into my mouth.

"What if all the invisible animals, even those still underground, have conquered their fear of heights, then what good is your Snake tower with its walls or your giant sleeping platform?"

Sweat glistened on her tail and her hair was shaped like a fish going upstream. She waved her arms as if drowning. She yelled at me:

"Where is your precious Blackrobe, Huron puppy? Do you know if he'll come back to our village? Does he have any of his own tobacco yet or will he trade us secret information? Does he still believe in the Great River treaty?"

Wrinkled Black Skin had changed so much since Frog Snake's disappearance. I could only answer one of her questions. I told her Blackrobe had promised me he'd be back by winter.

Jumping Snake walked up to me in a daze and started licking my hands with his cold slimy tongue. My hungry nails took bits of mushroom and fish off his tongue, as I watched all three of his eyeballs rapidly change places. He was becoming more like Full Moon everyday. Blue smoke strings surrounded his neck and shoulders. Around his stomach-trunk he wore a belt of forks.

"Little Spoon, I've seen burning birch trees in my dreams for three nights in a row. They knocked down our great tower and their flames wouldn't go out. . . ."

Jumping Snake started flopping around in the dust like a fish. This happened so often now in the Snake village that no one paid any attention to it. When Jumping Snake finally quieted down, he immediately proceeded to another dream:

"I walked through an open door and saw many lights and spinning circles. In the center of this bright nowhere a muskrat and killer yellow dog were fighting over the Giant Snake's magic box. Your manhood was inside it, Huron puppy, surrounded by chunks of invisible flesh.

"I struggled very hard to get the box. And when I opened it up your manhood changed into the face of Blackrobe, but his beard was white and his skin was as black as mine. The rest of the satchel was filled with ice-cold smoke."

Jumping Snake dove down to my feet, scratching and searching for stray hairs. He pulled out a few and examined them carefully. He said:

"I see dark and invisible poems written here, and your hairs feel like pages torn from a damp book."

"That's enough, Jumping Snake," Wrinkled Black Skin commanded . . . this was the first time she raised her voice to him. "Don't tell this slave captive anything else. He might learn some invisible tricks from your dreams and use them against us."

Jumping Snake's face was suddenly split in half by the upward rush of a ladder. I saw the webbed hands of a stray invisible animal grab his belt of forks, but then Jumping Snake popped out his middle eye and threw it at the creature, which instantly burned up with the ladder.

Black medicine bundles, discarded snakeskins, mushrooms, roots, forks and fish tumbled out of Jumping Snake's missing eye. I couldn't control myself, I acted like a village dog at supper time. I had already eaten the black medicine bundles when Jumping Snake finally knocked me down and started dancing on my stomach. It didn't bother me in the least, except when he spread his legs and tried to choke me with his bad smells. . . .

Suddenly the air was filled with the sounds of two warriors blowing off their tails. Everyone looked towards the mushroom fields, where a small crop was waiting. I knew what these Snake cries meant . . . help, something awful has happened! There was a sickly sweet smell in the air . . . everyone was irresistibly drawn to it.

Partridge with Snake Tooth and Birch Bark in his canoe rushed past me. I knew what they were thinking. It was possible that these helpless warriors might shed their skins at any moment, and some stray invisible animals pick them up and secretly take over their bodies.

The two warriors, Curly Head and Snake Nose, were brought inside the village and rolled along the ground like medicine balls. Their stomach trunks were cut in half like René Goupil and their hands rested by their feet . . . a sure sign of defeat. But the most remarkable thing about these two was the color of their skin . . . it was no longer black. It had returned to its original slimy mushroom color. They spoke together:

"We were the only ones to escape. . . ."

I heard many hissing noises join together from everywhere in the Snake village. It was their Song of Mourning . . . when they finished it they would forget all about their dead. It was a very sad song to hear, although my heart soared to the sky at news of their defeat. Very slowly my wishes and dreams disappeared into thoughtless spots of light. . . .

This had been Curly Head's first mission as a captain, and he looked so bad that I wouldn't have recognized him except for his nail-studded tail and his bloody mouth. He picked up his head, then threw it back down in the dust. Wrinkled Black Skin rushed over to help the rest of him stand up. She splashed water on his head, then she stretched herself around Curly Head. A slimy juice started to drip out of her extended body. The head in the dust spoke up:

"Our fishing party reached Mushroom Lake with only two small fights. . . ."

Snake Tooth's sliding teeth shot out of his mouth and dived into Curly Head's lips, shutting them with a hard crunch. Then Snake Tooth picked up the head and put it back where it belonged. As he took back his teeth, he said:

"Curly Head, some things are best said with your head on your shoulders, especially now when we are all forced to live out of snakeskin satchels. . . ."

Wrinkled Black Skin collected some of the slime juice off her body and rubbed it into Curly Head's mouth. He moved his lips around ever so slowly before he spoke again:

"We were fishing with good results and stuffing everything into our snakeskin satchels. We hadn't spotted any burning birch trees or invisible animals. . . ."

Snake Tooth shook his head:

"A very bad sign in cold weather."

Curly Head's tail curled around his feet as he continued:

"We misinterpreted all the signs . . . the beavers tried to warn us, but they came too late and died there at Mushroom Lake. We were attacked by an overwhelming number of Hurons and French, who were unlike any I had ever seen before. . . ."

My manhood started rising in the air like the Snake tower . . . it was much bigger than life. Snake warriors stepped back in amazement, their eyes bulging past anything ever mentioned in their ancient stories. Several Snake women were smiling and whispering about so many pieces of meat.

Snake Tooth was popping out of his chest. His head became another bone inside itself, then his body weaved in and out as though he were examining dead leaves. He was once a Huron, so he must have known better than to believe that the Hurons would break a sacred treaty without first sliding their medicine hoops into the Snake village, then hanging their eyes underneath the Snake kettles. I could tell he was wondering about the French. He rubbed his bones, then nodded his head. I thought he was holding back something. . . .

I did not believe that the Hurons and French would do such a thing. I knew that without Eustace, my father, and Blackrobe, my people could not possibly bring together such a large force so quickly. I felt sure that William Coutre and Ignatius Owanago could not do this. It was very hard and took much bravery and magic. . . .

Meanwhile the Snake warriors continued to be amazed at the size of my manhood, which was now as long and as big as a Snake captain's tail, but unlike a Snake captain I could make my manhood smoke by touching its tip. I was almost a man. All the Snake warriors either wanted to throw my manhood on a pile of discarded snakeskins or push it off a narrow platform.

Curly Head ripped off one of his arms and beat my manhood many times until he was tired, and it was soft again and smoke stopped seeping out its tip. I picked up a snakeskin satchel, tied it around my waist and tucked my manhood into it. I thought about what Curly Head had said, and I also remembered my other father's hands . . . how nice and smooth and holy they once were, and how even now they made me a better boy each time they touched me. I decided to find out who had really attacked Curly Head's party.

My voice dropped into my hard stomach. I was growing up . . . everyone listened when I asked:

"Curly Head, did these Hurons and French have hairy shadows in their eyes, and did they have round black stones curled under their fingers?"

Curly Head put his arm back where it belonged while he kept his tail straight and nodded at me.

"Yes they did and when they ate those stones, they'd jump into the fight with such a vengeance that their shadows would fill up half the sky."

"Did they have sharp axes sticking out of their bones?"

"Yes they did. And if one of my party was wounded and not yet dead, these Hurons and French would roll over and over the wounded warriors and their stone axes would rip open our Snake flesh. Huron puppy, how do you know all these things? Did Blackrobe give you some secret information?"

I chewed on a fork as I thought over what I should say. I was growing up . . . there were many short distances in the air. Invisible war cries were pounding in my ears. I swallowed hard to make sure that I would be loud enough so everyone could hear, even if they were on top of the sleeping platform, or out guarding the mushroom fields. My voice became man-size:

"Curly Head, they were not the Hurons and French I know. I think it was a trick of the invisible animals. They knew where you were all the time . . . it was a trap, no doubt about it."

I snapped my fingers then put my bands across my shoulders. There was something inside me that made me sound so convincing that for a moment I thought it was another muskrat. I continued:

"A very clever trap, not just something thrown together by ducks. And remember that the invisible animals would certainly like the distance from here to Mushroom Lake. It could become their base camp to start serious attacks on your village without being seen."

Much to my surprise Snake Tooth slithered over to me and sniffed the snakeskin satchel between my legs. He said:

"I believe Little Spoon is right . . . I think he's a very smart Huron."

I smiled in secret delight as many Snake warriors nodded their approval. They believed that Blackrobe had given me secret information about the invisible animals. They were more stupid than village dogs. I looked at Snake Tooth and he smiled at me almost like a Huron, but then he yanked me towards him and swiftly punched in the snakeskin satchel that protected my manhood. I thought my body would snap in two. It was divided up equally beyond my elbows, so I couldn't breathe or see the upper world. Incredible pains were shooting through my manhood, but my own powers were great that day because I thought of my other father's promise to let me be his helper when he returned from his invisible mission. I did not scream out in agony like I had done once or twice before, instead I rested on my legs as if my thighs had nothing to do with my knees. I wasn't going to let my manhood be swept off its feet.

Snake Tooth's hands dropped to his side . . . he was impressed by the power of my manhood. I quickly pulled up my snakeskin satchel and held on tight just in case I might yell out in pain. Snake Tooth turned away from me and spoke to all the Poison Snake People:

"Hey-Ho-Hey! Our plans for winter will not fail. We must fortify the Snake tower. We will need more food. Maybe we should send out small raiding parties to attack our enemies, then run back to the village. . . ."

Several Snake captains voiced their disapproval of running. Black Magic called for a Snake council. Snake Tooth raised himself into the air and spoke in all directions:

"Tonight will be the last Snake council. To me they are a big waste of time. They are drowning us in wave after wave of invisible words that only make us disagree. I am the chief of the Poison Snake People, and I say that we will die quickly if we don't agree. Only if we agree do we stand a chance against our invisible enemies."

He returned to the ground and began stroking my snakeskin satchel as though there were an invisible animal inside dying to get out. After a few strokes I didn't feel any more pain so I let go of my snakeskin satchel, and as I did Snake Tooth grabbed it and picked me up. He started swinging me around, brushing the sleeping ground to the sky. His teeth sank into the satchel. I let out a grunt. It was painful, yet there was also some pleasure there. He opened his chest before he spoke:

"Hey-Ho-Hey! My brave people, as soon as I touched Little Spoon's snakeskin satchel, I knew what was lurking behind it . . . invisible designs with hair which might suddenly appear twenty feet away like dark memories passing from warrior to warrior.

"We need to do something unexpected. I will lead a fishing party to the Great River. We will break through the circle of invisible animals and bring back more than enough fish for winter."

Snake Tooth paused long enough to close his chest and let the Snake warriors cheer like crazy, then he continued:

"O my people, we should be of one mind to think straight in the winter time, so we must stick together or we'll crack like ice. . . ."

Then he whirled me around again and threw me up towards the Snake women's sleeping platform.

"I think this Huron would be useful sleeping with the Snake women on those certain nights when the crazy full moon stands still in the sky. His manhood contains many strange powers. It reminds me of our poison flesh treaty paddle, and it is the sign of a great Huron chief. . . ."

I was hanging from the bottom of the platform. My whole body seemed to wander away just beyond my reach as I heard Snake Tooth remember:

"I challenged the boy's father once. Eustace had two legs then and his manhood was the biggest in the tribe. The fight lasted for hours, and in the end Blackrobe had to secretly help him, but not before I had broken one of his legs. Afterwards I became an apostate and left for the hills of the killer yellow dogs. . . ."

I let go of the sleeping platform . . . my body hit the ground like a village dog. Snake Tooth peeled off a layer of his skin and used it to wipe his hands. He was surely the greatest chief of the Poison Snake People. As I crawled back together a thought struck me that not only Snake Tooth but also the invisible animals must hate my other father's poems.

I stared at Snake Tooth's chest as it opened up again. A piece of paper fell out, shriveled up, and turned to dust. I was left to myself at the edge of the Snake tower. My feet felt like they belonged to two different stones. My heart was like a clump of hair hovering outside a snakeskin satchel, then it quieted down and I fell asleep for a little bit. . . .

By evening a piece of the moon was already eaten up. Some mushrooms were being dried and stretched. The last crazy Snake council was starting under the Snake women's sleeping platform. Their minds were being prepared for winter. The older Snake captains and warriors were unraveling their dreams.

"Aaaiii! . . . the last Snake council. . . ."

"The Giant Snake's snakeskin box . . . the Great River treaty. . . ."

"Hundreds of fish under our tails. . . ."

"Here swallow these mushrooms. . . ."

"No! . . ."

This was the greatest weakness of the Poison Snake People . . . they always liked to argue and disagree. Their beliefs were divided like a pair of spreading antlers. Their minds were twisted into circles and burning with insults and torture fires . . . they were very hot-headed. . . .

For the last time at a council the Snake captains took off their heads, and each head wandered around asking for something from their dreams. Then all the heads lined up in a row and the Snake captains danced on their tails while the heads chanted a dance song. I grew dizzy watching. . . .

Black Magic tossed his green feather headdress into the air after Snake Tooth left the council fire to check the mushroom fields. The feathers were slowly twirling around like strings of smoke as he bent forward from his stomach trunk and with his mouth he pretended to bite his tail on both sides. Shadows jumped out of his hairless head. He spoke to the council, claiming that Blackrobe was the cause of all trouble. He concluded:

"The Giant Snake's magic box must be found, then the Hurons and French should be totally destroyed. . . ."

Laughter slid down my throat and into the snakeskin satchel between my legs. How could the Poison Snake People destroy my people during winter time. I slapped my head against my thighs. Outside the village I heard a low warning cry. I knew something big was going to happen before this last council was over, and I wanted to be there, but not as a grinding stone or a storage basket.

I needed to eat . . . I was so hungry I was chasing my elbows and touching my knuckles to the ground. I made a grab for something in the dark and swallowed it right up. Later on I dreamed it was the heart of an invisible animal, but I really didn't have any idea what it was. . . .

I was wide-awake as Snake Tooth came rushing back, fire sparking out of his hands and his chest beating like a drum. He said that he had just beaten off an invisible attack against the mushroom fields. He handpicked the warriors to go defend the fields . . . they were all supporters of Black Magic. After they left, he told the council that the invisible animals he fought were disguised as Huron and French . . . he knew for sure. . . .

Everyone there started arguing. Hey-Ho-Hey! I listened to their invisible madness crumbling around my feet like mushrooms left too long in the ground. The rivalry between Snake Tooth and Black Magic had to be settled one way or another because if one of them gave an opinion, the other would surely oppose it. Black Magic said he was sure that the Hurons and French had really attacked the mushroom fields. Snake Tooth and Black Magic started flattening out their messages and screaming at open spaces or hidden edges that couldn't be explained. . . .

I agreed with Snake Tooth for a change, but it didn't matter. I looked through the other side of a ladder. I found myself becoming more aware of Snake Tooth's scars and sliding teeth. The top of the sky was dark . . . the night was getting colder. There were no more feelings of warmth left lying around on the ground. . . .

A cracking voice shot down from the Snake women's sleeping platform. It quickly shut down my thoughts. It was Kettle Skin, her upper body vaguely framed by torchlight in a trap door. Snake warriors started examining their tails . . . it was not a pleasant sight. All the arguments of this last Snake council were rolled into pictures right in front of Kettle Skin's eyes, which were shining like cooking fires. There were more spoons inside her body than forks . . . she looked uglier than ever. She was determined to address this last Snake council:

"Hey-Ho-Hey! O mighty Snake captains, I have two minds about all the things you have said. I have seen the invisible animals in my dreams. I have touched them. I even tasted their flesh. . . .

"I am old and hateful, but my heart softened into a basket when

I saw in my dreams how many of us will die in the snow."

Some Snake warriors started slashing the ground with their manhoods . . . they each made a small space, fell down in it, and started squirming around. They worked themselves up to a frenzy, their bodies moist with slime. When they finally collapsed and shed their skins, Kettle Skin pushed her voice into the crowd:

"Hey-Ho-Hey! The Snake women believe that the tower and walls must be fortified for the winter. We should wait until spring to slaughter the Hurons and French, but we should make a thorough search of the village right now for the Giant Snake's magic box that Blackrobe stole from us."

My other father didn't steal the box, I wanted to shout out but didn't. He had won the invisible tricks contest . . . that's why Kicking Snake was tricked into giving the box to him. Meanwhile shadows were moving around in the dark like spoons and forks. Rotten pieces of fish were popping up between rocks and out of discarded snakeskins. I was dying of hunger. I thought the future looked very dim for anyone left out of the Snake tower during wintertime. . . .

Kettle Skin was now sitting on the edge of the sleeping platform. She was the oldest Snake woman, she had been so for many years. She picked up her thoughts and tied them together inside her mouth.

"I think Blackrobe is the source of all our troubles, and all he ever wants is more and more tobacco. I'm sure he won't even tell us anything important about the invisible animals that we don't know already. I saw him in my dreams three nights in a row . . . he was pacing back and forth in front of the Giant Snake's magic box. He looked tired. He was pinching his skin and pulling slimy green feathers out of his body until only the smell of tobacco was left."

Kettle Skin paused to catch her breath . . . she needed an extra snakeskin or longer fork. More than just curiosity rushed through everyone's bones. Snake warriors were smearing tobacco juice on their faces, and it was very crowded around the council fire.

"Hey-Ho-Hey! Listen to me again, Poison Snake People. I agree with Snake Tooth. There are far too many arguments. I am tired of this invisible life without any real Snake babies hanging in the air."

Then she pushed herself off the sleeping platform. She exploded like an arquebus. Her hairless shoulders, neck and head quickly caught fire as though they had been rubbed with Snake slime. Everyone stood completely still for a moment, then the bottom of the village deepened with the stunning shock of cold water as Kettle Skin landed on the council fire. A Song of Mourning descended to the ground. All the Snake warriors sang it too, huddled together in circles, tails pointing to the center. I watched Kicking Snake for signs of grief . . . he was playing with his tail while a fish was hanging out of his mouth. I searched around where I was sitting until I found a rotten fish. I acted like a village dog. . . .

Finally Wrinkled Black Skin climbed down from the sleeping platform. She was wearing the ceremonial Snake robe made from the manhoods of many dead enemies. A fork was stuck in her hair, which was shaped like a birch tree . . . her eyes had collected many legends. She said:

"Kettle Skin is dead . . . her neck will never touch her open thighs again. She was the oldest woman in our village, and the first one to ever kill herself."

She looked at Snake Tooth, then she continued:

"By tomorrow she'll be forgotten and her kettle will be given away. . . ."

Already her body smelled like rotten fish. I moved closer with my tongue hanging out. I spotted many gray hairs on the bottom of her feet . . . that was something I had never noticed before.

With one quick yank Wrinkled Black Skin peeled off the dead snakeskin and stuffed it back into Kettle Skin's mouth, then she took the fork from her own hair and drove it past the burnt outer layers of Kettle Skin's flesh. The power of her hand was so strong that she pulled out Kettle Skin's heart with her fork without letting it drop to the ground. She held it in front of her face. It was a very big slimy piece of meat, and strings of blue smoke were seeping out of it. Wrinkled Black Skin took a deep breath and in a calm flat voice said:

"Once I was trapped in a snake pit begging for hair. I wasn't afraid to wait because I could still wrap my knees around each other for warmth and sleep fitfully at the bottom of the pit. It was a long cold night, and my hair wasn't shaped like a storage basket, so I had to eat my heart out to stay alive . . . like this. . . ."

She swallowed the heart without moving her lips. My stomach settled into a number of dreams, it was ready to swallow anything. We had stayed up the whole giant night. The sky was getting lighter without any rolling in the dust. . . .

Wrinkled Black Skin gently rubbed her ceremonial robe, making some of the dead manhoods come alive. She cut up the remains of Kettle Skin and distributed the flesh pieces among the Snake warriors. She gave Kicking Snake the biggest piece. He devoured it instantly. Then she turned to me, stretching out her arms like paddles. My body felt like a swift canoe . . . my manhood was shaking in its snakeskin satchel. She shouted at me:

"Little Spoon, come here. You can eat the bottoms of Kettle Skin's feet . . . your stomach is tough enough."

She watched me as I chewed with all my might on Kettle Skin's last remains. When I finished I looked up to see Wrinkled Black Skin comparing several holes in her tail, as if steady nerves were a substitute for clear thinking. She growled at me:

"Huron puppy, if you have anything to do with the Giant Snake's magic box, as sure as I'm standing here I'll cut off your manhood."

Wrinkled Black Skin would have threatened me some more, but Black Magic cut her short. He was crouched near the ground, trembling with invisible dreams. He picked up a stone and put it on his face. He looked hurt and surprised because Kettle Skin, his best ally in his power struggles, had killed herself. He was more than helpless with many signs of grief dying out on the ground. Now he was the oldest in the Snake village. . . .

Black Magic turned his body inside out and started chanting

something about the dangers of birch trees planted by the mouth of a cave. Next he invited Birch Bark to sit close to him and share a pipeful of special tobacco, but Birch Bark shook his head furiously as though he were being asked to change places with an invisible animal.

Black Magic shut his eyes tight and suddenly his face resembled a water jar, which had been cracked by a heavy stone. He sat there silently curving over a log, his face digging into the earth. When he finally stood up, he claimed that a dream-vision had just stretched itself through his head.

"Hey-Ho-Hey! I saw a birch tree surrounded by swarms of burning flies in an open field. Its bark was peeling off and its leaves had departed into other dreams. Flames were swirling out along its branches. Many discarded snakeskins and bits of tobacco were lying all around it. Suddenly Blackrobe walked out of its trunk, carrying the Giant Snake's magic box in front of him, and as he stooped down to pick up some tobacco I noticed that there were fish heads sticking out of his neck.

"Then I watched footprints crossing the field, and when they reached Blackrobe they became three stray invisible animals with many teeth. Most of their other features were missing. They surrounded him and charged . . . passing right through him. Blackrobe was also in their dreams. I was lucky to come back alive."

Black Magic pressed his hands against his heart. Everyone was waiting for him to say more. It was already morning and my stomach had flattened itself into animal teeth. Black Magic built another fire where Kettle Skin had landed. He interpreted his own vision:

"O my people, I am sure that Blackrobe has passed through the invisible animals since in my vision they passed through him. He's been a long time underground, but I'm sure he knows nothing new that could help us through winter. He might even have made a treaty with them, you never know. I still think we should attack the Hurons and French immediately, and if Blackrobe comes back here, he should die right away. These are my final thoughts in this Snake council, which I hope won't be the last. . . ."

Snake Tooth was furious. His head jumped into a cloud of tobacco smoke. Everyone stepped aside as the smoke circled around the fire, but Black Magic seemed stuck in the ground like a fork. The smoke drifted back and forth, then Snake Tooth's voice rang out from everywhere:

"Hey-Ho-Hey! The Poison Snake People can no longer disagree. I will say it again . . . there will be no more Snake councils. Now I must find an invisible sign near the ground. . . ."

Snake Tooth slammed on his head and dropped to my feet. He was holding a fishing pole, hoping to catch some secret information. Had he eaten any rotten fish? I felt my whole life might slip away if his pole was able to sink into my thoughts. His warm breath covered my body. I struggled to get loose, and as I was shaking in a mad dance my manhood began to rise by itself out of its snakeskin satchel. It quickly became hard and full size and started to smoke.

Snake Tooth got on my manhood with his fishing pole and started riding it like a canoe. Then he was choking it just below the head . . . I was helpless, and my manhood became soft very quickly. Snake Tooth had something at the end of his line. He pushed me out from under him, and I fell back into a heap of discarded snakeskins.

Snake Tooth's hairless feet came rushing back to his body as he stood up, holding a squirming fish. He spoke to it:

"My little brother, I know you've been sent to me by the Giant Snake . . . how can I stop all these arguments?"

He put the fish close to his ear, and a smile slipped across his face as his head nodded up and down, sometimes so hard it seemed like it would snap halfway off his neck. I started chewing on an old snakeskin hoping against hope that some food might reappear in between my toes . . . none did. My stomach exploded across the late morning sky as I heard Snake Tooth thanking his magic fish in four directions. What an apostate! Then he rubbed snake slime into the fish's body and swallowed it down in one big gulp. I almost cried. He spoke to all:

"Hey-Ho-Hey! My little brother has told me many things. Some of them were very bad . . . more Snake women will kill themselves like Kettle Skin, jumping off their kettle platform and feeding the invisible hunger of our enemies. . . .

"My little brother told me I will lead a large fishing party to the Great River. We will slide in and out of the invisible animals."

He paused and stared at Black Magic before he continued:

"It also said Blackrobe would help us back to our village, and we will bring home half the fish in the river . . . more than enough for all our needs in winter time. There is only one condition for this victory . . . as long as the Snake tower is finished before we get back, otherwise the fish will turn into Snake slime and rot away. . . .

"My little brother also told me that the Giant Snake's magic box will be found before we leave. It will help us, but now only Blackrobe knows its secret power."

Snake Tooth whirled and pointed at me. He told me to hide my manhood more securely in its snakeskin satchel . . . it would be needed later on.

"Huron puppy, you surprise me more and more. My little brother had much to say about you. . . ."

I did not believe him so I rolled around on the ground to become very hairy. It didn't work, and Snake Tooth kicked me until I got back up.

"Big Spoon . . . that's what my fish brother called you. It told me what's in your snakeskin satchel might be helpful at night with the Snake women. Of course I thought of that before . . . my little brother wants you and the warriors who survived the Mushroom Lake massacre to sleep with them during the crazy full moon."

I did not want to sleep with the Snake women . . . it would be wrong to have their hair around my manhood. Snake Tooth was very shrewd and knew all the invisible dreams of the Poison Snake People. . . .

Meanwhile Black Magic was stretching himself over a kettle . . . a few handfuls at a time. I knew he was afraid because his eyes grew cloudy like snake slime or yesterday's awful tasting dinner. Strings of blue smoke started curling around Snake Tooth's head. He walked around in small circles, painting red spots on his shoulders. He was building up his anger. He wanted to settle all the arguments of the Poison Snake People. His sliding teeth edged closer and closer to Black Magic. They formed words which opened up like a snakeskin satchel:

"Black Magic, my little brother told me you are the cause of all our disagreements."

"No! No!" Black Magic screamed as Snake Tooth ripped off his headdress of slimy green feathers and popped off his necklace of French keys. Next Snake Tooth wrapped himself and Black Magic in a cocoon of his own skin, and they became shadows in the sky above the Snake tower.

Snake Tooth's voice thundered into the growing afternoon:

"I am the only chief of the Poison Snake People chosen by the Giant Snake in a sacred ceremony. There will be no more councils. I will rule alone and tell you who will take my place when that time is fated. Hey-Ho-Hey!"

Snake Tooth pulled himself free from his own skin cocoon, his flesh dripping, but Black Magic was still caught. Snake warriors were slapping their manhoods with their tails . . . a gruesome sight. Ugh! None of their manhoods could grow and smoke like mine.

Snake Tooth was dancing in the sky. Black Magic was helpless, and he appeared to be no more than a long dark lash of hair. Snake Tooth brought him down to earth. He covered Black Magic's face with his mouth, then sucked it off until it was blank except for two wide eye holes and two small nose holes. He chewed on Black Magic's mouth for a while, then spit it out into my slime hole. I know I saw it go in there, but when I searched for it later on I couldn't find it at all. Had it become invisible? . . .

Snake Tooth threw Black Magic back up in the air right into the skin cocoon. Birch Bark brought the sacred treaty paddle. Snake Tooth whirled it around over his head, flames leaping out and darting like tongues among the Snake warriors. Next he put it against his own hairless thigh and repeated:

"There will be no more Snake councils!"

I could see his burning flesh curling back from his bones . . . he had made another flesh paddle, fusing them together like logs in a birch bark chapel. He waved it over his head and shouted:

"This will take care of everything!"

Snake Tooth had made another great sign of his strength, a powerful paddle-club. In one smooth motion he pitched it at Black Magic, who was still hanging like a Snake baby inside the cocoon. The flesh club hit exactly where Snake Tooth wanted it to, and returned back to his hand, while his skin readjusted itself to his body, completely healing his thighs, but leaving a thick patch of white hair.

Black Magic fell in a heap on the fire he had started, putting it out instantly without any smoke escaping. In one smart stroke Snake Tooth had ended all their disagreements . . . there would be no more quick opinions or doubts. Black Magic's face had vanished, and I could see clear through his head, yet he was still alive. He got up and bowed to Snake Tooth, who had proven himself once again to be the only rightful chief of the Poison Snake People. . . .

An evening chill was slipping in from the northeast. No one paid any attention to me. I quietly searched for food. Everywhere Snake warriors were shedding their skins. Snake Tooth watched this Snake madness, leaning heavily on his magic flesh paddle-club. He released it several times to chew up the ground . . . it was try-ing to search out and destroy any stray invisible animal. Finally he stood back and looked over all the warriors jumping up and down without their skins. He laughed to himself . . . it was a hideous sight in the nighttime fires. Then he went on with his work as chief . . . he checked the mushroom fields and counted the burning birch trees outside the village. He came back and sat under the growing Snake tower and lost himself in visionary dreams. He made sharp little noises with his teeth. He shook his head in disbelief whenever he looked up. Then he said:

"Snake warriors, you are worse than Huron dogs in wintertime arguing over a bone. The Giant Snake chose me as your chief to defend you against the invisible animals. I have already beaten them in battle with my magic tricks and confused their narrow purposes. Now I've learned from the Giant Snake's little fish brother that the invisible animals have very bad eyesight and can only see for a little distance straight in front of themselves. . . ."

All the Poison Snake People hissed their approval. Snake Tooth waved his flesh paddle-club . . . the whole tribe was quiet. Then he pointed his club at me. . . .

A wild magic surged through my manhood, which forcefully ripped open a circle in the center of its snakeskin satchel . . . it started to rise, but no one was paying any attention to me. . . .

Torches were lit and pipes of tobacco were passed around. Snake Tooth made a sign to Birch Bark and Partridge. They paddled right over to me and picked me up by my manhood. I was forced to lie on my back while Snake Tooth towered over me in the canoe, rubbing my manhood until it was just a quivering tower of flesh, much longer than before. It was smoking and burning hot with unspeakable feelings dying to be turned loose.

Snake Tooth's slimy tongue was sliding up and down my manhood. My feelings were wide open with the excitement of night. The first fiery spurts from my manhood jerked my body so hard that I kept on shaking out more heavy splashes until my manhood collapsed with a thud back into its snakeskin satchel. I am truly the son of a great Huron chief . . . all my spurts and splashes formed a puddle over Black Magic's dead fire. . . .

Snake Tooth painted a big red circle on the unripped side of my satchel. I lay in the canoe, exhausted, unable to move without falling into dreams of eating my other father's mangled hands. I watched Snake Tooth step out of the canoe. He raised his flesh paddle-club way over his head, and with a flying leap he came down hard right smack in the middle of the dead fire, splattering cold ashes and the pool of liquid made by my manhood. . . .

Snake Tooth was waiting for something to happen. He appeared slimy and hideous in the dancing torch lights, but nothing happened. I wanted to go to sleep in the worst way, but Partridge was now keeping his eye on me. Anytime I closed my eyes for more than a few seconds, he would utter a terrible scream and whack me over my head or across my manhood with his white paddle. . . .

Snake Tooth took another shot at the wet ashes, this time driving his club deep into the ground. A stream of fresh water poured out of the hole . . . now the Snake women wouldn't have to melt snow outside the tower during winter. Snake Tooth was fortifying the Snake tower with magic.

Everyone tasted the water but me. Partridge only sprinkled a few drops on the tip of my tongue. He was isolated from the rest of the Poison Snake People now that he no longer protected the poison flesh paddle of the Great River treaty. . . .

Meanwhile Snake Tooth and Birch Bark were quietly talking through Snake signs. They were sitting face to face with two torches stuck in the ground between them, so I was able to understand most of what they were saying. Snake Tooth gave off little sparks when he made the Snake sign for birch trees. Birch Bark rolled his head in a circle. Slime dripped from his matted fur, and his tongue was hanging out between his teeth. He seemed very mysterious as he told Snake Tooth that he wasn't sure these burning birch trees were allies of the invisible animals, but he also signaled that he didn't have to get right next to them to feel their heat was burning hot. . . .

Snake Tooth stood up and stroked his own manhood . . . it grew with a quick snap of his tongue. He had high hopes for it, but it wasn't anything like mine. He helped Birch Bark up and gently rubbed his paws. He spoke slowly so Birch Bark could read his lips.

"Birch Bark, my old warrior friend, remember the days in the hills when we could shake out our bodies without any effort, and smell our own delicious smells. Where's Hot Dog?"

Hot Dog came running and embraced Snake Tooth's manhood,

licking it as though it were a piece of meat cooked on a stick. Snake Tooth leaned back inside his flesh, picking at his thoughts like a bird. A lot of water was sloshing around in his stomach.

"Birch Bark, Hot Dog, I want you to find out for sure if the birch trees are invisible or not, and if and when they plan to attack. You should inspect everything for burning hairs, yet still be careful not to get too close."

Birch Bark and Hot Dog immediately cut their flesh, and their tails touched each other's paws. Birch Bark stretched himself across his face . . . this was the strongest he had looked in a long time. They slipped out of the Snake tower, making sure to erase their trail. . . .

Everyone waited in silence, which was only interrupted by the low hissings of Snake women on the sleeping platform or the loud whacks of Partridge's paddle to keep me awake. . . .

My eyes were straining in the distance. I saw thirty dancing lights. Snake warriors rubbed their forks just in case of a dawn attack. After a very long time of no change, one of the birch trees suddenly burned up in its own flames. Snake Tooth blew his breath hard into his hands, making strange noises that slid sideways through his mouth. . . .

Hot Dog came running back, panting hard, his fur side burned completely off. Strips of his flesh were trailing behind him in the last plunging darkness of night.

"Birch Bark . . . he touched one of those evil trees and burned up like a slab of fat. He couldn't even let out a quick scream."

Snake Tooth wept . . . I was amazed and almost touched. Snake women hissed their soothing Song of Mourning. Hot Dog solemnly gave Snake Tooth part of Birch Bark's charred tail. Snake Tooth tied it around his neck like a French ribbon. He looked grimly at Hot Dog and said:

"You must go home to our old mountain holes and bring back all the killer yellow dogs. I am now certain that the birch trees burning outside our village have been uprooted and hollowed out, then filled with invisible animals. . . .

"The Poison Snake People will need winter help scouting outside the tower. My killer yellow dogs will prowl around in circles sniffing both the ground and the air."

Hot Dog got ready for his journey without any painful shivers. He put on his best snakeskin robe to cover his burnt skin. He was proud to obey Snake Tooth's command. . . .

I dragged myself back to my slime hole. No one bothered me. I picked up a rotten fish along the way and swallowed it down like a village dog. Bits of tobacco started falling from the sky. My thoughts wandered . . . burning birch tree attack . . . invisible pieces of flesh that could feed a tribe . . . no more fish in the Great River. . . .

When I finally settled into my slime hole I was thinking that the Poison Snake People made many mistakes because they were hot-headed and fight-crazy, but Snake Tooth was now their greatest leader. I searched for the remains of Black Magic's face . . . as usual I was hungry. I didn't find the face and my eyes kept closing and my chin bumping against my chest. . . .

I remember my last drifting thought was I could probably sleep for two days straight. . . .

It is good to sleep. . . .

I, Tarcisius Tandihetsi, say so.

CHAPTER XXIII
FISH

In which Snake Tooth wakes up Tarcisius after letting him sleep for two days . . . he drags Tarcisius around by his manhood . . . Snake slime spread on the mushroom fields, lookouts on the sleeping platform . . . the changes inside and outside the Snake tower . . . Snake Tooth makes Kicking Snake dive into boiling slime hole to retrieve the Giant Snake's magic box . . . Blackrobe pops out of the magic box . . . his skin has turned black and he wears a halo of tobacco smoke . . . Black Magic's teeth are also hidden in the box, they bite Snake Tooth . . . another missed meal . . . Snake Tooth stuffs Blackrobe's poems inside his head . . . he wants to understand the language of the invisible animals . . . Blackrobe demands his own kettle and Tarcisius as a helper . . . he says the invisible animals have lost their incredible fear of heights . . . frozen fish . . . Partridge and Jumping Snake guard the Giant Snake's magic box . . . Blackrobe and Tarcisius spend the night in their kettle . . . Blackrobe tells Tarcisius he must escape . . . Tarcisius' mission . . . the next day is unusually hot . . . Snake Tooth's magic dream . . . the Great River fishing party leaves . . . work work work in Snake village . . . torture kettles where Black Magic's eyes used to be . . . the Snake tower is finally built and fortified for the winter . . . everything has been brought inside . . . Wrinkled Black Skin wants Tarcisius' manhood . . . he recaptures his own stomach and Wrinkled Black Skin is carried away forever inside a snakeskin cocoon . . . many Snake women volunteer to become invisible scouts . . . Partridge's vision . . . horrible invisible smell . . . Black Magic kills Partridge . . . Tarcisius jumps off the Snake tower . . . the first snow of winter . . . Snake women pick up Tarcisius as they race back to tower.

"**H**uron puppy, get up," Snake Tooth's voice rattled my dreams. "You've been asleep two days and that's enough . . . there's plenty of work to be done."

He had a firm grip on my snakeskin satchel . . . it wasn't very nice to be dragged around the Snake village once again by my manhood. When we finally stopped in the mushroom fields, I noticed that their small crop had been picked and snake slime spread on the fields. This really puzzled me more than any powerful Snake magic. I couldn't figure out why I hadn't been forced to do this work. Snake Tooth let me sleep! . . .

As I was wondering about all this Snake Tooth carved his name on my rock stomach, then he danced on my face. His feet smelled awful and I began thinking that it might be good to be young and go to God immediately. . . .

From on top of the sleeping platform a large drum boomed into the morning stillness. How did that drum get there? Snake Tooth was now fortifying the whole Snake village. I saw Curly Head and Snake Nose standing lookout on the sleeping platform. Snake women were gathered around them.

Snake slime rolled off my body although none of it got inside my snakeskin satchel. The rip had been sealed. More birch trees were burning beyond the fields. Out of nowhere a heavy wind started knocking against the cold ground. Many voices were hidden in the air. I couldn't understand what they were saying, but Snake Tooth seemed to know what was going on inside every possible thought. He beat the drum inside his chest as he dragged me back to my slime hole.

Many warriors were gathered there . . . they were waiting for Snake Tooth to speak. No council fire was burning. The Snake tower was proudly waking up to my gaze . . . it had grown quite a bit in my two days of sleep. Many kettles including Wrinkled Black Skin's had been moved from the village. They were inside the Snake tower . . . each one on its own platform, rising in the air and connected by many ladders. The Snake women were going to sleep inside the tower during winter.

Some warriors were chewing on slimy green feathers, while some others were letting out their breath just above their horrible dreams. I saw Black Magic off by himself putting his fingers through his empty eyes. My tongue was quivering for the taste of anything. The cold breath of hunger rushed madly through my stomach. . . .

Snake Tooth shook his head as though there were no other choice. He was still wearing Birch Bark's charred tail around his neck. He told Partridge to pile up fish next to my slime hole. Others he told to heat up some fires . . . soon it became extraordinarily hot. I was licking Snake slime off the ground when the fish started smoking and the slime in my sleeping hole started boiling and splashing.

Snake Tooth's voice cracked through the flames:

"Kicking Snake, come here and paint yourself red. Then you'll take a snakeskin satchel and find the Giant Snake's magic box. The Giant Snake told me this in a dream."

Kicking Snake protested:

"Snake Tooth, I've searched the village many times. . . ."

Snake Tooth waved his flesh club, and Kicking Snake quickly painted himself red and picked up a snakeskin satchel. He stood nearby tugging at his manhood with his head locked in a door.

Snake Tooth spread his legs across the slime hole, and pointing to the bottom told Kicking Snake to go under . . . there he'd find the Giant Snake's magic box. Snake Tooth added:

"Kicking Snake, make sure you put the box into the satchel as fast as you can and push it up to the surface right away. Then you can reach out to the edge of the ground and your life will be painlessly short . . . one deep red spurt of vomit and blood."

Kicking Snake was about to yell bloody murder, but Snake Tooth stopped him short:

"Kicking Snake, you answered Blackrobe's question the way he wanted you to. You gave him the Giant Snake's magic box. You're even soaked with Saving Waters. Ugh! You're the oldest after Black Magic."

Kicking Snake stretched his face and sadly shook his tail. He jumped into the boiling slime, and only his voice was left echoing in the heat, aimlessly protesting his fate. . . .

I looked away. The distances behind this day were already lost. My body shook as the snakeskin satchel rose to the surface. Everyone waited, not moving at all, but Kicking Snake was out of reach forever. . . .

Snake Tooth opened the satchel and took out the Giant Snake's box . . . there was a red circle painted on it. He plucked off some slimy green feathers, then he told everyone there to go to the spot where Blackrobe had disappeared into the ground. He started to sing a song about tobacco. He carried the magic box with one hand, and with the other he dragged me by my manhood. His flesh paddle-club was tied to his leg. . . .

When everyone was finally assembled at Blackrobe's invisible spot, Snake Tooth opened the magic box. Clouds of tobacco smoke poured out, and both sides of the sky suddenly stopped moving. The tobacco smoke was very cold. Belly Skin and Wrinkled Black Skin crawled into their hair. I shivered under my breath. I wondered if my other father was paying attention to the tricks of the invisible animals or just quietly spitting into their mouths? . . .

When the cold tobacco smoke cleared I saw Blackrobe's face and shoulders squirming out of the magic box. What a change! His skin was as black as any Snake warrior's. A small cloud of tobacco smoke shaped like a halo had settled in over his head. Long ago when Saving Waters were poured on my forehead my other father had shown me many French pictures of holy people with shiny halos over their heads. These holy people would be turned every which way, yet their halos stayed right with them. . . .

I kept my pounding heart under control. My other father turned to me and said:

"Tarcisius, my little son, I have come back just like I promised. It is very cold in here. The first snows of winter are coming. Are you still a Christian and a Huron, the son of a great chief?"

"Yes!" I yelled proudly while Blackrobe smiled and his chest popped out of the magic box. But Snake Tooth wasn't smiling at all, both his hands were resting on his flesh club. Belly Skin, Wrinkled Black Skin and several other Snake women shaped their hair into big noses, which pulled them around, making them smell things all over the tower. They seemed to be afraid of too many ladders. They brought Curly Head and Snake Nose down from the sleeping platform and huddled around them protectively. . . .

Blackrobe jumped out of the magic box. Now I saw the change completely. His hair, robe and beard were white, and white fur was growing on his mangled hands, but all his skin that I could see had turned black. My arms went out like two branches on a limb, yet before I could touch my other father or give out any sort of warning, Snake Tooth hit him over the head with his powerful flesh club. Aaaaiii! Snake Tooth was such an awful enemy . . . he did not fear any combination of words.

"Blackrobe, I hope you haven't forgotten that you are a hostage of the Great River Treaty. . . ."

The patch of white fur on his thigh gleamed in the afternoon. He looked inside the magic box and saw something move. His sharp fingers dug deep.

"EEEEEE-eeeeee!"

He quickly pulled back his hand . . . Black Magic's teeth could still bite. They had hidden themselves in the magic box. My manhood quivered in its satchel. I heard Blackrobe praying in his secret language, while Snake Tooth shook off Black Magic's teeth, which turned into slimy green feathers when they hit the ground. Jumping Snake pushed past me, and before I could even get up he had eaten all the feathers. Another missed meal. Snake Tooth's fingers were half falling off as he danced in pain. He opened my snakeskin satchel and slid his hand inside. He sighed with relief as his head seemed to be floating into feathers. . . .

Finally he pulled his hand out . . . it was completely healed. Black Magic had gone into hiding. Snake Tooth told me to take out whatever else might be in the box. I took out the little bit of elkskin robe I had put in there and Blackrobe's book of poems. I gave them to Snake Tooth who raised his leg like a village dog. He swallowed the elkskin, then he cut a circle in the back of his head, folded up the poems and stuffed them inside. For a moment his head was spinning, then he threw up his arms and said:

"Your poems hurt my head, Blackrobe, and I know that at any moment they might fill up the sky. Now if you really want them back, you better give me some secret information."

Slowly Blackrobe leaned over the edge of his feet. His head drifted northwards with the cold wind, but his stomach stayed in the same position. He still didn't wear his hands over his wrists or jump without a doubt. Finally he spoke and his voice filled up the village.

"Your tower is tremendous . . . I have seen nothing like it in France . . . it's truly a monument to the genius and appetites of the Poison Snake People. Snake Tooth is your greatest chief!"

All of a sudden everyone including me saw the Snake tower differently, and I was even proud I was working on it.

Blackrobe resumed:

"Snake Tooth, I want my poems back in their proper order without any red marks or heavy blankets. The invisible animals have put together fresh tracks. The only way you can save yourselves is by letting me pour Saving Waters over your heads."

"Ugh!" Snake Tooth grunted, his face flushed with the French alphabet. "It didn't save Kicking Snake." Then he grabbed my other father's white beard as he spoke between his sliding teeth:

"Don't say anything more about your water slime. I know what Saving Waters can do. Its magic isn't as strong as my flesh club, which can knock you off your feet more than a dozen times."

Snake Tooth rubbed the charred piece of Birch Bark's tail stretched around his neck. Slimy green feathers fell out of his head. He picked them up and made a pair of wings for his flesh club . . . circles of magical effort, breath and life broken into hair and deep wishes. . . .

"Blackrobe, don't let your dreams run away with you. I want you to teach me the language of the invisible animals."

My fingers were full of prayers as I thought about my other father's promises and Snake Tooth's threat to make me spend the nights of the crazy full moon sleeping with the Snake women. I felt soft and round inside like a little boy. I cried out:

"Blackrobe, Blackrobe . . . don't let them make me sleep with the Snake women."

Under my breath I also said, "They stink!"

My other father bent down and touched his feet. I followed his halo of tobacco smoke as it adjusted itself to his movements. He stood up and said:

"Poison Snake People, I know everything that's happened in your village. I am still a hostage of the Great River treaty, so there are plenty of things I'm not allowed to do. I cannot lie, cheat and steal, or stuff dirt into an open wound. . . .

"I will tell you all, but first you must give me my own kettle and let Tarcisius stay with me as a helper. He is too young to sleep with the Snake women."

Suddenly Curly Head and Snake Nose stepped forward and spoke together:

"Snake Tooth, we don't want the Huron puppy sleeping with our Snake women. His manhood is very strange. We'll kill ourselves like Kettle Skin if he does."

Blackrobe was pacing back and forth on the other side of his feet.

"Remember, Snake Tooth, if the invisible animals get me first, Tarcisius will help you out later. . . ."

In my head I repeated:

"I will never help the Poison Snake People. I will never help the Poison Snake People."

Snake Tooth was swaying back and forth, gathering secret information and thinking about his own desires. I was listening as hard as a deer in springtime. He said:

"Blackrobe, you and I will strike up a bargain like two traders. I will give you one or two things and you will give me three or four things."

Drops of blood appeared on my other father's white robe. Snake Tooth stated his conditions . . . he understood ideas better than anyone else's hair.

"Blackrobe, I never want you to mention Saving Waters again . . . if you do, my flesh club will change your face.

"Now I want you to think things over and tell me what you know about the invisible animals. The Poison Snake People need to prepare their winter defenses."

My other father followed a path of red circles around some water jars. He opened one and took a drink, his head moving slowly into deeper water. Meanwhile Partridge brought Black Magic back into the Snake tower. A group of warriors surrounded Black Magic and were slowly disappearing inside their own tobacco smoke. I had no idea what they were doing. I had never seen so many people disappear into smoke before. Blackrobe finally spoke:

"The invisible animals have lost their incredible fear of heights by cutting up their flesh into tiny pieces as they become more visible, then they mass it together like hunks of French bread specked with blood and slime. They will attack the Snake village in the dead of winter. The burning birch trees are now their allies. . . ."

Belly Skin started screaming and crying, then all the Snake women did. Blackrobe reached under his white robe and pulled out a long pipe. He filled it up with sacred tobacco sprinkled with white powder. He got a light from a cooking fire . . . several were burning all the time now in the tower. He inhaled the rising smoke through his nose, his face almost disappeared in a showering explosion of light. He offered the pipe to Snake Tooth with this advice:

"Apostate, you should try to live your life without getting stuck in the snow."

Snake Tooth quickly sniffed up the smoke and his face almost disappeared. He gave it back to Blackrobe who offered it to me. I was greatly honored, but the smoke itself was so strong I almost sneezed my whole face out through my nose. I gave it back to my other father who passed it on to the nearest Snake warrior. Everyone was going to have a chance to smoke it and almost disappear. . . .

Snake Tooth started to examine the Giant Snake's magic box.

"Blackrobe, why is it hot on the outside and cold on the inside?"

My other father took the box from Snake Tooth, then dipped his hand into it and pulled out several fish, each one frozen in tobacco leaves. He threw them at me. I ate them up right away. Blackrobe flowed in and out of a water jar with the magic box. He was dripping wet and arranging notes in his head as he explained:

"Snake Tooth, you can put all the fish you catch on the Great River inside this box and they will not turn to slime all winter. The invisible animals will certainly try to stop you, but if I help you and we move fast in one direction they won't be able to."

He handed the box back to Snake Tooth and said:

"Use it to store fish and you won't have so many snakeskin satchels weighing you down."

Snake Tooth put the box in Partridge's canoe. He ordered Partridge and Jumping Snake to guard it all the time. Then he returned to Blackrobe and said:

"You'll come with me tomorrow to the Great River and teach me the language of the invisible animals on the way."

My other father nodded in agreement and pointed to me. Snake Tooth called to Wrinkled Black Skin and ordered her to give me to Blackrobe as a treaty helper. She came up to me to stick one last fork into my snakeskin satchel, luckily missing my sleeping manhood. Blackrobe touched it and it healed itself. His halo of smoke shifted with his head. It was already evening and it had been a busy day.

"Tarcisius, my son, let's go up and clean out our kettle, the one that once belonged to Kettle Skin. "

We climbed up the many ladders which were already twisting through the Snake tower. We smelled fish and mushrooms cooking on the small kettle platforms. We were pretty high up, about the height of seven birch trees. . . .

Blackrobe and I were left alone to clean out the kettle, talk and pray. But before we even set foot inside my other father put red sticks on top of my head and turned me around in his dreams. He told me nothing about his invisible adventures . . . only to prepare for the worst, and that I knew enough already. He was more interested in searching for tobacco. . . .

When we were finally settled in, Snake Tooth himself brought us some food. My hand went up to my mouth . . . this was unbelievable. I tried to force myself not to dive on what he put down in front of us. One, two, three . . . I couldn't control myself, I gobbled it all down. It was good, and I didn't die. . . .

Snake Tooth started talking about old times in my Huron village. He said that he liked the times before Blackrobe came the best . . . they were the good old days to him. Suddenly he became very angry and warned Blackrobe not to try any invisible tricks on the fishing trip, because if the party didn't come back on time Partridge would give me up to the pleasures and tortures of the Snake women. He spoke directly to me:

"Little Spoon, from now on I won't pull you around by your manhood because when I come back from the Great River I will sleep with the Snake women myself. My power is growing, even now my flesh club is more powerful than a French arquebus. . . ."

He turned again to my other father:

"Blackrobe, why has your skin turned black and how come your black robe is white?"

My other father hadn't answered these questions when I asked him before, but now he replied:

"First give me some tobacco, then I'll answer you."

Snake Tooth knocked Blackrobe off his feet with his powerful flesh club. I licked my face in fear, but then I was astonished to see him bend down and help Blackrobe to his feet. He gave him two hunks of tobacco, one for now and one for later. Blackrobe put one hunk under his robe, then quickly smoked up the other. His voice was jumpy with tobacco.

"Snake Tooth . . . I am prepared to meet God more positively than just a mere cloud of smoke."

"Me too," I said under my breath.

My other father continued:

"I changed the color of my skin not the invisible animals. I am a missionary to the Poison Snake People and a hostage to the Great River treaty."

That made no sense to me at all, but I didn't say a word. I looked down at my feet . . . water covered my ankles. There were a great many shadows around my knees. I pounded on my stomach until my hands hurt. I was hungry again and nervous as an arrow unable to draw strength from the bottom of a canoe. . . .

Partridge and Jumping Snake paddled into our kettle, white wings painted on both sides of the canoe. They had come for Snake Tooth. The Giant Snake's magic box was tied down between them. Partridge's head was drifting to the east, while Jumping Snake's drifted to the west. As the canoe passed by Partridge slapped my snakeskin satchel, then he tried to hit my other father, but his slimy webbed hands only slid over the dark surfaces. Blackrobe touched my manhood and my mind dropped midway between a point and a hole. I liked that feeling very much. . . .

Snake Tooth left in the canoe. He sat on the magic box. I listened to my other father as I fell asleep . . . my head resting in the back of my throat.

"Tarcisius, I know you can learn how to stir up your dreams and jump from side to side. But all this won't really matter unless you escape from here. I know in my secret heart that I will never leave this Snake tower."

"AAAaaaiiiiii!" I wailed, suddenly wide awake and shivering. Blackrobe touched my manhood again. Slimy green feathers fell out of my snakeskin satchel.

"Tarcisius, be careful . . . I will try to get a message to William

Coutre along the Great River. I can no longer help you or tell you any secrets. You're growing up and I'm dying with a quiet eager joy that you can't understand. . . ."

I felt worse than a village dog or a discarded snakeskin, my shoulders almost disappeared. My other father instructed me:

"When I come back from this desperate fishing trip Snake Tooth will give me back my poems as he promised. They are very important to me and I will give them to you . . . it's your first mission. Hide my book in your snakeskin satchel. No one will know where they are unless your manhood pops up unexpectedly and you should be able to control that soon. I want you to take my poems with you when you escape. . . ."

My hands were shaking into drops of water . . . I opened my eyes, then closed them again. Sleep was finally pulling me down through my stomach into the edges of my dreams. . . .

The next morning we stood on our kettle's small platform and looked down. I heard sounds that sounded very far off. I stretched my arms across my chest, which didn't feel any wider than my name. It was an unnaturally hot day for this time of year. I touched my other father's mangled hands, then pointed below where Snake Tooth was walking down a line of Snake women, embracing as many as possible and encouraging them to work harder on the Snake tower . . . it was almost finished. He told them all his magic dream:

"Last night the Giant Snake visited me deep inside my dreams . . . it dragged my sliding teeth under its skin and I fell across its slimy neck. It told me that our lakes, our valleys, our great trees were changing invisibly, but I didn't know what that meant so I asked if it would turn out good or bad for us. It wouldn't tell me exactly, but it did say our only chance to survive the winter was inside the Snake tower. It should be finished by the time I come back from this fishing trip, and if we can keep the invisible animals out until springtime, they will no longer threaten us or hold our legs apart. Then our Giant Snake will return to us. . . ."

Snake Tooth touched the back of his head where he had stuffed Blackrobe's poems. He painted a white fish there. It would give him extra magic to catch more fish. He continued to talk to the Snake women. He insisted on the possibility of resisting the invisible animals. Then he said that in the spring the Poison Snake People might attack the Hurons and French. . . .

The fishing party was ready to go . . . each Snake warrior had painted a white fish on his body. Many fish would be needed for the winter. Snake Tooth pointed up to our small kettle platform and shouted:

"Blackrobe . . . jump down here right now."

My other father did as he was told, and I was right behind him. I saw drops of blood on the back of his neck. We landed at Snake Tooth's feet.

"Blackrobe, you will lead us through the blockade of burning birch trees, around any clumps of invisible animals, right to the Great River and there I will trick the fish into the Giant Snake's magic box. . . ."

He touched the white fish painted on his head and swept his powerful flesh club in a circle four times. The fishing party marched off with many canoes and storage baskets. Curly Head and Snake Nose were guarding my other father.

The birch trees massed outside the village stopped burning. Either they were letting the fishing party through because of my other father's magic, or they were setting up a trap. I wasn't going to know for several long weeks. . . .

Partridge was left behind in charge of everything. His black skin was falling off in many small patches instead of shedding all at once. His hands and feet were completely webbed. Snake Tooth had told him to make sure everyone worked except Black Magic . . . a very grave insult. All the mushrooms had to be stored in snakeskin satchels, water jars collected and filled, the Snake tower finished, and everything brought inside by the time the fishing party came back. . . .

The Snake tower was getting huge . . . it was already the size of ten birch trees one on top of the other. The Snake women's sleeping platform moved up with the tower. Many kettles were now hanging up inside, placed on small platforms connected to each other by at least six different ladders. Snake women were moving down from their sleeping platform as the tower grew. . . .

Work, work, work . . . that was all I did, and so did everyone else except Black Magic. The Poison Snake People rushed around with all sorts of crazy ideas. Things were changing before my eyes . . . heavy rocks moved like mushrooms, ladders broke in half, and the Snake baby visions disappeared. Partridge took credit for this disappearance since Snake Tooth no longer believed these visions were gifts of the Giant Snake. . . .

Black Magic hardly spoke or looked at anyone . . . invisible noises had entered his heart. At night after their work was done, Belly Skin and several other Snake women but never Wrinkled Black Skin would sit in a circle around Black Magic and smoke so much tobacco that they would almost disappear. After a week I noticed two half-built torture kettles where Black Magic's eyes used to be. I didn't dare ask him if they were for anyone special. I tried to think along with him, but it was hopeless. . . .

And then one cold clear evening everything was finished . . . the Snake tower completely built and fortified for the winter. It looked magnificent standing tall like a giant manhood in the middle of a big circle of open land, where the mushroom fields and the Snake village had been. Both were filled with Snake slime and crossed by many flying walls and burning mounds of tobacco. . . .

All the water jars had been filled, a few were even set aside. Partridge and Black Magic blew their fiery breath inside them. The spring, which Snake Tooth revealed with two mighty blows of his flesh club, was still trickling out so the water jars could be constantly refilled.

I had finished my work too . . . all the mushroom satchels were filled to the brim. Even Black Magic finished the torture kettles in his blank eyes. Now he would grab the Snake women who smoked around him and point to where his eyes had been, sometimes poking the kettles and sometimes passing right through them. His sense of distances was as empty as my stomach. . . .

Everything had been brought inside the Snake tower . . . you could've thrown a stone underground and no one would've paid any attention to it. Only a few warriors were lying around, while everyone else celebrated the Snake tower with each breath. Three of the special water jars were opened.

I was allowed to go to my kettle with some real food, which Belly Skin gave me. I was surprised by the way she looked at me. I had already sewn up the skin around my heart and shaped an armful of circles. I pressed myself against the middle of the kettle as I wolfed down the raw meat. Suddenly bubbles of water rushed up from the bottom of the kettle . . . Wrinkled Black Skin appeared. I waved my arms and feet without getting up. She was wearing the sacred ceremonial robe made from the captured manhoods of many enemies. Her hair was shaped like my snakeskin satchel and strings of blue smoke poured out of her body.

"Little Spoon, you don't have to shake or tremble . . . I'm not here to play tricks on you or use your feet like a pair of antlers. I want to give back your stomach. New feelings and desires are burning up my body. . . ."

She moved towards me, her body thundering like a storm which could pin any kind of shadows between my legs. A crazy full moon was fixed above the large smoke-hole at the top of the Snake tower. I saw my stomach stuck between her legs and under her tail. Her eyes gleamed like village dogs before a meal. She barked at me:

"Your satchel, Little Spoon . . . open your manhood satchel! You are my fresh meat . . . I want your giant tower!"

She pointed between my legs and froze for a moment. Outside the crazy noises of tower celebration grew louder . . . they were very far into their dreams. I heard weird cries which sounded like someone being skinned alive. I glanced up and saw an empty snakeskin cocoon floating inside the tower. Then Wrinkled Black Skin dripping with slime rushed me, grabbed my shoulders and wiped her face with my hands. She rubbed her robe and the manhoods snapped straight up, whereupon the robe slipped off her shoulders, brushed my toes and was swallowed up in the mud at the bottom of my kettle.

I stared from hunger at my own stomach. It was not a pretty sight. Wrinkled Black Skin shed her skin. The darkness was no longer neatly laid out like a blanket. Cold water splashed inside my head as I dove for my stomach. I captured it and swallowed it whole, then I looked up and saw Wrinkled Black Skin lifted bodily in the air like a Frenchwoman and carried away inside the snakeskin cocoon. I also noticed a few white hairs growing between my toes. . . .

I needed more to eat so I climbed out of the kettle, but Black Magic grabbed hold of me and bounced me back inside. He forced me to stare at the holes in his face where his eyes had been . . . I saw my name written across one torture kettle and Partridge across the other. My mind curled up to the sky while darkness spread through my snakeskin satchel. I think I would've died then and there if so many Snake women hadn't jumped into the kettle looking for Wrinkled Black Skin. I told them what happened. They looked at me like fresh meat until Partridge leaned over the top of the kettle. Black Magic quickly hid in a corner. Partridge's voice splashed through the kettle:

"Snake women, Snake Tooth told me what to say . . . I need you to be like warriors. I want you to be invisible scouts and sneak into the birch trees and pick up some secret information."

All the Snake women shouted their approval except Belly Skin. It was a great honor to be an invisible scout. Partridge gave them instructions and they all left on assigned tasks. Black Magic was the last to leave, his withered manhood shifted back and forth across my footsteps. I did not think many Snake women would survive the winter. . . .

Partridge dragged me out of the kettle. He said:

"Huron puppy, you will stay with me until Snake Tooth comes back, then he can decide whether to roll you up like paper or spit you out like tobacco. From now on I'm the chief protector of the Great River treaty!"

More invisible madness! It was almost dawn . . . I could feel a stiff frost in the air. The first big snow would be coming soon . . . the fishing party and my other father should be back. . . .

Partridge jumped on my back and forced me to climb up towards the now abandoned sleeping platform. I caught a passing glimpse of Black Magic climbing into his own kettle. His head was hanging a short distance above his withered manhood. He reminded me of Full Moon. . .

Partridge paddled me upwards like a canoe. The Snake tower was nearly deserted . . . only a few small eyes flashed restlessly under their dreams. It was very very cold on the sleeping platform. Only the large drum had been left there. I looked up and saw a handful of dripping lights at a great distance. They seemed like streaks of fire burning slowly along the edges of the earth. Beyond the mushroom fields the birch trees ignited themselves again.

Partridge thought this was a bad sign so he tied me over his narrow hips and down onto his tail, which felt so slimy it made me shiver. He started checking out the platform for any stray invisible animals that might be squirming around, but he found none.

I screamed out:

"Partridge, I'm hungry . . . I need something to eat."

Partridge ignored me. Strings of blue smoke were streaming out of his body. He spoke to the air above us:

"We might as well forget it if the invisible animals get inside the tower. Snake Tooth better come back soon, and the killer yellow dogs too. If there are any invisible animals nearby they'll smell them out for sure. . . ."

Partridge started swinging his tail like a paddle. A horrible new smell overwhelmed our senses. My face was swept towards the edge of the smokehole while clouds held back the morning light. Partridge was choking:

"I have never smelled this kind of air before. It makes me dizzy and I see black in front of my face. The invisible animals are nearby."

His skin crumpled like tobacco, his lips were cracked with scratches, and his voice needed sleep.

"They will attack us for sure and might bury us with their weight. We might be drowned or choked to death by their smell."

He crossed his eyes and dropped his tail, banging my head against the platform.

"This invisible smell is awful. . . ."

His thoughts disappeared into pagan shadows, while my mind collected nothing. He held his dreams against the wind and saw a vision:

"Snake Tooth and the fishing party are fighting their way back from the Great River, and your Blackrobe is helping them with magic tricks that fold into ladders."

I listened inside my head for a message from my other father . . . my ears were folded down to my face, but it was Partridge's fearful voice I heard:

"Black Magic!"

Black Magic had climbed up to the sleeping platform . . . he was carrying a hunting fork in one hand and with the other he was slapping a fish between his legs. Long shadows passed through his empty face, and strings of blue smoke floated out of the torture kettles in his blank eyes.

He rushed Partridge and stabbed him in the chest, and as Partridge tumbled over he poked him in the back right above where my feet were tied. He wildly coughed fire into the air as he died, burning the snakeskin knots half off my ankles and wrists. . . .

My tongue was trembling so much I was forced to drag my teeth under my skin, then I struggled to get free. Partridge's dead body instantly smelled awful, but it still was nothing compared to the other invisible smell which was more than unbearable. It made me feel like a lump of rotting meat no smaller than a wall. I unraveled myself from Partridge's tail and pushed him off the Snake tower. He was never seen again. . . .

Black Magic made a grab for my manhood. I couldn't look him in the face so I jumped into his feet, separating his words then plunging towards the bottom of his dreams. It was worse than awful. I threw myself far off the sleeping platform, my shoulders pushed around by strong winds. I landed on my snakeskin satchel. Slimy green feathers were scattered on the ground. I devoured them without a thought. . . .

All the burning birch trees were shaking or moving in place. Snake women were running across the slime-filled mushroom fields. There was more than just a handful of dripping lights in the sky. I couldn't bear the uproar in my heart. I started flopping around on the cold ground and didn't stop until I realized I was covered with snow and bits of my body were cracking like ice. . . .

I felt a great fear as invisible cries pounded in my ears. I wanted to sleep for the rest of winter and stick to the darkness of my own dreams like a rabbit. The Snake women picked me up as they ran towards the Snake tower. I didn't expect to live very long. . . .

I, Tarcisius Tandihetsi, say so.

CHAPTER XXIV
INVISIBLE SLIME

IN WHICH THE FISHING PARTY RETURNS FROM THE GREAT RIVER . . .
SNAKE TOOTH LOOKS DIFFERENT . . . THE KILLER YELLOW DOGS
WILL BE INVISIBLE SCOUTS OUTSIDE THE SNAKE TOWER . . . ALL
THE FISH CAUGHT IN THE GREAT RIVER POUR INSIDE THE GIANT
SNAKE'S MAGIC BOX . . . SNAKE TOOTH GIVES BACK BLACKROBE'S
POEMS . . . A BIRCH BARK PLATFORM IS BUILT INSIDE THE SNAKE
TOWER . . . CURLY HEAD AND SNAKE NOSE ARE DEAD . . . BLACK
MAGIC TURNS INTO A TORTURE KETTLE . . . BLACKROBE GIVES
TARCISIUS HIS POEMS . . . SNAKE TOOTH DECIDES TO KILL
BLACKROBE . . . THE INVISIBLE ANIMALS BREAK THROUGH THE
BIRCH BARK PLATFORM . . . THE FIGHT IS OVER VERY QUICKLY,
ONLY A SCOUTING ATTACK . . . TARCISIUS IS GROWING RAPIDLY . . .
BLACKROBE IS TIED INTO TORTURE KETTLE THAT ONCE WAS BLACK
MAGIC'S . . . BELLY SKIN WANTS TO FLOP AROUND WITH TARCISIUS'
MANHOOD . . . ANOTHER INVISIBLE ATTACK, THIS TIME THROUGH
THE SMOKEHOLE . . . BELLY SKIN IS KILLED . . . THE BURNING BIRCH
TREES ATTACK THE SNAKE TOWER . . . THE FIGHT IS A LONG ONE
. . . SNAKE TOOTH PUSHES HIS THOUGHTS THROUGH HIS HEAD LIKE
MUSHROOMS . . . BLACKROBE SMILES FOR THE LAST TIME . . .
EVERYONE HAS A TURN WHACKING BLACKROBE WITH SNAKE
TOOTH'S MAGIC FLESH CLUB . . . BLACKROBE GIVES TARCISIUS HIS
MANGLED HANDS AND DIES . . . SNAKE WARRIORS SCOOP UP THE
BOILING SLIME FROM THE TORTURE KETTLE AND THEIR SKINS
CHANGE BACK TO ORIGINAL MUSHROOM COLOR . . . HOT DOG OPENS
THE GIANT SNAKE'S MAGIC BOX AND INSTEAD OF FISH OUT POURS
A STREAM OF INVISIBLE SLIME THAT NEVER STOPS . . . THE FINAL
ATTACK . . . JUMPING SNAKE DIES . . . TARCISIUS FIGHTS TO EAT . . .
THE BIG SKY MOUTH . . . BLACKROBE GOES TO GOD . . . THE
INVISIBLE ANIMALS FILL UP THE SNAKE TOWER WITH TURNING
POINTS AND CIRCLES . . . MORE AND MORE ROWS OF CUTTING SHARP
TEETH APPEAR . . . SNAKE TOOTH LOSING HIS MAGICAL POWERS . . .
HOT DOG, THE LAST KILLER YELLOW DOG, DIES . . . A GIGANTIC RUSH
OF INVISIBLE SLIME . . . EVERYONE FLEES TOWARDS THE SMOKEHOLE,
THEN ONLY SNAKE TOOTH AND TARCISIUS ARE LEFT . . . SNAKE

Now it was snowing full blast outside the Snake tower. Early morning clouds were hanging out as though they had hair. Everything was freezing and turning white except that awful smell. I suffered many disagreements between grips and blows. All the Poison Snake People's thoughts had one common center . . . the invisible animals! . . .

Several hours raced noiselessly over the snow while pagan memories shifted back and forth across the Snake women's footsteps. They were standing outside the tower. Black Magic was asking lots of questions. Every so often he would pull on the snakeskin rope he had tied around my neck. I was his eyes. Once while he was talking snake slime, three dirty green feathers dropped out of his armpit. I got down on my hands and knees like a village dog and swallowed them whole. I acted like a foolish boy. . . .

Suddenly the drum on top of the Snake tower boomed out a warning. My nose cracked like a butterfly. The invisible smell drifted away . . . it was replaced by a new one. Fish! The birch trees stopped burning. A magic trick of my other father. Snake Tooth and Blackrobe with the Giant Snake's magic box led the charge through the birch trees just like Partridge predicted. They were followed by the killer yellow dogs and the rest of the Great River fishing party, then sliding right behind everyone were thousands of frozen fish melting slowly in all different directions. My stomachs felt raw, empty and irresistibly drawn to the fish. I was on my hands and knees again. I threw my dreams to the wind and my body turned over a new leaf. I screamed even louder with my feet.

"Blackrobe . . . Blackrobe, help me!"

I opened my snakeskin satchel. White hairs had grown up around my manhood. The ground under my feet started crawling backwards, but it stopped when my other father stood in front of me. His skin was still black and his robe white but with many added bloodstains. I was sure that he had been cruelly tortured on the trail. . . .

My manhood was pounding between my legs . . . it started to rise. It felt wet and slimy like a fish. Blackrobe gently touched it and said:

"Control yourself, Tarcisius. You are a Christian and the son of a great chief."

I put my manhood back in its snakeskin satchel. I felt like a good boy again, just received Saving Waters. . . .

Black Magic pulled hard on the snakeskin rope around my neck. Snake Tooth was standing in front of us, holding the magic box. He looked much different. The top of his head was covered by flames but not burning. Mushrooms were growing all over his body except around the patch of white fur on his thigh. His manhood kept jumping up and down. He still wore Birch Bark's tail as a necklace, and more white fish were painted on his chest and shoulders. He knew everything that happened. Crowded behind him were the killer yellow dogs and the fishing party. First Snake Tooth, nodding to Blackrobe, cut the rope from around my neck, then he gave Black Magic such a whack with his flesh club that I thought he killed him, but Black Magic blindly crawled back inside the Snake tower. . . .

Next Snake Tooth ordered all the Poison Snake People inside the tower. He positioned the killer yellow dogs while Hot Dog remained at his side. His language was beginning to change the lines of his body.

"My faithful killer yellow dogs, I have brought you here to protect the Poison Snake People. You will be our invisible scouts with a terrible strength that can fly through the air like my flesh club."

He walked through them scratching their necks and touching

as many as he could with his flesh club. He continued to instruct them:

"Dig as many holes as you can and keep your roaring voices ready to crack through the sky."

The killer yellow dogs growled fiercely and many forks were collected. Snake Tooth opened the magic box and called all the fish inside. The fish kept pouring in, wave after wave of very deep breaths. I was incredibly hungry. It was early afternoon when Snake Tooth finally closed the magic box . . . all the fish were inside and the box was no bigger than before. . . .

Snake Tooth dragged me into the tower by my snakeskin satchel while Blackrobe carried the magic box, followed closely by Hot Dog. Many cooking fires were burning on the kettle platforms but everywhere it was cold. Snake Tooth spoke:

"My people, the Snake tower is too cold. We have to build a platform from the ground up to the lowest kettles. We need wood and we can get it now while the birch trees aren't burning."

He looked at Blackrobe who answered:

"I can stop the fire inside the birch trees for about three hours, but first, Snake Tooth, give me back my poems."

My mind passed beyond any invisible recognition. I thought surely my other father would go to God, but instead Snake Tooth gave back the poems. Blackrobe wrapped his face with them and touched the bottom of his feet, then he put them under his blood-stained robe. . . .

Blackrobe sat in the middle of the Snake tower while Snake Tooth directed all the warriors. Many birch trees were cut down. I helped with Belly Skin watching me. Everyone was very scared and afraid, but my other father's magic was very strong. I did not see Curly Head or Snake Nose . . . the lines on their bodies had probably disappeared into another language. . . .

The birch bark platform was finished that night and it was warmer inside but not as warm as a Huron cabin in wintertime. Snake Tooth danced on the platform, his dreams hidden under the mushrooms stuck like armor to his skin. His manhood kept rising and falling, surrounded by blue smoke strings. . . .

He gathered together all the warriors from the Great River fishing party . . . there weren't many left. I was sure now that Curly Head and Snake Nose were dead. Snake Tooth rubbed the painted white fish off everyone. Jumping Snake was last. Snake Tooth told him to find Black Magic. He set off right away, jumping from one kettle platform to the next. Small forks started dropping out of the mouths of the fishing party warriors. Others picked them up and used them to eat their fish. . . .

"Black Magic!"

Snake Tooth was swinging his magic flesh club. It flew out of his hand and hit Black Magic's empty face, then it flew back to Snake Tooth. The next few seconds softened into waiting. He turned to Hot Dog and told him to fetch a water jar Black Magic had flamed when the Snake tower was finished. Hot Dog opened one . . . there was dust not water inside. Snake Tooth sprinkled it on Black Magic's face . . . many slimy green feathers fell out.

Hot Dog scooped them all up for Snake Tooth, who broke one in half and listened inside the feather until his own invisible thoughts grew into a language. He spoke:

"Black Magic, for a long time I've treated you like a Snake captain and respected your age. No more. You've been taken over by the invisible animals. The water you flamed turned to dust . . . your face hasn't grown back and slimy green feathers fell out of it. I broke one open and it told me everything."

Black Magic couldn't stop shaking and many bits of his skin fell off as he shaped his body into a torture kettle. His own name was written across it . . . a suggestion of sacrifice. Black Magic died without a fight and he remained a torture kettle. . . .

My other father carried me on his shoulders up to our kettle platform. Once there I asked:

"Blackrobe, do you have anything to eat?"

I felt my body lose control of my mind. He grabbed me and

rolled me through an invisible hoop. He opened my snakeskin satchel and touched my manhood. I threw my head back to open up my mind. Blackrobe was staring over the edge of my forehead as he uncovered my secret dreams and rubbed my manhood with his poems. He spread his shoulders from a whisper into a language of invisible words as he spoke:

"I want to give you my poems. I'll feed them into your head like a Huron feast, then you'll hide them in your snakeskin satchel."

His fingers continued running between my legs while words were chewed up like tobacco and spit into my head, then he stuck his poems under my manhood. Terrible fears developed in my bones as my body went flat against my chest, my mouth rolling under my manhood like a cloud. My head was leaning against my snakeskin satchel. The future looked horrible but I was too hungry to care. Blackrobe gave me fish to eat. I ate quite a few of them. Just before I fell asleep I felt my manhood growing bigger inside its snakeskin satchel. . . .

The next morning I woke up too big for the kettle. Blackrobe was already up and at it like the French stories tell of Jesus. I looked up at the smokehole . . . it was snowing. The Snake tower seemed to be falling out of a storage basket. I was incredibly hungry. I heard my other father below talking to Belly Skin and a small group of Snake women. They were standing next to the torture kettle that once was Black Magic.

"The only way you can survive and raise Snake babies again is to have Saving Waters poured over your heads."

Snake Tooth's flying flesh club knocked my other father down. Snake Tooth stood over him.

"You've broken our agreement. The Great River treaty is dead."

Blackrobe almost disappeared into thoughtless spots of light. A snake hoop silently rolled through his head. My teeth hurt and my whole body was growing, even my snakeskin satchel. Snake Tooth pointed at me and yelled:

"Huron puppy, you'll be next if you keep on growing."

Suddenly the warning drum on top of the tower boomed out, and my face was split in half by the upward rush of a ladder. My skin felt like pages torn from a book. That hideous invisible smell returned, now even thicker than mud or snake slime. Outside the Snake tower the killer yellow dogs were yelling and growling fiercely . . . an invisible attack. My voice dropped into my stomachs when the invisible animals broke through the birch bark platform. . . .

Everywhere you looked there were slimy pieces of invisible flesh squeezed together like frenchbread. It was easy to rip them in half and eat them up. Plenty of slime juice dripped to the birch bark platform then turned into slimy green feathers. I ate them too . . . now they tasted like rotten fish. I know I killed many invisible animals. I helped the Poison Snake People without thinking about it. . . .

Snake Tooth shouted instructions not to let any invisible shapes join together. I didn't. I attacked between their invisible parts, breathing deeply with my mouth wide open. I never moved directly in front of them. I liked best of all smashing down on them so their slimy juices would splash right into my mouth. . . .

The fight was over very quickly. I was sure it had been only a scouting attack. The birch bark platform was repaired. My other father had not helped one way or the other. He floated in and out of the kettles, above it all, and only came back down to the platform after the fight was over. . . .

I turned to Snake Tooth. I felt proud of killing so many invisible animals. I was growing up but not as a good Christian. Snake Tooth's head was still burning, yet not on fire. His face was pierced by chunks of invisible flesh, completely invisible to whatever they touched. His manhood was still rising and falling, no bigger than before, with strings of blue smoke surrounding it. He shook my hand like a Frenchman. I didn't know what he meant, but I did notice I had grown up to his shoulder. He walked away without saying a word to me. . . .

My other father crawled up to me like a child. I kissed his mangled hands. He whispered in my ear:

"Tarcisius, listen carefully. On the Great River we saw a trading party of Hurons and French with William Coutre in the first canoe. Snake Tooth made me turn the other way, but I got a secret message to them anyway."

Snake Tooth came back with Hot Dog, Jumping Snake and other Snake warriors. Jumping Snake tied me to a large standing torture fork. I was a head taller than him and very hungry. My thoughts were cooking into all sorts of different meals. Snake Tooth dragged my other father around the birch bark platform then tied him into the torture kettle that once was Black Magic. Snake Tooth smeared tobacco juice on top of Blackrobe's head, then he spit fire on it. The flames stayed burning there until he put them out with his face, all the time sucking up the smoke. The white hairs on Blackrobe's face were completely burned off. I felt his poems scratching underneath my manhood. My other father's eyes closed from the pain and his halo of smoke rested on the back of his head. He slept. . . .

Snake Tooth and the others left us there helplessly drifting off to one side like two shadows without any oars. I looked up the smoke-hole. I thought I saw a large bird diving towards me with its head moving much faster than its body. . . .

Belly Skin stepped out of a kettle not far above my head. She climbed down and untied my hands. Her hair was shaped like a cooking fire and her body filled the air. She told me to open my snakeskin satchel. Her tail was wrapped around her neck. She wanted to flop around with my manhood, showing me all her dark secrets. A soft light crept into her eyes. I was beginning to see things differently. The Poison Snake People could no longer draw strength from the bottom of their dreams. Their Giant Snake had fled into the vast deep spaces of their earth. Meanwhile here and now I was thinking that Belly Skin looked plump and juicy. I licked my lips. My heart was in quite an uproar. . . .

Suddenly again the warning drum, the thick invisible smell, and the howling of the killer yellow dogs outside . . . Jumping Snake came running towards us. He reminded me of Full Moon. My other father woke up and started to pray in his secret language. Hunks of invisible flesh dropped down from the smokehole. An unexpected attack. Several landed on Belly Skin and quickly formed themselves into an invisible animal. All that was visible were its slimy head and neck and its webbed hands and feet. It knocked her to the ground and jumped on top of her. Jumping Snake didn't help her, instead he cut me loose. He was itching with messages but more invisible pieces of flesh were stuck between his words:

"The birch trees are coming!"

I felt a tremendous noise. The Snake tower itself shuddered, then an avalanche of withering yells and howls. The killer yellow dogs were suffering great pains. I heard Snake Tooth screaming to let them in or they would be burnt up forever. . . .

I stopped thinking of anything but food. I tore the invisible animal from between Belly Skin's legs and devoured it whole. I enjoyed having pieces of invisible animal flesh stuck between my teeth like frenchbread. I was worse than a pagan. Belly Skin was dead . . . I ate her too.

Meanwhile Jumping Snake had knocked down another invisible animal, killing it under its throat. It turned into many slimy green feathers. Before Jumping Snake could even jump one foot I had all the feathers eaten up. More and more hunks of invisible flesh fell through the smokehole. Their smell was sickening. The killer yellow dogs were let into the tower. Feet and paws were flying everywhere. . . .

The fighting continued up and down and all over the Snake tower, which was now thick with invisible animals. I had a feast with fast moves to the throat and an ever increasing hunger. . . .

"BOOM! BOOM! BOOM!"

The burning birch trees banged against the tower and made it shake underground. Snake Tooth yelled above the noise:

"The Giant Snake warned me in my dreams. My people, form water lines to every opening in our tower. Use the jars that are already full. The birch trees will die quickly in the cold."

The pieces of invisible flesh suddenly stopped dropping down from the smokehole. I stopped eating and suddenly remembered my other father. I rushed back to the torture kettle and untied his mangled hands. Very briefly I felt happy and holy inside my feet, but nothing came out I could eat, so after Blackrobe was free I left him to go back to fight and eat. I was growing up and even the magic of my other father's mangled hands could not hold it back. . . .

I feasted on everything. Meanwhile many water lines were formed and the banging of the burning birch trees against the tower grew weaker. I saw a Snake warrior grab one of the water jars fire-dusted by Black Magic. I watched it move up a line without anyone noticing, then it disappeared through a hole to the outside. An explosion crashed through the Snake tower, knocking everyone down. It made a big hole. Several burning birch trees broke through . . . many things caught fire. Snake Tooth reformed the water lines and they put out all the fires. The birch trees that broke through were coated with fish and a heavy snake slime. They helped fill in the hole. . . .

The fight was over . . . it had been a big attack and lasted many hours. I had eaten an enormous amount of invisible flesh and slimy green feathers, yet I was still hungry. . . .

Hot Dog spoke up for the killer yellow dogs:

"Snake Tooth, don't send us back outside, or else we'll be killed in the snow by the invisible animals."

Snake Tooth pushed his thoughts through his head like mushrooms. It was no longer on fire. Jumping Snake stood behind him, boiling a little, with his tail stuck in his mouth. I looked down at my feet . . . white hairs were filling up the spaces between my toes. . . .

All the remaining Poison Snake People gathered around. It was very smoky but not hard to see. Many Snake warriors were slapping fish against their manhoods and spitting at my other father in the torture kettle. His mangled hands were turning stiff just below his hips. His whole body dripped slime and mud, but I could hear his voice on both sides of my head.

"Tarcisius, nothing is tiresome that's endured for tobacco, and I will have plenty of tobacco when I go to God. I will smoke with Eustace, your father. . . ."

A fire started smoking around the torture kettle. Snake slime, pieces of invisible flesh, mushrooms, splinters of wood, fish bones and discarded snakeskins were thrown into the kettle. It was getting bigger. My other father tried to comfort me:

"Don't worry, Tarcisius, my son, there are plenty of short distances in this tower. You will survive and grow old in your own village. I have offered some tobacco. . . ."

My mind tumbled into spots . . . I was too hungry to talk. Blackrobe went back to praying for more tobacco. Snake Tooth stood on a ladder and spoke to his people. I noticed most of his teeth were missing.

"Blackrobe will die, but I want every one to get a good whack at him before he's boiled in snake slime."

Snake Tooth's flesh club went flying towards Blackrobe, smashing his halo of smoke into bits of tobacco. My other father smiled for the last time. . . .

Hot Dog was the first to whack Blackrobe with Snake Tooth's magic flesh club. Everyone had a turn, letting out their breath just above their horrible dreams. A snake hoop rolled silently through my head when the torture kettle began to boil and splash. I heard words that I'm sure no one else heard. The torture kettle that once was Black Magic was chanting:

"The invisible animals are coming apart.

The Poison Snake People must fight.

I was invisible.

Death! Death!"

Jumping Snake was the last to whack Blackrobe. My other father's bones crumpled like tobacco. Snake Tooth was speaking again:

"A heavy brush has gone over my eyes. All this might be deeper than just the invisible animals. . . ."

I stopped listening . . . nighttime suddenly dropped into the Snake tower like a bundle of tobacco. A crazy full moon stood above the smokehole. My other father was dying. I moved closer to the torture kettle. One side of his skin had rolled completely under his bones. I could no longer recognize his face or for that matter any part of his body except his mangled hands.

I bent over and embraced him . . . his body was hot but the boiling slime water was cool. I knew right away that he had poured in Saving Waters. While embracing he hid his mangled hands inside my snakeskin satchel. For several long seconds my thoughts devoured them in my head, but then I remembered myself and who I really was. . . .

I looked at my other father again. He was dead and his mangled hands were his last gift to me before he went to God. . . .

Some Snake warriors to show how brave they were scooped up the boiling slime from the torture kettle without screaming or jumping into their dreams. Very quickly their skins changed back to its original mushroom color. All the Poison Snake People cheered, they thought this was a good sign. Then everyone except Snake Tooth rushed to the torture kettle and drank up the remains. They even started fighting among themselves. I watched all this as though my stomachs, which were slowly melting into one just right for my size, had nothing to do with my thoughts. . . .

Snake Tooth's mushroom armor, which was harder than stone, had many chips. His manhood looked like a bone inside a mushroom. He was feeling triumphant, picking off bits of Blackrobe's flesh from his magic flesh club and dropping them into his mouth. I felt awful. . . .

Hot Dog started growling and jumping in the air. He barked:

"Snake Tooth, Snake Tooth . . . the boiling slime wasn't hot and it made me very hungry."

Everyone agreed. Me too. I was very hungry. Snake Tooth didn't pay much attention, finally he pointed to the Giant Snake's magic box and said:

"If you're hungry, Hot Dog, eat."

Hot Dog ran to the magic box and opened it up. He died instantly . . . the horrible smell must have killed him first. Out poured a stream of invisible slime and it never stopped. No one was prepared for this kind of attack not even Snake Tooth. The slime was yellowish white and gave off its own bright light. In it boiled pieces of invisible flesh, tufts of hair, slimy green feathers, and rows of cutting sharp teeth. All the fish from the Great River had turned invisible. . . .

Snake Tooth yelled out instructions. Jumping Snake flattened out his feet and leaped towards the Giant Snake's magic box, hoping to shut off the invisible flow. It didn't work. The pieces of flesh formed themselves into invisible animals and pulled Jumping Snake down into their stream of slime. He screamed out his last breath as he drowned. The invisible stream kept flowing out of the Giant Snake's magic box into both the open spaces and hidden edges of the Snake tower. . . .

I climbed up to the second level of kettle platforms. No one bothered me because they all were fighting for their lives. Without flying Snake Tooth was everywhere striking at the invisible animals as they formed themselves out of the boiling slime. The smells were so bad they could rip your teeth out if you opened your mouth for too long. . . .

I thought Snake Tooth had really wasted his life. He could have stayed a Huron and a Christian and none of this would have happened. Now his mushroom flesh was opening into many small red circles. He couldn't use his teeth anymore and the fire from his hands was no help at all in close quarters. . . .

The invisible animals' tactics were very clear. Their slime would flood the Snake tower while their pieces of flesh jumped out of the shining hot liquid, formed their invisible bodies, attacked a victim and dragged him back into the slime. I joined the fighting below hoping for something to eat . . . my hunger was bigger than my body. With these invisible enemies I was careful not to fight too openly. Invisible slime dripped off each and every bit of their invisible flesh. The birch bark platform was hot and slippery. The Poison Snake People retreated to their kettles. I controlled my desire to run away and I didn't turn my head in any direction but straight up. I saw the Big Sky Mouth, the same one that took Blackrobe off the sacred mountain, waiting below the crazy full moon.

I looked back to the torture kettle that had once been Black Magic. I felt my other father's mangled hands rubbing my manhood inside my snakeskin satchel. The kettle was floating on the rising invisible slime tide. Several invisible animals formed themselves and attacked the kettle, but even in death Blackrobe's magic was great. These attackers fell back and dissolved in their own slime. Then the kettle rose in the air, skillfully avoiding the platforms filled with Poison Snake People and killer yellow dogs and sailed safely through the smokehole. There it bounded up and away as the Big Sky Mouth opened wide and swallowed up Blackrobe's last remains. My other father had truly gone to God. . . .

My manhood started to rise and smoke, but Blackrobe's mangled hands forced it back into its snakeskin satchel. It was getting very crowded in the Snake tower. Too many bad smells. The Giant Snake's magic box had disappeared from sight, but the flow of invisible slime didn't stop. I quickly opened and closed my mouth without lifting my legs. My eyes were lost in thought under my feet, and whenever I stretched out my arms an invisible animal would form itself and leap towards my manhood. The invisible animals were hungry too. They were filling up the Snake tower with turning points and circles. . . .

I saw many Snake warriors flopping around in the invisible slime, emptying their bodies into strings of blue smoke, then their tails would be thrown aside. More and more rows of cutting sharp teeth appeared. I retreated to the kettle platforms. The hideous smells were choking me. Then Snake Tooth was choking me . . . there were holes inside the red circles on his mushroom armor. He still looked strong, his manhood rising and falling with only a few blue smoke strings dying out. He hissed at me:

"Huron dog, it's your time to die forever. It was my biggest mistake to let you and Blackrobe live so long among the Poison Snake People. It would've been better if you had been tortured to death and your manhood flung into the Great River."

He threw me against a kettle, then he leaned over me, swinging his magic flesh club. I would've died instantly if several invisible animals hadn't formed themselves out of the slime and jumped on Snake Tooth's back, almost knocking him off the platform. . . .

I hid behind the kettle. Snake Tooth was a beautiful fighter to watch. He knew so many magic fighting tricks . . . he even tricked two of his invisible attackers into killing each other. He looked down to the kettle platforms underneath . . . the Snake warriors and killer yellow dogs fighting there weren't doing so good. I knew it was time for serious escape when Snake Tooth shouted at me as he dove into the invisible fight:

"I'll be back to kill you, if it's the last thing I ever do."

It was now or never. I jumped onto the nearest ladder and started climbing to the next kettle platform. I looked down at Snake Tooth looking up at me. We stared at each other. It was then that I knew for sure that Snake Tooth was losing his magical powers . . . he could no longer fly. There was some shiny invisible slime on his back. . . .

I saw that only five killer yellow dogs were left in the Snake tower. The stream of invisible slime had grown into a boiling lake. I climbed up some more and again looked down. The first two kettle platform levels had gone under the tide of invisible flesh. The Poison Snake People were losing the battle. . . .

Then I saw Hot Dog, the last killer yellow dog, pulled into the yellowish filth by many rows of invisible teeth. Only Snake Tooth kept on killing the enemies, but he was wounded in many places. He saw me watching and threw his flesh club. I ducked and it hit a kettle, making a noise like the bang of an arquebus, then it returned to him. This triggered a gigantic rush of invisible slime which started to devour whole kettles, platforms and ladders. I saw three Snake warriors caught in a whirlpool of invisible flesh and swallowed up without a fight. My face fell into my throat. I had to flee for my life, so did Snake Tooth and the rest of the Poison Snake People still alive. I was three ladders ahead of them. . . .

As we climbed invisible animals formed themselves and pulled down the Poison Snake People one at a time until only Snake Tooth was left. Then he slipped and fell but he wasn't swallowed up. He was able to swim a few strokes on the rising tide of invisible flesh, his flesh club over his head, but the weight of his mushroom armor was pulling him down. He pleaded:

"Tarcisius, help me."

I stretched out my arm, but it was no use. I took out one of my other father's mangled hands, but it was only able to touch his fingertips. Snake Tooth was being sucked in by his worst enemies. I heard him, an apostate, actually pray to God as he was sinking. Many half-formed invisible animals jumped out of the slime and dove on him, the last and greatest chief of the Poison Snake People. But in the end Snake Tooth screamed for mercy and died like the village dog that he was. . . .

No more Snake Tooth! No more Blackrobe! No more Poison Snake People! No more killer yellow dogs! I took out my other father's mangled hands and rubbed my legs with them as I climbed from ladder to ladder. The flood of invisible slime flesh was chasing me towards the smokehole, but no invisible animal jumped at me because they were too busy underneath picking apart Snake Tooth. . . .

Poor Snake Tooth . . . he was a Huron and the bravest of the brave all the way until the end. I didn't blame him for yelling out for help. I was afraid of the invisible slime too. I thought about my other father . . . how he had tricked the Poison Snake People, but in the end he did let them drink up his Saving Waters. . . .

I kept on thinking to myself as I climbed closer to the smokehole, even though the invisible slime was gaining on me. I realized that Snake Tooth and Blackrobe were alike in so many ways I had scarcely thought about before. They both had a lot of magic power in their heads and both had known what was going on inside every possible thought. This was where my other father had been much greater than Snake Tooth because he could hide his real thoughts behind other thoughts. I remembered that neither one of them had ever lost his voice in a drop of water, and when they talked a lot about the invisible animals they suggested feathers. . . .

I stopped thinking . . . it was too dangerous. A rush of invisible flesh slime was boiling the kettle platform below me. I couldn't divide myself like an invisible animal. My head was shaking as though there were no other possibilities. I put my other father's mangled hands back in my snakeskin satchel with his beloved poems. My last thought was that it was better to be a Huron and a Christian than an invisible animal. . . .

Suddenly four invisible animals sprang up from the raging filth, trying to capture me. I smashed them like a Huron. They made incredible noises under their tufts of hair. They smelled worse than the invisible slime if that was possible. I was very near the top. I prayed to my other father not to let the invisible slime overflow the tower. Everywhere it was getting hotter as I leaped through the smokehole. I just made it in time. The tide reached the top right behind me, but there it stopped. I cried out:

"Thank God . . . and my other father!"

It was a little past dawn . . . the shadows of night were softening into a continuous gray. The crazy full moon had disappeared and it was snowing again. I noticed that the great warning drum was cracked in half. I should have been very cold dressed in snakeskin rags, but underneath the invisible animals were boiling furiously. The charred remains of the birch bark trees were scattered around the Snake tower. . . .

I leaned back inside myself and locked my head in a door. Distances were stretched through my hair and through the other side of my feet. I howled like a village dog and yelled for help . . . my voice echoing back many times until it sounded as if the sky were laughing at me. . . .

Suddenly the tower shook from very deep inside the earth. Blue smoke strings and hideous slimy smells were belching out of the smokehole. I heard my other father's voice inside my head:

"Tarcisius, throw my hands into the invisible slime when the Giant Snake appears."

I was trembling like a shadow. Invisible animals half-formed themselves and tried to jump through the smokehole, but their bodies only stretched up a little bit. They couldn't leave the boiling slime. My manhood started to rise. I opened my snakeskin satchel, calmed myself, rearranged Blackrobe's poems and took out his mangled hands. The hairs around my manhood were no longer white. Meanwhile the Snake tower was getting hotter and hotter, I was dancing on my toes and wondering if I could magically climb into the sky like my other father. I was desperate . . . hairy shadows were dripping through my flesh, my thoughts had gone where the dead crabs go. I glanced down and saw the Giant Snake struggling through the invisible slime. For several moments I wrapped myself in dreams and tried to climb out of my feet. . . .

Now daylight was everywhere with rolling clouds cold and gray as my last trailing thoughts. I was coiling and uncoiling my body like a snake. I remembered my other father's instructions. I knew what to do. I heard a deep roaring moan that sounded like countless owls dying in torment. . . .

The Giant Snake's head broke through the smokehole. Blackrobe's voice whispered inside my head again:

"Tarcisius, the Giant Snake has found its manhood. Be careful. Help is corning. Throw my hands on its slimy neck."

I did as I was told. Blackrobe's mangled hands started choking the life out of the Giant Snake. No one worshipped it anymore. It quickly sank down out of sight forever. A deep explosion rocked the Snake tower. For a brief moment among all the filthy odors I could smell water far away. I felt better instantly. My manhood was waving in the air. Invisible animals tried to escape, but instead disappeared forever in the invisible slime, their own rows of cutting sharp teeth eating them up. At the same time kettles, platform, ladders, mushrooms and fish came spitting out. I also saw many cut-up parts of the Poison Snake People and killer yellow dogs. There was another deep explosion and another. I knew it was only a matter of time before the Snake tower itself exploded. I had to escape. Suddenly I smelled water again, but this time not so far away. I thought that being roasted alive in the wintertime was a crazy way to die. . . .

I danced over to the edge of the Snake tower, my eyes searching the sky. I saw something moving this way. Inside my head I was building a birch bark chapel. I was saved. William Coutre was coming in a canoe, not just paddling through the air like Partridge used to do, but with a constant stream of water underneath. He embraced me and helped me into his magic canoe. He told me he already knew that Blackrobe had gone to God. More explosions but this time closer to the surface. Invisible slime splashed through the smokehole and the hideous smells nearly choked us to death.

"Let's go!"

My thoughts were heading in a straight line to my village. We shot out of there just in time. The Snake tower finally exploded, and the whole country of the Poison Snake People disappeared through the smokehole. The earth below us was soft and slimy with no snow and no blue smoke strings, only a few red circles, fish bones and rows of broken teeth. . . .

My stomach seemed to sink into the sky as the canoe picked up speed. I remembered all the Huron and French slave captives tortured and killed in the Snake village. Everything that happened to me since the beaver fight on the Great River passed out of my eyes, filling the sky with magic and collecting many lines. My eyes were shining in the cold. I whispered a prayer:

"Blackrobe, please never let me be hungry again. When I get

home to my village I will read all your poems and tell everyone the true story of your mangled hands. . . ."

I, Tarcisius Tandihetsi, say so.

WRITING WITHOUT THUMBS

A Conversation with
Johnny Stanton and Elinor Nauen
by George Salis

Aside from him having written the neglected masterpiece Mangled Hands, *published by Sun & Moon Press in 1985, I was fascinated by Johnny Stanton because there was very little information about him except for that one book, which was described as having had an underground reputation even before its publication. What info I could dig up was immensely interesting; for instance, that Johnny had started a newspaper called* Siamese Banana *in the early '70s which turned into a press then a "gang." But beyond these morsels, Stanton was even more mysterious than Thomas Pynchon, having only published a single novel which was virtually unlike anything else I've read. Ultimately, I discovered that Stanton was thankfully alive and married to a poet named Elinor Nauen who happened to be active on social media. Not only did Stanton turn out to be an interesting and funny character in his own right, but I was transported to a world I had little to no knowledge of: the New York City scene of literature in the mid and late 20th century (not to mention Stanton and Nauen have a beautiful and powerful relationship). Thus, from Pynchon to possible, I proudly present this interview, which is the product of enchantment, research, and a dedication to shining a light on wrongly-neglected writers and their work.*

[The following phone conversation was lightly edited for concision and clarity.]

GEORGE SALIS: The man of the hour! Hey Johnny, how are you doing?

JOHNNY STANTON: Okay, good.

GS: Thank you so much for agreeing to this. It means a lot to me. So my first question is, while Tarcisius, the 14-year-old Huron protagonist of the novel, has an "other father" in the French priest "Blackrobe," *Mangled Hands* is dedicated to "my other father, Neil Boyton, S.J." As it happens, Boyton was the author of *Mangled Hands: A Story of the New York Martyrs*, which came out in January 1926 and is a fictional account of Isaac Jogues and others who interacted with Native American populations. Can you talk about your relationship with Boyton and the relationship between these two books?

JS: He was a local parish priest that used to do a lot of things with kids during the summer. He would bring us to this park in Coney Island, Steeplechase Park, and he'd give us free tickets. We'd go in the swimming pool, a saltwater swimming pool. As we came out of the swimming pool he would be there with cheese and Ritz crackers and some juice for everybody and he would bring 30 to 40 kids every weekend during the summer.

GS: So he was like another father for you, a father figure?

JS: Yeah, exactly. Also, I wanted to rewrite his book. I wanted to give it the Burroughs touch.

GS: And when did you read that one? Do you remember?

JS: Oh, when I was in grammar school.

GS: And then was this something that had a big effect on you? Did you think "maybe I could improve on it"? How did that go?

JS: No, I just wanted to make another work.

Elinor Nauen: Can I ask a question?

GS: Sure!

EN: Did this have anything to do with Ted Berrigan's *Clear the Range* and Ron Padgett's *Motor Maids Across the Continent*? Was it the same time that those guys were doing those cut-up books?

JS: No, this was before that.

EN: Oh, do you think they got the idea from you?

JS: I doubt it. I mean, it is Burroughs.

EN: Right, okay.

GS: So that was what I was going to ask because there was a review in *The Washington Post* that described it as a "cut and fold-in method" or a "collage novel." What was that process actually like?

JS: I would take a lot of texts like Joyce, Ford Madox Ford, and Henry James, and cut them up and try to make something out of it but none of those guys did anything for me so I reverted to my favorite fantasy, the stories of Conan the Barbarian.

GS: Oh wow. So you didn't just use Boyton's *Mangled Hands*.

JS: *(Laughs)* No. I used as much trash as possible.

GS: *(Laughs)* And then you turned it into pure gold.

JS: Yeah, well. . . .

EN: *(Laughs)*

GS: Don't be modest!

JS: I was hoping for bronze!

GS: So my next question is about the marketing lingo on the back of the book. *Mangled Hands* has been compared to Sterne's *Tristram Shandy* and Marquez's *One Hundred Years of Solitude*. Were these an influence and did you cut them up too?

JS: No, I didn't cut them up. And that's more Doug Messerli media production [founder of Sun & Moon Press].

EN: You had read *Tristram Shandy* though, right?

JS: Oh yeah! I've read all of those books. Even the ones I didn't cut up. *(Laughs)*

EN: But didn't *One Hundred Years of Solitude* come out after? I thought that one came out much later than *Mangled Hands*.

JS: I don't think so. I don't remember.

GS: Do you remember when you started working on *Mangled Hands*?

JS: Oh Jesus, I don't know.

EN: It must've been the mid-'60s.

JS: Yeah. It was slow going.

GS: How long did it take?

JS: I'm too embarrassed to tell you.

EN: He's gonna tell!

JS: How long have I been married to you?

EN: Too long!

JS: That's my answer! *(Everyone laughs)*

GS: Hey, that stuff takes time. You can't do magic overnight.

EN: So what did it take, like 10 years?

JS: Yeah, probably. I was working and everything at the time. I also had the Siamese Banana Gang and the press.

GS: I can't wait to talk about that. I recently interviewed Wendy Walker and she took 10 to 15 years to write her first novel because, you know, life gets in the way. You can't fully dedicate yourself to your work, in most cases at least.

JS: Yeah.

EN: There are different kinds of books that take 10 years or one year. I mean, both are fine if that's how long it takes you. If it takes 10 years, it takes 10 years. Who cares?

GS: Exactly.

JS: One of the things I wanted to do from the cutups and with the background of the Jesuit relations in North America was make a fantasy. A completely different fantasy and I guess I succeeded at that.

GS: I would say so! Your book actually reminded me a lot of Ben Okri's *The Famished Road* except even more concentrated in the mythology.

JS: Oh, I don't know that book, but I will since Elinor has it.

GS: Oh really? And can you talk about any other spirits that animated you as you wrote the novel?

EN: Alice's tits.

JS: Huh? Whose tits?

EN: Alice's. [Born in Arizona and raised in Needles, California, according to the Poetry Foundation, "Alice Notley has become one of America's greatest living poets. She has long written in narrative and epic and genre-bending modes to discover new ways to explore the nature of the self and the social and cultural importance of disobedience. The artist Rudy Burckhardt once wrote that Notley may be 'our present-day Homer.'" Stanton describes a reading given by Notley in a partly autobiographical story titled "Radar Love" (*Transfer*, ed. Gary Lenhart, Fall/Winter 1989/90, Vol 2 #2), and at the end of the reading: "He felt a warm tearing wave of affection between his legs. If only he could make love to Alice, he'd be a much better writer. . . ."]

JS: What? No! *(They laugh)*

EN: So which spirits? Other books?

JS: Hmm, I don't know.

GS: Can you talk about your interest in Native American mythology? Did you just make it all up?

JS: No. I went to a grammar school run by the Jesuits. I went to two years of this Jesuit high school before I went to Columbia. The Indians could've been cutting off their thumbs and they'd still be writing. A lot was going on. They have tons of books on the Jesuit relations.

GS: And that was about the Jesuits and their interactions with the Native Americans?

JS: Yeah, that's what the original *Mangled Hands* is about.

EN: So all those priests who settled my part of the country and Canada were Jesuits? Chevrolet?

JS: *(Singing)* See the USA, Chevrolet!

EN: All those cars were named after priests?

JS: Buick? Oh, a big Buick. He has a big Buick baby! *(Everyone laughs)*

EN: The priests in the Detroit area, they were all Jesuits? I didn't know that!

GS: I was surprised when Elinor told me that you have Irish ancestry.

JS: Oh yes, my parents came over here in 1929, just in time for the Depression.

GS: And were the bedtime stories Joyce, *Finnegans Wake*?

JS: *(Everyone laughs)* No, I don't know if they were more about the transport workers union and their president Red Mike Quill.

EN: And the IRA. His dad was involved in that. They came over the same year? I thought your dad came a little sooner.

JS: I thought it was '29.

EN: Oh, could be.

GS: So *Mangled Hands* is a cutup like you were saying. Do you remember if you had a rigid structure or like you said you were just pulling randomly out of all of these different sources?

JS: Well I would pull sentences from the cutups and if they worked with the fantasy that was going on in my head then I would put them in. If not, I didn't.

GS: So whole sentences or just fragments or just one word?

JS: It depends.

GS: One thing that was really interesting that also comes from the back of the book is how it said *Mangled Hands* was passed among New York poets and fiction writers in manuscript form and it had some kind of underground reputation. Can you talk about that?

JS: Well, it had been published in a few places. *Columbia Review* published a couple of chapters.

GS: I actually remember that Elinor had a magazine, what was it called?

EN: *Koff Magazine.*

GS: Did you publish any of his pieces?

EN: Our plan for *Koff* was not to publish people who had already had a fair amount of publishing and I didn't really know him at that point. We met toward the end of *Koff* and he was too big time for me, for *Koff*. I don't think he would've published in *Koff*, would you?

JS: Oh, take my clothes off for you guys? Oh shit, yeah!

EN: You know what he's referring to, George? We did a calendar of naked poets in one issue.

GS: Oh I didn't know about that. That was in *Koff*?

EN: We had a naked centerfold.

GS: Oh my gosh, competing with *Playboy*?

JS: Yeah, I thought it was pretty boring myself. *(Everyone laughs)*

EN: Well, we thought poetry was pretty boring and we thought it would be enlivened by looking at naked men!

GS: So *Playgirl Magazine*?

EN: Yeah! *Playpoet*.

GS: So I also found a blog post from Douglas Messerli and he said, "I read just a few sections of [Stanton's] lost book, *Mangled Hands* in a magazine, and with great audacity called him up to ask if the book was ever completed. Yes, it's under my bed, he responded. Please send it to me, and I published it." How did it end up under your bed?

JS: *(Laughs)* You know what, I lied. I hadn't finished it then so I immediately got up and started to finish it.

EN: Johnny had a lot of people living in his house and I think under the bed was probably the only place where it was safe from the kids, right?

GS: So was there a point where you just gave up on it or life got in the way and you stopped working on the project?

JS: Well, it had gotten in the way, yes, because I started working with kids, a kind of social work bullshit.

GS: I'm assuming that took up a lot of time.

JS: Yeah, it did. They were always over at my house smoking grass.

GS: Did you smoke any with them? Peace pipe?

JS: *(Laughs)* Once I started the Siamese Banana Gang, yeah.

GS: I can't wait to get to that one. So there was an underground reputation for your book. What was the literary scene in New York like around that time?

JS: It was mostly poetry on the Lower East Side. There was Ted Berrigan, Dick Gallup, Peter Schjeldahl, Ron Padgett. Yeah, and who . . . *Fuck You* [subtitled *A Magazine of the Arts*, which was published by the poet Ed Sanders in the '60s], what was . . . Ed Sanders had a bookstore ["the Peace Eye Bookstore, located at 147 Avenue A in the Lower East Side of NYC. The sign was created by noted artist Spain Rodriguez. Peace Eye was a well-known cultural center for its era. Peace Eye also served as a community print center, and was a stopping off point for the underground railroad helping people flee the war. America's first LeMar demonstrations were organized out of Peace Eye"].

GS: So you were the odd man out as a novelist then.

JS: Yeah. Though I did take a poetry course from Ted Berrigan over at his house.

GS: And that helped you with *Mangled Hands* in some way?

JS: Oh, hell yeah!

EN: The class was just him, and Ted had him writing a lot.

JS: I can't remember what else was helpful except that the class made me realize I wasn't a poet. It was a lot of work. The culmination of the class was me reading at Cafe Metro and I have to say I think Ted was rather proud of me.

GS: Because the book reads like pure poetry every page and that's the kind of novel I like reading. Sun & Moon Press usually published novels from playwrights and poets. Were those the glory days of publishing compared to now?

JS: For mimeograph publishing. It was pretty cheap publishing. I had started a newspaper called *Siamese Banana*.

GS: That was the first incarnation, right?

JS: Yeah. I would use electric stencils to get all of the different pictures I would use in the newspaper and it was pretty cheap.

GS: And you wouldn't be able to do that now if you wanted? Is it more expensive now?

JS: Oh, I don't know!

EN: It's just different technology now. All of the poetry magazines were done with mimeo and that might be before your time, George, but you would type it on this blue paper and then there would be a mimeo machine. It was like negatives almost. So then you would run it through the machine and actual paper would come out. We didn't have computers or any way to make multiples. There weren't really any copy shops. So that was the way to make multiple copies. The nice thing was that everybody's poems looked the same. You couldn't pick a font. It was just the mimeo so if you didn't put names on things, your poem looked just as good as anybody else's!

GS: It sort of levels the playing field a little maybe.

EN: Yeah, it really did, and so people would do magazines and mimeo books and then there'd be collating parties because you'd print out 100 copies of each page and then stack them on the table and everybody would go around. That's why I only have one copy of my first mimeo book and the cover is on upside down. *(Everyone laughs)*

GS: I bet that could throw readers for a loop.

EN: Yeah, so some of those magazines printed short excerpts of fiction. They wouldn't print 40 pages because that would be ridiculous to do. It would probably be like a page or two by you, right Johnny?

JS: Yeah, or something small.

GS: That's what I did with my first novel. I tried to get little pieces in magazines or online here and there just to get something out there while I spent so much time working on one project.

JS: I'd like to talk about who I'd like to see revived. Tom Veitch's *The Louis Armed Story* and Ted Berrigan's *Clear the Range*.

GS: This is your answer for the question about books that deserve more readers?

JS: Yes!

EN: *Clear the Range* is supposed to come out again.

GS: What made you choose those two?

JS: Those were things I really liked and they were by friends.

GS: Nepotism!

JS: Oh, sure! *(Everyone laughs)* I mean, come on, it's a small neighborhood! You get to know everybody!

EN: Ted's granddaughters are my granddaughters by the way. Not through any shenanigans, but it's the nepotism part.

JS: Oh, the truth comes out!

EN: The truth?

JS: The truth! *(Laughs)*

GS: I'm not familiar with those books of course. Can you tell me a little bit about them?

JS: Ah, no. Go get them! *(Laughs)*

EN: You know Tom Veitch, he's also a comic book writer.

GS: Oh, I'll go get them! So I only have a few more questions about *Mangled Hands* and then we can move on. *Mangled Hands* is suffused with dream logic and surreal scenes. How do you view the importance of dreams, particularly in the context of literature?

JS: Not much.

EN: Really?

JS: Yeah, no.

EN: Did you at the time?

JS: I kept a dream journal.

GS: How did that go? How long did you keep that going?

JS: Not that long, maybe a couple of years.

GS: I would say that's long! I remember I tried doing that and after a couple of entries I was finished.

JS: *(Laughs)* Then let me change my answer. A couple of days! *(All laugh)*

GS: I can't remember who said it, but there's that adage, "Tell a dream, lose a reader" which I never believed in.

JS: Wow, I never heard that one before!

GS: Do you agree with that?

JS: No, I don't agree with that. I was a big fan of the Dadaists and the surrealists. Give me a break. I always thought that dreams were pretty cool!

GS: I have to agree with that. So we have a guest question since I like to bring in some people from the community to participate. This question comes from S. D. Stewart: "Toward the end of the book, Snake Tooth takes Blackrobe's poems and stuffs them in the back of his head, then uses his possession of them as leverage to get secret information from Blackrobe. Snake Tooth claims the poems hurt his head and says he knows 'at any moment they might fill up the sky.' Yet later he appears to use the magical strength of the poems to help the fishing party catch more fish. When the fishing party arrives back at the village, Snake Tooth returns the poems as promised to Blackrobe, who in turn gives them to Tarcisius. The level of significance of the poems to Blackrobe is clear, as well as their greater power within the mythology of the book. What meaning do you see in Blackrobe's poems and why do you think Snake Tooth, an apostate who consistently defies Blackrobe's 'saving waters,' still seems to hold a certain amount of reverence for them?"

JS: Actually I think that that might've been influenced by John Ashberry and Ted, about the poems. Snake Tooth was getting interested in the religion. He was interested in Blackrobe. Maybe he wanted to kill him, maybe he wanted to have sex with him, I don't know.

GS: He was an apostate but maybe he still believed. Is that what you're saying?

JS: Yeah, something like that. *(Laughs)*

EN: An apostate who still had a relationship with belief.

JS: Yeah, an apostate can be a heretic or someone who was excommunicated.

GS: And there's only really one instance where we get a glimpse of Blackrobe's poetry. How did you write that? In juxtaposition with the rest of the book it didn't feel like poetry. *(JS laughs)* Not to insult you or Blackrobe, but compared with the rest of the book.

EN: Well, the book was poetry but the poetry wasn't, in other words.

JS: *(Laughs)* I plead the fifth.

GS: No problem.

EN: Do you not remember?

JS: No.

EN: *(Laughs)* He doesn't remember. The fifth he's pleading is about memory, not about that.

JS: Well, I'm getting old!

EN: Yeah, we all know that.

GS: So my last question is playful: Where do the dead crabs go? Do you know?

JS: Hmm, I think the beavers ate them.

GS: They were causing a lot of trouble.

JS: Yes, yes, and it worked on a sexual level too.

GS: There was a lot of manhood touching. What made you put so much of that in the book?

EN: He had the fire down below. I can attest to that. *(JS bursts into laughter)*

JS: Ah, something like that.

GS: Okay, so, moving on, *(JS laughs more)* Elinor told me that you've been getting quite a few tattoos, including a line from *Mangled Hands:* "I, Tarcisius Tandihetsi, say so," which is repeated at the end of every chapter. What made you get that tattoo recently?

JS: I got my first tattoo when I was 70.

GS: So how did that start? I got mine when I graduated high school and I've only gotten one other since.

JS: Tattoos weren't as popular when I was growing up in the late '40s and '50s.

EN: Wait, so how did you start then?

JS: It was just this one!

EN: Oh, the *Koff Magazine* one?

JS: It's not a *Koff Magazine*.

EN: No, that was our logo!

JS: That wasn't your logo. It was the Consumptive Poets one.

EN: Right, so his first tattoo was the logo of the Consumptive Poets which was the publisher of *Koff Magazine* so it's the symbol of the American Lung Association, you know like a cross with two bars but the end of it is a pen dripping with a drop of blood. But that is a great question, what made you start getting tattoos?

JS: Oh, I was thinking about you, I was thinking deeply about you! It was probably something you did to annoy me.

GS: Revenge tattoo?

EN: He also has the title of a book of mine tattooed on his back.

GS: And which one was that?

EN: It's *So Late into the Night*.

GS: Is it on the lower back, a tramp stamp?

JS: No, the middle back!

EN: It's very large. It's as big as the line from *Mangled Hands*.

JS: And I have a tattoo of the Siamese Banana Gang.

EN: *(Laughs)* He's showing it to you! Each time we say a tattoo, he's showing it. I'm like, okay, he doesn't see it, but that's okay! That's right, he has the Siamese Banana Gang. Somebody saw that and went, "Wait!"

GS: Somebody recognized it?

EN: Somebody who knew the Siamese Banana Gang saw that, but maybe they didn't know you?

JS: I don't know.

GS: That's strange. How many tattoos do you have in total?

EN: Oh that's a good question.

JS: Uh, one, two, three, four, five, six, seven!

EN: No, more than that.

JS: Oh, eight, nine!

EN: That's it?

JS: Isn't that enough?

GS: You have me outnumbered. Are you thinking of getting any more?

JS: Only if I get inspired.

EN: Yeah, right now things aren't really happening.

JS: Yeah. No tattoo parlors are open.

GS: How are you handling the quarantine? You're still locked up tight?

JS: Yeah and I'm beginning to shake. Ooh, shake it baby! One time for me! *(Everyone laughs)*

GS: I feel you! I haven't left the house in two months or more.

JS: Oh, God.

GS: Time is just melting for me.

JS: Yeah, it is strange.

GS: And yet I see people outside my window acting like everything is normal and they're not doing what they're supposed to.

EN: Yeah, Florida seems to be . . .

GS: Really bad.

EN: Yeah. At least in New York most people are pretty—

JS: Oh yeah!

EN: You know, because we're all on top of each other. Plus I don't think there's anyone who doesn't know anyone who hasn't been sick or died so it does sober you up when it's not abstract. I mean it's sort of abstract anyway and when you don't know anyone who's gotten sick it feels like "this has nothing to do with me." But here, we all feel like it has something to do with us. You really haven't been out? How are you getting food?

GS: Delivery from Instacart and Walmart delivery.

EN: Oh wow, do you have a big house and backyard and stuff?

GS: No, actually I'm in an apartment complex so I have to take out the trash at night and it's like *Mission: Impossible* because I don't trust anyone to keep their distance.

EN: Right.

JS: Really? Wow!

EN: You know he lives near Peter? He lives in Daytona.

JS: Oh, you live in Daytona? Where is my brother living, New Smyrna Beach?

GS: Well, if you guys are down here when the pandemic is over I'll buy you a drink.

JS: Oh, good, whoo! *(Laughs)*

GS: A margarita sounds pretty good.

EN: Wait, you were going to ask something more about Siamese Banana.

GS: Yeah, I have a couple more. So there was actually very little information about you when I was first Googling you and I actually didn't even know if you were still alive! It was like Pynchon, you're like a Pynchon figure.

EN: I think it's because he doesn't have a social media presence.

GS: Yeah, and there was no bio or anything for me to find. But there was this random thing on a website from 1997 I think it was, where you were describing the history briefly of Siamese Banana.

JS: Oh, right. It was a book about the underground press.

EN: Was that the secret history book?

JS: Yeah, something butter balls.

GS: Because you said you worked at a neighborhood youth center. That was earlier, before the social work or was that related?

JS: Yes, that's exactly where I was working.

GS: So you had already started working on *Mangled Hands* by then.

JS: Yeah, I wrote it when I lived on 89th Street.

GS: And a fearless director barked at you *(Woofs)*, "Jumping butter balls! *(All laugh)* You're supposed to be a writer, why don't you start a center newspaper?" Why did that person say you're supposed to be a writer? Did they know that you were working on this project then?

JS: No, they just knew that I was a writer.

GS: So this person had an influence on you? That was the impetus for starting the whole press?

JS: Yeah, well, starting the newspaper, it turned out to be so great I wanted to publish books too.

GS: What kind of news did you publish?

JS: Oh, things from around the neighborhood. It was completely local to the children center.

GS: And what kind of reception did you get?

JS: I got a lot of laughs. *(Laughs)*

GS: So it was mostly a comedic newspaper. "If the facts don't fit, change them."

JS: Remember, young teenagers can be really snotty or sarcastic. Actually, everybody really liked it.

GS: And that inspired you to take it to the next level?

JS: Yeah, and then I was able to get Joe Brainard to publish his first books.

GS: And I think Elinor mentioned Paul Auster? He made it pretty big.

JS: Oh, yeah. Later on he put out a big book of French surrealist poetry but what I published was a little anthology of French surrealist poetry so it was the start of that big book.

GS: So not his work specifically then, just an anthology he curated?

JS: His translations, yes.

GS: Ah, interesting. I'll have to see if I can get my hands on that or maybe just go for the big one.

EN: That book is very available. I've got it right here. It's the anthology of 20th-century French poetry.

JS: Yeah, he was talking about the Siamese Banana one.

EN: No, I know, but the big one that I have. Oh, I see. I don't know if you can get the little one, the Siamese Banana one.

JS: See, it's not that we have too many books around here. *(All laugh)* You know how the walls kind of feel like they're closing in on you? When you're sitting at the desk with all of the books you're looking at and they're coming towards you.

GS: Mine are right at my back. Mine loom behind me. So did you call Paul and say, "You're mine because I published you first"?

JS: Oh, no! Why would I do that? *(Laughs)* You know what? He has a book out, *4 3 2 1*. There's a section in there about me and the Siamese Banana Press. I mean he calls it something else. It gets to 89th Street and, well, it'll be easy to recognize me. I'm the handsome one in the book!

GS: Of course. *(Laughs)* So what are some other notable things you published when Siamese Banana was a press?

JS: Stuff by Anne Waldman and Joe Brainard and a guy from Columbia University, Hilton Obenzinger, David Anderson. It was a good time! Lord Scum's Hotel by John Weingarten. He was from Colombia too.

GS: How big did this press get? What was the biggest print run you did of a book?

JS: Oh, Jesus. Well 100, 200, I don't know.

GS: Interesting, so it did take off a bit?

JS: Oh yeah. I think I published around 8 to 10 books.

GS: And that includes some of yours as well? Because I saw some online.

JS: Yeah, one of mine. *The Day Our Turtle Was Kidnapped.*

GS: They're a little out of my price range but I'm saving my lunch money.

JS: Jesus, really?

GS: Yeah, it depends. There's a couple of them floating around.

JS: Uh-huh.

GS: And they're rare, so. Have you held onto any of these things that you've published?

JS: Hmmmm. Some of them.

EN: They might be in that box that Bill brought out of storage. Now I don't know where that book is. I usually can put my hands on it because I like to look at that book but it's, I don't know, it might turn up.

GS: So it went from newspaper to press then finally a gang!

JS: A theater group.

GS: Ah, because when I hear gang I'm thinking more tattoos and chains.

JS: No, only because I have tattoos now! But that's what we called ourselves. It would be something that I wrote, maybe stories, plays that would be performed behind me while I read.

GS: Where did you do this, at a park or something?

JS: No, I did it at the Poetry Project, on cable television, Off Broadway. [Stanton mentions these performances in the above-mentioned story "Radar Love": "She had once read with Stanton at a loft in Soho. He had these teenage kids perform stories as he read. They were hilarious: controlled anarchy, spontaneous drama scripted with props, much better than the Living Theater. No Lie. What the hell was their name? She quickly remembered: The Siamese Banana Gang."]

GS: Very cool. And were you the only one who was writing these plays or were there other people involved?

JS: Well, there wasn't too much of that going around at the time, no. As a matter of fact, actually one of our best productions wasn't something by me, it was by Henry Carey, *Chrononhotonthologos: The Most Tragical Tragedy That ever was Tragediz'd by any Company of Tragedians.*

GS: That sounds like a lot!

JS: Yeah! *(Laughs)* It was an 18th-century play.

EN: That was when I met Johnny, when he was in a poets' theater in 1979 and I was in some poets' plays. He had directed this play, and that was where we met. I was taking my clothes off in everybody's plays. My other strength as an actor was fainting. I wasn't very good at acting at all, but I did two things that people always wanted, taking my dress off and fainting. I would've met him eventually because all of our friends were friends in common but that was where we met and soon after that somebody we knew was in a play up in Connecticut and he had a truck because he worked for a moving company and I didn't have a car at that point so a bunch of us drove up to see the play and I ended up sitting in the front and we were talking. [In Elinor Nauen's nonfiction book *My Marriage A to Z: A Big-City Romance*, she writes "Johnny drove us in his work truck and I insisted on sitting up front because I like watching the highway go by. It gave him the wrong idea. The first time we went somewhere together, just the two of us, he almost killed us racing home, thinking he was about to get in my pants. I thought he was a great driver, but when he ran the light at 42nd and First, I knew it was sex not automotive prowess that powered him."] We just became friends and here's the shallow part of the story. So Johnny had this big, black beard that covered his whole face and I did not find him attractive. He always asked me out for years and I would hang out with him as friends. Then one day I went to a reading at the church and I said, "Oh! Who's that over there?" and whoever was with me said, "That's Johnny!" and I said, "No, that cute guy." And they said, "No, that's Johnny. He shaved!" I didn't recognize him, his grown sons didn't recognize him. I mean he really looked so different and after that I was like "Okay, I'll go out with you!" *(Laughs)*

GS: He came out of the chrysalis.

EN: He did! So now he always thinks I'm shallow because I wouldn't go out with him until he was cute! But yeah, Johnny is a very unusual person, which you can get from his books. There's nobody that I admire more. It's like he is himself every minute without consideration for what people think he should do or not do.

GS: Did you ever write these plays down, Johnny, or are they just lost to the air?

JS: Hmm, I don't know.

GS: I'll have to do a little more Googling! So what is your fondest memory of Siamese Banana. What sticks out to you from that history?

JS: Oh, Jeez. The Henry Carey thing because it was a big deal, it was a big production. It was in an Off Broadway theater.

GS: And that was received very well, I'm assuming?

JS: There were a lot of women taking their clothes off there, including my wife, my present wife.

EN: I took my clothes off for about five different plays! It wasn't a lot of women, it was just me! *(All laugh)*

GS: Oh, my! So as I mentioned earlier, there's this blog post by Douglas Messerli from June 2019: "I'm almost speechless here. The indescrible [sic] fiction writer Johnny Stanton. [...] He wrote a second book, and we typeset it, sending him the proofs, but he pulled it from publication; to this day I don't quite know why. He's a true genius. And I loved his company; we went for Chinese in D.C. with Elinor Nauen and he showed up to several of our NYC parties. Johnny where are you? I miss you so much. *Mangled Hands* is a classic of American fiction in case you didn't know." Can you tell me about that?

EN: Johnny continued writing more and more edits in the margins of the galley and he just ended up never sending it back.

JS: Yeah. I didn't like it anymore. I actually didn't like writing anymore.

GS: That was my next question. If you continue to write or if you don't write anymore, what was the decision behind stopping?

JS: I didn't like it. I didn't make money at it.

GS: And it just didn't bring you any more joy?

JS: No.

GS: Did it become a chore?

JS: Uh, yeah, I guess so. That's a good word. [Answering the question of "Why I Like to Write ?!" in a mimeograph, Johnny Stanton once wrote, "I like to write because I feel a deep need within me every night to express my love and abiding interest in mankind. Each man, woman, and child deserves to be the subject of a great story. I wish I had more time, less sleep. [...] Whenever I sit down at my desk to write a story I always try to keep in mind the parts men play as individuals, not as mere abstractions, in the universe that surrounds them. This is exactly the thing that gives history its true and proper value, poetry some of its merit, and the stories I write their only reason for existing."]

GS: Yeah, once you suck the joy out of something then why continue to do it? What can you tell me about the book you pulled? What was the title?

JS: It was called *Sons of Xavier Keep Marching*.

GS: That sounds very interesting to me!

JS: Yeah, and then there was another book that I put together called *Johnny Stanton vs the Big Guys*.

GS: Are these both short story collections?

JS: Yeah. With the second one, I was reading a lot of stories, such as Chekhov, and ones that I really liked I would decide to write a story off of them so in a way it was still part of that cutup technique.

GS: Hmm, but in that method you weren't actually pulling words or sentences.

JS: Yeah, no.

GS: So kind of like ekphrastic in a way where you look at the paintings and then write a poem based on that.

JS: Right!

GS: Can anyone convince you to publish these?

JS: Well, I would have to find them. I have no idea where they are.

GS: Oh, my! Elinor do you know where they are?

JS: No, she's still looking for that other book! *(Laughs)* By the way, it was published by Random House.

GS: So you decided to stop writing. Do you express yourself artistically in any other way? Or just binge Netflix?

JS: *(Laughs)* Well, I better leave on that note!

GS: Phew, I really appreciate you talking to me, Johnny! And I appreciate your efforts too, Elinor. Thank you so much!

EN: Oh, it's exciting for me too! A lot of this stuff I've never heard before or I haven't heard for such a long time. It's kind of a thrill because every once in a while I meet somebody and they'll say, "Wait, you're married to Johnny Stanton?"

JS: A woman's dream!

EN: This is such a great thing that you're doing, George. I love that these are the kinds of books that you're interested in and you're right, the mainstream books don't need advocates.

GS: Yeah, I feel a communion with these writers because I feel like I'm going to eventually be one of them once my work comes out. It's inevitable. Another reason is that they tend to write without inhibitions.

EN: Right, it's what the great Turkish poet Murat Nemet Nejat said, "If no one's buying the bread you're baking, you can make it as salty as you want." *(Both laugh)*

GS: Exactly, I prefer writers who stay true to their vision, whatever that turns out to be.

Special thanks to S.D. Stewart for helping me track down Johnny Stanton and to Nicole Melchionda for transcribing the conversation.

Johnny Stanton was born in 1943 in Manhattan, the son of Irish immigrants from Galway. He was an altar boy and Eagle Scout who attended Catholic schools and eventually graduated from Columbia University, where he fell in with many poets and writers of the New York School, including Kenneth Koch, Ted Berrigan, Ron Padgett, and Paul Auster. He published many of them, some for the first time, in his Siamese Banana Press, which started as a newspaper in 1972 and ended as a performance gang in 1978. He is the author of many short stories and the novel *Mangled Hands*, neglected by critics yet highly acclaimed by the readers who discover it. He has lived in the East Village for 30 years with his wife, the poet Elinor Nauen, a cat (currently Lefty), and a lot of art.

Elinor Nauen's books include *My Marriage A to Z: A Big-City Romance, So Late into the Night, Cars and Other Poems, American Guys, Now That I Know Where I'm Going,* and, as editor, *Ladies, Start Your Engines: Women Writers on Cars and the Road* (Faber & Faber, 1997) and *Diamonds Are a Girl's Best Friend: Women Writers on Baseball* (Faber & Faber, 1994). Her work has appeared in *New Ameri-*

can Writing, FICTION, Exquisite Corpse, The World, KOFF, and other magazines and anthologies. She has been a teacher/guest lecturer in writing workshops and classes in colleges, secondary and primary schools, and adult workshops at the Pingry School, Martinsville, NJ, where she was the visiting poet for several years; Washington State University, University of South Dakota, and elsewhere.

ACKNOWLEDGMENTS

The publisher extends his profound thanks to the following for their generous financial support, which helped to defray some of this book's production costs:

Clayton Achterberg, Kevin Adams, Ted Adams,
Jamey Adirim, elif ağanoğlu, AGT, Daniel David Allred,
Adrian Astur Álvarez, Ben Ament, Karen M Anderhalt,
JD Andersen, Jeffrey Atkins, Captain Awesome, AWS, CK Baker,
Reverend Justin Alexander Baldwin-Bonney, Cameron Bennett,
Thomas Young Barmore Jr, Nick Barry, Kian Bergstrom, BH,
Alfred Bie, Dustin Bingaman, Suzie Blaut, Matthew Boe,
Derek Bogdanoff, Brian R. Boisvert, Bonriguez,
Giacomo Boschelle, Shannon Leigh Broughton-Smith,
Matthew Brown, David Brownless, Nathaniel Buckholz,
Wayne L. Budgen, Peter Bushyeager, Blake Butler,
Byougennojiyuu, Linda Byrne, Anthony C, Chris Call,
Stephen Camp, Jeffrey Canino, Tobias Carroll, Andrew Casher,
Elaine M. Cassell, Scott Chiddister, Wesley Chien,
Tony Tony Chopper, Chelsea Clifton, Adam Coale, Alex Cobb,
daniel cockrell, Tyler Cohn, C. Colla, Stephen Collins Jr,
John Morris Coombs, Jangus C. Cooper, Tom Coppock,
Jarad Whitney Cornett, Sheri Costa, Michael T. Costello,
Randy Cox, Sandra Lassle Crisp, Parker & Malcolm Curtis,
Robert Dallas, Victoria Elizabeth Francis De Maria,
Frank Derfield Jr., Daniel Dion, Stew Dirtsaw,
Sam & Dylan Doomwarre, Joe Dreshar, Michael Ducker,
James Duncan, Danny Durtsche, dynk, Curtis B. Edmundson,
Matthew Egerton, Isaac Ehrlich, Todd Emmenegger,
Joshua James Erb, Lisa Marie Ernst, FATHOMBOOKS,
Richard Faught, Pops Feibel, Rhonda Field, Fred Filios,

Landon Finch, Anthony Fletcher, Dennis Forsgren,
Robert Patrick Frerich, Miriam Fridman, Stephen Fuller,
Dave G, Peyton G., Nathan "N.R." Gaddis, Zac Gall,
Justin Gallant, Mitchell G Gallinger, John M. Gamble,
A. M. Garcia, Katja Gifford, Sheryl Giordano, Stephan Glander,
GmarkC, Saif Gohir, Lindsay Gomes, Damian Gordon,
Sara D Gore, Fernando Boxhoorn Goulart, David Greenberg,
Chloe Grubel, Mary Teresa Guilfoyle, Richard L. Haas III,
Ham, Mahan Harirsaz, Erik Hemming, Aric Herzog,
Mark Hoffe, Wesley Hoffman, Yonina Hoffman, Walter Holland,
Hall Hood, Jonathan Hope, Elijah House, Evelyn House,
Victoria Hoyle, Bill Hsu, John Hunchak, I love you Mom!,
Ja, Neil Jacobson, Brian Jagodzinski, R. Jazz. Clayton Johnson,
Erik T Johnson, Fred W Johnson, Haya .K., Gautham Kalva,
Simon Kavanagh, Laura E. Kenkel, MD, Kevin,Tom Kiefer,
Marshall Knauf, Sergey Kochergan, Stephanie Koenig,
Ethan L. Koss-Smith, Nathan Kouri, M.D. Kuehn, Paul Kuliev,
Gen Kumana, Kyle, Mark Lamb, Tara Lannen-Stanton,
J.J. Larrea, Dana West Lawlor, Dorian David Leigh,
George H. Lieber, Ben Lieberman, Felix Lopez, LordHog,
Daniel T. Losey, Luzius23, Mancini M.,
Brian de León Macchiarelli, Mo Mangini,
Maria C. Rodríguez Mas, Greg Masters, Elizabeth Maxim,
Joe McAlhany, Jim McElroy, Donald McGowan,
Shawn P. McMurray, Henry "Hank" McNeil, Jack Mearns,
Sergio Mendez-Torres, Dr. Melvin "Steve" Mesophagus,
Jason Miller, Mark Mills, John Miyasato, Spencer F Montgomery,
Geoffrey Moses, Gregory Moses, Scott Murphy,
Matt "Devilboy" Murray, Colin Myers, Clyde Nads, Marc Nasdor,
April Neal, Steve Nesselroth, Annie Ngo, Irwing Nieto,
Colin Nisbet, Anthony Notaro, Ryan D. O'Connor, Rick Ohnemus,
John Ross Olsen, Michael O'Shaughnessy, L. Ostick, Daniel Pack,
Peter Palmer, Marshall Parks, Zach Pattison-Gordon,
Andrew Pearson, Erik Pfeiffer, Ry Pickard, Phil Piotrowski,

Poems-For-All, Poffertje the cat, Pedro Ponce, Philipp Potocki,
Stephen Press, Waylon M. Prince, Jennifer Pritchett,
Nickolas Promitzer, Michael "Mikeystein" Ramage,
Michelle A. Raymond, Patrick M Regner, Paul Richardson,
Michael J. Richmond, Mr. Richter, Diana Rickard, Ricky,
Kyle William Riley, Andrew Robertson, John H Robinson,
Kara Roncin & James Wheeler, Doug Ross, Matthew Ross,
Owen Rowe, John Salis, Rebecca S, Sebastian Sarti,
Christopher H. Sartisohn, Spencer Saunders, Kristen Scanlan,
Scott Seago, Jeremiah Serafin, Brendan Sheehan, Mark M Sheehan,
Phil Skinn, H&A Skogstad, Chris Slajus,
Stephen J Sligo-Gibson, Jason Smith, Michael C. Snead,
Kelly Snyder, Yvonne Solomon, seth stahl,
Caitlin, Sean, and Meagan Stanton (we love you Grand-Daddyo!),
Martin E Stein & Scott A Saxon, Alexander Stewart, Sean Stewart,
Eric William Stillway, Joel Stimpson, K. L. Stokes, Leah Sylvester,
Sean Sylvester, Evan Thomas, Skye Thorleifson, Kate Torgerson,
Kathy Trankle, Lauren Kelsey Trumble, Sydney Umaña,
Daniel Vallejo, Chris Via, Chris Vola, Ashley Walker,
Jordan J Walker, Kim Wander, Jack Waters, William Waters,
Elijah Watson, Rachel Wells, Rommel Wells, Eric Westerlind,
Christopher Wheeling, Isaiah Whisner, Charlie C. Wilcox,
Charles Wilkins, Stephen S Williamson, Jeff Wilson, Ian Wissman,
Keith Withers, Marshall E. Woertz, Ian Eric Wojcikiewicz,
Chris Wolf, T.R. Wolfe, Stephen M. Wolterstorff, Michael Wood,
William T Wright, Sara Zeglin, The Zemenides Family,
Justin Zigenis, and Anonymous

9 780578 859422